STOCKTON-ON-TEES BOROUGH LIBRARIES

A FINE WILL BE CHARGED IF THE BOOK IS
RETURNED AFTER THE DATE ON WHICH IT IS DUE

This book should be returned on or before the latest date
stamped. It may, if not required by another reader, be
renewed on request for a further loan period.

005019449 6

THE MAVERICK

BY
DIANA PALMER

Published in Great Britain 2010
Harlequin Mills & Boon Limited,
Eton House, 18-24 Paradise Road, Richmond, Surrey TW9 1SR

© Diana Palmer 2009

ISBN: 978 0 263 88187 5

51-1210

Harlequin Mills & Boon policy is to use papers that are natural, renewable
and recyclable products and made from wood grown in sustainable forests.
The logging and manufacturing processes conform to the legal environmental
regulations of the country of origin.

Printed and bound in Spain
by Litografía Rosés S.A., Barcelona

Diana Palmer has a gift for telling the most sensual tales with charm and humor. With more than forty million copies of her books in print, Diana is one of North America's most beloved authors and considered one of the top ten romance authors in the United States. Diana's hobbies include gardening, archeology, anthropology, art, astronomy and music. She has been married to James Kyle for over thirty-five years. They have one son, Blayne, who is married to the former Christina Clayton, and a granddaughter, Selena Marie.

To Julie Benefiel, who designed my cowboy quilt
(hand pieced by Nancy Caudill),

To Nancy Mason, who quilted it,

And to Janet Borchert, who put together a 2007
hardcover book of all my covers, including foreign
ones, along with Jade, Tracy, Nancy, Carey, Amy,
Renata, Maria, LeeAnn, Efy, Kay, Peggy, Hang,
Ronnie, Mona and Debbie of the Diana Palmer
Bulletin Board.

Also to everyone who participated in the compendium
summaries of all my books, and to Nancy for the
quilted covers for the loose-leaf notebooks.

With many thanks and much love.

Dear Reader,

Of all the characters I have created over the past thirty years, Harley Fowler has been the most complex. He started life in *Mercenary's Woman* as a cowboy who worked for mercenary Eb Scott's friend, the enigmatic Cy Parks. He was a braggart, a blowhard and a pain in the neck, but we got glimpses of the man he might become. In *The Winter Soldier*, he grew up. When confronted by violent drug dealers, he discovered that, while he was pretending to be a professional soldier, Cy Parks, his reclusive boss, was the real article. Harley swallowed his pride and walked bravely into gunfire beside Cy Parks, Micah Steele and Eb Scott to take down a dangerous drug distribution center.

I have had many readers ask for Harley's own book, but until now I hadn't found just the right venue for him. Sometimes if you rush a story into publication, you do damage to the character it is intended to spotlight. I waited until I was certain I had the right story for Harley. Now I am.

I hope all of you who wanted to know more about Cy Parks's mysterious foreman will be pleased at the revelations. As you might notice, this book is the beginning of a murder mystery that will unravel in subsequent books, most notably in the story of Kilraven and Winnie Sinclair and in the following year's novel about Kilraven's half-brother, Jon Blackhawk. Don't be impatient. It's going to be a good ride. I promise.

Love to all of you from your biggest fan,

Diana Palmer

One

Harley Fowler was staring so hard at his list of chores that he walked right into a young brunette as he headed into the hardware store in Jacobsville, Texas. He looked up, shocked, when she fell back against the open door, glaring at him.

"I've heard of men getting buried in their work, but this is too much," she told him with a speaking look. She smoothed over her short black hair, feeling for a bump where she'd collided with the door. Deep blue eyes glared up into his pale blue ones. She noticed that he had light brown hair and was wearing a baseball cap that seemed to suit him. He was sexy-looking.

"I'm not buried in my work," he said curtly. "I'm trying to get back to work, and shopping chores are keeping me from it."

"Which doesn't explain why you're assaulting women with doors. Does it?" she mused.

His eyes flared. "I didn't assault you with a door. You walked into me."

"I did not. You were staring at that piece of paper so hard that you wouldn't have seen a freight train coming." She peered over his arm at the list. "Pruning shears? Two new rakes?" She pursed her lips, but smiling blue eyes stared at him. "You're obviously somebody's gardener," she said, noting his muddy shoes and baseball cap.

His eyebrows met. "I am not a gardener," he said indignantly. "I'm a cowboy."

"You are not!"

"Excuse me?"

"You don't have a horse, you're not wearing a cowboy hat, and you don't have any chaps." She glanced at his feet. "You aren't even wearing cowboy boots!"

He gaped at her. "Did you just escape from intense therapy?"

"I have not been in any therapy," she said haughtily. "My idiosyncrasies are so unique that they couldn't classify me even with the latest edition of the DSM-IV, much less attempt to pyschoanalize me!"

She was referring to a classic volume of psychology that was used to diagnose those with mental challenges. He obviously had no idea what she was talking about.

"So, can you sing, then?"

He looked hunted. "Why would I want to sing?"

"Cowboys sing. I read it in a book."

"You can read?" he asked in mock surprise.

"Why would you think I couldn't?" she asked.

He nodded toward the sign on the hardware store's door that clearly said, in large letters, PULL. She was trying to push it.

She let go of the door and shifted her feet. "I saw that," she said defensively. "I just wanted to know if you were paying attention." She cocked her head at him. "Do you have a rope?"

"Why?" he asked. "You planning to hang yourself?"

She sighed with exaggerated patience. "Cowboys carry ropes."

"What for?"

"So they can rope cattle!"

"Don't find many head of cattle wandering around in hardware stores," he murmured, looking more confident now.

"What if you did?" she persisted. "How would you get a cow out of the store?"

"Bull. We run purebred Santa Gertrudis bulls on Mr. Parks's ranch," he corrected.

"And you don't have any cows?" She made a face. "You don't raise calves, then." She nodded.

His face flamed. "We do so raise calves. We do have cows. We just don't carry them into hardware stores and turn them loose!"

"Well, excuse me!" she said in mock apology. "I never said you did."

"Cowboy hats and ropes and cows," he muttered. He opened the door. "You going in or standing out here? I have work to do."

"Doing what? Knocking unsuspecting women in the head with doors?" she asked pleasantly.

His impatient eyes went over her neat slacks and wool jacket, to the bag she was holding. "I said, are you going into the store?" he asked with forced patience, holding the door open.

"Yes, as a matter of fact, I am," she replied, moving closer. "I need some tape measures and Super Glue and matches and chalk and push pins and colored string and sticky tape."

"Don't tell me," he drawled. "You're a contractor."

"Oh, she's something a little less conventional than that, Harley," Police Chief Cash Grier said as he came up the steps to the store. "How's it going, Jones?" he asked.

"I'm overflowing in DBs, Grier," she replied with a grin. "Want some?"

He held up his hands. "We don't do a big business in homicides here. I'd like to keep it that way." He scowled. "You're out of your territory a bit, aren't you?"

"I am. I was asked down here by your sheriff, Hayes Carson. He actually does have a DB. I'm working the crime scene for him per his request through the Bexar County medical examiner's office, but I didn't bring enough supplies. I hope the hardware store can accommodate me. It's a long drive back to San Antonio when you're on a case."

"On a case?" Harley asked, confused.

"Yes, on a case," she said. "Unlike you, some of us are professionals who have real jobs."

"Do you know him?" Cash asked her.

She gave Harley a studied appraisal. "Not really. He came barreling up the steps and hit me with a door. He says he's a cowboy," she added in a confidential tone. "But just between us, I'm sure he's lying. He doesn't have a horse or a rope, he isn't wearing a cowboy hat or boots, he says he can't sing, and he thinks bulls roam around loose in hardware stores."

Harley stared at her with more mixed emotions than he'd felt in years.

Cash choked back a laugh. "Well, he actually is a cowboy," Cash defended him. "He's Harley Fowler, Cy Parks's foreman on his cattle ranch."

"Imagine that!" she exclaimed. "What a blow to the image of Texas if some tourist walks in and sees him dressed like that!" She indicated Harley's attire with one slender hand. "They can't call us the cowboy capital of the world if we have people working cattle in baseball caps! We'll be disgraced!"

Cash was trying not to laugh. Harley looked as if he might explode.

"Better a horseless cowboy than a contractor with an attitude like yours!" Harley shot back, with glittery eyes. "I'm amazed that anybody around here would hire you to build something for them."

She gave him a superior look. "I don't build things. But I could if I wanted to."

"She really doesn't build things," Cash said. "Harley, this is Alice Mayfield Jones," he introduced. "She's a forensic investigator for the Bexar County medical examiner's office."

"She works with dead people?" Harley exclaimed, and moved back a step.

"Dead bodies," Alice returned, glaring at his obvious distaste. "DBs. And I'm damned good at my job. Ask him," she added, nodding toward Cash.

"She does have a reputation," Cash admitted. His dark eyes twinkled. "And a nickname. Old Jab-'Em-in-the-Liver Alice."

"You've been talking to Marc Brannon," she accused.

"You did help him solve a case, back when he was still a Texas Ranger," he pointed out.

"Now they've got this new guy, transferred up from Houston," she said on a sigh. "He's real hard going. No sense of humor." She gave him a wry look. "Kind of like you used to be, in the old days when you worked out of the San Antonio district attorney's office, Grier," she recalled. "A professional loner with a bad attitude."

"Oh, I've changed." He grinned. "A wife and child can turn the worst of us inside out."

She smiled. "No kidding? If I have time, I'd love to see that little girl everybody's talking about. Is she as pretty as her mama?"

He nodded. "Oh, yes. Every bit."

Harley pulled at his collar. "Could you stop talking about children, please?" he muttered. "I'll break out in hives."

"Allergic to small things, are you?" Alice chided.

"Allergic to the whole subject of marriage," he emphasized with a meaningful stare.

Her eyebrows arched. "I'm sorry, were you hoping I was going to ask you to marry me?" she replied pleasantly. "You're not bad-looking, I guess, but I have a very high standard for prospective bridegrooms. Frankly," she added with a quick appraisal, "if you were on sale in a groom shop, I can assure you that I wouldn't purchase you."

He stared at her as if he doubted his hearing. Cash Grier had to turn away. His face was going purple.

The hardware-store door opened and a tall, black-haired, taciturn man came out it. He frowned. "Jones? What the hell are you doing down here? They asked for Longfellow!"

She glared back. "Longfellow hid in the women's restroom and refused to come out," she said haughtily. "So they sent me. And why are you interested in Sheriff Carson's case? You're a fed."

Kilraven put his finger to his lips and looked around hastily to make sure nobody was listening. "I'm a policeman, working on the city force," he said curtly.

Alice held up both hands defensively. "Sorry! It's so hard to keep up with all these secrets!"

Kilraven glanced at his boss and back at Alice. "What secrets?"

"Well, there's the horseless cowboy there—" she pointed at Harley "—and the DB over on the Little Carmichael River…"

Kilraven's silver eyes widened. "On the river? I thought it was in town. Nobody told me!"

"I just did," Alice said. "But it's really a secret. I'm not supposed to tell anybody."

"I'm local law enforcement," Kilraven insisted. "You can tell me. Who is he?"

Alice gave him a bland look and propped a hand on her hip. "I only looked at him for two minutes before I realized I needed to get more investigative supplies. He's male and dead. He's got no ID, he's naked, and even his mother wouldn't recognize his face."

"Dental records…" Kilraven began.

"For those, you need identifiable teeth," Alice replied sweetly.

Harley was turning white.

She glanced at him. "Are you squeamish?" she asked hopefully. "Listen, I once examined this dead guy whose girlfriend caught him with a hooker. After she offed him, she cut off his… Where are you going?"

Harley was making a beeline for the interior of the hardware store.

"Bathroom, I imagine." Grier grinned at Kilraven, who chuckled.

"He works around cattle and he's squeamish?" Alice asked, delighted. "I'll bet he's a lot of fun when they round up the calves!"

"Not nice," Kilraven chided. "Everybody's got a weak spot, Jones. Even you."

"I have no weak spots," she assured him.

"No social life, either," Grier murmured. "I heard you tried to conduct a postmortem on a turkey in North Carolina during a murder investigation there."

"It met with fowl play," she said, straight-faced.

Both men chuckled.

"I have to get to work," she said, becoming serious. "This is a strange case. Nobody knows who this guy is or where he came from, and there was a serious attempt to make him unidentifiable. Even with DNA, when I can get a profile back from state—and don't hold your breath on the timetable—I don't know if we can identify him. If he has no criminal record, he won't be on file anywhere."

"At least we don't get many of these," Kilraven said quietly.

Jones smiled at him. "When are you coming back up to San Antonio?" she asked. "You solved the Pendleton kidnapping and helped wrap up the perps."

"Just a few loose ends to tie up," he said. He nodded at her and his boss. "I'll get back on patrol."

"Brady's wife made potato soup and real corn bread for lunch. Don't miss it."

"Not me, boss."

Alice stared after the handsome officer. "He's a dish. But isn't he overstaying his purpose down here?" she asked Cash.

He leaned down. "Winnie Sinclair works for the 911 center. Local gossip has it that he's sweet on her. That's why he's finding excuses not to leave."

Alice looked worried. "And he's dragging around a whole past that hardly anybody knows about. He's pretending it never happened."

"Maybe he has to."

She nodded. "It was bad. One of the worst cases I ever worked. Poor guy." She frowned. "They never solved it, you know. The perp is still out there, running around loose. It must have driven Kilraven and his brother, Jon Blackhawk, nuts, wondering if it was somebody they arrested, somebody with a grudge."

"Their father was an FBI agent in San Antonio, before he drank himself to death after the murders. Blackhawk still is," Cash replied thoughtfully. "Could have been a case any one of the three men worked, a perp getting even."

"It could," she agreed. "It must haunt the brothers. The guilt would be bad enough, but they wouldn't want to risk it happening again, to someone else they got involved with. They avoid women. Especially Kilraven."

"He wouldn't want to go through it again," Cash said.

"This Sinclair woman, how does she feel about Kilraven?"

Cash gave her a friendly smile. "I am not a gossip."

"Bull."

He laughed. "She's crazy about him. But she's very young."

"Age doesn't matter, in the long run," Alice said with

a faraway look in her eyes. "At least, sometimes." She opened the door. "See you around, Grier."

"You, too, Jones."

She walked into the hardware store. There at the counter was Harley, pale and out of sorts. He glared at her.

She held up both hands. "I wasn't even graphic," she said defensively. "And God only knows how you manage to help with branding, with that stomach."

"I ate something that didn't agree with me," he said icily.

"In that case, you must not have a lot of friends…."

The clerk doubled over laughing.

"I do not eat people!" Harley muttered.

"I should hope not," she replied. "I mean, being a cannibal is much worse than being a gardener."

"I am not a gardener!"

Alice gave the clerk a sweet smile. "Do you have chalk and colored string?" she asked. "I also need double-A batteries for my digital camera and some anti-bacterial hand cleaner."

The clerk looked blank.

Harley grinned. He knew this clerk very well. Sadly, Alice didn't. "Hey, John, this is a real, honest-to-goodness crime scene investigator," he told the young man. "She works out of the medical examiner's office in San Antonio!"

Alice felt her stomach drop as she noted the bright fascination in the clerk's eyes. The clerk's whole face became animated. "You do, really? Hey, I watch all those CSI shows," he exclaimed. "I know about DNA profiles. I even know how to tell how long a body's been dead just by identifying the insects on it…!"

"You have a great day, Ms. Jones," Harley told Alice, over the clerk's exuberant monologue.

She glared at him. "Oh, thanks very much."

He tipped his bibbed cap at her. "See you, John," he told the clerk. Harley picked up his purchases, smiling with pure delight, and headed right out the front door.

The clerk waved an absent hand in his general direction, never taking his eyes off Alice. "Anyway, about those insects," he began enthusiastically.

Alice followed him around the store for her supplies, groaning inwardly as he kept talking. She never ran out of people who could tell her how to do her job these days, thanks to the proliferation of television shows on forensics. She tried to explain that most labs were understaffed, under-budgeted, and that lab results didn't come back in an hour, even for a department like hers, on the University of Texas campus, which had a national reputation for excellence. But the bug expert here was on a roll and he wasn't listening. She resigned herself to the lecture and forced a smile. Wouldn't do to make enemies here, not when she might be doing more business with him later. She was going to get even with that smug cowboy the next time she saw him, though.

The riverbank was spitting out law enforcement people. Alice groaned as she bent to the poor body and began to take measurements. She'd already had an accommodating young officer from the Jacobsville Police Department run yellow police tape all around the crime scene. That didn't stop people from stepping over it, however.

"You stop that," Alice muttered at two men wearing deputy sheriff uniforms. They both stopped with one foot in the air at the tone of her voice. "No tramping around on my crime scene! That yellow tape is to keep people *out*."

"Sorry," one murmured sheepishly, and they both went back on their side of the line. Alice pushed away a strand of sweaty hair with the back of a latex-gloved hand and muttered to herself. It was almost Christmas, but the weather had gone nuts and it was hot. She'd already taken off her wool jacket and replaced it with a lab coat, but her slacks were wool and she was burning up. Not to mention that this guy had been lying on the riverbank for at least a day and he was ripe. She had Vicks Salve under her nose, but it wasn't helping a lot.

For the hundredth time, she wondered why she'd ever chosen such a messy profession. But it was very satisfying when she could help catch a murderer, which she had many times over the years. Not that it substituted for a family. But most men she met were repelled by her profession. Sometimes she tried to keep it to herself. But inevitably there would be a movie or a TV show that would mention some forensic detail and Alice would hold forth on the misinformation she noted. Sometimes it was rather graphic, like with the vengeful cowboy in the hardware store.

Then there would be the forced smiles. The excuses. And so it went. Usually that happened before the end of the first date. Or at least the second.

"I'll bet I'm the only twenty-six-year-old virgin in the whole damned state of Texas," she muttered to herself.

"Excuse me?" one of the deputies, a woman, exclaimed with wide, shocked eyes.

"That's right, you just look at me as if I sprouted horns and a tail," she murmured as she worked. "I know I'm an anachronism."

"That's not what I meant," the deputy said, chuckling. "Listen, there are a lot of women our ages with that attitude. I don't want some unspeakable condition that I catch from a man who passes himself around like a dish of peanuts at a bar. And do you think they're going to tell you they've got something?"

Alice beamed. "I like you."

She chuckled. "Thanks. I think of it as being sensible." She lowered her voice. "See Kilraven over there?" she asked, drawing Alice's eyes to the arrival of another local cop—even if he really was a fed pretending to be one. "They say his brother, Jon Blackhawk, has never had a woman in his life. And we think we're prudes!"

Alice chuckled. "That's what I heard, too. Sensible man!"

"Very." The deputy was picking up every piece of paper, every cigarette butt she could find with latex gloves on, bagging them for Alice for evidence. "What about that old rag, Jones, think I should put it in a bag, too? Look at this little rusty spot."

Alice glanced at it, frowning. It was old, but there was a trace of something on it, something newer than the rag. "Yes," she said. "I think it's been here for a while, but that's new trace evidence on it. Careful not to touch the rusty-looking spot."

"Blood, isn't it?" She nodded.

"You're good," Alice said.

"I came down from Dallas PD," she said. "I got tired of big-city crime. Things are a little less hectic here. In fact, this is my first DB since I joined Sheriff Carson's department."

"That's a real change, I know," Alice said. "I work

out of San Antonio. Not the quietest place in the world, especially on weekends."

Kilraven had walked right over the police tape and came up near the body.

"What do you think you're doing?" Alice exclaimed. "Kilraven…!"

"Look," he said, his keen silver eyes on the grass just under the dead man's right hand, which was clenched and depressed into the mud. "There's something white."

Alice followed his gaze. She didn't even see it at first. She'd moved so that it was in shadow. But when she shifted, the sunlight caught it. Paper. A tiny sliver of paper, just peeping out from under the dead man's thumb. She reached down with her gloved hand and brushed away the grass. There was a deep indentation in the soft, mushy soil, next to his hand; maybe a footprint. "I need my camera before I move it," she said, holding out her hand. The deputy retrieved the big digital camera from its bag and handed it to Alice, who documented the find and recorded it on a graph of the crime scene. Then, returning the camera, she slid a pencil gently under the hand, moving it until she was able to see the paper. She reached into her kit for a pair of tweezers and tugged it carefully from his grasp.

"It's a tiny, folded piece of paper," she said, frowning. "And thank God it hasn't rained."

"Amen," Kilraven agreed, peering at the paper in her hand.

"Good eyes," she added with a grin.

He grinned back. "Lakota blood." He chuckled. "Tracking is in my genes. My great-great-grandfather was at Little Big Horn."

"I won't ask on which side," she said in a loud whisper.

"No need to be coy. He rode with Crazy Horse's band."

"Hey, I read about that," the deputy said. "Custer's guys were routed, they say."

"One of the Cheyenne people said later that a white officer was killed down at the river in the first charge," he said. "He said the officer was carried up to the last stand by his men, and after that the soldiers seemed to lose heart and didn't fight so hard. They found Custer's brother, Tom, and a couple of ranking officers from other units, including Custer's brother-in-law, with Custer. It could indicate that the chain of command changed several times. Makes sense, if you think about it. If there was a charge, Custer would have led it. Several historians think that Custer's unit made it into the river before the Cheyenne came flying into it after them. If Custer was killed early, he'd have been carried up to the last stand ridge—an enlisted guy, they'd have left there in the river."

"I never read that Custer got killed early in the fight," the deputy exclaimed.

"I've only ever seen the theory in one book—a warrior was interviewed who was on the Indian side of the fight, and he said he thought Custer was killed in the first charge," he mused. "The Indians' side of the story didn't get much attention until recent years. They said there were no surviving eyewitnesses. Bull! There were several tribes of eyewitnesses. It was just that nobody thought their stories were worth hearing just after the battle. Not the massacre," he added before the deputy could speak. "Massacres are when you kill unarmed people. Custer's men all had guns."

The deputy grinned. "Ever think of teaching history?"

"Teaching's too dangerous a profession. That's why I joined the police force instead." Kilraven chuckled.

"Great news for law enforcement," Alice said. "You have good eyes."

"You'd have seen it for yourself, Jones, eventually," he replied. "You're the best."

"Wow! Did you hear that? Take notes," Alice told the deputy. "The next time I get yelled at for not doing my job right, I'm quoting Kilraven."

"Would it help?" he asked.

She laughed. "They're still scared of you up in San Antonio," she said. "One of the old patrolmen, Jacobs, turns white when they mention your name. I understand the two of you had a little dustup?"

"I threw him into a fruit display at the local supermarket. Messy business. Did you know that blackberries leave purple stains on skin?" he added conversationally.

"I'm a forensic specialist," Alice reminded him. "Can I ask why you threw him into a fruit display?"

"We were working a robbery and he started making these remarks about fruit with one of the gay officers standing right beside me. The officer in question couldn't do anything without getting in trouble." He grinned. "Amazing, how attitudes change with a little gentle adjustment."

"Hey, Kilraven, what are you doing walking around on the crime scene?" Cash Grier called from the sidelines.

"Don't fuss at him," Alice called back. "He just spotted a crucial piece of evidence. You should give him an award!"

There were catcalls from all the officers present.

"I should get an award!" he muttered as he went to join his boss. "I never take days off or vacations!"

"That's because you don't have a social life, Kilraven," one of the officers joked.

Alice stood up, staring at the local law enforcement uniforms surrounding the crime scene tape. She recognized at least two cars from other jurisdictions. There was even a federal car out there! It wasn't unusual in a sleepy county like Jacobs for all officers who weren't busy to congregate around an event like this. It wasn't every day that you found a murder victim in your area. But a federal car for a local murder?

As she watched, Garon Grier and Jon Blackhawk of the San Antonio district FBI office climbed out of the BuCar—the FBI's term for a bureau car—and walked over the tape to join Alice.

"What have you found?" Grier asked.

She pursed her lips, glancing from the assistant director of the regional FBI office, Grier, to Special Agent Jon Blackhawk. What a contrast! Grier was blond and Blackhawk had long, jet-black hair tied in a ponytail. They were both tall and well-built without being flashy about it. Garon Grier, like his brother Cash, was married. Jon Blackhawk was unattached and available. Alice wished she was his type. He was every bit as good-looking as his half brother Kilraven.

"I found some bits and pieces of evidence, with the deputy's help. Your brother," she told Jon, "found this." She held up the piece of paper in an evidence bag. "Don't touch," she cautioned as both men peered in. "I'm not unfolding it until I can get it into my lab. I won't risk losing any trace evidence out here."

Blackhawk pulled out a pad and started taking notes. "Where was it?" he asked.

"Gripped in the dead man's fingers, out of sight. Why are you here?" she asked. "This is a local matter."

Blackhawk was cautious. "Not entirely," he said.

Kilraven joined them. He and Blackhawk exchanged uneasy glances.

"Okay. Something's going on that I can't be told about. It's okay." She held up a hand. "I'm used to being a mushroom. Kept in the dark and fed with…"

"Never mind," Garon told her. He softened it with a smile. "We've had a tip. Nothing substantial. Just something that interests us about this case."

"And you can't tell me what the tip was?"

"We found a car in the river, farther down," Cash said quietly. "San Antonio plates."

"Maybe his?" Alice indicated the body.

"Maybe. We're running the plates now," Cash said.

"So, do you think he came down here on his own, or did somebody bring him in a trunk?" Alice mused.

The men chuckled. "You're good, Alice," Garon murmured.

"Of course I am!" she agreed. "Could you," she called to the female deputy, "get me some plaster of Paris out of my van, in the back? This may be a footprint where we found the piece of paper! Thanks."

She went back to work with a vengeance while two sets of brothers looked on with intent interest.

Two

Alice fell into her bed at the local Jacobsville motel after a satisfying soak in the luxurious whirlpool bathtub. Amazing, she thought, to find such a high-ticket item in a motel in a small Texas town. She was told that film crews from Hollywood frequently chose Jacobs County as a location and that the owner of the motel wanted to keep them happy. It was certainly great news for Alice.

She'd never been so tired. The crime scene, they found, extended for a quarter of a mile down the river. The victim had fought for his life. There were scuff marks and blood trails all over the place. So much for her theory that he'd traveled to Jacobsville in the trunk of the car they'd found.

The question was, why had somebody brought a man down to Jacobsville to kill him? It made no sense.

She closed her eyes, trying to put herself in the shoes of the murderer. People usually killed for a handful of reasons. They killed deliberately out of jealousy, anger or greed. Sometimes they killed accidentally. Often, it was an impulse that led to a death, or a series of acts that pushed a person over the edge. All too often, it was drugs or alcohol that robbed someone of impulse control, and that led inexorably to murder.

Few people went into an argument or a fight intending to kill someone. But it wasn't as if you could take it back even seconds after a human life expired. There were thousands of young people in prison who would have given anything to relive a single incident where they'd made a bad choice. Families suffered for those choices, along with their children. So often, it was easy to overlook the fact that even murderers had families, often decent, law-abiding families that agonized over what their loved one had done and paid the price along with them.

Alice rolled over, restlessly. Her job haunted her from time to time. Along with the coroner, and the investigating officers, she was the last voice of the deceased. She spoke for them, by gathering enough evidence to bring the killer to trial. It was a holy grail. She took her duties seriously. But she also had to live with the results of the murderer's lack of control. It was never pleasant to see a dead body. Some were in far worse conditions than others. She carried those memories as certainly as the family of the deceased carried them.

Early on, she'd learned that she couldn't let herself become emotionally involved with the victims. If she started crying, she'd never stop, and she wouldn't be effective in her line of work.

She found a happy medium in being the life of the

party at crime scenes. It diverted her from the misery of her surroundings and, on occasion, helped the crime scene detectives cope as well. One reporter, a rookie, had given her a hard time because of her attitude. She'd invited him to her office for a close-up look at the world of a real forensic investigator.

The reporter had arrived expecting the corpse, always tastefully displayed, to be situated in the tidy, high-tech surroundings that television crime shows had accustomed him to seeing.

Instead, Alice pulled the sheet from a drowning victim who'd been in the water three days.

She never saw the reporter again. Local cops who recounted the story, always with choked-back laughter, told her that he'd turned in his camera the same day and voiced an ambition to go into real estate.

Just as well, she thought. The real thing was pretty unpleasant. Television didn't give you the true picture, because there was no such thing as smell-o-vision. She could recall times when she'd gone through a whole jar of Vicks Salve trying to work on a drowning victim like the one she'd shown the critical member of the Fourth Estate.

She rolled over again. She couldn't get her mind to shut down long enough to allow for sleep. She was reviewing the meager facts she'd uncovered at the crime scene, trying to make some sort of sense out of it. Why would somebody drive a murder victim out of the city to kill him? Maybe because he didn't know he was going to become a murder victim. Maybe he got in the car voluntarily.

Good point, she thought. But it didn't explain the crime. Heat of passion wouldn't cover this one. It was too deliberate. The perp meant to hide evidence. And he had.

She sighed. She wished she'd become a detective instead of a forensic specialist. It must be more fun solving crimes than being knee-deep in bodies. And prospective dates wouldn't look at you from a safe distance with that expression of utter distaste, like that gardener in the hardware store this afternoon.

What had Grier called him, Fowler? Harley Fowler, that was it. Not a bad-looking man. He had a familiar face. Alice wondered why. She was sure she'd never seen him before today. She was sure she'd remember somebody that disagreeable.

Maybe he resembled somebody she knew. That was possible. Fowler. Fowler. No. It didn't ring any bells. She'd have to let her mind brood on it for a couple of days. Sometimes that's all it took to solve such puzzles—background working of the subconscious. She chuckled to herself. *Background workings,* she thought, *will save me yet.*

After hours of almost-sleep, she got up, dressed and went back to the crime scene. It was quiet, now, without the presence of almost every uniformed officer in the county. The body was lying in the local funeral home, waiting for transport to the medical examiner's office in San Antonio. Alice had driven her evidence up to San Antonio, to the crime lab, and turned it over to the trace evidence people, specifically Longfellow.

She'd entrusted Longfellow with the precious piece of paper which might yield dramatic evidence, once unfolded. There had clearly been writing on it. The dead man had grasped it tight in his hand while he was being killed, and had managed to conceal it from his killer. It must have something on it that he was desperate to preserve. Amazing. She wanted to know what it was. Tomorrow, she promised herself, their best trace evidence specialist, Longfellow, would have that paper turned every which way but loose in her lab, and she'd find answers for Alice. She was one of the best CSI people Alice had ever worked with. When Alice drove right back down to Jacobsville, she knew she'd have answers from the lab soon.

Restless, she looked around at the lonely landscape, bare in winter. The local police were canvassing the surrounding area for anyone who'd seen something unusual in the past few days, or who'd noticed an out-of-town car around the river.

Alice paced the riverbank, a lonely figure in a neat white sweatshirt with blue jeans, staring out across the ripples of the water while her sneakers tried to sink into the damp sand. It was cooler today, in the fifties, about normal for a December day in south Texas.

Sometimes she could think better when she was alone at the crime scene. Today wasn't one of those days. She was acutely aware of her aloneness. It was worse now, after the death of her father a month ago. He was her last living relative. He'd been a banker back in Tennessee, where she'd taken courses in forensics. The family was from Floresville, just down the road from San Antonio. But her parents had moved away to Tennessee when she was in her last year of high school, and that had been a wrench. Alice had a crush on a boy in her class, but the move killed any hope of a relationship. She really had been a late bloomer, preferring to hang out in the biology lab rather than think about dating. Amoeba under the microscope were so much more interesting.

Alice had left home soon after her mother's death, the year she started college. Her mother had been a live wire, a happy and well-adjusted woman who could do almost anything around the house, especially cook. She despaired of Alice, her only child, who watched endless reruns of the old TV show *Quincy,* about a medical examiner, along with archaic *Perry Mason* episodes. Long before it was popular, Alice had dreamed of being a crime scene technician.

She'd been an ace at biology in high school. Her science teachers had encouraged her, delighting in her bright enthusiasm. One of them had recommended her to a colleague at the University of Texas campus in San Antonio, who'd steered her into a science major and helped her find local scholarships to supplement the small amount her father could afford for her. It had been an uphill climb to get that degree, and to add to it with courses from far-flung universities when time and money permitted; one being courses in forensic anthropology at the University of Tennessee in Knoxville. In between, she'd slogged away with other techs at one crime scene after another, gaining experience.

Once, in her haste to finish gathering evidence, due to a rare prospective date, she'd slipped up and mislabeled blood evidence. That had cost the prosecution staff a conviction. It had been a sobering experience for Alice, especially when the suspect went out and killed a young boy before being rearrested. Alice felt responsible for that boy's death. She never forgot how haste had put the nails in his coffin, and she never slipped up again. She gained a reputation for being precise and meticulous in evidence-gathering. And she never went home early again. Alice was almost always the last person to leave the lab, or the crime scene, at the end of the day.

A revved-up engine caught her attention. She turned as a carload of young boys pulled up beside her white van at the river's edge.

"Lookie there, a lonely lady!" one of them called. "Ain't she purty?"

"Shore is! Hey, pretty thing, you like younger men? We can make you happy!"

"You bet!" Another one laughed.

"Hey, lady, you feel like a party?!" another one cat-called.

Alice glared. "No, I don't feel like a party. Take a hike!" She turned back to her contemplation of the river, hoping they'd give up and leave.

"Aww, that ain't no way to treat prospective boy-friends!" one yelled back. "Come on up here and lie down, lady. We want to talk to you!"

More raucous laughter echoed out of the car.

So much for patience. She was in no mood for teen-agers acting out. She pulled out the pad and pen she always carried in her back pocket and walked up the bank and around to the back of their car. She wrote down the license plate number without being obvious about it. She'd call in a harassment call and let local law enforcement help her out. But even as she thought about it, she hesitated. There had to be a better way to handle this bunch of loonies without involving the law. She was overreacting. They were just teenagers, after all. Inspiration struck as she reemerged at the driver's side of the car.

She ruffled her hair and moved closer to the tow-headed young driver. She leaned down. "I like your tires," she drawled with a wide grin. "They're real nice. And wide. And they have treads. I *like* treads." She wiggled her eyebrows at him. "You like treads?"

He stared at her. The silly expression went into eclipse. "Treads?" His voice sounded squeaky. He tried again. "Tire…treads?"

"Yeah. Tire treads." She stuck her tongue in and out and grinned again. "I *reeaaally* like tire treads."

He was trying to pretend that he wasn't talking to a lunatic. "Uh. You do. Really."

She was enjoying herself now. The other boys seemed even more confused than the driver did. They were all staring at her. Nobody was laughing.

She frowned. "No, you don't like treads. You're just humoring me. Okay. If you don't like treads, you might like what I got in the truck," she said, lowering her voice. She jerked her head toward the van.

He cleared his throat. "I might like what you got in the truck," he parroted.

She nodded, grinning, widening her eyes until the whites almost gleamed. She leaned forward. "I got bodies in there!" she said in a stage whisper and levered her eyes wide-open. "Real dead bodies! Want to see?"

The driver gaped at her. Then he exclaimed, "Dead… bod…. Oh, Good Lord, no!"

He jerked back from her, slammed his foot down on the accelerator, and spun sand like dust as he roared back out onto the asphalt and left a rubber trail behind him.

She shook her head. "Was it something I said?" she asked a nearby bush.

She burst out laughing. She really did need a vacation, she told herself.

* * *

Harley Fowler saw the van sitting on the side of the road as he moved a handful of steers from one pasture to another. With the help of Bob, Cy Parks's veteran cattle dog, he put the little steers into their new area and closed the gate behind him. A carload of boys roared up beside the van and got noisy. They were obviously hassling the crime scene woman. Harley recognized her van.

His pale blue eyes narrowed and began to glitter. He didn't like a gang of boys trying to intimidate a lone woman. He reached into his saddlebag and pulled out his gunbelt, stepping down out of the saddle to strap it on. He tied the horse to a bar of the gate and motioned Bob to stay. Harley strolled off toward the van.

He didn't think he'd have to use the pistol, of course. The threat of it would be more than enough. But if any of the boys decided to have a go at him, he could put them down with his fists. He'd learned a lot from Eb Scott and the local mercs. He didn't need a gun to enforce his authority. But if the sight of it made the gang of boys a little more likely to leave without trouble, that was all right, too.

He moved into sight just at the back of Alice's van. She was leaning over the driver's side of the car. He couldn't hear what she said, but he could certainly hear what the boy exclaimed as he roared out onto the highway and took off.

Alice was talking to a bush.

Harley stared at her with confusion.

Alice sensed that she was no longer alone, and she turned. She blinked. "Have you been there long?" she asked hesitantly.

"Just long enough to see the Happy Teenager Gang

take a powder," he replied. "Oh, and to hear you asking a bush about why they left." His eyes twinkled. "Talk to bushes a lot in your line of work, do you?"

She was studying him curiously, especially the low-slung pistol in its holster. "You on your way to a gunfight and just stopped by to say hello?"

"I was moving steers," he replied. "I heard the teenagers giving you a hard time and came to see if you needed any help. Obviously not."

"Were you going to offer to shoot them for me?" she asked.

He chuckled. "Never had to shoot any kids," he said with emphasis.

"You've shot other sorts of people?"

"One or two," he said pleasantly, but this time he didn't smile.

She felt chills go down her spine. If her livelihood made him queasy, the way he looked wearing that sidearm made her feel the same way. He wasn't the easygoing cowboy she'd met in town the day before. He reminded her oddly of Cash Grier, for reasons she couldn't put into words. There was cold steel in this man. He had the self-confidence of a man who'd been tested under fire. It was unusual, in a modern man. Unless, she considered, he'd been in the military, or some paramilitary unit.

"I don't shoot women," he said when she hesitated.

"Good thing," she replied absently. "I don't have any bandages."

He moved closer. She seemed shaken. He scowled. "You okay?"

She shifted uneasily. "I guess so."

"Mind telling me how you got them to leave so quickly?"

"Oh. That. I just asked if they'd like to see the dead bodies in my van."

He blinked. He was sure he hadn't heard her right. "You asked if…?" he prompted.

She sighed. "I guess it was a little over the top. I was going to call Hayes Carson and have him come out and save me, but it seemed a bit much for a little catcalling."

He didn't smile. "Let me tell you something. A little catcalling, if they get away with it, can lead to a little harassment, and if they get away with that, it can lead to a little assault, even if drugs or alcohol aren't involved. Boys need limits, especially at that age. You should have called it in and let Hayes Carson come out here and scare the hell out of them."

"Well, aren't you the voice of experience!"

"I should be," he replied. "When I was sixteen, an older boy hassled a girl in our class repeatedly on campus after school and made fun of me when I objected to it. A few weeks later, after she'd tried and failed to get somebody to do something about him, he assaulted her."

She let out a whistle. "Heavy stuff."

"Yes, and the teacher who thought I was overreacting when I told him was later disciplined for his lack of response," he added coldly.

"We live in difficult times," she said.

"Count on it."

She glanced in the direction the car had gone. "I still have the license plate number," she murmured.

"Give it to Hayes and tell him what happened," he encouraged her. "Even if you don't press charges, he'll keep an eye on them. Just in case."

She studied his face. "You liked that girl."

"Yes. She was sweet and kind-natured. She…"

She moved a little closer. "She…?"

"She killed herself," he said tightly. "She was very religious. She couldn't live with what happened, especially after she had to testify to it in court and everyone knew."

"They seal those files…" she began.

"Get real," he shot back. "It happened in a small town just outside San Antonio, not much bigger than Jacobsville. I was living there temporarily with a nice older couple and going to school with her when it happened. The people who sat on the jury and in the courtroom were all local. They knew her."

"Oh," she said softly. "I'm sorry."

He nodded.

"How long did the boy get?"

"He was a juvenile," he said heavily. "He was under eighteen when it happened. He stayed in detention until he was twenty-one and they turned him loose."

"Pity."

"Yes." He shook himself as if the memory had taken him over and he wanted to be free of it. "I never heard anything about him after that. I hope he didn't prosper."

"Was he sorry, do you think?"

He laughed coldly. "Sorry he got caught, yes."

"I've seen that sort in court," she replied, her eyes darkening with the memory. "Cocky and self-centered, contemptuous of everybody around them. Especially people in power."

"Power corrupts," he began.

"And absolute power corrupts absolutely," she finished for him. "Lord Acton," she cited belatedly.

"Smart gent." He nodded toward the river. "Any new thoughts on the crime scene?"

She shook her head. "I like to go there alone and

think. Sometimes I get ideas. I still can't figure how he died here, when he was from San Antonio, unless he came voluntarily with someone and didn't know they were going to kill him when they arrived."

"Or he came down here to see somebody," he returned, "and was ambushed."

"Wow," she said softly, turning to face him. "You're good."

There was a faint, ruddy color on his high cheekbones. "Thanks."

"No, I mean it," she said when she saw his expression. "That wasn't sarcasm."

He relaxed a little.

"We got off to a bad start, and it's my fault," Alice admitted. "Dead bodies make me nervous. I'm okay once I get started documenting things. It's the first sight of it that upsets me. You caught me at a bad time, at the hardware store. I didn't mean to embarrass you."

"Nothing embarrasses me," he said easily.

"I'm sorry, just the same."

He relaxed a little more.

She frowned as she studied his handsome face. He really was good-looking. "You look so familiar to me," she said. "I can't understand why. I've never met you before."

"They say we all have a doppelgänger," he mused. "Someone who looks just like us."

"Maybe that's it," she agreed. "San Antonio is a big city, for all its small-town atmosphere. We've got a lot of people. You must resemble someone I've seen."

"Probably."

She looked again at the crime scene. "I hope I can get enough evidence to help convict somebody of this. It was a really brutal murder. I don't like to think of people who can do things like that being loose in society."

He was watching her, adding up her nice figure and her odd personality. She was unique. He liked her. He wasn't admitting it, of course.

"How did you get into forensic work?" he asked. "Was it all those crime shows on TV?"

"It was the *Quincy* series," she confessed. "I watched reruns of it on TV when I was a kid. It fascinated me. I liked him, too, but it was the work that caught my attention. He was such an advocate for the victims." Her eyes became soft with reminiscence. "I remember when evidence I collected solved a crime. It was my first real case. The parents of the victim came over and hugged me after the prosecutor pointed me out to them. I always went to the sentencing if I could get away, in cases I worked. That was the first time I realized how important my work was." She grinned wickedly. "The convicted gave me the finger on his way out of the courtroom with a sheriff's deputy. I grinned at him. Felt good. Really good."

He laughed. It was a new sound, and she liked it.

"Does that make me less spooky?" she asked, moving a step closer.

"Yes, it does."

"You think I'm, you know, normal?"

"Nobody's really normal. But I know what you mean," he said, and he smiled at her, a genuine smile. "Yes, I think you're okay."

She cocked her head up at him and her blue eyes twinkled. "Would you believe that extraordinarily handsome Hollywood movie stars actually call me up for dates?"

"Do they, really?" he drawled.

"No, but doesn't it sound exciting?"

He laughed again.

She moved another step closer. "What I said, about not purchasing you if you were on sale in a groom shop…I didn't really mean it. There's a nice ring in that jewelry shop in Jacobsville," she said dreamily. "A man's wedding ring." She peered up through her lashes. "I could buy it for you."

He pursed his lips. "You could?"

"Yes. And I noticed that there's a minister at that Methodist Church. Are you Methodist?"

"Not really."

"Neither am I. Well, there's a justice of the peace in the courthouse. She marries people."

He was just listening now. His eyes were wide.

"If you liked the ring, and if it fit, we could talk to the justice of the peace. They also have licenses."

He pursed his lips again. "Whoa," he said after a minute. "I only met you yesterday."

"I know." She blinked. "What does that have to do with getting married?"

"I don't know you."

"Oh. Okay. I'm twenty-six. I still have most of my own teeth." She displayed them. "I'm healthy and athletic, I like to knit but I can hunt, too, and I have guns. I don't like spinach, but I love liver and onions. Oh, and I'm a virgin." She smiled broadly.

He was breathless by this time. He stared at her intently.

"It's true," she added when he didn't comment. She scowled. "Well, I don't like diseases and you can't look at a man and tell if he has one." She hesitated. Frowned worriedly. "You don't have any…?"

"No, I don't have any diseases," he said shortly. "I'm fastidious about women."

"What a relief!" she said with a huge sigh. "Well, that covers all the basics." Her blue eyes smiled up at him and she batted her long black eyelashes. "So when do we see the justice of the peace?"

"Not today," he replied. "I'm washing Bob."

"Bob?"

He pointed toward the cattle dog, who was still sitting at the pasture gate. He whistled. Bob came running up to him, wagging her long, silky tail and hassling. She looked as if she was always smiling.

"Hi, Bob," Alice said softly, and bent to offer a hand, which Bob smelled. Then Alice stroked the silky head. "Nice boy."

"Girl," he corrected. "Bob's a girl."

She blinked at him.

"Mr. Parks said if Johnny Cash could have a boy named Sue, he could have a girl dog named Bob."

"He's got a point," she agreed. She ruffled Bob's fur affectionately. "You're a beaut, Bob," she told the dog.

"She really is. Best cattle dog in the business, and she can get into places in the brush that we can't, on horseback, to flush out strays."

"Do you come from a ranching family?" she asked absently as she stroked the dog.

"Actually I didn't know much about cattle when I went to work for Mr. Parks. He had one of his men train me."

"Wow. Nice guy."

"He is. Dangerous, but nice."

She lifted her head at the use of the word and frowned slightly. "Dangerous?"

"Do you know anything about Eb Scott and his outfit?"

"The mercenary." She nodded. "We all know about his training camp down here. A couple of our officers use his firing range. He made it available to everyone in law enforcement. He's got friends in our department."

"Well, he and Mr. Parks and Dr. Micah Steele were part of a group who used to make their living as mercenaries."

"I remember now," she exclaimed. "There was a shoot-out with some of that drug lord Lopez's men a few years ago!"

"Yes. I was in it."

She let out a breath. "Brave man, to go up against those bozos. They carry automatic weapons."

"I noticed." That was said with a droll expression worth a hundred words.

She searched his eyes with quiet respect. "Now, I really want to see the justice of the peace. I'd be safe anywhere."

He laughed. "I'm not that easy. You haven't even brought me flowers, or asked me out to a nice restaurant."

"Oh, dear."

"What?"

"I don't get paid until Friday, and I'm broke," she said sorrowfully. She made a face. "Well, maybe next week? Or we could go dutch…"

He chuckled with pure delight. "I'm broke, too."

"So, next week?"

"We'll talk about it."

She grinned. "Okay."

"Better get your van going," he said, holding out a palm-up hand and looking up. "We're going to get a rain shower. You could be stuck in that soft sand when it gets wet."

"I could. See you."

"See you."

She took off running for the van. Life was looking up, she thought happily.

Three

Harley went back to the ranch house with Bob racing beside his horse. He felt exhilarated for the first time in years. Usually he got emotionally involved with girls who were already crazy about some other man. He was the comforting shoulder, the listening ear. But Alice Jones seemed to really like him.

Of course, there was her profession. He felt cold when he thought about her hands working on dead tissue. That was a barrier he'd have to find some way to get past. Maybe by concentrating on what a cute woman she was.

Cy Parks was outside, looking over a bunch of young bulls in the corral. He looked up when Harley dismounted.

"What do you think, Harley?" he asked, nodding toward several very trim young Santa Gertrudis bulls.

"Nice," he said. "These the ones you bought at the

auction we went to back in October? Gosh, they've grown!"

He nodded. "They are. I brought them in to show to J. D. Langley. He's looking for some young bulls for his own herd. I thought I'd sell him a couple of these. Good thing I didn't have to send them back."

Harley chuckled. "Good thing, for the seller. I remember the lot we sent back last year. I had to help you deliver them."

"Yes, I remember," Cy replied. "He slugged you and I slugged him."

Harley resisted a flush. It made him feel good, that Mr. Parks liked him enough to defend him. He could hardly recall his father. It had been years since they'd had any contact at all. He felt a little funny recalling how he'd lied to his boss about his family, claiming that his mother could help brand cattle and his father was a mechanic. He'd gone to live with an older couple he knew after a fight with his real folks. It was a small ranch they owned, but only the wife lived on it. Harley had stayed in town with the husband at his mechanic's shop most of the time. He hadn't been interested in cattle at the time. Now, they were his life and Mr. Parks had taken the place of his father, although Harley had never put it into words. Someday, he guessed, he was going to have to tell his boss the truth about himself. But not today.

"Have any trouble settling the steers in their new pasture?" Cy asked.

"None at all. The forensic lady was out at the river."

"Alice Jones?"

"Yes. She said sometimes she likes to look around crime scenes alone. She gets impressions." He smiled.

"I helped her with an idea about how the murder was committed."

Parks looked at him and smiled. "You've got a good brain, Harley."

He grinned. "Thanks."

"So what was your idea?"

"Maybe the victim was here to see somebody and got ambushed."

Parks's expression became solemn. "That's an interesting theory. If she doesn't share it with Hayes Carson, you should. There may be somebody local involved in all this."

"That's not a comforting thought."

"I know." He frowned as he noted the gun and holster Harley was wearing. "Did we have a gunfight and I wasn't invited?"

"This?" Harley fingered the butt of the gun. "Oh. No! There were some local boys trying to harass Alice. I strapped it on for effect and went to help her, but she'd already sent them running."

"Threatened to call the cops, huh?" he asked pleasantly.

"She invited them to her van to look at bodies," he said, chuckling. "They left tread marks on the highway."

He grinned back. "Well! Sounds like she has a handle on taking care of herself."

"Yes. But we all need a little backup, from time to time," Harley said.

Cy put a hand on Harley's shoulder. "You were mine, that night we had the shoot-out with the drug dealers. You're a good man under fire."

"Thanks," Harley said, flushing a little with the praise. "You'll never know how I felt, when you said that, after we got home."

"Maybe I do. See about that cattle truck, will you? I

think it's misfiring again, and you're the best mechanic we've got."

"I'll do it. Just don't tell Buddy you meant it," he pleaded. "He's supposed to be the mechanic."

"Supposed to be is right," Cy huffed. "But I guess you've got a point. Try to tell him, in a nice way, that he needs to check the spark plugs."

"You could tell him," Harley began.

"Not the way you can. If I tell him, he'll quit." He grimaced. "Already lost one mechanic that way this year. Can't afford to lose another. You do it."

Harley laughed. "Okay. I'll find a way."

"You always do. Don't know what I'd do without you, Harley. You're an asset as a foreman." He studied the younger man quietly. "I never asked where you came from. You said you knew cattle, but you really didn't. You learned by watching, until I hooked you up with old Cal and let him tutor you. I always respected the effort you put in, to learn the cattle business. But you're still as mysterious as you were the day you turned up."

"Sometimes it's better to look ahead, and not backward," Harley replied.

Parks smiled. "Enough said. See you later."

"Sure."

He walked off toward the house where his young wife, Lisa, was waiting with one preschool-aged boy and one infant boy in her arms. Of all the people Harley would never have expected to marry, Mr. Parks was first on his list. The rancher had been reclusive, hard to get along with and, frankly, bad company. Lisa had changed him. Now, it was impossible to think of him as anything except a family man. Marriage had mellowed him.

Harley thought about what Parks had said, about how mysterious he was. Maybe Mr. Parks thought he was running from the law. That was a real joke. Harley was running from his family. He'd had it up to his neck with monied circles and important people and parents who thought position was everything. They'd argued heatedly one summer several years ago, when Harley was sixteen, about Harley's place in the family and his lack of interest in their social life. He'd walked out.

He had a friend whose aunt and uncle owned a small ranch and had a mechanic's shop in Floresville. He'd taken Harley down there and they'd invited him to move in. He'd had his school files transferred to the nearest high school and he'd started his life over. His parents had objected, but they hadn't tried to force him to come back home. He graduated and went into the Army. But, just after he returned to Texas following his release from the Army, he went to see his parents and saw that nothing had changed at all. He was expected to do his part for the family by helping win friends and influencing the right people. Harley had left that very night, paid cash for a very old beat-up pickup truck and turned himself into a vagabond cowhand looking for work.

He'd gone by to see the elderly couple he'd lived with during his last year of high school, but the woman had died, the ranch had been sold and the mechanic had moved to Dallas. Discouraged, Harley had been driving through Jacobsville looking for a likely place to hire on when he'd seen cowboys working cattle beside the road. He'd talked to them and heard that Cy Parks was hiring. The rest was history.

He knew that people wondered about him. He kept his silence. It was new and pleasant to be accepted at

face value, to have people look at him for who he was
and what he knew how to do rather than at his background. He was happy in Jacobsville.

He did wonder sometimes if his people missed
him. He read about them in the society columns.
There had been a big political dustup just recently and
a landslide victory for a friend of his father's. That had
caught his attention. But it hadn't prompted him to try
to mend fences. Years had passed since his sudden
exodus from San Antonio, but it was still too soon for
that. No, he liked being just plain Harley Fowler,
cowboy. He wasn't risking his hard-won place in Jacobsville for anything.

Alice waited for Hayes Carson in his office, frowning
as she looked around. Wanted posters. Reams of paper-
work. A computer that was obsolete, paired with a
printer that was even more obsolete. An old IBM Selec-
tric typewriter. A battered metal wastebasket that looked
as if it got kicked fairly often. A CB unit. She shook her
head. There wasn't one photograph anywhere in the
room, except for a framed one of Hayes's father, Dallas,
who'd been sheriff before him. Nothing personal.

Hayes walked in, reading a sheet of paper.

"You really travel light, don't you?" Alice mused.

He looked up, surprised. "Why do you say that?"

"This is the most impersonal office I've ever walked
into. Wait." She held up a hand. "I take that back. Jon
Blackhawk's office is worse. He doesn't even have a
photograph in his."

"My dad would haunt me if I removed his." He
chuckled, sitting down behind the desk.

"Heard anything from the feds?"

"Yes. They got a report back on the car. It was reported missing by a woman who works for a San Antonio politician yesterday. She has no idea who took it."

"Damn." She sighed and leaned back. "Well, Longfellow's working on that piece of paper I found at the crime scene and we may get something from the cast I made of the footprint. We did find faint sole markings, from a sneaker. FBI lab has the cast. They'll track down which company made the shoe and try to trace where it was sold."

"That's a damned long shot."

"Hey, they've solved crimes from chips of paint."

"I guess so."

She was deep in thought. "Odd, how that paper was pushed into the dirt under his hand."

"Somebody stepped on it," Hayes reminded her.

"No." Her eyes narrowed. "It was clenched in the victim's hand and hidden under it."

Hayes frowned. "Maybe the victim was keeping it hidden deliberately?"

She nodded. "Like, maybe he knew he was going to die and wanted to leave a clue that might bring his killer to justice."

Hayes chuckled. "Jones, you watch too many crime dramas on TV."

"Actually, to hear the clerk at the hardware tell it I don't watch enough," she sighed. "I got a ten-minute lecture on forensic entomology while he hunted up some supplies I needed."

"Bug forensics?" he asked.

She nodded. "You can tell time of death by insect activity. I've actually taken courses on it. And I've solved at least one murder with the help of a bug expert." She pushed back a stray wisp of dark hair. "But what's really interesting, Carson, is teeth."

He frowned. "Teeth?"

She nodded. "Dentition. You can tell so much about a DB from its teeth, especially if there are dental records available. For example, there's Carabelli's cusp, which is most frequently found in people of European ancestry. Then there's the Uto-Aztecan upper premolar with a bulging buccal cusp which is found only in Native Americans. You can identify Asian ancestry in shovel-shaped incisors... Well, anyway, your ancestry, even the story of your life, is in your teeth. Your diet, your age..."

"Whether you got in bar fights," he interrupted.

She laughed. "Missing some teeth, are we?"

"Only a couple," he said easily. "I've calmed right down in my old age."

"You and Kilraven," she agreed dubiously.

He laughed. "Not that yahoo," he corrected. "Kilraven will never calm down, and you can quote me."

"He might, if he can ever slay his demons." She frowned thoughtfully and narrowed her eyes. "We have a lot of law enforcement down here that works in San Antonio." She was thinking out loud. "There's Garon Grier, the assistant SAC in the San Antonio field office. There's Rick Marquez, who works as a detective for San Antonio P.D. And then there's Kilraven."

"You trying to say something?" he asked.

She shook her head. "I'm linking unconnected facts. Sometimes it helps. Okay, here goes. A guy comes down here from San Antonio and gets whacked. He's driving somebody else's stolen car. He's messed up so badly that his own mother couldn't identify him. Whoever killed him didn't want him ID'd."

"Lots of reasons for that, maybe."

"Maybe. Hear me out. I'm doing pattern associations." She got up, locked her hands behind her waist, and started pacing, tossing out thoughts as they presented themselves. "Of all those law enforcement people, Kilraven's been the most conspicuous in San Antonio lately. He was with his brother, Jon, when they tried to solve the kidnapping of Gracie Marsh, Jason Pendleton's stepsister…"

"Pendleton's wife, now," he interrupted with a grin.

She returned it. "He was also connected with the rescue of Rodrigo Ramirez, the DEA agent kidnapping victim whose wife, Glory, was an assistant D.A. in San Antonio."

Hayes leaned back in his chair. "That wasn't made public, any of it."

She nodded absently.

"Rick Marquez has been pretty visible, too," he pointed out. He frowned. "Wasn't Rick trying to convince Kilraven to let him reopen that murder case that involved his family?"

"Come to think of it, yes," she replied, stopping in front of the desk. "Kilraven refused. He said it would only resurrect all the pain, and the media would dine out on it. He and Jon both refused. They figured it was a random crime and the perp was long gone."

"But that wasn't the end of it."

"No," she said. "Marquez refused to quit. He promised to do his work on the QT and not reveal a word of it to anybody except the detective he brought in to help him sort through the old files." She grimaced. "But the investigation went nowhere. Less than a week into their project, Marquez and his fellow detective were told to drop the investigation."

Hayes pursed his lips. "Now isn't that interesting?"

"There's more," she said. "Marquez and the detective went to the D.A. and promised to get enough evidence to reopen the case if they were allowed to continue. The D.A. said to let him talk to a few people. The very next week, the detective who was working with Marquez on the case was suddenly pulled off Homicide and sent back to the uniformed division as a patrol sergeant. And Marquez was told politely to keep his nose out of the matter and not to pursue it any further."

Hayes was frowning now. "You know, it sounds very much as if somebody high up doesn't want that case reopened. And I have to ask why?"

She nodded. "Somebody is afraid the case may be solved. If I'm guessing right, somebody with an enormous amount of power in government."

"And we both know what happens when power is abused," Hayes said with a scowl. "Years ago, when I was still a deputy sheriff, one of my fellow deputies—a new recruit—decided on his own to investigate rumors of a house of prostitution being run out of a local motel. Like a lamb, he went to the county council and brought it up in an open meeting."

Alice grimaced, because she knew from long experience what most likely happened after that. "Poor guy!"

"Well, after he was fired and run out of town," Hayes said, "I was called in and told that I was not to involve myself in that case, if I wanted to continue as a deputy sheriff in this county. I'd made the comment that no law officer should be fired for doing his job, you see."

"What did you do?" she asked, because she knew Hayes. He wasn't the sort of person to take a threat like that lying down.

"Ran for sheriff and won," he said simply. He grinned. "Turns out the head of the county council was getting kickbacks from the pimp. I found out, got the evidence and called a reporter I knew in San Antonio."

"That reporter?" she exclaimed. "He got a Pulitzer Prize for the story! My gosh, Hayes, the head of the county council went to prison! But it was for more than corruption…"

"He and the pimp also ran a modest drug distribution ring," he interrupted. "He'll be going up before the parole board in a few months. I plan to attend the hearing." He smiled. "I do so enjoy these little informal board meetings."

"Ouch."

"People who go through life making their money primarily through dishonest dealings don't usually reform," he said quietly. "It's a basic character trait that no amount of well-meaning rehabilitation can reverse."

"We live among some very unsavory people."

"Yes. That's why we have law enforcement. I might add, that the law enforcement on the county level here is exceptional."

She snarled at him. He just grinned.

"What's your next move?" she asked.

"I'm not making one until I know what's in that note. Shouldn't your assistant have something by now, even if it's only the text of the message?"

"She should." Alice pulled out her cell phone and called her office. "But I'm probably way off base about Kilraven's involvement in this. Maybe the victim just ticked off the wrong people and paid for it. Maybe he had unpaid drug bills or something."

"That's always a possibility," Hayes had to agree.

The phone rang and rang. Finally it was answered. "Crime lab, Longfellow speaking."

"Did you know that you have the surname of a famous poet?" Alice teased.

The other woman was all business, all the time, and she didn't get jokes. "Yes. I'm a far-removed distant cousin of the poet, in fact. You want to know about your scrap of paper, I suppose? It's much too early for any analysis of the paper or ink…"

"The writing, Longfellow, the writing," Alice interrupted.

"As I said, it's too early in the analysis. We'd need a sample to compare, first, and then we'd need a handwriting expert…"

"But what does the message *say?*" Alice blurted out impatiently. Honest to God, the other woman was so ponderously slow sometimes!

"Oh, that. Just a minute." There was a pause, some paper ruffling, a cough. Longfellow came back on the line. "It doesn't say anything."

"You can't make out the letters? Is it waterlogged, or something?"

"It doesn't have letters."

"Then what does it have?" Alice said with the last of her patience straining at the leash. She was picturing Longfellow on the floor with herself standing over the lab tech with a large studded bat…

"It has numbers, Jones," came the droll reply. "Just a few numbers. Nothing else."

"An address?"

"Not likely."

"Give me the numbers."

"Only the last six are visible. The others apparently

were obliterated by the man's sweaty palms when he clenched it so tightly. Here goes."

She read the series of numbers.

"Which ones were obliterated?" Alice asked.

"Looks like the ones at the beginning. If it's a telephone number, the area code and the first of the exchange numbers is missing. We'll probably be able to reconstruct those at the FBI lab, but not immediately. Sorry."

"No, listen, you've been a world of help. If I controlled salaries, you'd get a raise."

"Why, thank you, Jones," came the astonished reply. "That's very kind of you to say."

"You're very welcome. Let me know if you come up with anything else."

"Of course I will."

Alice hung up. She looked at the numbers and frowned.

"What have you got?" Hayes asked.

"I'm not sure. A telephone number, perhaps."

He moved closer and peered at the paper where she'd written those numbers down. "Could that be the exchange?" he asked, noting some of the numbers.

"I don't know. If it is, it could be a San Antonio number, but we'd need to have the area code to determine that, and it's missing."

"Get that lab busy."

She glowered at him. "Like we sleep late, take two-hour coffee breaks, and wander into the crime lab about noon daily!"

"Sorry," he said, and grinned.

She pursed her full lips and gave him a roguish look. "Hey, you law enforcement guys live at doughnut shops and lounge around in the office reading sports magazines and playing games on the computer, right?"

He glowered back.

She held out one hand, palm up. "Welcome to the stereotype club."

"When will she have some more of those numbers?"

"Your guess is as good as mine. Has anybody spoken to the woman whose car was stolen to ask if someone she knew might have taken it? Or to pump her for information and find out if she really loaned it to him?" she added shrewdly.

"No, nobody's talked to her. The feds in charge of the investigation wanted to wait until they had enough information to coax her into giving them something they needed," he said.

"As we speak, they're roping Jon Blackhawk to his desk chair and gagging him," she pronounced with a grin. "His first reaction would be to drag her downtown and grill her."

"He's young and hotheaded. At least to hear his brother tell it."

"Kilraven loves his brother," Alice replied. "But he does know his failings."

"I wouldn't call rushing in headfirst a failing," Hayes pointed out.

"That's why you've been shot, Hayes," she said.

"Anybody can get shot," he said.

"Yes, but you've been shot twice," she reminded him. "The word locally is that you'd have a better chance of being named king of some small country than you'd have getting a wife. Nobody around here is rushing to line up and become a widow."

"I've calmed down," he muttered defensively. "And who's been saying that, anyway?"

"I heard that Minette Raynor was," she replied without quite meeting his eyes.

His jaw tautened. "I have no desire to marry Miss Raynor, now or ever," he returned coldly. "She helped kill my brother."

"She didn't, and you have proof, but suit yourself," she said when he looked angry enough to say something unforgivable. "Now, do you have any idea how we can talk to that woman before somebody shuts her up? It looks like whoever killed that poor man on the river wouldn't hesitate to give him company. I'd bet my reputation that he knew something that could bring down someone powerful, and he was stopped dead first. If the woman has any info at all, she's on the endangered list."

"Good point," Hayes had to admit. "Do you have a plan?"

She shook her head. "I wish."

"About that number, you might run it by the 911 operators," he said. "They deal with a lot of telephone traffic. They might recognize it."

"Now that's constructive thinking," she said with a grin. "But this isn't my jurisdiction, you know."

"The crime was committed in the county. That's my jurisdiction. I'm giving you the authority to investigate."

"Won't your own investigator feel slighted?"

"He would if he was here," he sighed. "He took his remaining days off and went to Wyoming for Christmas. He said he'd lose them if he didn't use them by the end of the year. I couldn't disagree and we didn't have much going on when I let him go." He shook his head. "He'll punch me when he gets back and discovers that we had a real DB right here and he didn't get to investigate it."

"The way things look," she said slowly, "he may still

get to help. I don't think we're going to solve this one in a couple of days."

"Hey, I saw a murder like this one on one of those CSI shows," he said with pretended excitement. "They sent trace evidence out, got results in two hours and had the guy arrested and convicted and sent to jail just before the last commercial!"

She gave him a smile and a gesture that was universal before she picked up her purse, and the slip of paper, and left his office.

She was eating lunch at Barbara's Café in town when the object of her most recent daydreams walked in, tall and handsome in real cowboy duds, complete with a shepherd's coat, polished black boots and a real black Stetson cowboy hat with a brim that looked just like the one worn by Richard Boone in the television series *Have Gun Will Travel* that she used to watch videos of. It was cocked over his eyes and he looked as much like a desperado as he did a working cowboy.

He spotted Alice as he was paying for his meal at the counter and grinned at her. She turned over a cup of coffee and it spilled all over the table, which made his grin much bigger.

Barbara came running with a towel. "Don't worry, it happens all the time," she reassured Alice. She glanced at Harley, put some figures together and chuckled. "Ah, romance is in the air."

"It is not," Alice said firmly. "I offered to take him to a movie, but I'm broke, and he won't go dutch treat," she added in a soft wail.

"Aww," Barbara sympathized.

"I don't get paid until next Friday," Alice said,

dabbing at wet spots on her once-immaculate oyster-white wool slacks. "I'll be miles away by then."

"I get paid this Friday," Harley said, straddling a chair opposite Alice with a huge steak and fries on a platter. "Are you having a salad for lunch?" he asked, aghast at the small bowl at her elbow. "You'll never be able to do any real investigating on a diet like that. You need protein." He indicated the juicy, rare steak on his own plate.

Alice groaned. He didn't understand. She'd spent so many hours working in her lab that she couldn't really eat a steak anymore. It was heresy here in Texas, so she tended to keep her opinions to herself. If she said anything like that, there would be a riot in Barbara's Café.

So she just smiled. "Fancy seeing you here," she teased.

He grinned. "I'll bet it wasn't a surprise," he said as he began to carve his steak.

"Whatever do you mean?" she asked with pretended innocence.

"I was just talking to Hayes Carson out on the street and he happened to mention that you asked him where I ate lunch," he replied.

She huffed. "Well, that's the last personal question I'll ever ask him, and you can take that to the bank!"

"Should I mention that I asked him where *you* ate lunch?" he added with a twinkle in his pale eyes.

Alice's irritated expression vanished. She sighed. "Did you, really?" she asked.

"I did, really. But don't take that as a marriage proposal," he said. "I almost never propose to crime scene investigators over lunch."

"Crime scene investigators?" a cowboy from one of the nearby ranches exclaimed, leaning toward them.

"Listen, I watch those shows all the time. Did you know that they can tell time of death by…!"

"Oh, dear, I'm so sorry!" Alice exclaimed as the cowboy gaped at her. She'd "accidentally" poured a glass of iced tea all over him. "It's a reflex," she tried to explain as Barbara came running, again. "You see, every time somebody talks about the work I do, I just get all excited and start throwing things!" She picked up her salad bowl. "It's a helpless reflex, I just can't stop…"

"No problem!" the cowboy said at once, scrambling to his feet. "I had to get back to work anyway! Don't think a thing about it!"

He rushed out the door, trailing tea and ice chips, leaving behind half a cup of coffee and a couple of bites of pie and an empty plate.

Harley was trying not to laugh, but he lost it completely. Barbara was chuckling as she motioned to one of her girls to get a broom and pail.

"I'm sorry," Alice told her. "Really."

Barbara gave her an amused glance. "You don't like to talk shop at the table, do you?"

"No. I don't," she confessed.

"Don't worry," Barbara said as the broom and pail and a couple of paper towels were handed to her. "I'll make sure word gets around. Before lunch tomorrow," she added, still laughing.

Four

After that, nobody tried to engage Alice in conversation about her job. The meal was pleasant and friendly. Alice liked Harley. He had a good personality, and he actually improved on closer acquaintance, as so many people didn't. He was modest and unassuming, and he didn't try to monopolize the conversation.

"How's your investigation coming?" he asked when they were on second cups of black coffee.

She shrugged. "Slowly," she replied. "We've got a partial number, possibly a telephone number, a stolen car whose owner didn't know it was stolen and a partial sneaker track that we're hoping someone can identify."

"I saw a program on the FBI lab that showed how they do that," Harley replied. He stopped immediately as soon as he realized what he'd said. He sat with his fork poised in midair, eyeing Alice's refilled coffee mug.

She laughed. "Not to worry. I'll control my reflexes. Actually the lab does a very good job running down sneaker treads," she added. "The problem is that most treads are pretty common. You get the name of a company that produces them and then start wearing out shoe leather going to stores and asking for information about people who bought them."

"What about people who paid cash and there's no record of their buying them?"

"I never said investigation techniques were perfect," she returned, smiling. "We use what we can get."

He frowned. "Those numbers, it shouldn't be that hard to isolate a telephone number, should it? You could narrow it down with a computer program."

"Yes, but there are so many possible combinations, considering that we don't even have the area code." She groaned. "And we'll have to try every single one."

He pursed his lips. "The car, then. Are you sure the person who owned it didn't have a connection to the murder victim?"

She raised her eyebrows. "Ever considered a career in law enforcement?"

He laughed. "I did, once. A long time ago." He grimaced, as if the memory wasn't a particularly pleasant one.

"We're curious about the car," she said, "but they don't want to spook the car's owner. It turns out that she works for a particularly unpleasant member of the political community."

His eyebrows lifted. "Who?"

She hesitated.

"Come on. I'm a clam. Ask my boss."

"Okay. It's the senior U.S. senator from Texas who lives in San Antonio," she confessed.

Harley made an ungraceful movement and sat back in his chair. He stared toward the window without really seeing anything. "You think the politician may be connected in some way?"

"There's no way of knowing right now," she sighed. "Everybody big in political circles has people who work for them. Anybody can get involved with a bad person and not know it."

"Are they going to question the car owner?"

"I'm sure they will, eventually. They just want to pick the right time to do it."

He toyed with his coffee cup. "So, are you staying here for a while?"

She grimaced. "A few more days, just to see if I can develop any more leads. Hayes Carson wants me to look at the car while the lab's processing it, so I guess I'll go up to San Antonio for that and come back here when I'm done."

He just nodded, seemingly distracted.

She studied him with a whimsical expression. "So, when are we getting married?" she asked.

He gave her an amused look. "Not today. I have to move cattle."

"My schedule is very flexible," she assured him.

He smiled. "Mine isn't."

"Rats."

"Now, that's interesting, I was just thinking about rats. I have to get cat food while I'm in town."

She blinked. "Cat food. For rats?"

"We keep barn cats to deal with the rat problem," he

explained. "But there aren't quite enough mice and rats to keep the cats healthy, so we supplement."

"I like cats," she said with a sigh and a smile. "Maybe we could adopt some stray ones when we get married." She frowned. "Now that's going to be a problem."

"Cats are?"

"No. Where are we going to live?" she persisted. "My job is in San Antonio and yours is here. I know," she said, brightening. "I'll commute!"

He laughed. She made him feel light inside. He finished his coffee. "Better work on getting the bridegroom first," he pointed out.

"Okay. What sort of flowers do you like, and when are we going on our first date?"

He pursed his lips. She was outrageously forward, but behind that bluff personality, he saw something deeper and far more fragile. She was shy. She was like a storefront with piñatas and confetti that sold elegant silverware. She was disguising her real persona with an exaggerated one.

He leaned back in his chair, feeling oddly arrogant at her interest in him. His eyes narrowed and he smiled. "I was thinking we might take in a movie at one of those big movie complexes in San Antonio. Friday night."

"*Ooooooh,*" she exclaimed, bright-eyed. "I like science fiction."

"So do I, and there's a remake of a 1950's film playing. I wouldn't mind seeing it."

"Neither would I."

"I'll pick you up at your motel about five. We'll have dinner and take in the movie afterward. That suit you?"

She was nodding furiously. "Should I go ahead and buy the rings?" she asked with an innocent expression.

He chuckled. "I told you, I'm too tied up right now for weddings."

She snapped her fingers. "Darn!"

"But we can see a movie."

"I like movies."

"Me, too."

They paid for their respective meals and walked out together, drawing interest from several of the café patrons. Harley hadn't been taking any girls around with him lately, and here was this cute CSI lady from San Antonio having lunch with him. Speculation ran riot.

"They'll have us married by late afternoon," he remarked, nodding toward the windows, where curious eyes were following their every move.

"I'll go back in and invite them all to the wedding, shall I?" she asked at once.

"Kill the engine, dude," he drawled in a perfect imitation of the sea turtle in his favorite cartoon movie.

"You so totally rock, Squirt!" she drawled back.

He laughed. "Sweet. You like cartoon movies, too?"

"Crazy about them," she replied. "My favorite right now is *Wall-E,* but it changes from season to season. They just get better all the time."

"I liked *Wall-E,* too," he agreed. "Poignant story. Beautiful soundtrack."

"My sentiments, exactly. That's nice. When we have kids, we'll enjoy taking them to the theater to see the new cartoon movies."

He took off his hat and started fanning himself. "Don't mention kids or I'll faint!" he exclaimed. "I'm already having hot flashes, just considering the thought of marriage!"

She glared at him. "Women have hot flashes when they enter menopause," she said, emphasizing the first word.

He lifted his eyebrows and grinned. "Maybe I'm a woman in disguise," he whispered wickedly.

She wrinkled her nose up and gave him a slow, interested scrutiny from his cowboy boots to his brown hair. "It's a really good disguise," she had to agree. She growled, low in her throat, and smiled. "Tell you what, after the movie, we can undress you and see how good a disguise it really is."

"Well, I never!" he exclaimed, gasping. "I'm not that kind of man, I'll have you know! And if you keep talking like that, I'll never marry you. A man has his principles. You're just after my body!"

Alice was bursting at the seams with laughter. Harley followed her eyes, turned around, and there was Kilraven, in uniform, staring at him.

"I read this book," Kilraven said after a minute, "about a Scot who disguised himself as a woman for three days after he stole an English payroll destined for the turncoat Scottish Lords of the Congregation who were going to try to depose Mary, Queen of Scots. The family that sheltered him was rewarded with compensation that was paid for centuries, even after his death, they say. He knew how to repay a debt." He frowned. "But that was in the sixteenth century, and you don't look a thing like Lord Bothwell."

"I should hope not," Harley said. "He's been dead for over four hundred years!"

Alice moved close to him and bumped him with her hip. "Don't talk like that. Some of my best friends are dead people."

Harley and Kilraven both groaned.

"It was a joke," Alice burst out, exasperated. "My goodness, don't you people have a sense of humor?"

"He doesn't," Harley said, indicating Kilraven.

"I do so," Kilraven shot back, glaring. "I have a good sense of humor." He stepped closer. "And you'd better say that I do, because I'm armed."

"You have a great sense of humor," Harley replied at once, and grinned.

"What are you doing here?" Alice asked suddenly. "I thought you were supposed to be off today."

Kilraven shrugged. "One of our boys came down with flu and they needed somebody to fill in. Not much to do around here on a day off, so I volunteered," he added.

"There's TV," Alice said.

He scoffed. "I don't own a TV," he said huffily. "I read books."

"European history?" Harley asked, recalling the mention of Bothwell.

"Military history, mostly, but history is history. For instance," he began, "did you know that Hannibal sealed poisonous snakes in clay urns and had his men throw them onto the decks of enemy ships as an offensive measure?"

Harley was trying to keep a straight face.

Alice didn't even try. "You're kidding!"

"I am not. Look it up."

"I'd have gone right over the side into the ocean!" Alice exclaimed, shivering.

"So did a lot of the enemy combatants." Kilraven chuckled. "See what you learn when you read, instead of staying glued to a television set?"

"How can you not have a television set?" Harley exclaimed. "You can't watch the news…"

"Don't get me started," Kilraven muttered. "Corporate news, exploiting private individuals with personal problems for the entertainment of the masses! Look at that murder victim who was killed back in the summer, and the family of the accused is still getting crucified nightly in case they had anything to do with it. You call that news? I call it bread and circuses, just like the arena in ancient Rome!"

"Then how do you know what's going on in the world?" Alice had to know.

"I have a laptop computer with Internet access," he said. "That's where the real news is."

"A revolutionary," Harley said.

"An anarchist," Alice corrected.

"I am an upstanding member of law enforcement," Kilraven retorted. He glanced at the big watch on his wrist. "And I'm going to be late getting back on duty if I don't get lunch pretty soon."

Harley was looking at the watch and frowning. He knew the model. It was one frequently worn by mercs. "Blade or garrote?" he asked Kilraven, nodding at the watch.

Kilraven was surprised, but he recovered quickly. "Blade," he said. "How did you know?"

"Micah Steele used to wear one just like it."

Kilraven leaned down. "Guess who I bought it from?" he asked. He grinned. With a wave, he sauntered into the café.

"What were you talking about?" Alice asked curiously.

"Trade secret," Harley returned. "I have to get going. I'll see you Friday."

He turned away and then, just as suddenly turned back. "Wait a minute." He pulled a small pad and pencil out of his shirt pocket and jotted down a number. He tore off the paper and handed it to her. "That's my cell phone number. If anything comes up, and you can't make it Friday, you can call me."

"Can I call you anyway?" she asked.

He blinked. "What for?"

"To talk. You know, if I have any deeply personal problems that just can't wait until Friday?"

He laughed. "Alice, it's only two days away," he said.

"I could be traumatized by a snake or something."

He sighed. "Okay. But only then. It's hard to pull a cell phone out of its holder when you're knee-deep in mud trying to extract mired cattle."

She beamed. "I'll keep that in mind." She tucked the number in the pocket of her slacks. "I enjoyed lunch."

"Yeah," he said, smiling. "Me, too."

She watched him walk away with covetous eyes. He really did have a sensuous body, very masculine. She stood sighing over him until she realized that several pair of eyes were still watching her from inside the café. With a self-conscious grin in their direction, she went quickly to her van.

The pattern in the tennis shoes was so common that Alice had serious doubts that they'd ever locate the seller, much less the owner. The car was going to be a much better lead. She went up to the crime lab while they were processing it. There was some trace evidence that was promising. She also had Sergeant Rick Marquez, who worked out of San Antonio P.D., get as much information as he could about the woman the murdered man had stolen the car from.

The next morning in Jacobsville, on his way to work in San Antonio, Rick stopped by Alice's motel room to give her the information he'd managed to obtain. "She's been an employee of Senator Fowler for about two years," Rick said, perching on the edge of the dresser in front of the bed while she paced. "She's deeply religious. She goes to church on Sundays and Wednesdays. She's involved in an outreach program for the homeless, and she gives away a good deal of her salary to people she considers more needy." He shook his head. "You read about these people, but you rarely encounter them in real life. She hasn't got a black mark on her record anywhere, unless you consider a detention in high school for being late three days in a row when her mother was in the hospital."

"Wow," Alice exclaimed softly.

"There's more. She almost lost the job by lecturing the senator for hiring illegal workers and threatening them with deportation if they asked for higher wages."

"What a sweetheart," Alice muttered.

"From what we hear, the senator is the very devil to work for. They say his wife is almost as hard-nosed. She was a state supreme court judge before she went into the import/export business. She made millions at it. Finances a good part of the senator's reelection campaigns."

"Is he honest?"

"Is any politician?" Marquez asked cynically. "He sits on several powerful committees in Congress, and was once accused of taking kickbacks from a Mexican official."

"For what?"

"He was asked to oppose any shoring up of border security. Word is that the senator and his contact have their fingers in some illegal pies, most notably drug trafficking. But there's no proof. The last detective who tried to investigate the senator is now working traffic detail."

"A vengeful man."

"Very."

"I don't suppose that detective would talk to me?" she wondered aloud.

"She might," he replied surprisingly. "She and I were trying to get the Kilraven family murder case reopened, if you recall, when pressure was put on us to stop. She turned her attention to the senator and got kicked out of the detective squad." He grimaced. "She's a good woman. Got an invalid kid to look after and an ex-husband who's a pain in the butt, to put it nicely."

"We heard about the cold case being closed. You think the senator might have been responsible for it?" she wondered aloud.

"We don't know. He has a protégé who's just been elected junior senator from Texas, and the protégé has some odd ties to people who aren't exactly the crème of society. But we don't dare mention that in public." He smiled. "I don't fancy being put on a motorcycle at my age and launched into traffic duty."

"Your friend isn't having to do that, surely?" she asked.

"No, she's working two-car patrols on the night shift, but she's a sergeant, so she gets a good bit of desk work." He studied her. "What's this I hear about you trying to marry Harley?"

She grinned. "It's early days. He's shy, but I'm going to drown him in flowers and chocolate until he says yes."

"Good luck," he said with a chuckle.

"I won't even need it. We're going to a movie together Friday."

"Are you? What are you going to see?"

"The remake of that fifties movie. We're going to dinner first."

"You are a fast worker, Alice," he said with respect. He checked his watch. "I've got to get back to the precinct."

She glanced at his watch curiously. "You don't have a blade or a wire in that thing, do you?"

"Not likely," he assured her. "Those watches cost more than I make, and they're used almost exclusively by mercs."

"Mercs?" She frowned.

"Soldiers of fortune. They work for the highest bidder, although our local crowd had more honor than that."

Mercs. Now she understood Harley's odd phrasing about "trade secrets."

"Where did you see a watch like that?" he asked.

She looked innocent. "I heard about one from Harley. I just wondered what they were used for."

"Oh. Well, I guess if you were in a tight spot, it might save your life to have one of those," he agreed, distracted.

"Before you go, can you give me the name and address of that detective in San Antonio?" she asked.

He hesitated. "Better let me funnel the questions to her, Alice," he said with a smile. "She doesn't want anything to slip out about her follow-ups on that case. She's still working it, without permission."

She raised an eyebrow. "So are you, unless I miss my guess. Does Kilraven know?"

He shook his head. Then he hesitated. "Well, I don't think he does. He and Jon Blackhawk still don't want us nosing around. They're afraid the media will pick up the story and it will become the nightly news for a year or so." He shook his head. "Pitiful, how the networks don't go out and get any real news anymore. They just create it by harping on private families mixed up in tragedies, like living soap operas."

"That's how corporate media works," she told him. "If you want real news, buy a local weekly newspaper."

He laughed. "You're absolutely right. Take care, Alice."

"You, too. Thanks for the help."

"Anytime." He paused at the door and grinned at her. "If Harley doesn't work out, you could always pursue me," he invited. "I'm young and dashing and I even have long hair." He indicated his ponytail. "I played semiprofessional soccer when I was in college, and I have a lovely singing voice."

She chuckled. "I've heard about your singing voice, Marquez. Weren't you asked, very politely, to stay out of the church choir?"

"I wanted to meet women," he said. "The choir was full of unattached ones. But I can sing," he added belligerently. "Some people don't appreciate real talent."

She wasn't touching that line with a pole. "I'll keep you in mind."

"You do that." He laughed as he closed the door.

Alice turned back to her notes, spread out on the desk in the motel room. There was something nagging at her about the piece of paper they'd recovered from the murder victim. She wondered why it bothered her.

Harley picked her up punctually at five on Friday night for their date. He wasn't overdressed, but he had on slacks and a spotless sports shirt with a dark blue jacket. He wasn't wearing his cowboy hat, either.

"You look nice," she said, smiling.

His eyes went to her neat blue sweater with embroidery around the rounded neckline and the black slacks she was wearing with slingbacks. She draped a black coat with fur collar over one arm and picked up her purse.

"Thanks," he said. "You look pretty good yourself, Alice."

She joined him at the door. "Ooops. Just a minute. I forgot my cell phone. I was charging it."

She unplugged it and tucked it into her pocket. It rang immediately. She grimaced. "Just a minute, okay?" she asked Harley.

She answered the phone. She listened. She grimaced. "Not tonight," she groaned. "Listen, I have plans. I never do, but I really have plans tonight. Can't Clancy cover for me, just this once? Please? Pretty please? I'll do the same for her. I'll even work Christmas Eve…okay? Thanks!" She beamed. "Thanks a million!"

She hung up.

"A case?" he asked curiously.

"Yes, but I traded out with another investigator." She shook her head as she joined him again at the door. "It's been so slow lately that I forgot how hectic my life usually is."

"You have to work Christmas Eve?" he asked, surprised.

"Well, I usually volunteer," she confessed. "I don't have much of a social life. Besides, I think parents should be with children on holidays. I don't have any, but all my coworkers do."

He paused at the door of his pickup truck and looked down at her. "I like kids," he said.

"So do I," she replied seriously, and without joking. "I've just never had the opportunity to become a parent."

"You don't have to be married to have kids," he pointed out.

She gave him a harsh glare. "I am the product of generations of Baptist ministers," she told him. "My father was the only one of five brothers who went into business instead. You try having a modern attitude with a mother who taught Sunday School and uncles who spent their lives counseling young women whose lives were destroyed by unexpected pregnancies."

"I guess it would be rough," he said.

She smiled. "You grew up with parents who were free thinkers, didn't you?" she asked, curious.

He grimaced. He put her into the truck and got in beside her before he answered. "My father is an agnostic. He doesn't believe in anything except the power of the almighty dollar. My mother is just like him. They wanted me to associate with the right people and help them do it. I stayed with a friend's parents for a while and all but got adopted by them—he was a mechanic and they had a small ranch. I helped in the mechanic's shop. Then I went into the service, came back and tried to work things out with my real parents, but it wasn't possible. I ran away from home, fresh out of the Army Rangers."

"You were overseas during the Bosnia conflict, weren't you?" she asked.

He snapped his seat belt a little violently. "I was a desk clerk," he said with disgust. "I washed out of combat training. I couldn't make the grade. I ended up back in the regular Army doing clerical jobs. I never even saw combat. Not in the Army," he added.

"Oh."

"I left home, came down here to become a cowboy barely knowing a cow from a bull. The friends that I lived with had a small ranch, but I mostly stayed in town, working at the shop. We went out to the ranch on weekends, and I wasn't keen on livestock back then. Mr. Parks took me on anyway. He knew all along that I had no experience, but he put me to work with an old veteran cowhand named Cal Lucas who taught me everything I know about cattle."

She grinned. "It took guts to do that."

He laughed. "I guess so. I bluffed a lot, although I am a good mechanic. Then I got in with this Sunday merc crew and went down to Africa with them one week on a so-called training mission. All we did was talk to some guys in a village about their problems with foreign relief shipments. But before we could do anything, we ran afoul of government troops and got sent home." He sighed. "I bragged about how much I'd learned, what a great merc I was." He glanced at her as they drove toward San Antonio, but she wasn't reacting critically. Much the reverse. He relaxed a little. "Then one of the drug lords came storming up to Mr. Parks's house with his men and I got a dose of reality—an automatic in my face. Mr. Parks jerked two combat knives out of his sleeves and threw them at the two men who were holding me. Put them both down in a heartbeat." He shook his head, still breathless at the memory. "I never saw anything like it, before or since. I thought he was just a rancher. Turns out he went with Micah Steele and Eb Scott on real merc missions overseas. He listened to me brag and watched me strut, and never said a word. I'd never have known, if the drug dealers hadn't attacked. We got in a firefight with them later."

"We heard about that, even up in San Antonio," she said.

He nodded. "It got around. Mr. Parks and Eb Scott and Micah Steele got together to take out a drug distribution center near Mr. Parks's property. I swallowed my pride and asked to go along. They let me." He sighed. "I grew up in the space of an hour. I saw men shot and killed, I had my life saved by Mr. Parks again in the process. Afterward, I never bragged or strutted again. Mr. Parks said he was proud of me." He flushed a little. "If my father had been like him, I guess I'd still be at home. He's a real man, Mr. Parks. I've never known a better one."

"He likes you, too."

He laughed self-consciously. "He does. He's offered me a few acres of land and some cattle, if I'd like to start my own herd. I'm thinking about it. I love ranching. I think I'm getting good at it."

"So we'd live on a cattle ranch." She pursed her lips mischievously. "I guess I could learn to help with branding. I mean, we wouldn't want our kids to think their mother was a sissy, would we?" she asked, laughing.

Harley gave her a sideways glance and grinned. She really was fun to be with. He thought he might take her by the ranch one day while she was still in Jacobsville and introduce her to Mr. Parks. He was sure Mr. Parks would like her.

Five

The restaurant Harley took Alice to was a very nice one, with uniformed waiters and chandeliers.

"Oh, Harley, this wasn't necessary," she said quickly, flushing. "A hamburger would have been fine!"

He smiled. "We all got a Christmas bonus from Mr. Parks," he explained. "I don't drink or smoke or gamble, so I can afford a few luxuries from time to time."

"You don't have any vices? Wow. Now I really think we should set the date." She glanced at him under her lashes. "I don't drink, smoke or gamble, either," she added hopefully.

He nodded. "We'll be known as the most prudish couple in Jacobsville."

"Kilraven's prudish, too," she pointed out.

"Yes, but he won't be living in Jacobsville much

longer. He's been reassigned, we're hearing. After all, he's really a fed."

She studied the menu. "I'll bet he could be a heart-breaker with a little practice."

"He's breaking Winnie Sinclair's heart, anyway, by leaving," Harley said, repeating the latest gossip. "She's really got a case on him. But he thinks she's too young."

"He's only in his thirties," she pointed out.

"Yes, but Winnie's the same age as her brother's new wife," he replied. "Boone Sinclair thought Keely Welsh was too young for him, too."

"But he gave in, in the end. You know, the Ballenger brothers in Jacobsville both married younger women. They've been happy together, all these years."

"Yes, they have."

The waiter came and took their orders. Alice had a shrimp cocktail and a large salad with coffee. Harley gave her a curious look.

"Aren't you hungry?" he asked.

She laughed. "I told you in Jacobsville, I love salads," she confessed. "I mostly eat them at every meal." She indicated her slender body. "I guess that's how I keep the weight off."

"I can eat as much as I like. I run it all off," he replied. "Working cattle is not for the faint of heart or the out-of-condition rancher."

She grinned. "I believe it." She smiled at the waiter as he deposited coffee in their china cups and left. "Why did you want to be a cowboy?" she asked him.

"I loved old Western movies on satellite," he said simply. "Gary Cooper and John Wayne and Randolph Scott. I dreamed of living on a cattle ranch and having animals around. I don't even mind washing Bob when she gets dirty, or Puppy Dog."

"What's Puppy Dog's name?" she asked.

"Puppy Dog."

She gave him an odd look. "Who's on first, what's on second, I don't know's on third?"

"I don't give a damn's our shortstop?" he finished the old Abbott and Costello comedy routine. He laughed. "No, it's not like that. His name really is Puppy Dog. We have a guy in town, Tom Walker. He had an outlandish dog named Moose that saved his daughter from a rattlesnake. Moose sired a litter of puppies. Moose is dead now, but Puppy Dog, who was one of his offspring, went to live with Lisa Monroe, before she married my boss. She called him Puppy Dog and figured it was as good a name as any. With a girl dog named Bob, my boss could hardly disagree," he added on a chuckle.

"I see."

"Do you like animals?"

"I love them," she said. "But I can't have animals in the apartment building where I live. I had cats and dogs and even a parrot when I lived at home."

"Do you have family?"

She shook her head. "My dad was the only one left. He died a few months ago. I have uncles, but we're not close."

"Did you love your parents?"

She smiled warmly. "Very much. My dad was a banker. We went fishing together on weekends. My mother was a housewife who never wanted to run a corporation or be a professional. She just wanted a houseful of kids, but I was the only child she was able to have. She spoiled me rotten. Dad tried to counterbalance her." She sipped coffee. "I miss them both. I wish I'd had brothers or sisters." She looked at him. "Do you have siblings?"

"I had a sister," he said quietly.

"Had?"

He nodded. He fingered his coffee cup. "She died when she was seven years old."

She hesitated. He looked as if this was a really bad memory. "How?"

He smiled sadly. "My father backed over her on his way down the driveway, in a hurry to get to a meeting."

She grimaced. "Poor man."

He cocked his head and studied her. "Why do you say that?"

"We had a little girl in for autopsy, about two years ago," she began. "Her dad was hysterical. Said the television fell over on her." She lifted her eyes. "You know, we don't just take someone's word for how an accident happens, even if we believe it. We run tests to check out the explanation and make sure it's feasible. Well, we pushed over a television of the same size as the one in the dad's apartment. Sure enough, it did catastrophic damage to a dummy." She shook her head. "Poor man went crazy. I mean, he really lost the will to live. His wife had died. The child was all he had left. He locked himself in the bathroom with a shotgun one night and pulled the trigger with his toe." She made a harsh sound. "Not the sort of autopsy you want to try to sleep after."

He was frowning.

"Sorry," she said, wincing. "I tend to talk shop. I know it's sickening, and here we are in a nice restaurant and all, and I did pour a glass of tea on a guy this week for doing the same thing to me…"

"I was thinking about the father," he said, smiling to

relieve her tension. "I was sixteen when it happened. I grieved for her, of course, but my life was baseball and girls and video games and hamburgers. I never considered how my father might have felt. He seemed to just get on with his life afterward. So did my mother."

"Lots of people may seem to get over their grief. They don't."

He was more thoughtful than ever. "My mother had been a...lawyer," he said after a slight hesitation that Alice didn't notice. "She was very correct and proper. After my sister died, she changed. Cocktail parties, the right friends, the best house, the fanciest furniture...she went right off the deep end."

"You didn't connect it?"

He grimaced. "That was when I ran away from home and went to live with the mechanic and his wife," he confessed. "It was my senior year of high school. I graduated soon after, went into the Army and served for two years. When I got out, I went home. But I only stayed for a couple of weeks. My parents were total strangers. I didn't even know them anymore."

"That's sad. Do you have any contact with them?"

He shook his head. "I just left. They never even looked for me."

She slid her hand impulsively over his. His fingers turned and enveloped hers. His light blue eyes searched her darker ones curiously. "I never thought of crime scene investigators as having feelings," he said. "I thought you had to be pretty cold-blooded to do that sort of thing."

She smiled. "I'm the last hope of the doomed," she said. "The conscience of the murdered. The flickering candle of the soul of the deceased. I do my job so that murderers don't flourish, so that killers don't escape justice. I think of my job as a holy grail," she said solemnly. "I hide my feelings. But I still have them. It hurts to see a life extinguished. Any life. But especially a child's."

His eyes began to twinkle with affection. "Alice, you're one of a kind."

"Oh, I do hope so," she said after a minute. "Because if there was another one of me, I might lose my job. Not many people would give twenty-four hours a day to the work." She hesitated and grinned. "Well, not all the time, obviously. Just occasionally, I get taken out by handsome, dashing men."

He laughed. "Thanks."

"Actually I mean it. I'm not shrewd enough to lie well."

The waiter came and poured more coffee and took their orders for dessert. When they were eating it, Alice frowned thoughtfully.

"It bothers me."

"What does?" he asked.

"The car. Why would a man steal a car from an upstanding, religious woman and then get killed?"

"He didn't know he was going to get killed."

She forked a piece of cheesecake and looked at it. "What if he had a criminal record? What if he got involved with her and wanted to change, to start over? What if he had something on his conscience and he wanted to spill the beans?" She looked up. "And somebody involved knew it and had to stop him?"

"That's a lot of if's," he pointed out.

She nodded. "Yes, it is. We still don't know who the car was driven by, and the woman's story that it was stolen is just a little thin." She put the fork down. "I want to talk to her. But I don't know how to go about it. She works for a dangerous politician, I'm told. The feds have backed off. I won't do myself any favors if I charge in and start interrogating the senator's employee."

He studied her. "Let me see if I can find a way. I used to know my way around political circles. Maybe I can help."

She laughed. "You know a U.S. senator?" she teased.

He pursed his lips. "Maybe I know somebody who's related to one," he corrected.

"It would really help me a lot, if I could get to her before the feds do. I think she might tell me more than she'd tell a no-nonsense man."

"Give me until tomorrow. I'll think of something."

She smiled. "You're a doll."

He chuckled. "So are you."

She flushed. "Thanks."

They exchanged a long, soulful glance, only interrupted by the arrival of the waiter to ask if they wanted anything else and present the check. Alice's heart was doing double-time on the way out of the restaurant.

Harley walked her to the door of the motel. "I had a good time," he told her. "The best I've had in years."

She looked up, smiling. "Me, too. I turn off most men. The job, you know. I do work with people who aren't breathing."

"It doesn't matter," he said.

She felt the same tension that was visible in his tall, muscular body. He moved a step closer. She met him halfway.

He bent and drew his mouth softly over hers. When she didn't object, his arms went around her and pulled her close. He smiled as he increased the gentle pressure of his lips and felt hers tremble just a little before they relaxed and answered the pressure.

His body was already taut with desire, but it was too soon for a heated interlude. He didn't want to rush her. She was the most fascinating woman he'd ever known. He had to go slow.

He drew back after a minute and his hands tightened on her arms. "Suppose we take in another movie next week?" he asked.

She brightened. "A whole movie?"

He laughed softly. "At least."

"I'd like that."

"We'll try another restaurant. Just to sample the ones that are available until we find one we approve of," he teased.

"What a lovely idea! We can write reviews and put them online, too."

He pursed his lips. "What an entertaining thought."

"Nice reviews," she said, divining his mischievous thoughts.

"Spoilsport."

He winked at her, and she blushed.

"Don't forget," she said. "About finding me a way to interview that woman, okay?"

"Okay," he said. "Good night."

"Good night."

She stood, sighing, as he walked back to his truck. But when he got inside and started it, he didn't drive away. She realized belatedly that he was waiting until she went inside and locked the door. She laughed and waved. She liked that streak of protectiveness in him. It might not be modern, but it certainly made her feel cherished. She slept like a charm.

* * *

The next morning, he called her on his cell phone before she left the motel. "I've got us invited to a cocktail party tonight," he told her. "A fundraiser for the senator."

"Us? But we can't contribute to that sort of thing! Can we?" she added.

"We don't have to. We're representing a contributor who's out of the country," he added with a chuckle. "Do you have a nice cocktail dress?"

"I do, but it's in San Antonio, in my apartment."

"No worries. You can go up and get it and I'll pick you up there at six."

"Fantastic! I'll wear something nice and I won't burp the theme songs to any television shows," she promised.

"Oh, that's good to know," he teased. "Got to get back to work. I told Mr. Parks I had to go to San Antonio this afternoon, so he's giving me a half day off. I didn't tell him why I needed the vacation time, but I think he suspects something."

"Don't mention this to anybody else, okay?" she asked. "If Jon Blackhawk or Kilraven find out, my goose will be cooked."

"I won't tell a soul."

"See you later. I owe you one, Harley."

"Yes," he drawled softly. "You do, don't you? I'll phone you later and get directions to your apartment."

"Okay."

She laughed and hung up.

The senator lived in a mansion. It was two stories high, with columns, and it had a front porch bigger than Alice's whole apartment. Lights burned in every room, and in the gloomy, rainy night, it looked welcoming and beautiful.

Luxury sedans were parked up and down the driveway. Harley's pickup truck wasn't in the same class, but he didn't seem to feel intimidated. He parked on the street and helped Alice out of the truck. He was wearing evening clothes, with a black bow tie and highly polished black wingtip shoes. He looked elegant. Alice was wearing a simple black cocktail dress with her best winter coat, the one she wore to work, a black one with a fur collar. She carried her best black evening bag and she wore black pumps that she'd polished, hoping to cover the scuff marks. On her salary, although it was a good one, she could hardly afford haute couture.

They were met at the door by a butler in uniform. Harley handed him an invitation and the man hesitated and did a double take, but he didn't say anything.

Once they were inside, Alice looked worriedly at Harley.

"It's okay," he assured her, smiling as he cradled her hand in his protectively. "No problem."

"Gosh," she said, awestruck as she looked around her at the company she was in. "There's a movie star over there," she said under her breath. "I recognize at least two models and a Country-Western singing star, and there's the guy who won the golf tournament…!"

"They're just people, Alice," he said gently.

She gaped at him. "Just people? You're joking, right?" She turned too fast and bumped into somebody. She looked up to apologize and her eyes almost popped. "S-sorry," she stammered.

A movie star with a martial arts background grinned at her. "No problem. It's easy to get knocked down in here. What a crowd, huh?"

"Y-yes," she agreed, nodding.

He laughed, smiled at Harley, and drew his date, a gorgeous blonde, along with him toward the buffet table.

Harley curled his fingers into Alice's. "Rube," he teased softly. "You're starstruck."

"I am, I am," she agreed at once. "I've never been in such a place in my life. I don't hang out with the upper echelons of society in my job. You seem very much at home," she added, "for a man who spends his time with horses and cattle."

"Not a bad analogy, actually," he said under his breath. "Wouldn't a cattle prod come in handy around here, though?"

"Harley!" She laughed.

"Just kidding." He was looking around the room. After a minute, he spotted someone. "Let's go ask that woman if they know your employee."

"Okay."

"What's her name?" he whispered.

She dug for it. "Dolores."

He slid his arm around her shoulders and led her forward. She felt the warmth of his jacketed arm around her with real pleasure. She felt chilled at this party, with all this elegance. Her father had been a banker, and he hadn't been poor, but this was beyond the dreams of most people. Crystal chandeliers, Persian carpets, original oil paintings—was that a Renoir?!

"Hi," Harley said to one of the women pouring more punch into the Waterford crystal bowl. "Does Dolores still work here?"

The woman stared at him for a minute, but without recognition. "Dolores? Yes. She's in the kitchen, making canapés. You look familiar. Do I know you?"

"I've got that kind of face," he said easily, smiling.

"My wife and I know Dolores, we belong to her church. I promised the minister we'd give her a message from him if we came tonight," he added.

"One of that church crowd," the woman groaned, rolling her eyes. "Honestly, it's all she talks about, like there's nothing else in the world but church."

"Religion dies, so does civilization," Alice said quietly. She remembered that from her Western Civilization course in college.

"Whatever," the woman replied, bored.

"In the kitchen, huh? Thanks," Harley told the woman.

"Don't get her fired," came the quick reply. "She's a pain, sometimes, but she works hard enough doing dishes. If the senator or his wife see you keeping her from her job, he'll fire her."

"We won't do that," Harley promised. His lips made a thin line as he led Alice away.

"Surely the senator wouldn't fire her just for talking to us?" Alice wondered aloud.

"It wouldn't surprise me," Harley said. "We'll have to be circumspect."

Alice followed his lead. She wondered why he was so irritated. Perhaps the woman's remark offended his sense of justice.

The kitchen was crowded. It didn't occur to Alice to ask how Harley knew his way there. Women were bent over tables, preparing platters, sorting food, making canapés. Two women were at the huge double sink, washing dishes.

"Don't they have a dishwasher?" Alice wondered as they entered the room.

"You don't put Waterford crystal and Lenox china in a dishwasher," he commented easily.

She looked up at him with pure fascination. He didn't seem aware that he'd given away knowledge no working cowboy should even possess.

"How do we know which one's her?" he asked Alice.

Alice stared at the two women. One was barely out of her teens, wearing a nose ring and spiky hair. The other was conservatively dressed with her hair in a neat bun. She smiled, nodding toward the older one. She had a white apron wrapped around her. "The other woman said she was washing dishes," she whispered. "And she's a churchgoer."

He grinned, following her lead.

They eased around the curious workers, smiling.

"Hello, Dolores," Alice called to the woman.

The older woman turned, her red hands dripping water and soap, and started at the two visitors with wide brown eyes. "I'm sorry, do I know you?" she asked.

"I guess you've never seen us dressed up, huh? We're from your church," he told her, lying through his teeth. "Your minister gave us a message for you."

She blinked. "My minister…?"

"Could we talk, just for a minute?" Alice asked urgently.

The woman was suspicious. Her eyes narrowed. She hesitated, and Alice thought, *we've blown it.* But just then, Dolores nodded. "Sure. We can talk for a minute. Liz, I'm taking my break, now, okay? I'll only be ten minutes."

"Okay," Liz returned, with only a glance at the elegantly dressed people walking out with Dolores. "Don't be long. You know how he is," she added quickly.

Once they were outside, Dolores gave them a long look. "I know everyone in my church. You two don't go there," Dolores said with a gleam in her eyes. "Who are you and what do you want?"

Alice studied her. "I work for…out-of-town law enforcement," she improvised. "We found your car. And the man who was driving it."

The older woman hesitated. "I told the police yesterday, the car was stolen," she began weakly.

Alice stepped close, so that they couldn't be overheard. "He was beaten to death, so badly that his mother wouldn't know him," she said in a steely tone. "Your car was pushed into the river. Somebody didn't want him to be found. Nobody," she added softly, "should ever have to die like that. And his murderer shouldn't get away with it."

Dolores looked even sicker. She leaned back against the wall. Her eyes closed. "It's my fault. He said he wanted to start over. He wanted to marry me. He said he just had to do something first, to get something off his conscience. He asked to borrow the car, but he said if something happened, if he didn't call me back by the next morning, to say it was stolen so I wouldn't get in trouble. He said he knew about a crime and if he talked they might kill him."

"Do you know what crime?" Alice asked her.

She shook her head. "He wouldn't tell me anything. Nothing. He said it was the only way he could protect me."

"His name," Alice persisted. "Can you at least tell me his name?"

Dolores glanced toward the door, grimacing. "I don't know it," she whispered. "He said it was an alias."

"Then tell me the alias. Help me find his killer."

She drew in a breath. "Jack. Jack Bailey," she said. "He

said he'd been in jail once. He said he was sorry. I got him going to church, trying to live a decent life. He was going to start over…" Her voice broke. "It's my fault."

"You were helping him," Alice corrected. "You gave him hope."

"He's dead."

"Yes. But there are worse things than dying. How long did you know him?" Alice asked.

"A few months. We went out together. He didn't own a car. I had to drive…"

"Where did he live?"

Dolores glanced at the door again. "I don't know. He always met me at a little strip mall near the tracks, the Weston Street Mall."

"Is there anything you can tell me that might help identify him?" Alice asked.

She blinked, deep in thought. "He said something happened, that it was an accident, but people died because of it. He was sorry. He said it was time to tell the truth, no matter how dangerous it was to him…"

"Dolores!"

She jumped. A tall, imposing figure stood in the light from the open door. "Get back in here! You aren't paid to socialize."

Harley stiffened, because he knew that voice.

"Yes, sir!" Dolores cried, rushing back inside. "Sorry. I was on my break…!"

She ran past the elegant older man. He closed the door and came storming toward Alice and Harley, looking as if he meant to start trouble.

"What do you mean, interrupting my workers when I have important guests? Who the hell are you people and how did you get in here?" he demanded.

Harley moved into the light, his pale eyes glittering at the older man. "I had an invitation," he said softly.

The older man stopped abruptly. He cocked his head, as if the voice meant more to him than the face did. "Who…are you?" he asked huskily.

"Just a ghost, visiting old haunts," he said, and there was ice in his tone.

The older man moved a step closer. As he came into the light, Alice noticed that he, too, had pale eyes, and gray-streaked brown hair.

"H-Harley?" he asked in a hesitant tone.

Harley caught Alice's hand in his. She noticed that his fingers were like ice.

"Sorry to have bothered you, Senator," Harley said formally. "Alice and I know a pastor who's a mutual friend of Dolores. He asked us to tell her about a family that needed a ride to church Sunday. Please excuse us."

He drew Alice around the older man, who stood frozen watching them as they went back into the kitchen.

Harley paused by Dolores and whispered something in her ear quickly before he rejoined Alice and they sauntered toward the living room. The senator moved toward them before they reached the living room, stared after them with a pained expression and tried to speak.

It was too late. Harley walked Alice right out the front door. On the way, a dark-eyed, dark-haired man in an expensive suit scowled as they passed him. Harley noticed that the senator stopped next to the other man and started talking to him.

They made it back to the truck without being challenged, and without a word being spoken.

Harley put Alice inside the truck, got in and started it.

"He knew you," she stammered.

"Apparently." He nodded at her. "Fasten your seat belt."

"Sure." She snapped it in place, hoping that he might add something, explain what had happened. He didn't.

"You've got something to go on now, at least," he said.

"Yes," she agreed. "I have. Thanks, Harley. Thanks very much."

"My pleasure." He glanced at her. "I told Dolores what we said to the senator, so that our stories would match. It might save her job."

"I hope so," she said. "She seemed like a really nice person."

"Yeah."

He hardly said two words the whole rest of the way to her apartment. He parked in front of the building.

"You coming back down to Jacobsville?" he asked.

"In the morning," she said. "I still have some investigating to do there."

"Lunch, Monday, at Barbara's?" he invited.

She smiled. "I'd like that."

He smiled back. "Yeah. Me, too. Sorry we didn't get to stay. The buffet looked pretty good."

"I wasn't really hungry," she lied.

"You're a sweetheart. I'd take you out for a late supper, but my heart's not in it." He pulled her close and bent to kiss her. His mouth was hard and a little rough. "Thanks for not asking questions."

"No problem," she managed, because the kiss had been something, even if he hadn't quite realized what he was doing.

"See you Monday."

He went back to the truck and drove away. This time, he didn't wait for her to go in and close the door, an indication of how upset he really was.

Six

Harley drove back to the ranch and cut off the engine outside the bunkhouse. It had been almost eight years since he'd seen the senator. He hadn't realized what a shock it was going to be, to come face-to-face with him. It brought back all the old wounds.

"Hey!"

He glanced at the porch of the modern bunkhouse. Charlie Dawes was staring at him from a crack in the door. "You coming in or sleeping out there?" the other cowboy called with a laugh.

"Coming in, I guess," he replied.

"Well!" Charlie exclaimed when he saw how the other man was dressed. "I thought you said you were just going out for a drive."

"I took Alice to a party, but we left early. Neither of us was in the mood," he said.

"Alice. That your girl?"

Harley smiled. "You know," he told the other man, "I think she is."

Alice drove back down to Jacobsville late Sunday afternoon. She'd contacted Rick Marquez and asked if he'd do some investigating for her in San Antonio, to look for any rap sheet on a man who used a Jack Bailey alias and to see if they could find a man who'd been staying at a motel near the Weston Street Mall. He might have been seen in the company of a dark-haired woman driving a 1992 blue Ford sedan. It wasn't much to go on, but he might turn up something.

Meanwhile, Alice was going to go back to the crime scene and wander over it one more time, in hopes that the army of CSI detectives might have missed something, some tiny scrap of information that would help break the case.

She was dressed in jeans and sneakers and a green sweatshirt with CSI on it, sweeping the bank of the river, when her cell phone rang. She muttered as she pulled it out and checked the number. She frowned. Odd, she didn't recognize that number in any conscious way, but it struck something in the back of her mind.

"Jones," she said.

"Hi, Jones. It's Kilraven. I wondered if you dug up anything on the murder victim over the weekend?"

She sighed, her mind still on the ground she was searching. "Only that he had an alias, that he was trying to get something off his conscience, that he didn't own a car and he'd been in trouble with the law. Oh, and that he lived somewhere near the Weston Street Mall in San Antonio."

"Good God!" he exclaimed. "You got all that in one weekend?"

She laughed self-consciously. "Well, Harley helped. We crashed a senator's fundraiser and cornered an employee of his who'd been dating the… Oh, damn!" she exclaimed. "Listen, your brother will fry me up toasty and feed me to sharks if you tell him I said that. The feds didn't want anybody going near that woman!"

"Relax. Jon was keen to go out and talk to her himself, but his office nixed it. They were just afraid that some heavy-handed lawman would go over there and spook her. You share what you just told me with him, and I guarantee nobody will say a word about it. Great work, Alice."

"Thanks," she said. "The woman's name is Dolores. She's a nice lady. She feels guilty that he got killed. She never even fussed about her car and now it's totaled. She said she loaned him the car, but he told her to say it was stolen if he didn't call her in a day, in case somebody went after him. He knew he could get killed."

"He said he wanted to get something off his conscience," he reminded her.

"Yes. He said something happened that was an accident but that people died because of it. Does that help?"

"Only if I had ESP," he sighed. "Any more luck on that piece of paper you found in the victim's hand?"

"None. I hope to hear something in a few days from the lab. They're working their fingers to the bone. Why are holidays such a great time for murders and suicides?" she wondered aloud. "It's the holidays. You'd think it would make people happy."

"Sadly, as we both know, it doesn't. It just emphasizes what they've lost, since holidays are prime time for families to get together."

"I suppose so."

"We heard that you were going out with Harley Fowler," he said after a minute, with laughter in his deep voice. "Is it serious?"

"Not really," she replied pertly. "I mean, I ask him to marry me twice a day, but that's not what you'd call serious, is it?"

"Only if he says yes," he returned.

"He hasn't yet, but it's still early. I'm very persistent."

"Well, good luck."

"I don't need luck. I'm unspeakably beautiful, have great language skills, I can boil eggs and wash cars and… Hello? Hello!"

He'd hung up on her, laughing. She closed the flip phone. "I didn't want to talk to you, anyway," she told the phone. "I'm trying to work here."

She walked along the riverbank again, her sharp eyes on the rocks and weeds that grew along the water's edge. She was letting her mind wander, not trying to think in any conscious way. Sometimes, she got ideas that way.

The dead man had a past. He was mixed up in some sort of accident in which a death occurred that caused more deaths. He wanted to get something off his conscience. So he'd borrowed a car from his girlfriend and driven to Jacobsville. To see whom? The town wasn't that big, but it was pretty large if you were trying to figure out who someone a man with a criminal past was trying to find. Who could it be? Someone in law enforcement? Or was he just driving through Jacobsville on his way to talk to someone?

No, she discarded that possibility immediately. He'd

been killed here, so someone had either intercepted him or met him here, to talk about the past.

The problem was, she didn't have a clue who the man was or what he'd been involved in. She hoped that Rick Marquez came up with some answers.

But she knew more than she'd known a few days earlier, at least, and so did law enforcement. She still wondered at the interest of Jon Blackhawk of the San Antonio FBI office. Why were the feds involved? Were they working on some case secretly and didn't want to spill the beans to any outsiders?

Maybe they were working a similar case, she reasoned, and were trying to find a connection. They'd never tell her, of course, but she was a trained professional and this wasn't her first murder investigation.

What if the dead man had confessed, first, to the minister of Dolores's church?

She gasped out loud. It was like lightning striking. Of course! The minister might know something that he could tell her, unless he'd taken a vow of silence, like Catholic priests. They couldn't divulge anything learned in the confessional. But it was certainly worth a try!

She dug Harley's cell phone number out of her pocket and called him. The phone rang three times while she kicked at a dirt clod impatiently. Maybe he was knee-deep in mired cattle or something…

"Hello?"

"Harley!" she exclaimed.

"Now, just who else would it be, talking on Harley's phone?" came the amused, drawling reply.

"You, I hope," she said at once. "Listen, I need to talk to you…"

"You are," he reminded her.

"No, in person, right now," she emphasized. "It's about a minister…"

"Darlin', we can't get married today," he drawled. "I have to brush Bob the dog's teeth," he added lightly.

"Not that minister," she burst out. "Dolores's minister!"

He paused. "Why?"

"What if the murdered man confessed to him before he drove down to Jacobsville and got killed?" she exclaimed.

Harley whistled. "What if, indeed?"

"We need to go talk to her again and ask his name."

"Oh, now that may prove difficult. There's no party."

She realized that he was right. They had no excuse to show up at the senator's home, which was probably surrounded by security devices and armed guards. "Damn!"

"You can just call the house and ask for Dolores," he said reasonably. "You don't have to give your name or a reason."

She laughed softly. "Yes, I could do that. I don't know why I bothered you."

"Because you want to marry me," he said reasonably. "But I'm brushing the dog's teeth today. Sorry."

She glared at the phone. "Excuses, excuses," she muttered. "I'm growing older by the minute!"

"Why don't I bring you over here to go riding?" he wondered aloud. "You could meet my boss and his wife and the boys, and meet Puppy Dog."

She brightened. "What a nice idea!"

"I thought so myself. I'll ask the boss. Next weekend, maybe? I'll beg for another half day on Saturday and take you riding around the ranch. We've got plenty of spare horses." When she hesitated, he sighed. "Don't tell me. You can't ride."

"I can so ride horses," she said indignantly. "I ride horses at amusement parks all the time. They go up and down and round and round, and music plays."

"That isn't the same sort of riding. Well, I'll teach you," he said. "After all, if we get married, you'll have to live on a ranch. I'm not stuffing myself into some tiny apartment in San Antonio."

"Now that's the sort of talk I love to hear," she sighed.

He laughed. "Wear jeans and boots," he instructed. "And thick socks."

"No blouse or bra?" she exclaimed in mock outrage.

He whistled. "Well, you don't have to wear them on my account," he said softly. "But we wouldn't want to shock my boss, you know."

She laughed at that. "Okay. I'll come decently dressed. Saturday it is." She hesitated. "Where's the ranch?"

"I'll come and get you." He hesitated. "You'll still be here next Saturday, won't you?"

She was wondering how to stretch her investigation here by another week. Then she remembered that Christmas was Thursday and she relaxed. "I get Christmas off," she said. Then she remembered that she'd promised to work Christmas Eve already. "Well, I get Christmas Day. I'll ask for the rest of the week. I'll tell them that the case is heating up and I have two or three more people to interview."

"Great! Can I help?"

"Yes, you can find me two or three more people to interview," she said. "Meanwhile, I'll call Dolores and ask her to give me her minister's name." She grimaced. "I'll have to be sure I don't say that to whoever answers the phone. We told everybody we were giving her a message from her minister!"

"Good idea. Let me know what you find out, okay?"

"You bet. See you." She hung up.

She had to dial information to get the senator's number and, thank God, it wasn't unlisted. She punched the numbers into her cell phone and waited. A young woman answered.

"May I please speak to Dolores?" Alice asked politely.

"Dolores?"

"Yes."

There was a long pause. Alice gritted her teeth. They were going to tell her that employees weren't allowed personal phone calls during the day, she just knew it.

But the voice came back on the line with a long sigh. "I'm so sorry," the woman said. "Dolores isn't here anymore."

That wasn't altogether surprising, but it wasn't a serious setback. "Can you tell me how to get in touch with her? I'm an old friend," she added, improvising.

The sigh was longer. "Well, you can't. I mean, she's dead."

Alice was staggered. "Dead?!" she exclaimed.

"Yes. Suicide. She shot herself through the heart," the woman said sadly. "It was such a shock. The senator's wife found her… Oh, dear, I can't talk anymore, I'm sorry."

"Just a minute, just one minute, can you tell me where the funeral is being held?" she asked quickly.

"At the Weston Street Baptist Church," came the reply, almost in a whisper, "at two tomorrow afternoon. I have to go. I'm very sorry about Dolores. We all liked her."

The phone went dead.

Alice felt sick. Suicide! Had she driven the poor woman to it, with her questions? Or had she been depressed because of her boyfriend's murder?

Strange, that she'd shot herself through the heart. Most women chose some less violent way to die. Most used drugs. Suicides by gun were usually men.

She called Harley back.

"Hello?" he said.

"Harley, she killed herself," she blurted out.

"Who? Dolores? She's dead?" he exclaimed.

"Yes. Shot through the heart, I was told. Suicide."

He paused. "Isn't that unusual for a woman? To use a gun to kill herself, I mean?"

"It is. But I found out where her pastor is," she added. "I'm going to the funeral tomorrow. Right now, I'm going up to San Antonio to my office."

"Why?" he asked.

"Because in all violent deaths, even those ascribed to suicide, an autopsy is required. I wouldn't miss this one for the world."

"Keep in touch."

"You bet."

Alice hung up and went back to her van. She had a hunch that a woman as religious as Dolores wouldn't kill herself. Most religions had edicts against it. That didn't stop people from doing it, of course, but Dolores didn't strike Alice as the suicidal sort. She was going to see if the autopsy revealed anything.

The office was, as usual on holidays, overworked. She found one of the assistant medical examiners poring over reports in his office.

He looked up as she entered. "Jones! Could I get you to come back and work for us in autopsy again if I bribed you? It's getting harder and harder to find people who don't mind hanging around with the dead."

She smiled. "Sorry, Murphy," she said. "I'm happier with investigative work these days. Listen, do you have a suicide back there? First name Dolores, worked for a senator…?"

"Yep. I did her myself, earlier this evening." He shook his head. "She had small hands and the gun was a .45 Colt ACP," he replied. "How she ever cocked the damned thing, much less killed herself with it, is going to be one of the great unsolved mysteries of life. Added to that, she had carpal tunnel in her right hand. She'd had surgery at least once. Weakens the muscle, you know. We'd already ascertained that she was right-handed because there was more muscle attachment there—usual on the dominant side."

"You're sure it was suicide?" she pressed.

He leaned back in his chair, eyeing her through thick corrective lenses. "There was a rim burn around the entrance wound," he said, referring to the heat and flare of the shot in close-contact wounds. "But the angle of entry was odd."

She jumped on that. "Odd, how?"

"Diagonal," he replied. He pulled out his digital camera, ran through the files and punched up one. He handed her the camera. "That's the wound, anterior view. Pull up the next shot and you'll see where it exited, posterior."

She inhaled. "Wow!"

"Interesting, isn't it? Most people who shoot themselves with an automatic handgun do it holding the barrel to the head or under the chin. This was angled downward. And as I said before, her hand was too weak to manage this sort of weapon. There's something else."

"What?" she asked, entranced.

"The gun was found still clenched in her left hand."

"So?"

"Remember what I said about the carpel tunnel? She was right-handed."

She cocked her head. "Going to write it up as suspected homicide?"

"You're joking, right? Know who she worked for?"

She sighed. "Yes. Senator Fowler."

"Would you write it up as a suspected homicide or would you try to keep your job?"

That was a sticky question. "But if she was murdered…"

"The 'if' is subjective. I'm not one of those TV forensic people," he reminded her. "I'm two years from retirement, and I'm not risking my pension on a possibility. She goes out as a suicide until I get absolute proof that it wasn't."

Alice knew when that would be. "Could you at least put 'probable suicide,' Murphy?" she persisted. "Just for me?"

He frowned. "Why? Alice, do you know something that I need to know?"

She didn't dare voice her suspicions. She had no proof. She managed a smile. "Humor me. It won't rattle any cages, and if something comes up down the line, you'll have covered your butt. Right?"

He searched her eyes for a moment and then smiled warmly. "Okay. I'll put probable. But if you dig up something, you tell me first, right?"

She grinned. "Right."

Her next move was to go to the Weston Street Baptist Church and speak to the minister, but she had to wait until the funeral to do it. If she saw the man alone, someone might see her and his life could be in danger. It might be already. She wasn't sure what to do.

She went to police headquarters and found Detective Rick Marquez sitting at his desk. The office was almost empty, but there he was, knee-deep in file folders.

She tapped on the door and walked in at the same time.

"Alice!" He got to his feet. "Nice to see you."

"Is it? Why?" she asked suspiciously.

He glanced at the file folders and winced. "Any reason to take a break is a good one. Not that I'm sorry to see you," he added.

"What are you doing?" she asked as she took a seat in front of the desk.

"Poring over cold cases," he said heavily. "My lieutenant said I could do it on my own time, as long as I didn't advertise why I was doing it."

"Why are you doing it?" she asked curiously.

"Your murder down in Jacobsville nudged a memory or two," he said. "There was a case similar to it, also unsolved. It involved a fourteen-year-old girl who was driving a car reported stolen. She was also unrecognizable, but several of her teeth were still in place. They identified her by dental records. No witnesses, no clues."

"How long ago was this?" she asked.

He shrugged. "About seven years," he said. "In fact, it happened some time before Kilraven's family was killed."

"Could there be a connection?" she wondered aloud.

"I don't know. I don't see how the death of a teenage girl ties in to the murder of a cop's family." He smiled. "Maybe it's just a coincidence." He put the files aside. "Why are you up here?"

"I came to check the results of an autopsy," she said. "The woman who worked for Senator Fowler supposedly killed herself, but the bullet was angled downward, her hand was too weak to have pulled the trigger and the weapon was found clutched in the wrong hand."

He blew out his breath in a rush. "Some suicide."

"My thoughts, exactly."

"Talk to me, Jones."

"She was involved with the murder victim in Jacobsville, remember?" she asked him. "She wouldn't tell me his name, she swore she didn't know it. But she gave me the alias he used—the one I called and gave you—and she said he'd spoken to the minister of her church. He told her there was an accident that caused a lot of other people to die. He had a guilty conscience and he wanted to tell what he knew."

Marquez's dark eyes pinned hers. "Isn't that interesting."

"Isn't it?"

"You going to talk to the minister?"

"I want to, but I'm afraid to be seen doing it," she told him. "His life may be in danger if he knows something. Whatever is going on, it's big, and it has ties to powerful people."

"The senator, maybe?" he wondered aloud.

"Maybe."

"When did you talk to her?"

"There was a fundraiser at the senator's house. Harley Fowler took me..." She hadn't connected the names before. Now she did. The senator's name was Fowler. Harley's name was Fowler. The senator had recognized Harley, had approached him, had talked to him in a soft tone...

"Harley *Fowler?*" Marquez emphasized, making the same connection she did. "Harley's family?"

"I don't know," she said. "He didn't say anything to me. But the senator acted really strangely. He seemed to recognize Harley. And when Harley took me to my apartment, he didn't wait until I got inside the door. That's not like him. He was distracted."

"He comes from wealth and power, and he's working cattle for Cy Parks," Marquez mused. "Now isn't that a curious thing?"

"It is, and if it's true, you mustn't tell anybody," Alice replied. "It's his business."

"I agree. I'll keep it to myself. Who saw you talk to the woman at the senator's house?"

"Everybody, but we told them we knew her minister and came to tell her something for him."

"If she went to church every week, wouldn't that seem suspicious that you were seeing her to give her a message from her minister?"

Alice smiled. "Harley told them he'd asked us to give her a message about offering a ride to a fellow worshipper on Sunday."

"Uh, Alice, her car was pulled out of the Little Carmichael River in Jacobsville…?"

"Oh, good grief," she groaned. "Well, nobody knew that when we were at the party."

"Yes. But maybe somebody recognized you and figured you were investigating the murder," he returned.

She grimaced. "And I got her killed," she said miserably.

"No."

"If I hadn't gone there and talked to her…!" she protested.

"When your time's up, it's up, Jones," he replied philosophically. "It wouldn't have made any difference. A car crash, a heart attack, a fall from a high place…it could have been anything. Intentions are what matter. You didn't go there to cause her any trouble."

She managed a wan smile. "Thanks, Marquez."

"But if she was killed," he continued, "that fits into your case somehow. It means that the murderer isn't taking any chance that somebody might talk."

"The murderer…?"

"Your dead woman said the victim knew something damaging about several deaths. Who else but the murderer would be so hell-bent on eliminating evidence?"

"We still don't know who the victim is."

Marquez's sensuous lips flattened as he considered the possibilities. "If the minister knows anything, he's already in trouble. He may be in trouble if he doesn't know anything. The perp isn't taking any chances."

"What can we do to protect him?"

Marquez picked up the phone. "I'm going to risk my professional career and see if I can help him."

Alice sat and listened while he talked. Five minutes later, he hung up the phone.

"Are you sure that's the only way to protect him?" she asked worriedly.

"It's the best one I can think of, short of putting him in protective custody," he said solemnly. "I can't do that without probable cause, not to mention that our budget is in the red and we can't afford protective custody."

"Your boss isn't going to like it. And I expect Jon Blackhawk will be over here with a shotgun tomorrow morning, first thing."

"More than likely."

She smiled. "You're a prince!"

His eyebrows arched. "You could marry me," he suggested.

She shook her head. "No chance. If you really are a prince, if I kissed you, by the way the laws of probability work in my life, you'd turn right into a frog."

He hesitated and then burst out laughing.

She grinned. "Thanks, Marquez. If I can help you, anytime, I will."

"You can. Call my boss tomorrow and tell him that you think I'm suffering from a high fever and hallucinations and I'm not responsible for my own actions."

"I'll do that very thing. Honest."

The next morning, the local media reported that the pastor of a young woman who'd committed suicide was being questioned by police about some information that might tie her to a cold case. Alice thought it was a stroke of pure genius. Only a total fool would risk killing the pastor now that he was in the media spotlight. It was the best protection he could have.

Marquez's boss was, predictably, enraged. But Alice went to see him and, behind closed doors, told him what she knew about the murder in Jacobsville. He calmed down and agreed that it was a good call on his detective's part.

Then Alice went to see Reverend Mike Colman, early in the morning, before the funeral.

He wasn't what she expected. He was sitting in his office wearing sneakers, a pair of old jeans and a black sweatshirt. He had prematurely thinning dark hair, wore glasses, and had a smile as warm as a summer day.

He got up and shook hands with Alice after she introduced herself.

"I understand that I might be a candidate for admittance to your facility," he deadpanned. "Detective Marquez decided that making a media pastry out of me could save my life."

"I hope he's right," she said solemnly. "Two people have died in the past two weeks who had ties to this case. We've got a victim in Jacobsville that we can't even identify."

He grimaced. "I was sorry to hear about Dolores. I never thought she'd kill herself, and I still don't."

"It's sad that she did so much to help a man tortured by his past, and paid for it with her life. Isn't there a saying, that no good deed goes unpunished?" she added with wan humor.

"It seems that way sometimes, doesn't it?" he asked with a smile. "But God's ways are mysterious. We aren't meant to know why things happen the way they do at all times. So what can I do to help you?"

"Do you think you could describe the man Dolores sent to talk to you? If I get a police artist over here with his software and his laptop, can you tell him what the man looked like?"

"Oh, I think I can do better than that."

He pulled a pencil out of his desk drawer, drew a thick pad of paper toward him, peeled back the top and proceeded with deft strokes to draw an unbelievably lifelike pencil portrait of a man.

"That's incredible!" Alice exclaimed, fascinated by the expert rendering.

He chuckled as he handed it over to her. "Thanks. I wasn't always a minister," he explained. "I was on my way to Paris to further my studies in art when God tapped me on the shoulder and told me He needed me." He shrugged. "You don't say no to Him," he added with a kind smile.

"If there isn't some sort of pastor/confessor bond you'd be breaking, could you tell me what you talked about with him?"

"There's no confidentiality," he replied. "But he didn't really tell me anything. He asked me if God could forgive any sin, and I told him yes. He said he'd been a bad man, but he was in love, and he wanted to change. He said he was going to talk to somebody who was involved in an old case, and he'd tell me everything when he got back." He grimaced. "Except he didn't get back, did he?"

"No," Alice agreed sadly. "He didn't."

Seven

Alice took the drawing with her. She phoned Marquez's office, planning to stop by to show the drawing to him, but he'd already gone home. She tucked it into her purse and went to her own office. It was now Christmas Eve, and she'd promised to work tonight as a favor to the woman who'd saved her date with Harley.

She walked into the medical examiner's office, waving to the security guard on her way inside. The building, located on the University of Texas campus, was almost deserted. Only a skeleton crew worked on holidays. Most of the staff had families. Only Alice and one other employee were still single. But the medical examiner's office was accessible 24/7, so someone was always on call.

She went by her colleague's desk and grimaced as she saw the caseload sitting in the basket, waiting for her. It was going to be a long night.

She sat down at her own desk and started poring over the first case file. There were always deaths to investigate, even when foul play wasn't involved. In each one, if there was an question as to how the deceased had departed, it was up to her to work with the detectives to determine a cause of death. Her only consolation was that the police detectives were every bit as overloaded as she, a medical examiner investigator, was. Nobody did investigative work to get rich. But the job did have other rewards, she reminded herself. Solving a crime and bringing a murderer to justice was one of the perks. And no amount of money would make up for the pleasure it gave her to see that a death was avenged. Legally, of course.

She opened the first file and started working up the notes on the computer into a document easily read by the lead police detective on the case, as well as the assistant district attorney prosecuting it. She waded through crime scene photographs, measurements, witness statements and other interviews, but as she did, she was still wondering about the coincidence of Harley's last name and the senator's. The older man had recognized him, had called him Harley. They obviously knew each other, and there was some animosity there. But if the senator was a relation, why hadn't Harley mentioned it when he and Alice stopped by the house for the fundraiser?

Maybe he hadn't wanted Alice to know. Maybe he didn't want anyone to know, especially anyone in Jacobsville. Perhaps he wanted to make it on his own, without the wealth and power of his family behind him. He'd said that he no longer felt comfortable with the things his parents wanted him to do. If they were in politics and expected him to help host fundraisers and hang out with the cream of high society, he might have felt uncomfortable. She recalled her own parents and how much she'd loved them, and how close they'd been. They'd never asked her to do anything she didn't feel comfortable with. Harley obviously hadn't had that sort of home life. She was sad for him. But if things worked out, she promised herself that she'd do what she could to make up for what he missed. First step in that direction, she decided, was a special Christmas present.

She slept late on Christmas morning. But when she woke up, she got out her cell phone and made a virtual shopping trip around town, to discover which businesses were open on a holiday. She found one, and it carried just the item she wanted. She drove by there on her way down to Jacobsville.

Good thing she'd called ahead about keeping her motel room, she thought when she drove into the parking lot. The place was full. Obviously some locals had out-of-town family who didn't want to impose when they came visiting on the holidays. She stashed her suitcase and called Harley's number.

"Hello," came a disgruntled voice over the line.

"Harley?" she asked hesitantly.

There was a shocked pause. "Alice? Is that you?"

She laughed. "Well, you sound out of sorts."

"I am." There was a splash. "Get out of there, you walking steak platter!" he yelled. "Hold the line a minute, Alice, I have to put down the damn…phone!"

There was a string of very unpleasant language, most of which was mercifully muffled. Finally Harley came back on the line.

"I hate the cattle business," he said.

She grimaced. Perhaps she shouldn't have made that shopping trip after all. "Do you?" she asked. "Why?"

"Truck broke down in the middle of the pasture while I was tossing out hay," he muttered. "I got out of the truck and under the hood to see what was wrong. I left the door open. Boss's wife had sent me by the store on the way to pick up some turnip greens for her. Damned cow stuck her head into the truck and ate every damned one of them! So now, I'm mired up to my knees in mud and the truck's sinking, and once I get the truck out, I've got to go all the way back to town for a bunch of turnips on account of the stupid cow… Why are you laughing?"

"I thought you ran purebred bulls," she said.

"You can't get a purebred bull without a purebred cow to drop it," he said with exaggerated patience.

"Sorry. I wasn't thinking. Say, I'm just across the street from a market. Want me to go over and get you some more turnips and bring them to you?"

There was an intake of breath. "You'd do that? On Christmas Day?"

"I sort of got you something," she said. "Just a little something. I wanted an excuse to bring it to you, anyway."

"Doggone it, Alice, I didn't get you anything," he said shamefully.

"I didn't expect you to," she said at once. "But you took me to a nice party and I thought… Well, it's just a little something."

"I took you to a social shooting gallery and didn't even buy you supper," he said, feeling ashamed.

"It was a nice party," she said. "Do you want turnips or not?"

He laughed. "I do. Think you can find Cy Parks's ranch?"

"Give me directions."

He did, routing her the quickest way.

"I'll be there in thirty minutes," she said. "Or I'll call for more directions."

"Okay. Thanks a million, Alice."

"No problem."

She dressed in her working clothes, jeans and boots and a coat, but she added a pretty white sweater with a pink poinsettia embroidered on it, for Christmas. She didn't bother with makeup. It wouldn't help much anyway, she decided with a rueful smile. She bought the turnips and drove the few miles to the turnoff that led to Cy Parks's purebred Santa Gertrudis stud ranch.

Harley was waiting for her less than half a mile down the road, at the fork that turned into the ranch house. He was covered in mud, even his once-brown cowboy hat. He had a smear of mud on one cheek, but he looked very sexy, Alice thought. She couldn't think of one man out of thirty she knew who could be covered in mud and still look so good. Harley did.

He pushed back his hat as he walked up to the van, opening the door for her.

She grabbed the turnips in their brown bag and handed it to him. She jumped down with a small box in her hand. "Here," she said, shoving it at him.

"Wait a sec." He put the turnips in his truck and handed her a five-dollar bill. "Don't argue," he said at once, when she tried to. "I had money to get them with, even allowing for cow sabotage." He grinned.

She grinned back. "Okay." She put the bill in her slacks pocket and handed him the box.

He gave her an odd look. "What's it for?"

"Christmas," she said.

He laughed. "Boss gives me a bonus every Christmas. I can't remember the last time I got an actual present."

She flushed.

"Don't get self-conscious about it," he said, when he noticed her sudden color. "I just felt bad that I didn't get you something."

"I told you, the party…"

"Some party," he muttered. He turned the small box in his hands, curious. He pulled the tape that held the sides together and opened it. His pale eyes lit up as he pulled the little silver longhorn tie tack out of the box. "Hey, this is sweet! I've been looking for one of these, but I could never find one small enough to be in good taste!"

She flushed again. "You really like it?"

"I do! I'll wear it to the next Cattlemen's Association meeting," he promised. "Thanks, Alice."

"Merry Christmas."

"It is, now," he agreed. He slid an arm around her waist and pulled her against him. "Merry Christmas, Alice." He bent and kissed her with rough affection.

She sighed and melted into him. The kiss was warm, and hard and intoxicating. She was a normal adult woman with all the usual longings, but it had been a long time since a kiss had made her want to rip a man's clothes off and push him down on the ground.

She laughed.

He drew back at once, angry. "What the hell…!"

"No, it's not… I'm not laughing at you! I was wondering what you'd think if I started ripping your clothes off…!"

He'd gone from surprise to anger to indignation, and now he doubled over laughing.

"Was it something I said?" she wondered aloud.

He grabbed her up in his arms and spun her around, catching her close to kiss her hungrily again and again. He was covered in mud, and now she was covered in it, too. She didn't care.

Her arms caught around his neck. She held on, loving the warm crush of his mouth in the cold rain that was just starting to fall. Her eyes closed. She breathed, and breathed him, cologne and soap and coffee…

After a few seconds, the kiss stopped being fun and became serious. His hard mouth opened. His arm dragged her breasts against his broad chest. He nudged her lips apart and invaded her mouth with deliberate sensuality.

He nibbled her lower lip as he carried her to the pickup truck. He nudged the turnips into the passenger seat while he edged under the wheel, still carrying Alice. He settled her in his lap and kissed her harder while his hands slid under the warm sweater and onto her bare back, working their way under the wispy little bra she was wearing.

His hands were cold and she jumped when they found her pert little breasts, and she laughed nervously.

"They'll warm up," he whispered against her mouth.

She was going under in waves of pleasure. It had been such a long time since she'd been held and kissed, and even the best she'd had was nothing compared to this. She moaned softly as his palms settled over her breasts and began to caress them, ever so gently.

She held on for dear life. She hoped he wasn't going

to suggest that they try to manage an intimate session on the seat, because there really wasn't that much room. On the other hand, she wasn't protesting…

When he drew back, she barely realized it. She was hanging in space, so flushed with delight that she was feeling oblivious to everything else.

He was looking at her with open curiosity, his hands still under her top, but resting on her rib cage now, not intimately on her breasts.

She blinked, staring up at him helplessly. "Is something wrong?" she asked in a voice that sounded drowsy with passion.

"Alice, you haven't done much of this, have you?" he asked very seriously.

She bit her lip self-consciously. "Am I doing it wrong?"

"There's no right or wrong way," he corrected gently. "You don't know how to give it back."

She just stared at him.

"It's not a complaint," he said when he realized he was hurting her feelings. He bent and brushed his warm mouth over her eyelids. "For a brash woman, you're amazingly innocent. I thought you were kidding, about being a virgin."

She went scarlet. "Well, no, I wasn't."

He laughed softly. "I noticed. Here. Sit up."

She did, but she popped back up and grabbed the turnips before she sat on them. "Whew," she whistled. "They're okay."

He took them from her and put them up on the dash.

She gave him a mock hurt look. "Don't you want to ravish me on the truck seat?" she asked hopefully.

He lifted both eyebrows. "Alice, you hussy!" He laughed.

She grimaced. "Sorry."

"I was teasing!"

"Oh."

He drew her close and hugged her with rough affection. "Yes, I'd love to ravish you on the seat, but not on Christmas Day in plain view of the boss and any cowhand who wandered by."

"Are they likely to wander by?" she wondered out loud.

He let her go and nodded in the direction of the house. There were two cowboys coming their way on horseback. They weren't looking at them. They seemed to be talking.

"It's Christmas," she said.

"Yes, and cattle have to be worked on holidays as well as workdays," he reminded her.

"Sorry. I forgot."

"I really like my tie tack," he said. "And thanks a million for bringing me the turnips." He hesitated. "But I have to get back to work. I gave up my day off so that John could go and see his kids," he added with a smile.

She beamed. "I gave up my Christmas Eve for the same reason. But that's how I got to go to the party with you. I promised to work for him last night."

"We're both nice people," he said, smiling.

She sighed. "I could call a minister right now."

"He's busy," he said with a grin. "It's Christmas."

"Oh. Right."

He got out of the truck and helped her down. "Thanks for my present. Sorry I didn't get you one."

"Yes, you did," she said at once, and then laughed and flushed.

He bent and kissed her softly. "I got an extra one myself," he whispered. "Are we still going riding Saturday?"

"Oh, yes," she said. "At least, I think so. I've got to run up to San Antonio in the morning to talk to Rick Marquez. The minister of the murdered woman was able to draw the man she sent to him."

"Really?" he asked, impressed.

"Yes, and so now we have a real lead." She frowned thoughtfully. "You know, I wonder if Kilraven might recognize the guy. He works out of San Antonio. He might make a copy and show it to his brother, too."

"Good idea." He drew in a long breath. "Alice, you be careful," he added. "If the woman was killed because she talked to us, the minister might be next, and then you." He didn't add, but they both knew, that he could be on the firing line, too.

"The minister's okay. Marquez called a reporter he knew and got him on the evening news." She chuckled. "They'd be nuts to hurt him now, with all the media attention."

"Probably true, and good call by Marquez. But you're not on the news."

"Point taken. I'll watch my back. You watch yours, too," she added with a little concern.

"I work for a former mercenary," he reminded her drolly. "It would take somebody really off balance to come gunning for me."

"Okay. That makes me feel better." She smiled. "But if this case heats up in San Antonio, I may have to go back sooner than Saturday…"

"So? If you can't come riding, I can drive up there and we can catch a movie or go out to eat."

"You would?" she exclaimed, surprised.

He glowered at her. "We're going steady. Didn't you notice?"

"No! Why didn't you tell me?" she demanded.

"You didn't ask. Go back to the motel and maybe we can have lunch tomorrow at Barbara's. I'll phone you."

She grinned. "That would be lovely."

"Meanwhile, I've got more cattle to feed," he said on a weary sigh. "It was a nice break, though."

"Yes, it was."

He looked at the smears of mud on her once-pristine shirt and winced. "Sorry," he said.

She looked down at the smears and just laughed. "It'll wash," she said with a shy smile.

He beamed. He loved a woman who didn't mind a little dirt. He opened her van door and she climbed up into it. "Drive carefully," he told her.

She smiled. "I always do."

"See you."

"See you."

She was halfway back to the motel before she realized that she hadn't mentioned his connection to Senator Fowler. Of course, that might be just as well, considering that the newest murder victim had ties to the senator, and the original murder victim did, too, in a roundabout way.

On her way to see Hayes Carson at the sheriff's office, Alice phoned Marquez at home—well, it was a holiday, so she thought he might be at home with his foster mother, Barbara. She found out that Marquez had been called back to San Antonio on a case. She grimaced. She was never going to get in touch with him, she supposed.

She walked into Carson's office. He was sitting at his desk. He lifted both eyebrows. "It's December twenty-fifth," he pointed out.

She lifted both eyebrows. "Ho, ho, ho?" she said.

He chuckled. "So I'm not the only person who works holidays. I had started to wonder." He indicated the empty desks around his office in the county detention center.

"My office looked that way last night, too," she confessed. She sat down by his desk. "I questioned a woman who worked for Senator Fowler about the man who drove her car down here and got killed next to the river."

"Find out much?" he asked, suddenly serious.

"That I shouldn't have been so obvious about questioning her. She died of an apparent suicide, but I pestered the attending pathologist to put 'probable' before 'suicide' on the death certificate. She shot herself through the heart with the wrong hand and the bullet was angled down." She waited for a reaction.

He leaned back in his chair. "Wonders will never cease."

"I went to see her minister, who spoke to the man we found dead by the river. The minister was an art student. He drew me this." She pulled out a folded sheet of paper from her purse and handed it to him.

"Hallelujah!" he burst out. "Alice, you're a wonder! You should be promoted!"

"No, thanks, I like fieldwork too much," she told him, grinning. "It's good, isn't it? That's what your murder victim looks like." Her smile faded. "I'm just sorry I got the woman killed who was trying to help him restart his life."

He looked up with piercing eyes. "You didn't. Life happens. We don't control how it happens."

"You're good for my self-esteem. I was going to show that to Rick Marquez, but he's become rather elusive."

"Something happened in San Antonio. I don't know what. They called in a lot of off-duty people."

"Was Kilraven one of them, or do you know?" she asked.

"I don't, but I can find out." He called the dispatch center and gave Kilraven's badge number and asked if Kilraven was on duty.

"Yes, he is. Do you want me to ask him to place you a twenty-one?" she asked, referring to a phone call.

"Yes, thanks, Winnie," he said, a smile in his voice as he recognized dispatcher Winnie Sinclair.

"No problem. Dispatch out at thirteen hundred hours."

He hung up. "She'll have him call me," he told Alice. "What did the minister tell you about the murdered man?" he asked while they waited.

"Not much. He said the guy told him he'd been a bad man, but he wanted to change, that he was going to speak to somebody about an old case and that he'd talk to the minister again after he did it. It's a real shame. Apparently he'd just discovered that there was more to life than dodging the law. He had a good woman friend, he was starting to go to church—now he's lying in the morgue, unidentifiable."

"Not anymore," Hayes told her, waving the drawing.

"Yes, but he could be anybody," she replied.

"If he has a criminal background, he's got fingerprints on file and a mug shot. I have access to face recognition software."

"You do? How?" she asked, fascinated.

"Tell you what," he said, leaning forward. "I'll give you my source if you'll tell me how you got hold of that computer chip emplacement tech for tagging bodies."

She caught her breath. "Well! You do get around, don't you? That's cutting-edge and we don't advertise it."

"My source doesn't advertise, either."

"We'll trade," she promised. "Now, tell me…"

The phone rang. Hayes picked it up. He gave Alice a sardonic look. "Yes, the sheriff's office is open on Christmas. I just put away my reindeer and took off my red suit… Yes, Alice Jones is here with an artist's sketch of the murdered man… Hello? Hello?" He hung up with a sigh. "Kilraven," he said, answering the unasked question.

Alice sighed. "I get that a lot, too. People hanging up on me, I mean. I'll bet he's burning rubber, trying to get here at light speed."

"I wouldn't doubt it." He chuckled.

Sure enough, just a minute or two later, they heard squealing tires turning into the parking lot outside the window. A squad car with flashing blue lights slammed to a stop just at the front door and the engine went dead. Seconds later, Kilraven stormed into the office.

"Let's see it," he said without preamble.

Hayes handed him the drawing.

Kilraven looked at it for a long time, frowning.

"Recognize him?" Alice asked.

He grimaced. "No," he said gruffly. "Damn! I thought it might be somebody I knew."

"Why?" Hayes asked.

"I work out of San Antonio as a rule," he said. "And I was a patrol officer, and then a detective, on the police force there for some years. If the guy had a record in San Antonio, I might have had dealings with him. But I don't recognize this guy."

Hayes took the sketch back. "If I make a copy, could you show it to Jon and see if he looks familiar to him?"

"Sure." He glanced at Alice. "How'd you get a sketch of the dead man? Reconstructive artist?"

"No. That woman I talked to about him killed herself…"

"Like hell she did," Kilraven exclaimed. "That's too pat!"

"Just what I thought. I talked to the forensic pathologist who did the autopsy," she added. "He said she was right-handed, but shot herself through the heart with her left hand. Good trick, too, because she had carpal tunnel syndrome, plus surgery, and the gun was a big, heavy .45 Colt ACP. He said she'd have had hell just cocking it."

"He labeled it a suicide?"

She shook her head. "He's trying not to get caught up in political fallout. She worked for the senator, you know, and he's not going to want to be a media snack over a possible homicide that happened on his own property."

"The pathologist didn't label it a suicide?" he persisted.

"I got him to add 'probable' to the report."

"Well, that's something, I guess. Damned shame, about the woman. She might have been able to tell us more, in time." He smiled at Alice. "I'm glad you went to see her, anyway. What we have is thanks to you." He frowned. "But how did you get the sketch?"

"The woman's minister," she said simply. "He'd talked to the man who was killed and before he became a minister, he was an artist. He didn't add much to what the woman had already told me. He did say that the guy had a guilty conscience and he was going to talk to somebody about an old case."

Kilraven was frowning again. "An old case. Who was he going to talk to? People in law enforcement, maybe?"

"Very possibly," Alice agreed. "I'm not through digging. But I need to identify this man. I thought I might go to the motel where he was staying and start interviewing residents. It's a start."

"Not for you," Kilraven said sternly. "You've put yourself in enough danger already. You leave this to me and Jon. We get paid for people to shoot at us. You don't."

"My hero," Alice sighed, batting her eyelashes at him and smiling. "If I wasn't so keen to marry Harley Fowler, I swear I'd be sending you candy and flowers."

"I hate sweets and I'm allergic to flowers," he pointed out.

She wrinkled her nose. "Just as well, then, isn't it?"

"I'll copy this for you," Hayes said, moving to the copy machine in the corner. "We're low on toner, though, so don't expect anything as good as the original drawing."

"Why don't you get more toner?" Alice asked.

Hayes glowered. "I have to have a purchase order from the county commission, and they're still yelling at me about the last several I asked for."

"Which was for…?" Kilraven prompted.

Hayes made the copy, examined it and handed it to Kilraven. "A cat, and an electrician, and an exterminator."

Alice and Kilraven stared at him.

He moved self-consciously back to his desk and sat down. "I bought this cheap cat," he emphasized. "It only cost fifteen bucks at the pet store. It wasn't purebred or anything."

"Why did you buy a cat?" Alice asked.

He sighed. "Do you remember the mouse that lived in Tira Hart's house before she became Simon Hart's wife?"

"Well, I heard about it," Kilraven admitted.

"One of my deputies caught two field mice and was going to take them home to his kids for a science project. He put them in a wood box and when he went to get them out, they weren't there." Hayes sighed. "They chewed their way out of the box, they chewed up the baseboards and two electrical wires, and did about three hundred dollars worth of damage to county property. I called an electrician for that. Then I tried traps and they wouldn't work, so I bought a cat."

"Did the cat get the mice?" Alice asked.

Hayes shook his head. "Actually," he replied, "the mice lay in wait for the cat, chomped down on both his paws at the same time, and darted back into the hole in the wall they came out of. Last time I saw the cat, he was headed out of town by way of the city park. The mice are still here, though," he added philosophically. "Which is why I had to have authorization to pay for an exterminator. The chairman of our county commission found one of the mice sitting in his coffee cup." He sighed. "Would you believe, I got blamed for that, too?"

"Well, that explains why the commission got mad at you," Alice said. "I mean, for the cat and the electrician."

"No, that's not why they got mad."

"It wasn't?"

He looked sheepish. "It was the engine for a 1996 Ford pickup truck."

Alice stared at him. "Okay, now I'm confused."

"I had to call an exterminator. While he was looking for the mice, they got under the hood of his truck and did something—God knows what, but it was catastrophic. When he started the truck, the engine caught fire. It was a total loss."

"How do you know the mice did it?" Kilraven wanted to know.

"One of my deputies—the same one who brought the damned rodents in here in the first place—saw them coming down the wheel well of the truck just before the exterminator got in and started it."

Alice laughed. She got to her feet. "Hayes, if I were you, I'd find whoever bought Cag Hart's big albino python and borrow him."

"If these mice are anything like Tira's mouse, fat chance a snake will do what a cat can't."

As he spoke, the lights started dimming. He shook his head. "They're back," he said with sad resignation.

"Better hide your firearms," Kilraven advised as he and Alice started for the door.

"With my luck, they're better shots than I am." Hayes laughed. "I'm going to show this drawing around town and see if anybody recognizes the subject. If either of you find out anything else about the murdered man, let me know."

"Will do," Alice promised.

Eight

Alice followed Kilraven out the door. He stood on the steps of the detention center, deep in thought.

"Why did you think you might know the murder victim?" Alice asked him.

"I told you…"

"You lied."

He looked down at her with arched eyebrows.

"Oh, I'm psychic," she said easily. "You know all those shows about people with ESP who solve murders, well, I get mistaken for that dishy one all the time…"

"You're not psychic, Alice," he said impatiently.

"No sense of humor," she scoffed. "I wonder how you stay sane on the job! Okay, okay—" she held up both hands when he glowered "—I'll talk. It was the way you rushed over here to look at the drawing. Come on, give me a break. Nobody gets in that sort of hurry without a pretty sturdy reason."

He rested his hand on the holstered butt of his pistol. His eyes held that "thousand-yard stare" that was so remarked on in combat stories. "I've encouraged a former San Antonio detective to do some digging into the files on my cold case," he said quietly. "And you aren't to mention that to Marquez. He's in enough trouble. We're not going to tell him."

She wouldn't have dared mention that she already knew about the detective working on the case, and so did Marquez. "Have you got a lead?" she asked.

"I thought this case might be one," he said quietly. "A guy comes down here from San Antonio, and gets killed. It's eerie, but I had a feeling that he might have been looking for me. Stupid, I know…"

"There are dozens of reasons he might have driven down here," she replied. "And he might have been passing through. The perp might have followed him and ambushed him."

"You're right, of course." He managed a smile. "I keep hoping I'll get lucky one day." The smile faded into cold steel. "I want to know who it was. I want to make him pay for the past seven miserable years of my life."

She cocked her head, frowning. "Nothing will make up for that," she said quietly. "You can't take two lives out of someone. There's no punishment on earth that will take away the pain, or the loss. You know that."

"Consciously, I do," he said. He drew in a sharp breath. "I worked somebody else's shift as a favor that night. If I hadn't, I'd have been with them…"

"Stop that!" she said in a tone short enough to shock him. "Lives have been destroyed with that one, stupid word. *If!* Listen to me, Kilraven, you can't appropriate the power of life and death. You can't control the world. Sometimes people die in horrible ways. It's not right, but it's just the way things are. You have to go forward. Living in regret is only another way the perp scores off you."

He didn't seem to take offense. He was actually listening.

"I hear it from victims' families all the time," she continued. "They grieve, they hate, they live for vengeance. They can't wait for the case to go to trial so they can watch the guilty person burn. But, guess what, juries don't convict, or perps make deals, or sometimes the case even gets thrown out of court because of a break in the chain of evidence. And all that anger has no place to go, except in sound bites for the six-o'clock news. Then the families go home and the hatred grows, and they end up with empty lives full of nothing. Nothing at all. Hate takes the place that healing should occupy."

He stared down at her for a long moment. "I guess I've been there."

"For about seven years," she guessed. "Are you going to devote your life to all that hatred? You'll grow old with nothing to show for those wasted years except bitter memories."

"If my daughter had lived," he said in a harsh tone, "she'd be ten years old next week."

She didn't know how to answer him. The anguish he felt was in every word.

"He got away with it, Jones," he said harshly.

"No, he didn't," she replied. "Someone knows what happened, and who did it. One day, a telephone will ring in a detective's office, and a jilted girlfriend or boyfriend will give up the perp out of hurt or revenge or greed."

He relaxed a little. "You really think so?"

"I've seen it happen. So have you."

"I guess I have."

"Try to stop living in the past," she counseled gently. "It's a waste of a good man."

He lifted an eyebrow, and the black mood seemed to drop away. His silver eyes twinkled. "Flirting with me?"

"Don't go there," she warned. "I've seen too many wives sitting up watching the late show, hoping their husbands would come home. That's not going to be me. I'm going to marry a cattle rancher and sleep nights."

He grinned. "That's no guarantee of sleep. Baby bulls and cows almost always get born in the wee hours of the morning."

"You'd know," she agreed, smiling. "You and Jon have that huge black Angus ranch in Oklahoma, don't you?"

He nodded. "Pity neither of us wants to sit around and babysit cattle. We're too career conscious."

"When you get older, it might appeal."

"It might," he said, but not with any enthusiasm. "We hold on to it because Jon's mother likes to have company there." He grimaced. "She's got a new prospect for Jon."

"I heard." Alice chuckled. "He had her arrested in his own office for sexual harassment. I understand Joceline Perry is still making him suffer for it."

"It really was sexual harassment," Kilraven corrected. "The woman is a call girl. We both tried to tell my stepmom, but her best friend is the woman's mother. She won't believe us. Mom keeps trying to get her to the ranch, with the idea that Jon will like her better if he sees her in blue jeans."

"Fat chance," Alice said. "Jon should tell Joceline the truth."

"He won't lower his dignity that far. He said if she wants to think he's that much of a scoundrel, let her. They don't get along, anyway."

"No offense, but most women don't get along with your brother," she replied. "He doesn't really like women very much."

He sighed. "If you had my stepmother as a mom, you wouldn't, either." He held up a hand. "She has her good qualities. But she has blind spots and prejudices that would choke a mule. God help the woman who really falls in love with Jon. She'll have to get past Jon's mother, and it will take a tank."

She pursed her lips. "I hear Joceline has the personality of a tank."

He chuckled. "She does. But she hates Jon." He hesitated. "If you get any new leads, you'll tell me, right?"

"Right."

"Thanks for the lecture," he added with twinkling eyes. "You're not bad."

"I'm terrific," she corrected. "Just you wait. Harley Fowler will be rushing me to the nearest minister any day now."

"Poor guy."

"Hey, you stop that. I'm a catch, I am. I've got movie stars standing in line trying to marry me... Where are you going?"

"Back to work while there's still time," he called over his shoulder.

Before she could add to her bragging, he hopped into his squad car and peeled out of the parking lot.

Alice stared after him. "You'd be lucky if I set my sights on you," she said to nobody in particular. "It's your loss!" she called after the retreating squad car.

A deputy she hadn't heard came up behind her. "Talking to yourself again, Jones?" he mused.

She gave him a pained glance. "It's just as well that I do. I'm not having much luck getting people to listen to me."

"I know just how that feels," he said with a chuckle.

He probably did, she thought as she went back to her van. People in law enforcement were as much social workers as law enforcers. They had to be diplomatic, keep their tempers under extraordinary provocation, hand out helpful advice and firm warnings, sort out domestic problems, handle unruly suspects and even dodge bullets.

Alice knew she was not cut out for that sort of life, but she enjoyed her job. At least, she chuckled, she didn't have to dodge bullets.

Saturday, she was still in Jacobsville, waiting for one last piece of evidence that came from the site of the car that was submerged in the river. A fisherman had found a strange object near the site and called police. Hayes Carson had driven out himself to have a look. It was a metal thermos jug that the fisherman had found in some weeds. It looked new and still had liquid in it. Could have been that some other pedestrian lost it, Hayes confided, but it paid to keep your options open. Hayes had promised that Alice could have it, but she'd promised to go riding with Harley. So she'd told Hayes she'd pick it up at his office late that afternoon.

"And you think the sheriff himself sits at his desk waiting for people on a Saturday?" Hayes queried on the phone in mock horror.

"Listen, Hayes, I have it on good authority that you practically sleep at the office most nights and even keep a razor and toothbrush there," she said with droll humor. "So I'll see you about seven."

He sighed. "I'll be here, working up another budget proposal."

"See?" She hung up.

Cy Parks wasn't what she'd expected. He was tall and lean, with black hair showing just threads of gray, and green eyes. His wife, Lisa, was shorter and blonde with light eyes and glasses. They had two sons, one who was a toddler and the other newborn. Lisa was holding one, Cy had the oldest.

"We've heard a lot about you," Cy mused as Alice stood next to Harley. They were all wearing jeans and long-sleeved shirts and coats. It was a cold day.

"Most of it is probably true," Alice sighed. "But I have great teeth—" she displayed them "—and a good attitude."

They laughed.

"We haven't heard bad things," Lisa assured her, adjusting her glasses on her pert nose.

"Yes, we have." Cy chuckled. "Not really bad ones. Harley says you keep proposing to him, is all."

"Oh, that's true," Alice said, grinning. "I'm wearing him down, day by day. I just can't get him to let me buy him a ring."

Cy pursed his lips and glanced at Harley. "Hey, if you can get him in a suit, I'll give him away," he promised.

Harley grinned at him. "I'll remind you that you said that," he told his boss.

Cy's eyes were more kind than humorous. "I mean it."

Harley flushed a little with pleasure. "Thanks."

"Does that mean yes?" Alice asked Harley, wide-eyed.

He gave her a mock glare. "It means I'm thinking about it."

"Darn," she muttered.

"How's your murder investigation coming?" Cy asked suddenly.

"You mean the DB on the river?" she asked. "Slowly. We've got evidence. We just can't puzzle out what it means."

"There are some messed-up people involved, is my guess," Cy said, somber. "I've seen people handled the way your victim was. It usually meant a very personal grudge."

Alice nodded. "We've found that most close-up attacks, when they aren't random, are done by people with a grudge. I never cease to be amazed at what human beings are capable of."

"Amen." Cy slid an arm around Lisa. "We'd better get these boys back into a warm house. We've been through the mill with colds already." He chuckled. "Nice to meet you, Alice. If you can get him—" he pointed at Harley "—to marry you, I've already promised him some land and a seed herd of my best cattle."

"That's really nice of you," Alice said, and meant it.

Cy glanced at Harley warmly. "I'd kind of like to keep him close by," he said with a smile. "I'd miss him."

Harley seemed to grow two feet. "I'm not going anywhere," he drawled, but he couldn't hide that he was flattered.

"Come back again," Lisa told Alice. "It's hard to find two minutes to talk with little guys like these around—" she indicated her babies "—but we'll manage."

"I'd love to," Alice told her.

The Parks family waved and went into the house.

"They're nice," Alice said to Harley.

He nodded. "Mr. Parks has been more of a father to me than my own ever was."

Alice wanted to comment, to ask about the senator. But the look on Harley's face stopped her. It was traumatic. "I haven't been on a horse in about two years," she told him. "I had to go out with the Texas Rangers to look at some remains in the brush country, and it was the only way to get to the crime scene." She groaned. "Six hours on horseback, through prickly pear cactus and thorny bushes! My legs were scratched even through thick jeans and they felt like they were permanently bowed when I finally got back home."

"I've been there, too." He laughed. "But we won't go six hours, I promise."

He led her into the barn, where he already had two horses saddled. Hers was a pinto, a female, just the right size.

"That's Bean," he said. "Colby Lane's daughter rides her when she comes over here."

"Bean?" she asked as she mounted.

"She's a pinto," he said dryly.

She laughed. "Oh!"

He climbed into the saddle of a black Arabian gelding and led off down the trail that ran to the back of the property.

It was a nice day to go riding, she thought. It had rained the night before, but it was sunny today, if cold. There were small mud patches on the trail, and despite the dead grass and bare trees, it felt good to be out-of-doors on a horse.

She closed her eyes and smelled the clean scent of

country air. "If you could bottle this air," she commented, "you could outsell perfume companies."

He chuckled. "You sure could. It's great, isn't it? People in cities don't even know what they're missing."

"You lived in a city once, didn't you?" she asked in a conversational tone.

He turned his head sideways. Pale blue eyes narrowed under the wide brim of his hat as he pondered the question. "You've been making connections, Alice."

She flushed a little. "No, I really haven't. I've just noticed similarities."

"In names," he replied.

"Yes," she confessed.

He drew in a breath and drew in the reins. So did she. He sat beside her quietly, his eyes resting on the horizon.

"The senator is your father," she guessed.

He grimaced. "Yes."

She averted her gaze to the ground. It was just faintly muddy and the vegetation was brown. The trees in the distance were bare. It was a cold landscape. Cold, like Harley's expression.

"My parents were always in the middle of a cocktail party or a meeting. All my life. I grew up hearing the sound of ice clinking in glasses. We had politicians and other rich and famous people wandering in and out. I was marched out before bedtime to show everybody what a family man the politician was." He laughed coldly. "My mother was a superior court judge," he added surprisingly. "Very solemn on the bench, very strict at home. My sister died, and suddenly she was drinking more heavily than my father at those cocktail parties. She gave up her job on the bench to become an importer." He shook his head. "He changed, too. When he was younger, he'd play ball with me, or take me to the movies. After my sister died, everything was devoted to his career, to campaigning, even when he wasn't up for reelection. I can't tell you how sick I got of it."

"I can almost imagine," she said gently. "I'm sorry."

He turned back to her, frowning. "I never connected those two facts. You know, my sister's death with the changes in my parents. I was just a kid myself, not really old enough to think deeply." He glanced back at the horizon. "Maybe I was wrong."

"Maybe you were both wrong," she corrected. "Your father seemed very sad when he saw you."

"It's been almost eight years," he replied. "In all that time, not one card or phone call. It's hard to square that with any real regret."

"Sometimes people don't know how to reach out," she said. "I've seen families alienated for years, all because they didn't know how to make the first contact, take the first step back to a relationship that had gone wrong."

He sighed, fingering the bridle. "I guess that describes me pretty well."

"It's pride, isn't it?" she asked.

He laughed faintly. "Isn't it always?" he wondered aloud. "I felt that I was the wronged party. I didn't think it was up to me to make the first move. So I waited."

"Maybe your father felt the same way," she suggested.

"My father isn't the easiest man to approach, even on his good days," he said. "He has a temper."

"You weren't singing happy songs the day I called you, when the cow ate your turnips," she replied, tongue-in-cheek.

He laughed. "I guess I've got a temper, too."

"So do I. It isn't exactly a bad trait. Only if you carry it to extremes."

He looked down at his gloved hands. "I guess."

"They're not young people anymore, Harley," she said quietly. "If you wait too much longer, you may not get the chance to patch things up."

He nodded. "I've been thinking about that."

She hesitated. She didn't want to push too hard. She nudged her horse forward a little, so that she was even with him. "Have you thought about what sort of ring you'd like?"

He pursed his lips and glanced over at her. "One to go on my finger, or one to go through my nose?"

She laughed. "Stop that."

"Just kidding." He looked up. "It's getting cloudy. We'd better get a move on, or we may get caught in a rain shower."

She knew the warning was his way of ending the conversation. But she'd got him thinking. That was enough, for now. "Suits me."

He walked her back to the van, his hands in his pockets, his thoughts far away.

"I enjoyed today," she told him. "Thanks for the riding lesson."

He stopped at the driver's door of the van and looked down at her, a little oddly. "You don't push, do you?" he asked solemnly. "It's one of the things I like best about you."

"I don't like being pushed, myself," she confided. She searched his eyes. "You're a good man."

He drew his hand out of his pocket and smoothed back her windblown dark hair, where it blew onto her cheek. The soft leather of the glove tickled. "You're a good woman," he replied. "And I really mean that."

She started to speak.

He bent and covered her mouth with his before she could say anything. His lips parted, cold and hungry on her soft, pliable lips. She opened them with a sigh and reached around him with both arms, and held on tight. She loved kissing him. But it was more than affection. It was a white-hot fire of passion that made her ache from head to toe. She felt swollen, hot, burning, as his arms contracted.

"Oh, God," he groaned, shivering as he buried his mouth in her neck. "Alice, we're getting in too deep, too quick."

"Complaints, complaints," she grumbled into his coat.

He laughed despite the ache that was almost doubling him over. "It's not a complaint. Well, not exactly." He drew in a calming breath and slowly let her go. His eyes burned down into hers. "We can't rush this," he said. "It's too good. We have to go slow."

Her wide, dark blue eyes searched his languidly. She was still humming all over with pleasure. "Go slow." She nodded. Her eyes fell to his mouth.

"Are you hearing me?"

She nodded. Her gaze was riveted to the sensuous lines of his lips. "Hearing."

"Woman…!"

He caught her close again, ramming his mouth down onto hers. He backed her into the door of the van and ground his body against hers in a fever of need that echoed in her harsh moan.

For a long time, they strained together in the misting rain, neither capable of pulling back. Just when it seemed that the only way to go was into the back of the van, he managed to jerk his mouth back from hers and step away. His jaw was so taut, it felt as if his mouth might break. His pale blue eyes were blazing with frustrated need.

Her mouth was swollen and red. She leaned back against the door, struggling to breathe normally as she stared up at him with helpless adoration. He wasn't obviously muscular, but that close, she felt every taut line of his body. He was delicious, she thought. Like candy. Hard candy.

"You have to leave. Now." He said it in a very strained tone.

"Leave." She nodded again.

"Leave. Now."

She nodded. "Now."

"Alice," he groaned. "Honey, there are four pairs of eyes watching us out the window right now, and two pairs of them are getting a hell of a sex education!"

"Eyes." She blinked. "Eyes?"

She turned. There, in the living-room window, were four faces. The adult ones were obviously amused. The little ones were wide-eyed with curiosity.

Alice blushed. "Oh, dear."

"You have to go. Right now." He moved her gently aside and opened the door. He helped her up onto the seat. He groaned. "I'm not having supper in the big house tonight, I can promise you that," he added.

She began to recover her senses and her sense of humor. Her eyes twinkled. "Oh, I see," she mused. "I've compromised you. Well, don't you worry, sweetheart," she drawled. "I'll save your reputation. You can marry me tomorrow."

He laughed. "No. I'm trimming horses' hooves."

She glowered at him. "They have farriers to do that."

"Our farrier is on Christmas vacation," he assured her.

"One day," she told him, "you'll run out of excuses."

He searched her eyes and smiled softly. "Of course I will." He stepped back. "But not today. I'll phone you." He closed the door.

She started the engine and powered down the window. "Thanks for the ride."

He was still smiling. "Thanks for the advice. I'll take it."

"Merry Christmas."

He cocked his head. "Christmas is over."

"New Year's is coming."

"That reminds me, we have a New Year's celebration here," he said. "I can bring you to it."

"I'll be back in San Antonio then," she said miserably.

"I'll drive you down here and then drive you home."

"No. I'll stay in the motel," she said. "I don't want you on the roads after midnight. There are drunk drivers."

His heart lifted. His eyes warmed. "You really are a honey."

She smiled. "Hold that thought. See you."

He winked at her and chuckled when she blushed again. "See you, pretty girl."

She fumbled the van into gear and drove off jerkily. It had been a landmark day.

Nine

Alice was back in her office the following week. She'd turned the thermos from the river in Jacobsville over to Longfellow first thing in the morning. She was waiting for results, going over a case file, when the door opened and a tall, distinguished-looking gentleman in an expensive dark blue suit walked in, unannounced. He had black hair with silver at the temples, and light blue eyes. She recognized him at once.

"Senator Fowler," she said quietly.

"Ms. Jones," he replied. He stood over the desk with his hands in his pockets. "I wonder if you could spare me a few minutes?"

"Of course." She indicated the chair in front of her desk.

He took his hands out of his pockets and sat down,

crossing one long leg over the other. "I believe you know my son."

She smiled. "Yes. I know Harley."

"I… My wife and I haven't seen him for many years," he began. "We made terrible mistakes. Now, it seems that we'll never be able to find our way back to him. He's grown into a fine-looking young man. He… has a job?"

She nodded. "A very good one. And friends."

"I'm glad. I'm very glad." He hesitated. "We didn't know how to cope with him. He was such a cocky youngster, so sure that he had all the answers." He looked down at his shoes. "We should have been kinder."

"You lost your daughter," Alice said very gently.

He lifted his eyes and they shimmered with pain and grief. "I killed…my daughter," he gritted. "Backed over her with my car rushing to get to a campaign rally." He closed his eyes. "Afterward, I went mad."

"So did your wife, I think," Alice said quietly.

He nodded. He brushed at his eyes and averted them. "She was a superior court judge. She started drinking and quit the bench. She said she couldn't sit in judgment on other people when her own mistakes were so terrible. She was on the phone when it happened. She'd just told our daughter, Cecily, to stop interrupting her and go away. You know, the sort of offhand remark parents make. It doesn't mean they don't love the child. Anyway, Cecily sneaked out the door and went behind the car, unbeknownst to me, apparently to get a toy she'd tossed under it. I jumped in without looking to see if there was anybody behind me. I was late getting to a meeting… Anyway, my wife never knew Cecily was outside until I started screaming, when I knew what I'd done." He leaned forward. "We blamed each other. We had fights. Harley grieved. He blamed me, most of all. But he seemed to just get right on with his life afterward."

"I don't think any of you did that," Alice replied. "I don't think you dealt with it."

He looked up. His blue eyes were damp. "How do you know so much?"

"I deal with death every day," she said simply. "I've seen families torn apart by tragedies. Very few people admit that they need help, or get counseling. It is horrible to lose a child. It's traumatic to lose one the way you did. You should have been in therapy, all of you."

"I wasn't the sort of person who could have admitted that," he said simply. "I was more concerned with my image. It was an election year, you see. I threw myself into the campaign and thought that would accomplish the same thing. So did my wife." He shook his head. "She decided to start a business, to keep busy." He managed a smile. "Now we never see each other. After Harley left, we blamed each other for that, too."

She studied the older man curiously. "You're a politician. You must have access to investigators. You could have found Harley any time you wanted to."

He hesitated. Then he nodded. "But that works both ways, Ms. Jones. He could have found us, too. We didn't move around."

"Harley said you wanted him to be part of a social set that he didn't like."

"Do you think I like it?" he asked suddenly and gave a bitter laugh. "I love my job. I have power. I can do a lot of good, and I do. But socializing is part of that job. I do more business at cocktail parties than I've ever done in my office in Washington. I make contacts, I get

networks going, I research. I never stop." He sighed. "I
tried to explain that to Harley, but he thought I meant
that I wanted to use him to reel in campaign workers."
He laughed. "It's funny now. He was so green, so naive.
He thought he knew all there was to know about politics
and life." He looked up. "I hope he's learned that
nothing is black or white."

"He's learned a lot," she replied. "But he's been
running away from his past for years."

"Too many years. I can't approach him directly. He'd
take off." He clasped his hands together. "I was hoping
you might find it in your heart to pave the way for me.
Just a little. I only want to talk to him."

She narrowed her eyes. "This wouldn't have anything to do with the woman we talked to at your fund-
raising party…?"

He stared at her with piercing blue eyes just a shade
lighter than Harley's. "You're very quick."

"I didn't start this job yesterday," she replied, and
smiled faintly.

He drew in a long breath. "I gave Dolores a hard
time. She was deeply religious, but she got on my
nerves. A man who's forsaken religion doesn't like
sermons," he added, laughing bitterly. "But she was a
good person. My wife had a heart attack earlier this
year. I hired a nurse to sit with her, when she got home
from the hospital. Unknown to me, the nurse drugged
my wife and left the house to party with her boyfriend.
Dolores made sure I found out. Then she sat with my
wife. They found a lot to talk about. After my wife got
back on her feet, she began to change for the better. I
think it was Dolores's influence." He hung his head. "I
was harsh to Dolores the night of the fundraiser. That's

haunted me, too. I have a young protégé, our newest senator. He's got a brother who makes me very nervous…" He lifted his eyes. "Sorry. I keep getting off the track. I do want you to help me reconnect with my son, if you can. But that's not why I'm here."

"Then why are you here, Senator?" she asked.

He looked her in the eye. "Dolores didn't commit suicide."

Her heart jumped, but she kept a straight face. She linked her hands in front of her on the desk and leaned forward. "Why do you think that?"

"Because once, when I was despondent, I made a joke about running my car into a tree. She was eloquent on the subject of suicide. She thought it was the greatest sin of all. She said that it was an insult to God and it caused so much grief for people who loved you." He looked up. "I'm not an investigator, but I know she was right-handed. She was shot in the right side of her body." He shook his head. "She wasn't the sort of person to do that. She hated guns. I'm sure she never owned one. It doesn't feel right."

"I couldn't force the assistant medical examiner to write it up as a homicide. He's near retirement, and it was your employee who died. He's afraid of you, of your influence. He knows that you stopped the investigation on the Kilraven case stone-cold."

"I didn't," he said unexpectedly, and his mouth tightened. "Will Sanders is the new junior senator from Texas," he continued. "He's a nice guy, but his brother is a small-time hoodlum with some nasty contacts, who mixes with dangerous people. He's involved in illegal enterprises. Will can't stop him, but he does try to protect him. Obviously he thinks Hank knows something about the Kilraven case, and he doesn't want it discovered."

Alice's blue eyes began to glitter. "Murder is a nasty business," she pointed out. "Would you like to know what was done to Kilraven's wife and three-year-old daughter?" she added. "He saw it up close, by accident. But I have autopsy photos that I've never shown anyone, if you'd like to see what happened to them."

The senator paled. "I would not," he replied. He stared into space. "I'm willing for Kilraven to look into the case. Rick Marquez's colleague was sent to work in traffic control. I'm sorry for that. Will persuaded me to get her off the case. She's a bulldog when it comes to homicide investigation, and she stops at nothing to solve a crime." He looked up. "Will's rather forceful in his way. I let him lead me sometimes. But I don't want either of us being shown as obstructing a murder investigation, even one that's seven years old. He's probably afraid that his brother, Hank, may have knowledge of the perpetrator and Will's trying to shield him. He's done that all his life. But he has no idea what the media would do to him if it ever came out that he'd hindered the discovery of a murderer, especially in a case as horrific as this."

"I've seen what happens when people conceal evidence. It's not pretty," Alice said. "How can you help Kilraven?"

"For one thing, I can smooth the way for Marquez's colleague. I'll go have a talk with the police commissioner when I leave here. He'll get her reassigned to Homicide. Here." He scribbled a number on a piece of paper and handed it to her. "That's my private cell number. I keep two phones on me, but only a few people

have access to this number. Tell Kilraven to call me. Or
do you have his number?"

"Sure." She pulled out her own cell phone, pushed a
few buttons and wrote down Kilraven's cell phone number
on a scrap of paper. Odd, how familiar that number looked
on paper. She handed it to the senator. "There."

"Thanks. Uh, if you like," he added with a smile as
he stood up, "you could share my private number with
Harley. He can call me anytime. Even if I'm standing
at a podium making a speech somewhere. I won't mind
being interrupted."

She stood up, too, smiling. "I'm going down there
Wednesday for the New Year's Eve celebration in town,
as it happens, with Harley. I'll pass it along. Thanks,
Senator Fowler."

He shook hands with her. "If I can pave the way for
you in the investigation into Dolores's death, I'll be
glad to," he added.

"I'll keep you in mind. Kilraven will be grateful for
your help, I'm sure."

He smiled, waved and left.

Alice sat down. Something wasn't right. She pulled
up her notes on the Jacobsville murder investigation and
scrolled down to the series of numbers that Longfellow
had transcribed from the piece of paper in the victim's
hand. Gasping, she pulled up Kilraven's cell phone
number on her own cell phone and compared them.
The digits that were decipherable were a match for everything except the area code, which was missing. It
wasn't conclusive, but it was pretty certain that the
murder victim had come to contact Kilraven. Which
begged the question, did the victim know something
about the old murder case?

Her first instinct was to pick up the phone and call Kilraven. But her second was caution. Without the missing numbers, it could be a coincidence. Better to let the senator call Kilraven and get him some help—Marquez's detective friend—and go from there. Meanwhile, Alice would press Longfellow about the faded, wet portion of the paper where the first few numbers were, so far, unreadable. The FBI lab had the technology enabling them to pull up the faintest traces of ink. They might work a miracle for the investigation.

The thermos contained a tiny residue of coffee laced with a narcotic drug, Longfellow told Alice. "If it's connected to your case," the assistant investigator told Alice, "it could explain a lot. It would make the victim less able to defend himself from an attacker."

"Fingerprints?"

Longfellow shook her head. "It was clean. Wiped, apparently, and just tossed away. It's as if," she added, frowning, "the killer was so confident that he left the thermos deliberately, to show his superiority."

Alice smiled faintly. "I love it when perps do that," she said. "When we catch them, and get them into court, that cockiness usually takes a nosedive. It's a kick to see it."

"Indeed," Longfellow added. "I'll keep digging, though," she assured Alice.

"You do that. We'll need every scrap of evidence we have to pin this murder on somebody. The killer's good. Very good." She frowned. "He's probably done this before and never got caught."

"That might explain his efficiency," the other woman agreed. "But he missed that scrap of paper in the victim's hand."

"Every criminal slips up eventually. Let's hope this is his swan song."

"Oh, yes."

Alice drove down to Jacobsville in her personal car, a little Honda with terrific gas mileage, and checked in at the motel. She'd reserved a room, to make sure she got one, because out-of-town people came for the New Year's Eve celebration. Once she was checked in, she phoned Harley.

"I was going to come up and get you," he protested.

"I don't want you on the roads at night, either, Harley," she replied softly.

He sighed. "What am I going to do with you, Alice?"

"I have several suggestions," she began brightly.

He laughed. "You can tell me tonight. Barbara's Café is staying open for the festivities. Suppose I come and get you about six, and we'll have supper. Then we'll go to the Cattlemen's Association building where the party's being held."

"That sounds great."

"It's formal," he added hesitantly.

"No worries. I brought my skimpy little black cocktail dress and my sassy boa."

He chuckled. "Not a live one, I hope."

"Nope."

"I'll see you later, then," he said in a low, sexy tone.

"I'll look forward to it."

He hung up. So did she. Then she checked her watch. It was going to be a long afternoon.

Harley caught his breath when she opened the door. She was dressed in a little black silk dress with spaghetti straps and a brief, low-cut bodice that made the most of her pert breasts. The dress clung to her hips and fell to her knees in silky profusion. She wore dark hose and black slingback pumps. She'd used enough makeup to give her an odd, foreign appearance. Her lips, plumped with glossy red stay-on lipstick, were tempting. She wore a knitted black boa with blue feathery wisps and carried a small black evening bag with a long strap.

"Will I do?" Alice asked innocently.

Harley couldn't even speak. He nudged her back into the room, closed and locked the door, took off his hat and his jacket and pushed her gently onto the bed.

"Sorry," he murmured as his mouth took hers like a whirlwind.

She moaned as he slid onto her, teasing her legs apart so that he could ease up her skirt and touch the soft flesh there with a lean, exploring hand.

His mouth became demanding. His hands moved up and down her yielding body, discovering soft curves and softer flesh beneath. With his mouth still insistent on her parting lips, he brushed away the spaghetti straps and bared her to the waist. He lifted his head to look at her taut, mauve-tipped breasts. "Beautiful," he whispered, and his mouth diverted to the hardness, covered it delicately, and with a subtle suction that arched her off the bed in a stab of pleasure so deep that it seemed to make her swell all over.

She forced his head closer, writhing under him as the hunger built and built in the secret silence of the room. All she wanted was for him never to stop. She whispered it, moaning, coaxing, as the flames grew higher and higher, and his hands reached under her, searching for a waistband...

Her cell phone blared out the theme from the original *Indiana Jones* movie. They both jumped at the sound. Harley, his mind returning to normal, quickly drew his hands out from under Alice's skirt with a grimace, and rolled away. He lay struggling to get his breath while she eased off the bed and retrieved her purse from the floor, where she'd dropped it.

"Jones," she managed in a hoarse tone.

"Alice?" Hayes Carson asked, because she didn't sound like herself.

"Yes," she said, forcing herself to breathe normally. "Hayes?"

"Yes. I wanted to know if you found out anything about that thermos." He hesitated. "Did I call at a bad time?"

She managed a laugh. "We could debate that," she said. "Actually the thermos was clean. No fingerprints, but the liquid in it had traces of a narcotic laced in it," she replied. "But Longfellow's still looking. We've got the note at the FBI lab. Hopefully they'll be able to get the missing numbers for us. But they've got a backlog and it's the holidays. Not much hope for anything this week."

"I was afraid of that."

"Well, we live in hope," she said, and glanced at Harley, who was now sitting up and looking pained.

"We do. Coming to the celebration tonight?"

"Sure am. You coming?"

"I never miss it. Uh, is Harley bringing you?"

She laughed. "He is. We'll see you there."

"Sure thing." He hung up.

She glanced at Harley with a wicked smile. "Well, we can think of Hayes as portable birth control tonight, can't we?"

He burst out laughing despite his discomfort. He managed to get to his feet, still struggling to breathe normally. "I can think of a few other pertinent adjectives that would fit him."

"Unprintable ones, I'll bet." She went up to him and put her hands on his broad chest. She reached up to kiss him softly. "It was good timing. I couldn't have stopped."

"Yeah. Me, neither," he confessed, flushing a little. "It's been a long dry spell." He bent and brushed his mouth over hers. "But we've proven that we're physically compatible," he mused.

"Definitely." She pursed her lips. "So how about we get married tomorrow morning?"

He chuckled. "Can't. I'm brushing bulls for a regional show."

"Brushing bulls?" she wondered aloud.

"Purebred herd sires. They have to be brushed and combed and dolled up. The more ribbons we win, the higher we can charge for their, uh, well, for straws."

Of semen, he meant, but he was too nice to say it bluntly. "I know what straws are, Harley." She grinned. "I get the idea."

"So not tomorrow."

"I live in hope," she returned. She went to the mirror in the bathroom to repair her makeup, which was royally smeared. "Better check your face, too," she called. "This never-smear lipstick has dishonest publicity. It does smear."

He walked up behind her. His shirt was undone. She remembered doing that, her hands buried in the thick hair that covered his chest, tugging it while he kissed her. She flushed at the memory.

He checked his face, decided it would pass, and lowered his eyes to Alice's flushed cheeks in the mirror. He put his hands on her shoulders and tightened them. "We can't get married tomorrow. But I thought, maybe next week. Friday, maybe," he said softly. "I can take a few days off. We could drive down to Galveston. To the beach. Even in winter, it's beautiful there."

She'd turned and was staring up at him wide-eyed. "You mean that? It isn't you're just saying it so I'll stop harassing you?"

He bent and kissed her forehead with breathless tenderness. "I don't know how it happened, exactly," he said in a husky, soft tone. "But I'm in love with you."

She slid her arms around his neck. "I'm in love with you, too, Harley," she said in a wondering tone, searching his eyes.

He lifted her up to him and kissed her in a new way, a different way. With reverence, and respect, and aching tenderness.

"I'll marry you whenever you like," she said against his mouth.

He kissed her harder. The passion returned, riveting them together, locking them in a heat of desire that was ever more formidable to resist.

He drew back, grinding his teeth in frustration, and moved her away from him. "We have to stop this," he said. "At least until after the wedding. I'm really old-fashioned about these things."

"Tell me about it," she said huskily. "I come from a whole family of Baptist ministers. Need I say more?"

He managed a smile. "No. I know what you mean." He drew a steadying breath and looked in the mirror. He grimaced. "Okay, now I believe that publicity was a load of bull," he told her. "I'm smeared, too, and it's not my color."

"It definitely isn't," she agreed. She wet a washcloth and proceeded to clean up both of them. Then, while he got his suit coat back on, and his hair combed, she finished her own makeup. By the time she was done, he was waiting for her at the door. He smiled as she approached him.

"You look sharp," he said gently.

She whirled the boa around her neck and smiled from ear to ear. "You look devastating," she replied.

He stuck out an arm. She linked her hand into it. He opened the door and followed her out.

There was a band. They played regional favorites, and Harley danced with Alice. Practically the whole town had gathered in the building that housed the local Cattlemen's Association, to celebrate the coming of the new year. A pair of steer horns, the idea of Calhoun Ballenger, their new state senator, waited to fall when midnight came.

Hayes Carson was wearing his uniform, and Alice teased him about it.

"Hey, I'm on duty," he replied with a grin. "And I'm only here between calls."

"I'm not arguing. It's a big turnout. Is it always like this?"

"Always," Hayes replied. He started to add to that when a call came over his radio. He pressed the button on his portable and told the dispatcher he was en route to the call. "See what I mean?" he added with a sigh. "Have fun."

"We will," Harley replied, sliding an arm around her.

Hayes waved as he went out the door.

"Is he sweet on you?" Harley asked with just a hint of jealousy in his tone.

She pressed close to him. "Everybody but Hayes knows that he's sweet on Minette Raynor, but he's never going to admit it. He's spent years blaming her for his younger brother's drug-related death. She wasn't responsible, and he even knows who was because there was a confession."

"That's sad," Harley replied.

"It is." She looked up at him and smiled. "But it's not our problem. You said we'd get married next Friday. I'll have to ask for time off."

He pursed his lips. "So will I. Do you want to get married in church?"

She hesitated. "Could we?"

"Yes. I'll make the arrangements. What sort of flowers do you want, for your bouquet?"

"Yellow and white roses," she said at once. "But, Harley, I don't have a wedding gown. You don't want a big reception?"

"Not very big, no, but you should have a wedding gown," he replied solemnly. "If we have a daughter, she could have it for her own wedding one day. Or it could be an heirloom, at least, to hand down."

"A daughter. Children…" She caught her breath. "I hadn't thought about… Oh, yes, I want children! I want them so much!"

His body corded. "So do I."

"I'll buy a wedding gown, first thing when I get home," she said. "I'll need a maid of honor. You'll need a best man," she added quickly.

"I'll ask Mr. Parks," he said.

She smiled. "I don't really have many women friends. Do you suppose Mrs. Parks would be my matron of honor?"

"I think she'd be honored," Harley replied. "I'll ask them."

"Wow," she said softly. "It's all happening so fast." She frowned. "Not too fast, is it?" she worried aloud.

"Not too fast," he assured her. "We're the same sort of people, Alice. We'll fit together like a puzzle. I promise you we will. I'll take care of you all my life."

"I'll take care of you," she replied solemnly. "I want to keep my job."

He smiled. "Of course you do. You can commute, can't you?"

She smiled. "Of course. I have a Honda."

"I've seen it. Nice little car. I've got a truck, so we can haul stuff. Mr. Parks is giving me some land and some cattle from his purebred herd. There's an old house on the land. It's not the best place to set up housekeeping, but Mr. Parks said the minute I proposed, to let him know and he'd get a construction crew out there to remodel it." He hesitated. "I told him Saturday that I was going to propose to you."

Her lips parted. "Saturday?"

He nodded. "That's when I knew I couldn't live without you, Alice."

She pressed close into his arms, not caring what anybody thought. "I felt that way, too. Like I've always known you."

He kissed her forehead and held her tight. "Yes. So we have a place to live. The boss will have it in great shape when we get back from our honeymoon." He lifted his head. "Will you mind living on a ranch?"

"Are you kidding? I want to keep chickens and learn to can and make my own butter."

He laughed. "Really?"

"Really! I hate living in the city. I can't even keep a cat in my apartment, much less grow things there." She beamed. "I'll love it!"

He grinned back. "I'll bring you one of my chicken catalogs. I like the fancy ones, but you can get regular hens as well."

"Chicken catalogs? You like chickens?"

"Boss keeps them," he said. "I used to gather eggs for Mrs. Parks, years ago. I like hens. I had my mind on a small ranch and I thought chickens would go nicely with cattle."

She sighed. "We're going to be very happy, I think."

"I think so, too."

The Parkses showed up, along with the Steeles and the Scotts. Harley and Alice announced their plans, and the Parkses agreed with delightful speed to take part in the wedding. Other local citizens gathered around to congratulate them.

Midnight came all too soon. The steer horns lowered to the loud count by the crowd, out under the bright Texas stars to celebrate the new year. The horns made it to the ground, the band struck up "Auld Lang Syne" and everybody kissed and cried and threw confetti.

"Happy New Year, Alice," Harley whispered as he bent to kiss her.

"Happy New Year." She threw her arms around him and kissed him back.

He left her at her motel with real reluctance. "I won't come in," he said at once, grinning wickedly. "We've already discovered that I have no willpower."

"Neither do I," she sighed. "I guess we're very

strange. Most people who get married have been living together for years. We're the odd couple, waiting until after the ceremony."

He became serious. "It all goes back to those old ideals, to the nobility of the human spirit," he said softly. "Tradition is important. And I love the idea of chastity. I'm only sorry that I didn't wait for you, Alice. But, then, I didn't know you were going to come along. I'd decided that I'd never find someone I wanted to spend my life with." He smiled. "What a surprise you were."

She went close and hugged him. "You're the nicest man I've ever known. No qualms about what I do for a living?" she added.

He shrugged. "It's a job. I work with cattle and get sunk up to my knees in cow manure. It's not so different from what you do. We both get covered up in disgusting substances to do our jobs."

"I never thought of it like that."

He hugged her close. "We'll get along fine. And we'll wait, even if half the world thinks we're nuts."

"Speaking for myself, I've always been goofy."

"So have I."

"Besides," she said, pulling back, "I was never one to go with the crowd. You'll call me?"

"Every day," he said huskily. "A week from Friday."

She smiled warmly. "A week from Friday. Happy New Year."

He kissed her. "Happy New Year."

He got back into his car. He didn't drive away until she was safely inside her room.

Ten

Alice had forgotten, in the excitement, to tell Harley about the senator's message. But the following day, when he called, he didn't have time to talk. So she waited until Friday, when he phoned and was in a chatty mood.

"I have a message for you," she said hesitantly. "From your father."

"My father?" he said after a minute, and he was solemn.

"He said that he'd made some dreadful mistakes. He wants the opportunity to apologize for them. Your sister's death caused problems for both your parents that they never faced."

"Yes, and I never realized it. When did you talk to him?"

"He came to see me Monday, at my office. I like him," she added quietly. "I think he was sincere, about wanting to reconnect with you. He gave me his private cell phone number." She hesitated. "Do you want it?"

He hesitated, too, but only for a moment. "Yes."

She called out the numbers to him.

"I'm not saying I'll call him," he said after a minute. "But I'll think about it."

"That's my guy," she replied, and felt warm all over at the thought. She'd had some worries, though. "Harley?"

"Hmm?"

"You know that we've only known each other for a few weeks…" she began.

"And you're afraid we're rushing into marriage?"

She shrugged. "Aren't we?"

He laughed softly. "Alice, we can wait for several months or several years, but in the end, we'll get married. We have so much in common that no sane gambler would bet against us. But if you want to wait, honey, we'll wait." He cleared his throat. "It's just that my willpower may not be up to it. Just don't expect to get married in a white gown, okay?"

She remembered their close calls and laughed. "Okay, I'm convinced. We'll get married a week from Friday."

"Wear a veil, will you," he added seriously. "It's old-fashioned, but it's so beautiful."

"Say no more. I'll shop veils-are-us this very day."

"There's such a place?" he asked.

"I'll let you know."

"Deal. I'll call you tonight."

She felt a flush of warmth. "Okay."

"Bye, darlin'," he drawled, and hung up.

Alice held the phone close, sighing, until Longfellow walked by and gave her a strange look.

Alice removed the phone from her chest and put it

carefully on the desk. "Magnetism, Longfellow," she said facetiously. "You see, a burst of magnetism caught my cell phone and riveted it to my chest. I have only just managed to extricate it." She waited hopefully for the reply.

Longfellow pursed her lips. "You just stick to that story, but I have reason to know that you have recently become engaged. So I'll bet your boyfriend just hung up."

"Who told you I was engaged?" Alice demanded.

Longfellow started counting them off on her fingers. "Rick Marquez, Jon Blackhawk, Kilraven, Hayes Carson…"

"How do you know Kilraven?" Alice wanted to know.

"He keeps bugging me about that telephone number," she sighed. "As if the FBI lab doesn't have any other evidence to process. Give me a break!" She rolled her eyes.

"If they call you, get in touch with me before you tell Kilraven anything, okay?" she asked. "I want to make sure he's not running off into dead ends on my account."

"I'll do that," Longfellow promised. She stared at Alice. "If you want to shop for a wedding gown, I know just the place. And I'll be your fashion consultant."

Alice looked dubious.

"Wait a sec," Longfellow said. "I have photos of my own wedding, three years ago." She pulled them up on her phone and showed them to Alice. "That's my gown."

Alice caught her breath. "Where in the world did you find such a gown?"

"At a little boutique downtown, would you believe it? They do hand embroidery—although in your case, it will probably have to be machined—and they have a pretty good selection for a small shop."

"Can we go after work?" Alice asked enthusiastically.

Longfellow laughed. "You bet."

"Thanks."

"Not a problem."

Alice picked out a dream of a gown, white satin with delicate pastel silk embroidery on the hem in yellow and pink and blue. There was a long illusion veil that matched it, with just the ends embroidered delicately in silk in the same pastel colors. It wasn't even that expensive.

"Why aren't you on the news?" Alice asked the owner, a petite little brunette. "I've never seen such beautiful wedding gowns!"

"We don't appeal to everybody," came the reply. "But for the few, we're here."

"I'll spread the word around," Alice promised.

"I already have." Longfellow chuckled.

Outside the shop, with her purchase safely placed in the backseat of her car, Alice impulsively hugged Longfellow. "Thanks so much."

"It was my pleasure," Longfellow replied. "Where will you live?"

"He's got a small ranch," she said proudly. "We're going to raise purebred Santa Gertrudis cattle. But until we make our first million at it, he's going to go on working as a ranch foreman, and I'll keep my job here. I'll commute."

"You always wanted to live in the country," Longfellow recalled.

Alice smiled. "Yes. And with the right man. I have definitely found him." She sighed. "I know it sounds like a rushed thing. We've known each other just a short time…"

"My sister met her husband and got married in five

days," Longfellow said smugly. "They just celebrated their thirty-seventh wedding anniversary."

"Thirty-seven years?" Alice exclaimed.

"Well, he liked *Star Trek,* she said," Longfellow explained. "She said that told her everything she needed to know about him—that he was intelligent, tolerant, inquisitive, optimistic about the future, unprejudiced and a little quirky." She shrugged and laughed. "Not bad for a quick character reading, was it?"

"Not at all. Good for her!"

"You do the same," Longfellow lectured. "I don't want to see you in divorce court a month after you say your vows."

"I believe we can safely say that won't happen," Alice replied, and she felt and sounded confident. She frowned. "I wonder if he likes *Star Trek,*" she wondered aloud.

In fact, she asked him when he called that night. "I do," he replied. "All the series, all the movies, and especially the new one, about Kirk, Spock and McCoy as cadets." He paused. "How about you?"

"I love it, too." She laughed, and then explained why she'd asked the question.

He was serious then. "That's a long time," he said of Longfellow's sister's marriage. "We'll give her a run for her money, won't we, Alice?"

She smiled. "Yes, we will."

There was a long pause. "You're wondering if I called that number you gave me," Harley said.

She laughed in surprise. "You read minds! That's great! If we ever have an argument, you'll know why I was mad and just what to do about it!"

"I only read minds occasionally," he told her, "so

let's not have arguments. But I did call my father. We had a long talk. I think we may get together one day, with my mother, and try to iron things out."

"That's wonderful," she said softly.

"It won't be easy to get over the past, but at least we're all willing to try. I did mention the wedding to him."

"And?"

"He said that if he showed up, we'd be a media lunch. I have to agree," he added. "I don't want that. Neither do you. But we're invited to their house for a potluck dinner the day we get back from our honeymoon."

"I'd enjoy that."

"Me, too."

"I bought a wedding gown. With a veil. It's beautiful."

"On you, any gown would be. You're delicious, Alice."

She laughed softly. "That's just the right thing to say."

"I mean it, too."

"I know."

"Game for a movie tomorrow night?" he asked. "There's a Christmas-themed one we could go see."

"That would be fun. Yes."

"I'll pick you up at six and we'll have supper first."

"That's a date."

"Uh, and no stopping by your apartment after. I go home."

"Yes, Harley. You go home."

There was a brief pause and they both burst out laughing.

He did go home, but only after a heated session on her sofa that ended with him actually pulling away and running for the door. He waved as he slammed it behind him, leaving a disheveled Alice laughing her head off.

* * *

It was raining on their wedding day. Alice carried an umbrella over her gown and Lisa Parks held up the train as they rushed into the church just ahead of a thunderbolt. Cy Parks was waiting at the altar with Harley, who looked devastating in a tuxedo, a conventional black one with a white shirt and black bow tie. Harley couldn't take his eyes off Alice.

Lisa went to her seat. The full church quieted. Alice smiled as the Wedding March struck up on the organ and she adjusted her train before she picked up the pretty bouquet he'd ordered for her. The fingertip veil just hid the wetness in her eyes as she wished with all her heart that her parents had been here to see her marry.

She walked slowly down the aisle, aware of friendly, curious eyes admiring her dress. Leo Hart and his wife, Janie, were sitting on the aisle. Alice didn't know, but Janie had dated Harley while she was trying to get over Leo. It hadn't been serious. In fact, Harley had dated several local women, including one who'd cast him off like a wet shoe and hurt his pride. It had seemed to many people as if Harley would always be the stand-in for some other man. But here he was with a really pretty, professional woman, and she had a reputation as a keen investigator. Many people in Jacobsville watched the crime scene investigation shows. They grinned as they considered how nice it was going to be, having somebody local who could answer all those questions they wanted to ask about homicide investigation.

Alice paused at the altar, looked up at Harley and felt a moment of panic. They hardly knew each other. They were almost strangers. This was insane…!

Just then, as if he knew what she was feeling,

Harley's big hand reached over and linked itself unob-
trusively into her cold fingers and pressed them, very
gently. She looked into his eyes. He was smiling, with
love and pride and confidence. All at once, she relaxed
and smiled back.

The minister cleared his throat.

"Sorry," Alice mouthed, and turned her attention to
him instead of Harley.

The minister, who had a daughter just Alice's age,
grinned at her and began the service.

It was brief, but poignant. At the end of it, Harley
lifted the exquisite veil and kissed his bride. Alice
fought back tears as she returned the tender kiss.

They ran out of the church amid a shower of confetti
and well wishes.

"Good thing you aren't having a reception," Cash
Grier remarked as they waited for the limousine Cy
Parks had ordered to take them to the airport, one of
several wedding presents.

"A reception?" Alice asked, curious. "Why?"

"Our local district attorney, Blake Kemp, had one,"
Cash explained. "He and his wife went home instead to
dress for their honeymoon. While they were gone, there
was an altercation. One of my officers was wearing the
punch, another salvaged just the top layer of the
wedding cake and most of the guests went to jail." He
grinned. "Jacobsville weddings are interesting."

They both laughed, and agreed that it was probably
a good thing after all.

Cy Parks paused with Lisa when the limo drove up
and the driver came around to open the rear door.

Cy shook hands with Harley. "Your house will be ready
when you get back," he told Harley. "You did good."

Harley beamed. "You'll never know how much it meant to me, that you and Lisa stood up with us. Thanks."

Cy was somber. "You're a good man, Harley. I hope my sons will be like you."

Harley had to bite down hard. "Thanks," he managed.

"Go have a nice honeymoon," Cy told the couple. He grinned. "I won't let the Hart boys near your house, either."

"The Hart boys?" Alice parroted.

Leo Hart leaned over her shoulder. "We have a reputation for making weddings interesting," he told her, and grinned.

"Not so much these days." Janie grinned from beside him.

A tall, silver-eyed man in a police uniform walked up beside them. Kilraven. Grinning. "I'm giving the limo a police escort to the airport," he told them.

"That's very nice of you," Alice told him.

He sighed. "Might as well, since there's no reception. Weddings are getting really somber around here."

"Why don't you get married and have a reception?" Cash Grier suggested.

Kilraven gave him a look. "And have women throwing themselves over cliffs because I went out of circulation? In your dreams, Grier!"

Everybody laughed.

Corpus Christi was a beautiful little city on the Gulf of Mexico. It had a sugar-sand beach and seagulls and a myriad of local shops with all sorts of souvenirs and pretty things to buy. Harley and Alice never noticed.

They'd managed to get checked in and they looked out the window at the beach. Then they looked at each other.

Clothes fell. Buttons popped. Intimate garments went everywhere. Alice threw back the covers and dived in just a few seconds ahead of her brand-new husband. In a tangle of arms and legs, they devoured each other in a surging crescendo of passion that lasted for what seemed hours.

"What are you waiting for?" Alice groaned. "Come back here!"

"I was only…trying to make it easier…" he began.

"Easier, the devil!" She arched up, grimacing, because it really did hurt. But only for a few seconds. She stiffened, but then the fever burned right back up again, and she dragged him down with a kiss that knocked every single worry right out of his mind.

"Oh, wow," she managed when the room stopped spinning around them. She was lying half under Harley, covered in sweat even in the cool room, shivering with delight. "Now that was a first time to write about!" she enthused.

He laughed. "I was trying not to hurt you," he pointed out.

She pushed him over and rolled onto him. "And I appreciate every single effort, but it wasn't necessary," she murmured as she kissed him. "I was starving for you!"

"I noticed."

She lifted up and gave him a wicked look.

"I was starving for you, too," he replied diplomatically, and chuckled. "You were incredible."

"So were you." She sighed and laid her cheek on his broad, hairy chest. "No wonder people don't wait for wedding nights anymore."

"Some of them do."

"It isn't night, yet," she reminded him.

He laughed softly. "I guess not."

She kissed his chest. "Should we go down to the restaurant to eat?"

"Mr. Parks gave us a one-week honeymoon with room service. I do not think we should insult the man by not using it," he replied.

"Oh, I do agree. I would hate to insult Mr. Parks. Besides," she murmured, shifting, "I just thought of something we can do to pass the time until supper!"

"You did?" He rolled her over, radiant. "Show me!"

She did.

They arrived home bleary-eyed from lack of sleep and with only a few photos and souvenirs of where they'd been. In actuality, they'd hardly seen anything except the ceiling of their hotel room.

The ranch house was one level. It was old, but well-kept, and it had new steps and porch rails, and a porch swing. It also had a new coat of white paint.

"It's just beautiful," Alice enthused. "Harley, it looks like the house I lived in when I was a little girl, growing up in Floresville!"

"You grew up in Floresville?" he asked as he unlocked the door and opened it.

She looked up at him. "We don't know a lot about each other, do we? It will give us something to talk about when we calm down just a little."

He grinned and swept her up in his arms, to carry her into the house. "Don't hold your breath waiting for that to happen," he advised.

She smiled and kissed him.

He put her down in the living room. She sighed. "Oh, my," she said softly.

There were roses everywhere, vases full of them, in

every color. There were colorful afghans and two sweaters (his and hers), a big-screen color television set, a DVD player, an Xbox 360 gaming system and several games, and a basket of fruit. On the dining-room table, there were containers of breads and a propped-up note pointing to the refrigerator. It was full of cooked food. There was even a cake for dessert.

"Good grief," Harley whistled. He picked up the note and read it. "Congratulations and best wishes from the Scotts, the Parkses, the Steeles, all the Harts, and the Pendletons." He gaped at her. "The Pendletons! Jason Pendleton is a multimillionaire! I thought he was going to deck me in San Antonio…" He hesitated to tell his new wife that he'd tried to date Jason's stepsister Gracie, who was now Mrs. Pendleton. He chuckled. "Well, I guess he forgave me. His mother has a craft shop and she knits. I'll bet she made the afghans for us."

Alice fingered the delicate stitches. "I'll be still writing thank-you notes when our kids are in grammar school," she remarked. "Harley, you have so many friends. I never realized." She turned and smiled at him. "We're going to be so happy here."

He beamed. He opened his arms and Alice ran into them, to be held close and hugged.

"Are you hungry?" he asked.

She peered up at him and laughed. "We didn't get breakfast."

"And whose fault was that, Mrs. Fowler?" he teased.

"I said I was hungry, it just wasn't for food. Well, not then. I could eat," she added, peering past him at the cake on the table.

"So could I, and I noticed fried chicken in the fridge. It's my favorite."

"Mine, too," she agreed. "I don't cook much on the weekdays because I'm on call so often." She looked up at him worriedly.

"I can cook, Alice," he assured her, smiling. "And I will, when I need to."

"You're just the best husband," she sighed.

"Glad you think so." He chuckled. "Let's find some plates."

They watched television while they nibbled on all sorts of delicious things. It was a treat that they both liked the same sort of shows. But they didn't watch it for long. The trip back had been tiring, and in many ways, it had been a long week. They slept soundly.

The next day, Alice had to drive up to her office to check on what progress had been made into the murder investigation while Harley got back to work on the ranch. He had things to do, as well, not to mention getting his own present of purebred cattle fed and watered and settled before he went over to Mr. Parks's house to do his job.

Longfellow welcomed her at the door with a hug. "Did you have a nice trip?"

"Lovely," Alice assured her. "But it's good to get home. We had food and presents waiting for us like you wouldn't believe. Mr. Parks had Harley's house renovated and he actually gave him a small herd of purebred cattle for a wedding gift—not to mention the honeymoon trip. What a boss!"

Longfellow smiled. "Surprising, isn't it, how generous he is. Considering the line of work he used to be in, it's a miracle he survived to get married and have a family."

"Yes, I know what you mean," Alice replied. "Any word yet on that scrap of paper we sent to the FBI lab?"

She shook her head. "The holidays, you know, and we're not at the top of the line for quick results." She pursed her lips. "Didn't you once bribe people to get faster service?" she teased.

Alice laughed. "I did, but I don't think my new husband would appreciate it if I did that sort of thing now."

"Probably not."

"Anything on the woman who died at Senator Fowler's house?" Alice added.

Longfellow frowned. "Actually, the senator stopped by and left you a note. I think I put it in your middle desk drawer. He said you were going to be a terrific daughter-in-law… Oops, I'm not supposed to know that, am I?"

Alice's eyes widened. She hadn't considered that she was now the daughter-in-law of the senior senator from Texas. She sat down, hard. "Well, my goodness," she said breathlessly. "I hadn't thought about that."

"You'll have clout in high places, if you ever need it," the other woman said wickedly. "You can threaten people with him!"

Alice laughed. "You idiot."

"I'd threaten people with him," came the reply. She frowned. "Especially Jon Blackhawk," she added.

"What's Jon done to you?"

"He called me at home at midnight to ask if we had lab results back on that thermos that Sheriff Hayes gave you."

"Now why would he want to know about that?"

Longfellow's eyes sparkled. "The investigator who was working with Marquez on the Kilraven case re-called seeing one like it."

"Where? When?"

"At the home of her ex-husband, actually," she said. "Remember that spiral design on the cup? It was rather odd, I thought at the time, like somebody had painted it with acrylics."

"Can we find out who her ex-husband is?" Alice asked excitedly.

"I did. He died a few weeks ago. The woman he was living with couldn't tell her anything about his friends or visitors, or about the thermos. The investigator told me that the woman was so strung out on coke that she hardly knew where she was."

"Pity," Alice replied sadly.

"Yes, and apparently the ex-husband had a drug problem of his own. Poor woman," she added softly. "She worked her way up to sergeant in the homicide division, and lost her promotion when she helped Marquez reopen the Kilraven cold case files."

Alice was only half listening now. She recalled the note the senator had left, pulled it out, opened it and read it. He'd talked to the police commissioner, he wrote, who had promised the reinstatement of the investigator on the Kilraven case. He'd also spoken to his colleague, the junior senator, and informed him that they were not going to try to hinder any murder investigations, regardless of how old they were. He'd talked to the coroner as well, and the autopsy on the senator's kitchen worker had been reclassified as a homicide. He hoped this would help. He reminded her that she and Harley should call and let them know when they were coming to supper. They had a wedding gift to present.

Alice whistled softly. "He's been busy." She told Longfellow the results of the senator's intercession. "What a nice man."

"Lucky you, to be related to him." The other woman chuckled. "See, I told you that... Wait a sec."

Her phone was ringing. She picked it up, raised her eyebrows at Alice and pulled a pen and paper toward her. "That's very nice of you! We didn't expect to hear back so soon. Yes, I'm ready. Yes." She was writing. She nodded. "I've got it. Yes. Yes, that will be fine. Thank you!" She hung up. "The FBI lab!" she exclaimed. "They've deciphered the rest of the numbers on that slip of paper you found in the victim's hand in Jacobsville!"

"Really? Let me see!"

Alice picked up the slip of paper and read the numbers with a sinking feeling in her stomach. Now there was no doubt, none at all, who the victim had come to Jacobsville to see. The number was for Kilraven's cell phone.

Eleven

Kilraven waited for Alice in the squad room at the Jacobsville Police Department. Alice had driven down in the middle of the day. She didn't want him to have to wait for the news, but she didn't want to tell him over the phone, either.

He stood up when she walked in and closed the door behind her. "Well?" he asked.

"The number on that slip of paper in the dead man's hand," she said. "It was your cell phone number."

He let out a breath. His eyes were sad and bitter. "He knew something about the murder. He came to tell me. Somebody knew or suspected, and they killed him."

"Then they figured that Dolores, who worked for Senator Fowler, might have heard something from the man, and they killed her, too. This is a nasty business."

"Very," Kilraven replied. "But this case is going to

break the older one," he added. "I'm sure of it. Thanks, Alice," he added quietly. "I owe you one."

"I'll remember that," she said, smiling. "Keep me in the loop, will you? Oh, there's another thing, I almost forgot. That thermos that Sheriff Hayes found, the one wiped clean of prints? Your investigator in San Antonio actually recognized it! It belonged to her ex-husband!"

"Oh, boy," he said heavily. "That's going to cause some pain locally."

"It is? Why?"

"Her ex-husband is the uncle of Winnie Sinclair."

"Does Winnie know?" Alice asked, stunned.

"No. And you can't tell her." His eyes had an odd, pained look. "I'll have to do it, somehow."

"Was he the sort of person who'd get mixed up in murder?"

"I don't know. But he's dead now. Whatever he knew died with him. Thanks again, Alice. I will keep you in the loop," he promised.

She nodded and he left her standing there. She felt his pain. Her own life was so blessed, she thought. Kilraven's was a study in anguish. Maybe he could solve the case at last, though. And maybe little Winnie Sinclair would have a happier future than she expected. Certainly, Kilraven seemed concerned about her feelings.

Alice and Harley went to supper with the senator and his wife. They were hesitant at first, with Harley, but as the evening wore on, they talked. Old wounds were reopened, but also lanced. By the time the younger Fowlers left, there was a détente.

"It went better than I expected it to," Harley said. "I suppose all three of us had unrealistic expectations."

She smiled. "They were proud of you when they heard what you'd done with your life. You could tell."

He smiled. "I grew up. I was such a cocky brat when I went to work for Cy Parks." He chuckled. "But I grew up fast. I learned a lot. I'm still learning." He glanced at her as he drove. "Nice presents they gave us, too. A little unexpected."

"Yes. A telescope." She glanced through the back window of the pickup at it, in its thick cardboard box, lying in the bed of the truck. "An eight-inch Schmidt-Cassegrain, at that," she mused.

He stood up on the brakes. "You know what it is?" he burst out.

"Oh, yes, I took a course in astronomy. I have volumes in my office on…" She stopped. The senator had been in her office. She laughed. "My goodness, he's observant!"

"My present isn't bad, either."

They'd given Harley a new saddle, a very ornate one that he could use while riding in parades. "Somebody must have told them what you were doing for a living while we were on our honeymoon," she guessed.

"My father is a digger." He laughed. "I'm sure he asked around."

"We have to spend time with them," she told him. "Family is important. Especially, when you don't have any left."

"You have uncles," he reminded her.

"Yes, but they all live far away and we were never close. I'd like very much to have children. And they'll need a granny and granddaddy, won't they?"

He reached across the seat and linked her hand into his. "Yes." He squeezed her fingers. "We're going to be happy, Alice."

She leaned her head back and stared at him with utter delight. "We're going to be very happy, Harley," she replied. She closed her eyes with a sigh, and smiled. "Very happy."

* * * * *

"I'm taking you shopping," he said. "For whatever you need for this role."

"This role?" she echoed.

"As my lover, my girlfriend, my mistress, my woman. Which would you prefer?"

"No." She shook her head adamantly. "I won't do it. I would rather scrub floors."

"You came here tonight to ascertain your role as my employee." Suddenly his expression was decisive, his demeanor all brooking-no-argument business. "I do not need household help of any variety. I need you here, as my lover."

"Your *pretend* lover."

And when he closed down the space between them, she held her ground and held his gaze. "I have every confidence in you, Isabelle," he said evenly, but there was a hint of wicked in both voice and eyes as they drifted over her face. "I believe you will satisfy me in any role you take on, whether pretend or otherwise."

MAGNATE'S
MAKE-BELIEVE
MISTRESS

BY
BRONWYN JAMESON

All the characters in this book have no existence outside the imagination of the author, and have no relation whatsoever to anyone bearing the same name or names. They are not even distantly inspired by any individual known or unknown to the author, and all the incidents are pure invention.

Published in Great Britain 2010
Harlequin Mills & Boon Limited,
Eton House, 18-24 Paradise Road, Richmond, Surrey TW9 1SR

© Bronwyn Turner 2009

ISBN: 978 0 263 88187 5

51-1210

Harlequin Mills & Boon policy is to use papers that are natural, renewable and recyclable products and made from wood grown in sustainable forests. The logging and manufacturing processes conform to the legal environmental regulations of the country of origin.

Printed and bound in Spain
by Litografia Rosés S.A., Barcelona

Bronwyn Jameson spent much of her childhood with her head buried in a book. As a teenager, she discovered romance novels, and it was only a matter of time before she turned her love of reading them into a love of writing them. Bronwyn shares an idyllic piece of the Australian farming heartland with her husband and three sons, a thousand sheep, a dozen horses, assorted wildlife and one kelpie dog. She still chooses to spend her limited downtime with a good book. Bronwyn loves to hear from readers. Write to her at bronwyn@bronwynjameson.com or visit her website at www.bronwynjameson.com.

For the Maytoners; this pair of books
was blessed by your brainstorming.

Dear Reader,

Do you remember when you first started reading romance? I was young—I don't recall exactly how young, but my mother used to order the English *Woman's Weekly*, which carried serialized Mills & Boon novels. Waiting for the next issue to see what happened next was torturous, and I was soon seeking and devouring the books.

Many of my favorites were set in London and the English countryside, as were many of my family's television favorites of the time: *Upstairs, Downstairs, The Forsyte Saga, The Avengers*. This firmly seeded in me a love of all things English. The accents, the manners, the stately homes, the countryside and cottages and hedgerows. My favorite movie list includes *Love, Actually, Notting Hill, Four Weddings and a Funeral* and *Pride and Prejudice*.

Setting one or more of my books in England was inevitable, and the stories of sisters Isabelle and Chessie Browne fit perfectly. My first visit to England was for *my* sister's wedding, you see, and I was lucky enough to return a couple of years ago and revisit some of my favorite spots—and find some new ones—in and around London. These added to a lifetime of beloved reading and viewing experiences to create the world of this book.

It is an extremely affluent world, one Isabelle has only experienced as a housekeeper to the wealthy, and even then she's seen nothing like the townhouse or the country estate belonging to Cristiano Verón. She is swept into a world of polo and personal shoppers and charity benefits, a fairy-tale world she believes fits no better than the couture clothes and designer shoes.

I hope you enjoy Isabelle's Cinderella transformation.

Cheers,

Bronwyn

One

"Steady, baby, there is no rush. We have all the time in the world." Cristiano Verón shifted his weight over Gisele's back, the touch of his hand on her neck as deeply soothing as his voice. Between his legs, she quivered with contained excitement as their pace eased to a smooth, rolling rhythm.

"Good girl," he murmured. Another slow caress from ear to shoulder echoed his praise. "Perfect."

Gisele was so responsive, so biddable, so willing to please. So unlike the other females in his life, although that cynical observation did not dampen his bone-deep pleasure of this moment nor dim his satisfied smile. The verdant scent of spring filled his nostrils. Glorious sunshine warmed his back and arms for the first time in weeks. And when he swung his polo stick, the smack of contact with the ball fired exhilaration through his body.

Not better than sex, but hitting the polo field—even stick-

and-balling alone—ranked second on Cristo's personal pleasure scale.

Lately there'd been too few opportunities for pleasure. He could not recall the last weekend that wasn't built around business or family obligations, or the last Sunday he'd spent at his Hertfordshire estate. And, *Dios,* he missed his stables, he missed his ponies, he missed the passion and the controlled aggression of this game.

With a light press of his thighs, Cristo guided the favourite of his ponies through a series of sure-footed turns. As always, she responded sweetly, answering every command without argument. If only that were true of—

The thought stopped dead. Cristo's eyes narrowed on the lone figure standing dead centre of his practice pitch. Not one of the females hell-bent on driving him loco, but a near relation.

Hugh Harrington, his sister's fiancé.

Resigned to the interruption Cristo swore softly but without heat. It wasn't that he disliked his future brother-in-law. Hugh had pursued Amanda with the same single-minded purpose he displayed on the polo pitch, and that steadfast attitude had earned Cristo's grudging approval. Now if Hugh were standing midfield in his polo kit, Cristo would have welcomed his arrival with unbridled delight. But no, the younger man wore business clothes and an expression of grim determination on his pretty-boy face.

Another wedding drama, Cristo predicted. The damned event had turned into a circus of mammoth dimensions, and since Cristo was writing the cheques, he also suffered through the daily crises reported by Amanda and their mother.

He reminded himself it would be over in less than a month. Amanda would lose the manic bride-to-be tic. Vivi would resume her pursuit of husband number five. Life would return to normal.

Just twenty-eight more days…

Easing Gisele to a halt, he greeted his unexpected visitor with a laconically raised brow. "I thought you were casting your eye over a property in Provence."

"Finished the appraisal, flew home last night," Hugh said. Straightening his shoulders, he drew a breath that puffed out his chest. "I'm sorry to intrude on your practice, and on a Sunday. I won't keep you long, but I have to speak with you."

"That sounds ominous. What is it this time?" Cristo asked mildly. "Roses refusing to bloom? Caterer resigned in a snit? Another bridesmaid turned up pregnant?"

Hugh's south-of-France tan blanched. "Not a bridesmaid," he muttered.

"Amanda?"

"No, another woman. I don't know who she is," Hugh said in an agitated rush. "Except she's Australian and she called while I was away and left this bloody message on my voice mail. She says she's pregnant."

Gisele threw her head, alerting Cristo that he'd unconsciously tightened his grip on the reins. He gentled the pony's skittishness with a hand on her neck, but his gaze remained fixed on the younger man's harried countenance. "Are you telling me this woman is expecting your child?"

"That is her claim, but it's absolute bollocks."

"You said you don't know who she is." Cristo spoke slowly, each word a clear bite of disbelief. His voice was no longer mild. "Are you saying you have never met?"

"How can I say that for sure? You know I was in Australia for almost a month earlier this year, preparing for the Hillier estate sale."

Hugh travelled widely and often as a representative of his family's auction house, but Cristo did specifically remember the trip because of his lovelorn sister's response to her fiancé's

long absence. Amanda was a firm believer in the adage of
misery loves company.

"I daresay I met hundreds of people," Hugh continued.

"Some of them women, no doubt."

"I didn't meet them in that way. I was pointing out that I *may*
have met this woman, but I don't recall her by name. Since I
asked Amanda to be my wife, I haven't looked at anyone else.
Why would I risk everything that is my happiness?"

If not for his cynicism toward love and marriage, Cristo
might have swallowed that ardently delivered speech. But he
also subscribed to one of his stepfather's oft-quoted beliefs:
Where there's smoke, there is fire. "Does anyone else know
about this woman's claim?" he asked.

Hugh shook his head.

"You haven't told Amanda?"

"Are you serious? You know what state she is in with the
wedding preparations."

Sadly, Cristo did.

"She deserves nothing less than a perfect day. What if this
woman were to turn up here, on my doorstep, the day before
the wedding?"

"What are you planning to do?" Cristo asked. "Pay her off?"

Hugh blinked in astonishment, as if he'd not considered
that as an option. Cristo wondered if he'd considered any options. "I don't know what to do," he said, confirming that
judgement. "I would have consulted Justin, but he's in New
York patching up Harringtons' reputation. I couldn't lumber
him with another problem on top of this last year, which is
why I'm seeking your advice."

Cristo had no problem with that choice and acknowledged
it with a single nod. On top of his wife's death, Hugh's elder
brother was dealing with an internal scandal in the American

office of his family's venerable firm. According to rumours, the fallout was not pretty.

"Why me?" Hugh shook his head with apparent bemusement. "She must have chosen me for a reason."

Cristo could think of several billion. "Did she mention money?" he asked.

"She didn't mention much at all. She said she'd been trying to reach me for the past week. She asked if I remembered her—even spelt her name out, as if that were significant. Then she came right out with 'I'm pregnant.'"

"She sounds like a woman who doesn't mince words."

"She sounded like a woman who was ticked off. What should I do, Cristo? I can't risk Amanda finding out, nor can I ignore this…this…" Hugh raked a hand through his hair and expelled a broken breath. "Maybe it's a misunderstanding. Or a case of mistaken identity. Maybe I should just call her."

"Do you have her number?"

Hugh produced a sheet of notepaper from his inside jacket pocket. For a second, Cristo watched it shake in his hand. Despite the holiday tan, he looked wan and rattled, and Cristo had to wonder at the cause. Perhaps the old love-'em-and-leave-'em Hugh Harrington—the one his brother Justin had been called on to rescue from numerous past scrapes—had come out to play on that lengthy business trip.

A world away from home, a few too many drinks, a beautiful temptress who didn't mince words…

Perhaps that explained his reluctance to confide in Amanda, or to return the woman's call. Perhaps he'd come here today acting the part of bewildered innocence, confident that Cristo would pay off the momentary blunder and make her go away. He knew that family was everything to Cristo, that he would do anything to ensure his sister's happiness.

"Are you going to call her?" Hugh asked.

"I have a trip to Australia scheduled for early in June. I can bring it forward." Cristo made the decision on the spot, forming a plan of action as he spoke. "It would be desirable to meet this woman in person and as soon as possible. To discover exactly what she wants."

"You'd do that for me?"

"No," he replied tersely. "I'll do that for Amanda."

Leaning down, he plucked the fluttering page from Hugh's hand. *Isabelle Browne,* he read. Then a telephone number and what looked like a business name. "At Your Service?" Eyes narrowed, he looked up sharply. "Is this an escort agency?"

"I have no idea. I wrote that down from her message. I gather it's a business name, but it means nothing to me." Hugh's head came up a notch. A look of alarm pinched his expression. "You don't believe me, do you?"

"I don't *dis*believe you, but I prefer to make up my own mind."

"By trying to find this Isabelle Browne?"

"I will find her," Cristo corrected in a lethally low voice. "And I will discover the truth behind her allegation before I walk my sister down the aisle. If it turns out you are lying, there will be no payout, no hiding the truth and no wedding."

"Everything I have said is the truth, Cristo, I swear."

"Then you have nothing to worry about, do you?"

Isabelle Browne had spent twenty-four hours convincing herself she had nothing to worry about. The man who'd booked her as his housekeeper for the next week was CEO and Chairman of a private aviation firm. Any one of Chisholm Air's high-flying clients could have recommended her by name—they were precisely the sort who employed At

Your Service to make their arrangements when they visited Australia. This was not the first time she'd been handpicked. She was good—no, better than good, she was damn good—at her job.

But now he'd arrived, almost an hour early, catching her on the hop and reawakening a swarm of worries. For several seconds she closed her eyes and breathed deeply until the buzzing stopped and her hands steadied. *Just another client,* she told herself sternly, *with enough money and sense of entitlement to never accept "no" for an answer.*

Feeling calmer but no less curious, Isabelle pressed nearer to the window for a better view of the man emerging from the car downstairs. Absently she turned off her iPod, pulled the buds from her ears. The dance mix had been perfect to keep her moving as she prepared the house for his arrival, but now the breezy beat seemed inappropriate. Something like the theme from *Jaws* would be more fitting.

No.

A sliver of heat pierced her belly as she watched him yawn and stretch his long limbs like a big cat in a patch of sun. Nothing as cold-blooded as a shark. Nothing grey, either. From the sun-goldened tips of his deep brown hair to the toes of his hand-tooled leather loafers, he looked right at home ambling around the forecourt of the Mediterranean-style villa. His entrance music would be Ravel…or perhaps a Latin salsa. Something rich and vibrant, thick with the sultry beat of summer. Something befitting a Roman god.

Just another client? An ironic smile touched her lips. *She wished.*

With a name like Cristiano Verón, she should have been prepared for someone slightly more exotic than your average British business tycoon. Instead she'd been distracted by the

British part, by the London address, by the coincidence of timing that brought his booking and request for Isabelle and only Isabelle right after *that* phone call to another London number.

She shook her head and reassured herself for the trillionth time. *A coincidence, Isabelle. London is a big city.*

Unless Apollo downstairs gave her any reason to think otherwise, she would give him the benefit of the doubt and assume he had nothing to do with Hugh Harrington. She could remain wary without paranoia. Curious without crossing personal boundaries. Watching his arrival was okay. Eyeing his godlike derriere as he leaned into the low-slung car to retrieve his luggage, not so much.

Yet Isabelle could not wrench herself away from the window.

Her fingers curled into the plush fabric of the curtains at her side as he straightened, one modest suitcase in hand, and Isabelle caught her first glimpse of his face. Sharply slanted cheekbones, bold lips, dark aviator shades. Then he turned back to lock up the car, and she wanted more, a longer look, without the sunglasses.

As if that silent wish carried across the courtyard on the fluky autumn breeze, he paused to hook the glasses in the neckline of his chocolate brown sweater. And then he looked up, right at the window where she stood.

Isabelle took a rapid step back. Her heart raced, her backed-up breath released in an audible rush. "He couldn't have known I was watching him," she murmured, shaking her head to clear the shimmering heat. "He couldn't have seen me."

Heart pounding a mile a minute, she ventured a peek beyond the magenta velvet drapes, but he'd disappeared from sight. A ridiculous punch of disappointment hollowed her belly. Slowly her fingers released their grip. Less slowly her brain snapped back into gear.

He'd disappeared because he was striding toward the front entrance. Where she should be, cool and composed and collected, to greet his arrival. Miriam Horton would tear strips from her hide if Cristiano Verón were left cooling his heels on the doorstep. She glanced down at her feet and gave a yelp. Doubly so if she opened the door still wearing her slippers.

Scooping up the matronly shoes supplied with the At Your Service housekeeper's uniform, she bolted for the stairs.

Cristo noticed the woman when he drove through the porte cochere into the open courtyard. Not clearly, but as a distinctly feminine silhouette moving—no, not merely moving, she appeared to be dancing—past a window on the house's upper storey.

Sensing it was Isabelle Browne, he felt a sharp kick of anticipation. Suddenly the long trip and the business he'd spent his flight time rescheduling faded to a pin spot. Everything homed in on the woman inside the house.

When he'd discovered that At Your Service was a private concierge service favoured by the wealthy of Melbourne and their international visitors, he had found a possible link to Hugh Harrington. Tenuous, but hunches generally served him well. After contracting the agency to secure a house for his Melbourne stay, he'd tossed out the name Isabelle Browne as a recommendation from a friend. And struck pay dirt.

"I'm afraid Ms. Browne is on leave," the manager explained apologetically. "However, we do have other housekeepers with excellent references."

"Unless Ms. Browne is on sick leave," Cristo said, fishing for further information, "perhaps she could be persuaded to take this job."

"I'm sorry, Mr. Verón, but she has already turned down a position this week."

"Did that position offer double her usual wage?"

Money, as always, spoke with the sweetest of tongues. Less than an hour later, Cristo received a return call from At Your Service. He had his housekeeper of choice.

He also had a plan, one that followed the old adage about catching more flies with honey than with vinegar. By befriending her and asking the right questions, he would uncover what he needed to know about her alleged relationship with Hugh. Perhaps Isabelle Browne had worked as his housekeeper, perhaps for a house party he'd attended. Perhaps he didn't recognise her name because he hadn't bothered to ask.

As he pulled his luggage from the car, he sensed her scrutiny from an upstairs window. And he couldn't help wondering if she'd subjected Hugh to the same covert once-over. If she'd sized him up as potential prey for a pregnancy trap.

When he turned toward the house, he couldn't resist lifting his gaze to the window. He could no longer see her, but he knew she was there, watching him from behind the window's heavy frame of curtains. The hum of anticipation in his blood changed tenor, sharpening with a new intent.

Perhaps a more active approach would better serve his purpose. Patience, to his way of thinking, was an overrated virtue.

"Perhaps, Ms. Isabelle Browne—" his narrowed gaze raked the window one last time, and a faint smile ghosted across his lips as he strode toward the portico "—you are about to get more than you bargained for."

Two

At the airfield, Cristo had collected keys, car, directions and a large helping of flattery from the At Your Service manager. He'd wasted enough time deflecting that; he didn't intend wasting any more standing around beneath the portico. When his first press of the doorbell went unanswered, he used the supplied key. The heavy door swung open smoothly and silently, and he stepped into the foyer.

A woman—Isabelle Browne, he presumed—stood at the foot of the stairs. Poised on one leg, one hand on the banister for balance, she appeared to be midway through changing her shoes. That seemed the logical explanation for the mismatched pairing of one utilitarian lace-up and one sheepskin slipper.

The second shoe, in her hand, disappeared behind her back as she straightened. Standing on the short side of average, that did not take her long. Cristo allowed himself significantly longer to take her all in.

She was pretty in a wholesome, girl-next-door way. Sandy blond hair scraped back from her face revealed a high, smooth forehead and wide, startled eyes. Cheeks flushed, lips parted on a note of surprise, no makeup as far as he could tell. As for her body…he could tell even less. She wore an unflattering housekeeper's uniform, complete with starched apron.

She did not look like a temptress.

She did not look like Hugh Harrington's type at all.

When his gaze returned to her face, Cristo noted the hint of annoyance now glimmering in her eyes. Because of his long, leisurely perusal? Or because he'd caught her out?

"Welcome to Pelican Point, Mr. Verón," she said, releasing her grip on the banister and dipping into an awkward bob. The hand holding the shoe remained out of sight. "I am so sorry I wasn't downstairs to greet you at the door."

Professional obsequiousness, Cristo decided, did not suit a woman wearing mismatched shoes and an expression of barely disguised irritation.

"There's no need to apologise. As you can see, I am quite capable of opening—" he paused to kick the door shut behind him "—and closing the door."

"Of course, but one of my duties is to greet guests."

"I am happy for you to greet me here." Cristo closed the space between them in half a dozen unhurried strides. He extended his free hand along with a winning smile. "I am Cristo Verón."

Ignoring both his proffered hand and the smile, she ducked her head in acknowledgement. "May I take your bag, Mr. Verón?"

When she made a move toward his suitcase, he angled his body to block her path. Her hand grazed his flank, and she snatched it away. Her face pinkened into an unmistakable blush.

Had *she* felt that crackle of contact, too? Interesting.

"I'm sorry, Mr. Ver—"

"Please, call me Cristo," he interrupted, putting down his bag. Belatedly he wondered if there'd been a last-minute reassignment of staff. If Ms. Browne had changed her mind, or if her delicate condition meant she'd needed to pass up the sweet deal he'd offered for her services. "And you are Isabelle?"

"Ms. Browne."

So, no mistake. No changed arrangement. A pity, Cristo decided, because Ms. Browne wasn't anything like the woman he'd expected.

"Isn't that a little formal?" he asked.

"At Your Service prefers formality," she replied, as prim and starched as her attire.

"But what about you, Isabelle? Do you prefer this formality?" He gestured at the unfortunate grey uniform as he slowly circled her still, straight-backed form. Idly he recalled his impression of her dancing past the window, the swing of an arm and the bump of her hips. Then he leaned down to retrieve the discarded slipper from the bottom step. "Or is this more to your liking?"

"It doesn't matter whether I like the uniform," she replied, a bite of pique in both her voice and her eyes, "but I do have to wear it."

"What if I prefer a more casual dress code?"

What looked like suspicion flickered across her face before she looked down at the shapeless dress. "I would have to ask what is wrong with this. It is supplied and serviceable and…and…"

"Ugly?" he supplied helpfully when she struggled for description.

Surprise brought her head up, and their eyes met for a

moment, hers warm with suppressed humour. The transformation was remarkable. Cristo couldn't help but contemplate the effect of her full smile on an unsuspecting male.

"I was going to say comfortable," she said.

"Even the footwear?"

Consternation chased the smile from her eyes. "I'm sorry. I wasn't expecting you so soon. I didn't expect you would let yourself in. I—"

She pressed her lips together, shutting off the hurried defence. Her weight shifted from one mismatched foot to the other, and he could tell she was annoyed with herself for being drawn into an explanation. Probably contravened the rules of formality.

Cristo held out the slipper. "If these are more comfortable, wear them," he said, leaning forward to smile confidingly as he captured her gaze. He dropped his voice a half note. "I won't tell."

For a long moment she didn't do anything but blink, several slow sweeps of her silky dark lashes that failed to disguise the confusion in her hazel eyes. He really had thrown her. She really was nothing like he'd expected.

"All right." Despite the husky uncertainty in her voice, she gave a businesslike nod and straightened her shoulders. "Would you like me to show you through the house now?"

"By all means," Cristo said equitably. "Just as soon as you finish making your feet comfortable."

Call-me-Cristo Verón was nothing like the usual At Your Service client, Isabelle thought gloomily as she scuttled downstairs thirty minutes later. The thing with her uniform and shoes was only the start. During their tour of the spacious house he'd been all polite attention, but she'd felt a significant proportion of that attention concentrated on her rather than the features and fixtures she pointed out.

She'd never been more acutely aware of a client in ten-plus years of housekeeping. She'd never been more aware of a man in all her twenty-eight years. From the instant he'd come through the front door and caught her balancing on one leg like some kind of demented flamingo, he'd kept her off-balance.

It was more than being caught out by his unheralded entry and more than her curiosity about why he'd requested her as his only domestic. More even than his outrageously good looks, because there, too, he'd gone and thrown her. Up close the bump of an old break marred the strong line of his nose and a scar cut through one eyebrow.

Small imperfections that balanced the sensual beauty of his perfectly formed mouth and the rich underbelly of his voice.

Small reminders that he was not a god but a man.

Not just any man, Isabelle reminded herself, but a client. She had no business getting in a lather over that dark-honey voice or the way he softened the *s* in her name. Even if he weren't a client, she had no business. Her whole life was in flux at the moment. She'd taken time off work to sort out *what next,* but then she hadn't been able to refuse the money attached to this job.

Sure she'd been worried and wary, but she could not have anticipated this unlikely attraction. A heavy sigh escaped her lips. She'd been fine, relatively speaking, while he kept his distance. But then he would stand a little too near or look at her a little too long and her hormones would start dancing around in silly, look-at-me excitement. Reflexively she touched a hand to dance central, low in her belly. There'd been too many of those moments, when she'd forgotten her professional house-keeper's spiel and stumbled over her words. Or her feet.

The last she'd done just now in her rush to exit hi
bedroom. He'd started to pull off his sweater en route to the
bathroom and that glimpse of lithe muscles and olive skin and
silky, dark chest hair was more than enough for her imagi
nation. She didn't need to view any more interesting facets o
Cristo Verón, thank you very much!

The man was unpredictable…dangerously so.

"It will be okay," she told herself, fanning her hot face with
a rapidly flapping hand as she turned into the kitchen. Her
sanctuary. Her centre. "He's here for a week. Of business."

Isabelle knew the corporate drill. Long meetings, restau
rant meals; often she went days barely sighting her clients
She just needed a little time to get used to him and his overly
familiar ways.

Was he flirting? Oh, yes. Isabelle had no doubts on tha
score, but Cristo Verón struck her as the type who flirted in hi
sleep. Just like she was going through the motions now, piping
the mixture she'd prepared earlier into delicate petits fours
Sliding the perfectly aligned baking sheets into the oven.

Isabelle baked on autopilot; Cristo Verón flirted.

The insight cheered her. She set the timer and wiped the
countertop until the quartz gleamed. In her kitchen, she wa
in control and all was right with the world. Now she'd ac
knowledged the attraction for what it was—she was female
how could she not respond?—she could handle Cristiano
Verón and whatever he threw at her next…as long as tha
wasn't another article of clothing.

Rattled by the possibility of a complete striptease
Isabelle had fled his bedroom suite without asking if he pre
ferred coffee or tea. She made both. She set the table in the
breakfast nook that offered a spectacular view over Por
Phillip Bay, and by the time she heard his firm tread crossing

the parlour, she'd laid out a spread of roast beef and cress sandwiches, almond biscotti and lemon shortbread. The Swiss cakes were cooling on the benchtop. Everything looked perfect.

She wiped her hands, straightened her apron and drew a deep breath. This time she would act like a poised professional if it killed her. No stuttering, no staring, no stumbling.

He came through the archway via the wet bar: appropriately, since his hair was still slick from the shower. Wet and dark and longer than she'd realised. The ends grazed his collar and the front still bore the marks of his comb.

There was something indefinably intimate about that glimpse into his grooming, about knowing that minutes earlier he'd stood naked beneath a shower jet. Now he wore harmless dark trousers and a pure white shirt, but her insides tightened impurely, ambushed by bare-and-wet-skinned images. To her credit, Isabelle didn't stare, not at his freshly shaven jaw nor at the flare of his nostrils as he breathed in the scent of her baking. But then he picked up a petit four from the cooling tray and juggled it from one hand to the other as if judging the temperature, and that contrast of large, olive-skinned hands and tiny, delicate cake held her riveted.

Then he popped it in his mouth and murmured something low and indistinguishable and possibly foreign. Exact words didn't matter. His meaning was clear in the warm glimmer of his eyes and in the little finger-kissing gesture that followed.

It was very European and immensely flattering, and the way her hormones danced around in giddy response sounded a loud, clanging alarm in Isabelle's brain. She shook herself back into the real world, where the housekeeper didn't stare at her employer's hands and mouth and fantasise about that kiss on her skin.

When he reached for a second cake, she slid the tray out of reach.

"Is that silent chastisement?" he asked, smiling, unchastised. "Or is there a one-treat limit?"

She couldn't look at that smile; it would tie her tongue in knots. With quick hands, she transferred the remaining cakes to a serving plate, then slid it across the countertop. "Go your hardest," she invited.

One brow rose in a questioning arch. A wicked glint darkened his eyes. Isabelle gave herself a silent scolding. Obviously she needed to be on her mettle, to watch her tongue, to measure her words.

"They are all for you," she said more carefully. "And those." She gestured to the table at his back. "Would you prefer tea or coffee?"

Casting a quick eye over the offerings, he didn't address the question. Instead he asked, "Did you make the biscotti, Isabelle?"

His mouth turned the words over like a slow caress, and Isabelle caught herself watching, fascinated, for a second too long. For distraction she turned to the teapot. Whether he wanted tea or not, the measured actions gave her something to concentrate on other than the illusive wisp of an accent in his voice. She longed to ask about that, told herself it was not hers to know.

"Yes," she managed to answer. "They're all homemade." From the corner of her eye she saw him moving, not taking a seat at the table, but settling his hips against the countertop. His watchful silence was so unsettling that she found herself adding, "The biscotti is my gran's recipe."

"Did she teach you to bake?"

"She taught me everything."

It was a simple statement but so full of truth that Isabelle regretted opening her mouth. Not talking about herself, being just another efficient but invisible tool in a well-stocked household, was one of the things she liked about this job. That and the cooking-in-fabulously-equipped-kitchens part. "Would now be a good time to discuss menus?" she asked.

"What do you need to know?" he responded, still watching her instead of the menus she fanned out on the countertop. Still taking up too much space, his direct, dark-eyed gaze made her feel all too visible.

"It will help my planning if I know your schedule," Isabelle said. "I prefer notice on which meals you require me to cook, when you will be eating out, if you're expecting guests."

"Tonight I am eating out. I have a meeting in—" he shot a cuff and consulted an expensive-looking watch "—fifty minutes."

"Where is your meeting?" she asked automatically. "At this time of day, it will take more than an hour to drive into the city."

"Not the city. Brighton. It sounds as though you have a good local knowledge."

"I am a local. Do you need directions? I have a street directory in—"

"Thank you, but not necessary. My car has sat nav."

Of course it did. Isabelle gave herself a swift mental kick. She'd been too intent on the man, had barely noticed the car. No doubt it was as sleek, expensive and European as its driver.

"Would forty minutes be sufficient driving time?" he asked.

"I'd allow forty-five, minimum, to be sure."

Somehow he'd managed to trap her gaze, to hold it with the steady strength of his. "Is that your way, Isabelle? Are you the careful type who always makes allowances for the unexpected?"

"I believe that is efficient," she said carefully. "And sensible."

"Like your sensible and efficient uniform?"

Not really, but she did not want to indulge whatever issue he had with formality. The shapeless grey dress might be ugly, but it suited Isabelle just fine. "About the menus. Could we look at your preferences?"

She slid the breakfast list forward; he gave it one perfunctory glance and slid it back. "Juice, orange. Eggs, poached. Bacon, crisp but not too crispy. Coffee, Colombian, black."

So, he could *address the question efficiently when he chose to. Praise be.* "And lunch tomorrow?"

This time he didn't even glance at the menu choices. "Let's wing it."

"Wing it?" She frowned. "You must have some requirements, some preferences."

"Only one." With fluid grace he straightened his negligent posture and touched her Peter Pan collar with the knuckles of one hand. "This has to go."

"But I'm required to—"

"I would think that I am paying you enough to entitle me to dictate my own requirements, don't you?"

Isabelle nodded stiffly, then swallowed. He was too close, in her space. An insidious warmth pooled in her belly and thickened her voice when she spoke. "What are your requirements, Mr. Verón?"

"For a start, I don't stand on ceremony. There is no need to address me as Mr. Verón."

"But—"

He silenced her objection with a finger to her lips. "My name is Cristo. Let us start with that and work our way up, shall we?"

Shocked by his unexpected touch, fighting the temptation to lean into it, to open her mouth, Isabelle stared up at him for a full second before she could process the request and voice any form of response. "I can try," she said huskily.

"You strike me as very capable, Isabelle. I'm sure you will catch on."

Isabelle wasn't sure she wanted to catch on to something that involved the intimacy of first names and working their way up. But as he'd pointed out, he was the boss and paying her an obscenely generous wage, so she nodded in reluctant agreement. And focussed on the lesser of two evils. "What do you require me to wear instead of this uniform?"

"Whatever is comfortable," he said after considering the question far longer than it warranted. "As long as it is not grey."

Not grey Isabelle could do, but comfortable? No, she couldn't imagine ever being comfortable with this man. Not when her body still simmered from that simple glancing touch to her lips. Not after his sleepy-lidded eyes had glimmered with wicked intent while he considered the question of her work attire.

Was he picturing her without the uniform? Or in some sexy male-fantasy version? The possibilities should have appalled her, but instead they blazed in her mind as she watched him walk away.

His walk, like so much else about Cristo Verón, was confident and captivating. It grabbed her attention and didn't let go until the front door shut in his wake. Damn the man. He was like some sexy, six-foot, treacle-voiced magnetic field.

Isabelle should have been pleased to see the back of him, but after releasing the breath backed up in her lungs, she slumped into a chair. It was as though his departure had sucked the life force from the air and the stuffing from her legs. Ridiculous, she told herself. And when she ran that last exchange back over, she kicked herself for the missed opportunity.

If she'd been on her game, she would have asked *why* he was paying her the extravagant wage. Who had recommended her so glowingly that he would accept no substitute? Those were not questions she could ask Miriam Horton. At Your Service had a strict policy on discussing clients, but given that the client himself had brought it up, she could have angled in a polite query. Especially since he was pushing for informality in their working relationship. Next time the subject came up, she would not miss the opportunity.

Fortified by that decision, she cleared away the untouched afternoon-tea spread and did a run to the shops for breakfast supplies. Specifically, his requested blend of coffee. She thought about circling around to her home. It was only a ten-minute drive, and she could pick up some comfortable, non-grey clothes. It wasn't as though she needed to be in situ tonight. She didn't expect she would see her client—she could not bring herself to think of him as Cristo—again until breakfast.

But then she thought about her sister and the questions she was likely to ask, and turned her car back toward Mt Eliza. Tomorrow would be soon enough to face Chessie's inquisition.

She should have known her sister better.

Her call came late. No greeting, just an economical "Well?"

Isabelle didn't need any further explanation. They'd spent a lot of years with only each other; they spoke fluent sisterly shorthand. Chessie wanted details, a blow-by-blow of her first afternoon back at work and her impression of Cristiano Verón, but Isabelle found herself unaccountably shy for words.

"Can you not talk?" Chessie asked into the lengthening silence. "Is he there? Are you still working?"

Isabelle contemplated taking the coward's way out, but she couldn't do it. She couldn't lie to Chessie; she could only prevaricate. "No, he's not here, but I don't have anything to eport. He arrived this afternoon and went out to a business meeting soon after."

"And?" Chessie persisted. "You must have formed some impression."

A tumult of impressions tumbled over each other in Isabelle's mind, but only one singled itself out as relevant. "He's exactly like his name." Exotic, expensive, exclusively designer label. "He is Cristiano Verón."

"You did it? You took my advice and checked his passport?" Chessie sounded both shocked and impressed. "Outstanding!"

Isabelle pinched the bridge of her nose. "I did not look through his things," she said tightly. "I do not want to lose my job."

"You sounded so certain."

"I am. Don't ask me why, just trust my instincts on this," she said, struggling to sound reassuring when her stomach churned with uncertainty. She could have shared those feelings, but then Chessie was such a wild card. Isabelle did not need her arriving to suss the situation in her impulsive, to-hell-with-the-consequences way. She'd jeopardised Isabelle's position with At Your Service once already; she was not allowing her a second chance. "One thing I do know, he is not Hugh Harrington."

"That doesn't mean he's not a lackey," Chessie countered.

Releasing a short, humourless laugh, Isabelle shook her head. "Believe me, Chess, Cristiano Verón is nobody's lackey. I really do think this is a coincidence of timing, that he's a genuine client here on business. Anyone could have recommended me. The Thompsons, for a start."

"If you say so," Chessie said with a distinct lack of conviction.

"I *do* say so. And if anything happens that changes my mind, you will be the first to know."

Three

Was she pregnant?

From the entryway to the kitchen Cristo eyed his house-keeper's profile as she stretched to open an overhead cupboard. How in the name of all that was sacred could he tell when she insisted on wearing that sack of a dress? Today's version was not grey but an equally dull brown.

What kind of woman elected to wear something so unflattering when she had the go-ahead to choose anything she liked? One who honoured her rules of employment so rigidly that she would not risk her boss's censure? One who took pleasure in countermanding his request for informality?

Or one who didn't want to draw attention to a thickened waistline?

Cristo watched her cross the kitchen with a shimmy in her walk. She looked spry, not pale, with the effects of morning sickness. As she scooped coffee into the machine, she threw n a loose-jointed sway of her hips that turned his mouth dry. She was singing, too, in a disjointed but warmly tuneful one-word-here, one-hum-there manner that teased his lips into a smile that was quickly quashed. He did not want to be charmed by her or distracted from his purpose, and yet in the past two days she'd evaded his every effort at casual get-to-know-you conversation.

Today was Saturday. Time to step up the pressure.

Absorbed in her breakfast preparations, she still hadn't noticed him in the doorway, and when she stretched higher still, reaching into the overhead cupboard, he seized the opportunity to reveal his presence.

"Let me get that for you."

With a startled shriek she dropped the bowl, and Cristo hurried to steady her. His reaction was unnecessary, the placement of his hands on the soft curve between waist and hips deliberate, but then he looked down and lost himself in her deepwater eyes. On first meeting he'd thought them hazel, but he'd been wrong. Wrong, too, when he'd judged her merely pretty. That description did Isabelle Browne quite an injustice.

"I'm fine now," she said in a strangled voice. "Please take your hands off me."

Slowly Cristo released his grip. He took an equally measured step away. The impression of giving female flesh tingled in his palms as he held them up in a gesture of truce, but his attention was all on her hands that trembled visibly as she ripped earbuds from her ears and tossed them with her music device onto the countertop.

"I'm sorry for startling you." He dipped his head apologetically. "I didn't realise that you couldn't hear my offer to help." He'd been too intent on inspecting her waistline, and then on watching her dance moves, when he should have considered the source of the singing and dancing.

"You scared several years off my life." Her nostrils flared slightly as she drew a breath and let it go. Still rattled, but making a valiant effort to regather her composure. "You mentioned a later breakfast today. I didn't expect to see you downstairs this early."

"I'm a morning person. Waking early is a habit. I've been working for a while…as have you, it would seem." Cristo gestured at the evidence of her early morning industry. The fruit neatly cut. The coffee brewing. The oven's low hum and the sweet aroma of baking.

"My favourite time of day," she admitted. "I like the peace and the solitude. I can work to my own rhythm."

He arched a brow at her abandoned iPod, and Isabelle winced.

Had she been singing out loud? First the slippers and now impromptu karaoke. Talk about your consummate professional!

From now on she would be all business, all of the time.

"Your breakfast won't be long." Briskly she moved to the stove. Switched on the flame. "The morning papers are on the table, which I've set by the window. There are also two phone messages I took last night. If you would care to take a seat, I will bring your coffee."

In her peripheral vision she saw him glance toward the table, and willed him to follow the glance with his feet. How could she have been oblivious to his arrival? Fresh from his morning shower, he wore jeans—designer label, no doubt—and a black sweater that could, quite conceivably, be cashmere or silk or something equally delicate and soft to the touch. He, on the other hand, looked big and strong and completely male.

And she could still feel the imprint of his hands at her waist.

"With the coffee, please bring a second cup."

The unexpected request snapped Isabelle back to attention. "Will your guest be staying for breakfast?" she asked, and somehow she managed to sound polite, professional, unperturbed.

"My guest?" His dark gaze flicked over her face. "You misunderstand, Isabelle." Perhaps it was her imagination, but his voice seemed to deepen, to caress each note of her name. "The second cup is for you. I would like to discuss my weekend schedule, and I believe your local knowledge will be helpful."

Isabelle insisted on completing his breakfast, which she managed despite the distractingly deep hum of his voice returning one of last night's calls. Which one, she wondered? Vivi's call regarding Amanda's wedding, or Chloe calling about Gisele?

Neither was any of her business; she had no right to stew over that string of exotically feminine names. Even if the spark she felt was mutual, he was the wrong man at completely the wrong time. Yet she remained entirely too aware of him—the pull of worry that drew his brows together, the distracted tap of his fingers against the tabletop, his frowning eyes following her around the kitchen.

By the time she joined him at the table, her nerves were strung like a tightly quivering bow. She hated that he'd made her so self-aware. Especially here in the kitchen, *her* place, where she always felt at ease.

Once he'd established that she had already eaten and, no, she did not want coffee because she had given it up, he asked her to recommend a local restaurant. Isabelle's wariness eased. This was her territory. She settled back in her chair, not exactly relaxed but at least not perched on its lip like a sprinter on the blocks.

"Do you have a preference for any specific style of cuisine?" she asked.

"Good local food, nothing too fancy."

That described her local fish and chips shop, but Isabelle couldn't picture Cristo Verón—even in jeans—eating from a paper bundle on the picnic tables opposite Rosa and Joe's. She figured that her definition of "nothing fancy" might bear little acquaintanceship to his.

"There are a number of winery restaurants on the peninsula which fit that description. Is this for lunch or dinner?"

"Lunch, today. I'm driving to a farm near Geelong this morning to look at ponies. Is there somewhere between there and here, on the return drive?"

"Several," she replied, trying to quell her curiosity over his morning's plans. *Did he have children? Why else would a man look at ponies? But then why would he be looking in Australia?* "They're all very popular at the weekend, so I would suggest making a reservation."

He'd taken the seat facing out onto the terrace and gardens, and the morning sunlight softened eyes she'd thought black to a deep velvety brown. "You will be able to secure us a table at one of these places?"

Isabelle's heart did an anxious flutter before she realised that "us" had nothing to do with her. No doubt he'd be lunching with clients or perhaps his pony-farm friends. "At whichever you choose."

"Which would *you* choose, Isabelle?"

"I couldn't say without more information."

"For you."

Isabelle blinked. "For me?"

Easing back in his chair, he linked his fingers loosely over his chest. "I'm asking which of these restaurants would be your personal choice for lunch."

"None of the above," she admitted. When one dark brow rose

infinitesimally, she quickly added, "Not because I wouldn't want to eat there, but because they're not within my means."

"If you had the means?"

"Acacia Ridge." She named her wish-list number one without hesitation. "Their menu uses local produce in simple dishes with a twist. The cellar is legendary, the service superb and the outlook makes you forget you're so near the city."

"It sounds like a favourite."

"I've never eaten there, but it's a favourite with clients."

"We shall have to do something about that omission," he said easily, "so you can speak from firsthand knowledge."

"Perhaps I will treat myself after this week," she replied, although she knew there would be no treats. Her pay was earmarked for practical purposes, like medical bills and nursery essentials. "I have holiday time due," she added.

"Which I believe I interrupted, enticing you to take this job."

Isabelle sat up straighter. Unwittingly she had turned the conversation around and provided the perfect opening. Her heart rate kicked up, and she took a second to compose herself, striving to appear relaxed as she prepared the questions she'd been dying to ask. "If you don't mind me asking… Why did you do that? Why did you request me as your housekeeper?"

"Your name came up when I was talking to a friend." The hitch of one shoulder was elegantly nonchalant. "Why do you ask?"

Isabelle considered how to answer. She could hardly say: *Because I was wondering if you have some connection to Hugh Harrington, if you're here in response to an I'm-pregnant phone call, possibly to make that inconvenience go away.*

"Did you think the request unusual?" he continued when she didn't answer right away. "I find it hard to believe that this level of service—" his small gesture took in the table setting, the daffodils she'd picked fresh at dawn, the basket of cinnamon scrolls fresh from her oven and the coffee tray with milk in three strengths and four choices of sweetening "—would not earn you many glowing recommendations."

"Yes," she admitted, "but never for such a generous wage."

"You were on leave, presumably with holiday plans in place. I wanted to ensure my offer covered the inconvenience and made it worth your while. I interpreted your acceptance as meaning I had offered sufficient incentive and compensation." His gaze fixed on hers, no longer sleepy-lidded but direct and steady. "Am I to believe I was wrong?"

He thought she was complaining about the pay? "No," she replied adamantly, heat bleeding into her face at the thought. "You are paying me far too much to do far too little!"

"Then perhaps I need to look at increasing your workload."

"Of course," she said hurriedly. "Whatever you require. I would appreciate the chance to earn my pay."

For several seconds he seemed to consider that offer, his fingers linked loosely while his thumbs drummed a relaxed rhythm against his black-sweatered chest. But his eyes on hers were intent, and the mood had changed subtly, indescribably. "Do you have anything specific in mind?" he asked.

Isabelle felt a tightening in her skin. Awareness, she thought, that had nothing to do with business and everything to do with the undercurrents in that question. Her mind hazed over for a second of very specific images—*his hands, her waist, no black sweater, no ugly uniform*—and she had to clear the heat from her synapses before she could construct a businesslike answer. "Cooking is what I do best. If you have any special requests, or perhaps you might care to invite your business associates or friends here for dinner rather than a restaurant. I've also been called upon to shop. If there's anything you need for yourself or as a gift for your...anyone," she finished lamely.

One dark brow arched mockingly. "My...anyone?"

"Your wife," she supplied tartly, thinking of all those damned names on the phone messages again, "or your mistress. Sometimes I've shopped for both."

"Messy."

"I wouldn't know."

"Fortunately," he said slowly after a beat of pause, "I have neither."

She could do nothing to stop the absurd leap of gladness, nothing except pray it didn't show in her expression. His personal life was not her concern; she did not want to know about Vivi and company. No, she did not.

"No shopping and no dinner parties," he said, "but I do have something else in mind. Do you drive?"

"Yes, I do."

"Can you be ready to leave in half an hour?"

Isabelle felt as though she was being led blindfolded toward the cliff edge, but what could she do? She'd offered to earn her pay; it was too late to rescind the offer. She moistened her suddenly dry lips and plunged ahead. "Yes."

"Good," he said with a businesslike nod, and for a brief second Isabelle's qualms settled. He was sending her on an errand. A task to fill in part of a day that would otherwise be spent dusting and vacuuming a spotless house.

"Where will I be going?" she asked. "Do I need to change?"

"Out of that?" He favoured her uniform with a look of high disdain. "Please do."

"I don't have anything but jeans."

"Which will be fine for where we're going."

"We?"

In the process of refilling his coffee, he paused to capture her startled gaze. His was heavy-lidded, dark and languorous like his voice. "Did I not make myself clear? You, Isabelle, are driving me to Geelong."

No, that had not been clear, and looking into his unapologetic eyes she sensed that he knew it. What she didn't understand was why, and perhaps that showed in her face.

"I spent most of the last few nights on the phone and computer, working London hours. If I happen to doze off today, I would prefer that I were not behind the wheel."

"I can find you a professional driver," she suggested, searching for a way out.

"Why would I want a professional when I have you, Isabelle?" He unfolded his long frame and pushed to his feet. A hint of amusement glinted in his eyes. "There is no need to look so put-upon. In return for your chauffeuring duties, I am taking you to lunch at this restaurant you speak so highly of."

"I can't go to lunch with you," she choked out.

"Why not? Do you suspect I have ulterior motives? Is that why you questioned my reason for hiring you?" His gaze narrowed on the guilty heat flooding her face, and his voice dropped to a low, insulted tone. "What, exactly, do you think I am paying you for, Isabelle?"

"No, not that," she responded swiftly, but the warmth seeped from her face into her flesh as his meaning took vivid root in her imagination. "I don't expect you would ever need to pay."

His eyebrows shot up.

"I mean for a woman's company…to coax a woman to spend time in your company." Could she make a worse hash of explaining herself? She drew a deep breath and, avoiding the intent interest—and some amusement—in his eyes, smoothed her hands down her thighs before continuing in a less flustered tone. "You know what I mean, but that isn't why I'm squeamish about going to lunch with you."

"So, there is another reason?"

"I am the housekeeper."

"My housekeeper," he corrected, "who stated that she isn't doing enough to earn her pay. To make up for that, I have appointed you as my driver for today. Since I will be stopping for lunch, I am asking you to join me. If it helps, perhaps you can consider it professional development."

Four

"Is the menu not up to your expectations, Isabelle?"

In the hours spent crossing the bay by ferry, driving to the Armitage polo stables and then returning to the restaurant, Cristo hadn't dozed off in the passenger seat. He'd pressed his driver-for-the-day into conversation, asking about the sites they passed, about the local foods and wines, about driving and the rented Porsche that had caused her much I-can't-drive-this! trepidation at first. Deliberate topics that weren't too personal, that encouraged her to drop the professional reticence and relax in his company, and with her occupied behind the wheel Cristo was able to study the fine nuances of her expression. She gave away a lot with the set of her brows, by holding her mouth a certain way, or by distractedly chewing at her bottom lip.

"The menu is wonderful," she said now in answer to his question, but Cristo shook his head.

"You say it's wonderful, but you were worrying away at your lip—" he tapped a finger against his own bottom lip, indicating the exact spot where she habitually snagged the plushest point of hers "—just there."

"That is lack of orthodontic intervention, not a critique of the menu."

Cristo laughed softly at her quick answer. She'd surprised him many times this morning with her sharp observations once he'd encouraged her to say what she thought rather than what she thought was expected. The biggest surprise: how much he liked the real Isabelle he saw emerging from behind the polite, professional housekeeper. "In which case I applaud the lack of intervention."

"You prefer crooked teeth?" she asked, eyebrows rising with scepticism.

"Imperfections lend a face interest."

For a second she stared back at him. Then she shook her head, just once, and expelled an incredulous breath. "Suggesting that someone has an *interesting* face is not exactly flattering."

"And here I was thinking you would scoff at flattery," Cristo countered idly, but when their eyes met and held he sensed a new element in her regard. Surprise at his observation, yes, but also an acknowledgement that bordered on approval. For the first time he felt her honest response to him as a man, and he allowed himself to enjoy the elemental attraction that buzzed between them in that rare unguarded moment.

No harm, he told himself, since he fully intended to use that attraction to his own ends. "You strike me as a straightforward woman," he said.

"A straightforward woman with crooked teeth."

Entertained by the quick comeback, Cristo lolled back in his chair and allowed his gaze to drift to her lips. Full, plush, unenhanced by any cosmetic products as far as he could tell. And their softened set revealed a hint of those not-quite-straight teeth that he found so unexpectedly appealing. "You don't find flaws interesting?" he asked.

"That would depend on the story behind the flaw. My teeth, for example—" her tongue appeared to trace their underside, an innocent gesture that caused a not-so-innocent stirring low in Cristo's body "—just grew this way. Nothing of interest there."

"Your opinion."

Their gazes linked again, a moment longer, a spark warmer. "Is there a story behind your broken nose?" she asked.

"Not a particularly interesting one."

"Your opinion."

This time he laughed out loud. She was sharp. The kind of woman he would take a keen interest in pursuing, if she were any other woman. "The result of a fall from a horse," he admitted.

"You're kidding!"

He favoured her with an amused look. "If I intended inventing a tale, I would make it a trifle more heroic…or at least wild and daring. Sadly, it was the result of my backside and saddle parting company."

"After watching your b…*you,*" she corrected hastily, "this morning, I couldn't imagine you ever parting company with your saddle."

"So, you *were* watching."

Primitive male satisfaction drummed through Cristo as he observed the pretty flush that rose from her throat and into her face. "Yes," she admitted, "but I know nothing about polo. I didn't know you call the horses you ride ponies, for example." Then, after a beat of pause, "I suppose you were born with a silver polo stick in your hand."

Cristo laughed, low and genuinely entertained. "Not quite.

My father played professionally, so I was born with the scent of hay and horsehair in my blood if not quite wielding a mallet. I doubt my mother would have allowed that."

"She isn't into polo?"

"She had a passing fascination with the men who played," he supplied dryly. "Something about the Argentinean flair, I believe."

"I see."

The words were drawn out, thoughtful, and Cristo's gaze narrowed on hers. "What is it that you see, Isabelle?"

"Your name, your looks… I thought you might be Italian."

"Partly, although those genes are from my mother."

"She's Italian?"

"Vivi is half Italian, half English. All crazy."

Her eyes livened with interest, but he saw her rein that curiosity in. Her lips pressed together in self-restraint. Because family interest was getting too personal?

Too bad, Isabelle Browne. As far as personal goes, I'm only getting started.

"My father is Argentinean," he said, continuing from where he'd left off. Selective pieces of his personal story would serve as encouragement for when he zeroed in on hers. "Although my mother's second husband was more of a father to me."

"Is he English?" she asked after a moment, giving in to the curiosity that glowed bright in her eyes.

"Proudly. When he promoted Chisholm Air internationally, Alistair played shamelessly on every cliché of the English aristocracy."

"Alistair Chisholm," she asked with rising wonderment, "is your stepfather?"

"Was."

"Of course, I read about his death in the papers. I'm sorry."

"As am I," Cristo said. "My mother's best choice of husbands by far."

"So, you moved from Argentina to England?" she asked after a moment's reflection.

"And then to Italy after my mother's third marriage, and then back to my father's estancia for several years. That's where this happened."

He grazed a thumb lazily down the slope of his nose, saw Isabelle follow the action with reluctant interest in her eyes. She moistened her lips. "How?"

"On a dare from my brother, I took on an unbroken mare with an evil nature. Evil won."

"Machismo," she intoned, although the disapproving tone didn't quite ring true. Not with inquisitive interest glowing bright in her eyes. "Serves you right."

"The pain to my pride was considerable, but the sympathy I received more than made up for it."

"Female sympathy, I presume."

Cristo grinned lazily. "Is there any other kind?"

She let go a laugh full of disbelief, yet it still managed to slide under his skin. Beyond the nimbus of her hair—at some point of the morning the thick curls had sprung free of their usual ponytail restraint—he saw their waitress approaching, but he delayed her with the barest of signals. "What about you, Isabelle Browne with an *e*," he asked, deliberately choosing the phrase Hugh had quoted from her phone call. But he saw nothing in her eyes except lively amusement. "Have you lived around here for a long time?"

"I've lived in Melbourne most of my life, and here on the peninsula for the past six years."

"You really are a local."

"Yep." The smile in her eyes teased the corners of her mouth and tickled his libido. "In the past twenty years I haven't been any farther than one holiday to Bali."

"You have no ambition to see the world?"

"Oh, I'd love to travel, but I'm afraid that ambition has been put on hold. At the moment I have other priorities."

She spoke evenly, furnishing the information with matter-of-fact ease, but there was something going on behind her eyes and a tension in the edges of her smile. *Other priorities.* That could encompass a multitude of possibilities, but one blared loud in Cristo's mind.

Pregnancy.

The reminder of what had brought them to this place, this conversation, chilled the relaxed heat in his veins. He'd not forgotten his purpose, but he'd allowed his enjoyment of her company to colour his perception. No more. Straightening in his seat, he signalled the waitress. "We should order. What do you fancy?"

The worry creases between her brows deepened as she scanned the menu again. "Everything is so…much."

Everything was exactly as she'd described it that morning— simple ingredients, with a twist. "Do you mean the prices?" he asked, taking a second look before shrugging dismissively. "Compared with London, these are modest."

"Perhaps for you," she murmured.

"Since I'm paying, let's not make it a problem for you." He reached across and removed the menu from her hand. Leaning back in his chair, he smiled at the waitress. "What do you recommend, Kate?"

He took control of the ordering with the confident command Isabelle expected of a man from his background. Polo, wealth, privilege. Argentina, England, Italy. No wonder he'd struck her as exotic and expensive. Little wonder he'd taken zero-point-five seconds to charm the waitress, Kate, into a flirtatious smile. The pretty redhead had tripped over herself to assist with wine-matching recommendations along with the food choices.

This all served as a sobering reminder to Isabelle of the vast chasm in their circumstances. The kick she felt low in her belly when he looked at her a certain way, when he laughed at something she'd said, when he'd placed a hand low on her back to usher her toward their table—she wasn't used to having a delicious man like Cristo Verón pay attention to her. As he'd pointed out, she was not the type to respond to flattery. Not that she couldn't enjoy the experience, but she was too sensible to forget her place.

This was work, and she took the opportunity to reinforce that fact when the wine arrived. Even after saying she would be sticking to water, Cristo plucked the bottle from the ice bucket with an aim to pouring for her. She placed her hand over the glass and fixed him with a steady look. "I haven't changed my mind."

Apparently he took that as a challenge, because his gaze narrowed on hers. "You do not like my choice?"

"I'm sure it is a very fine choice—" after all of the confab between him and Kate, how could it not be? "—but I don't drink when I'm working."

"Surely one glass would not hurt."

"Surely you don't mean to tempt me when I'm acting as your driver."

For a long moment their gazes clashed, and she wondered if the dark intensity of his was a response to being thwarted. She couldn't imagine he heard *no* too often. But he did put down the wine, and in his eyes she read a measure of respect. "You do take your job seriously, don't you?"

"Of course," she replied briskly, sitting up straighter and folding her hands neatly in her lap as some sort of counterfoil to the pleasure his approval generated. "At Your Service would not employ me if I didn't."

"Do you like the job?"

"It's a good job."

"But do you *like* it?" he countered, his subtle emphasis demonstrating the distinction between the question he asked and the one she had answered.

"There are aspects I like very much and some I don't," she said carefully. "As with any job, I imagine."

Their starters arrived, and Isabelle was distracted by the plump prawns dressed in lime and hazelnut. She leaned closer to inhale the flavours and struggled not to drool.

"The cooking, I gather, is the part you like."

His insight brought her gaze up from her plate, and she didn't bother hiding her smile or the pleasure in her eyes. "You noticed."

"Impossible not to," he said, his mouth slanting into a responsive smile. "If food is your passion, then why do you not cook as a career?"

"Perhaps I would if I could work somewhere like this."

"And you can't…why?"

"Because they're rather selective," she said dryly, "and I don't have the training or qualifications."

"You could put together excellent references from your boss and clients, I imagine. If that is the direction you wished to take."

Isabelle's brow creased into a frown as she played her fork through her dish. How had he managed to home in on the exact question Chessie had been nagging her about for the past year? A question she'd been considering herself until her options had taken on new restrictions. "There is nothing wrong with being a housekeeper, and what I'm doing for At Your Service includes a lot of cooking in brilliantly equipped kitchens." Then, because her chest was tightening with the anxiety that came from thinking of the future and how she would cope, she had to lighten the mood. "Plus the pay and tips can be brilliant, as well."

"And money is important."

"Of course it is." She responded automatically, but then felt the weight of his gaze on her face. Was he judging her for placing too much importance on her pay packet? How easy for him, in his position. "That is how I pay the bills," she said with more than a touch of irritation. "And keep a roof over my head."

"Only your head, Isabelle?"

He asked easily enough, but there was something in his stillness and quiet attention that set her suspicions alight. Driving to the restaurant he'd said he was starving, yet he'd barely looked at his plate. Something was on his mind. This was more than small talk.

Frown deepening, Isabelle put down her fork and met his gaze. "What are you asking, exactly?"

"Only if you live alone," he replied smoothly. "Yesterday you mentioned a grandmother."

"Gran's been gone for six years."

Even after all those years, memories of Gran caused a thickening of emotion in Isabelle's chest and throat. Perhaps that showed in her voice or her eyes, because Cristo dipped his head slightly, in acknowledgement and perhaps respect for her loss, before asking, "Do you have other family?"

"A sister. We do share a roof," she added. "Just the two of us, at the moment."

The last phrase slipped out before she could stop herself. If she'd not been fixed on his face, drinking from the steady strength of his coal-dark gaze, she might have missed his response.

But she was fixed and she did notice the darkening of his eyes, the tightening in the lines that fanned from their corners, and the concerns he'd almost quashed with the power of his charismatic presence came flooding back. Her heart beat hard in her chest. A new tightness grabbed her by the throat, a mixture of suspicion and protective wariness.

Who are you, Cristiano Verón, and why are you so interested in my family?

From the corner of her eye she saw they were about to be interrupted, not by one of the waitstaff but by a man she pegged as the manager. Their barely touched plates had probably drawn his attention. Isabelle didn't pay complete heed to the man's quiet, apologetic words. *Sorry to interrupt, something about a phone call, yada yada.* Her eyes were trapped hard on Cristo's, awaiting the moment they were alone, while her mind whirred with questions of what to say next.

Could she risk this job, this pay packet from heaven, by confronting him? Perhaps she had imagined his reaction. Perhaps she'd misjudged the reason behind it. Perhaps it would be wise to let the conversation play out until all his cards were on the table....

Then she heard it—the one name guaranteed to snap her to instant, complete attention.

"Mr. Harrington," the manager continued in a sombre tone, "said I should tell you this is urgent and that it concerns Gisele."

Five

Before the manager finished speaking, Cristo had tossed his serviette aside and pushed back his chair. Isabelle's shock registered as a brief flash, like a snapshot taken and stored for later viewing, while his focus homed in on the waiting call.

When at breakfast he'd returned the call from Chloe, his head groom, she had expressed a slight concern over Gisele's lack of appetite. He'd asked her to keep him apprised, but he was unprepared for the grim news delivered by Hugh. The mare's life hung in the balance as a result of acute colic. When Chloe couldn't contact Cristo—he'd turned off his phone, not wanting interruptions to his conversation with Isabelle—in desperation she'd called on Hugh to track him down. They knew he would want to monitor the situation minute by minute. They knew him well.

He cut short their lunch. Then he spent the next five hours with a phone at his ear, talking to his stable staff and the vet, feeling distant and powerless. If getting on a plane could have achieved anything, he would have been airborne right now, taking the fastest route home. But he was a day away from England; the critical stage would have passed long before he arrived. So he returned to Pelican Point, and he paced and he sweated until the final call came through.

The tremendous courage and strength Gisele showed on the polo field had seen her through the worst. The crisis was over. For now she was safe.

A huge wave of relief washed through him, leaving Cristo spent and empty. The perfectly made bed at the centre of the room looked clean and wide and welcoming. Operating on autopilot, he shed his clothes en route to the bathroom. Perhaps it was the sight of that pristine bed or the act of getting naked or the fact that his mind was devoid of all that had occupied it during the long afternoon. Whatever the reason, the picture he'd stowed back at the restaurant suddenly reappeared in full, glossy, living detail.

Isabelle Browne, soft lips parted and eyes wide with shock at the mention of the Harrington name.

Standing with arms braced and hands splayed against the tiles while the shower streamed over the tense muscles of his shoulders and back, Cristo's mind darkened with all the other cues she'd given off over the past days. The baggy uniform. Her refusal to drink coffee or wine. How she'd counted her family as just one sister…at the moment.

There had been no mention of Hugh or their interrupted conversation on the drive home or in the hours since. She'd made several expeditions up the stairs with sandwiches, coffee and finally a dinner tray. He hadn't invited conversation, and she'd resumed her role as invisible housekeeper.

Yet he'd noticed. He'd noticed, and now he quietly seethed

because he'd allowed himself to be taken in by that straight-forward competence and by the other Isabelle with bright interest in her eyes and rhythm in her hips. Both sides attracted him, the antithesis intrigued him, and in that moment of stripped-bare honesty he acknowledged how badly he'd wanted the pregnancy allegation to be a misunderstanding.

If the phone call hadn't interrupted their conversation, he would have asked what she meant by "at the moment"; she would have owned up to impending motherhood; he would have revealed himself as Hugh Harrington's agent. This would be over, done and dusted.

Roughly he towelled himself dry and pulled on a pair of trousers. That was enough for now. On the balcony that sur-rounded the upper-floor suite of rooms, he dragged the chill air of late autumn into his lungs and welcomed its bite on his exposed chest and arms. Night fell quickly, darkening the waters of the bay and darkening his mind with self-reproach.

Dios, he'd handled this clumsily. He was an arrogant fool for thinking he could judge a woman's character from a few days' observation and one morning of conversation. He was a fool twice over for allowing his desire for the woman a say in that judgement.

Through the French doors came the faint tinkle of spoon against china, and all his senses flared with awareness. She had returned, possibly for the tray, probably with fresh coffee. It was the perfect opportunity to end the subterfuge.

In the doorway he paused, his gaze narrowing as he found her at his desk. Her back was to the door, her head bent forward in apparent concentration, her hands sifting busily through his papers. Suddenly they stopped. Her head came up a fraction as her backbone stiffened.

The burn of awareness in Cristo's blood turned to ice.

'Looking for anything in particular?" he asked, although he knew exactly what she had found.

Heart beating wildly with caught-out shock, Isabelle whipped around and found Cristo standing in the doorway leading to the terrace. He wasn't wearing a shirt. For a long moment the fascinating vista of smooth olive skin over honed muscle drove everything else from her consciousness.

She shouldn't stare. It was wrong to lick one's lips when eyeing one's employer. Wrong to be stung by a prickle of heat and the rampant desire to lick one's employer's chest.

Wrong to be caught red-handed going through his things.

She lifted one of those red hands to her thundering heart. "You have to stop doing that."

The words came in a rush of flustered awareness and guilt as he stepped through the doorway into the full light. "Doing…what?" he asked, his voice as silky as the trail of dark hair bisecting his abdomen.

Must. Not. Stare.

She forced her eyes down—dark trousers, beautifully tailored, perfectly fitted—then up again, all the way to his sleek, wet hair. Although he gave every appearance of relaxation, he wasn't lounging against the doorjamb. She sensed a coiled tension in every long, lean muscle. Like a pampas cat, sizing up his prey and ready to pounce.

A *danger, beware* tremor rippled through her flesh. She pressed her fingers harder against her chest. "Sneaking up on me. I don't know how someone your size moves so quietly."

He wore no shoes. She noticed that now as he silently crossed the room on those big, bare, sexy feet. Reflexively, she backed up a step, until the edge of the desk cut across the top of her thighs and halted her progress.

"Find what you were looking for?"

"I wasn't looking for anything in particular," she replied a little too quickly. It sounded like guilt. It sounded like a lie.

He came to a halt in front of her. So close she caught the scent of citrus and bergamot and recently showered male skin on an indrawn breath. So close she could see the scepticism in the slant of his mouth and the arch of one dark eyebrow. "Not even for me?" he asked.

"Well, yes. For you."

"And here I am," he said smoothly, touching fingertips to the centre of his chest. "Not on my desk."

Warmth flooded her face, but she kept her chin high. Her eyes fixed on his, not on his chest. "I brought coffee." She gestured vaguely toward the low table, where she'd left the pot. "And I wanted to check if you'd received any more news. About your horse."

"The crisis has passed."

"She will recover?"

"God willing."

"I am glad." A relieved half smile softened the tension in her face, and Isabelle thought she saw that same emotion echo momentarily in his eyes. "Seeing your anxiety this afternoon…" Her smile gathered warmth. "That horse must be very special."

"She is, but I would have felt the same for any member of my family, equine or human."

"That, I understand."

"Do you?" he asked softly, but there was a new hardness in his expression. A deepening of the creases that fanned from the corners of his eyes as he regarded her narrowly for several heartbeats. "I have to wonder about this sentiment, this show of concern, the coffee, the sustenance. How many times would you have hauled your pretty little backside up those stairs, waiting for an opportunity to search my desk?"

Finally he'd stopped circling and pounced. So unexpectedly that Isabelle was taken aback. She drew a quick, startled breath. And discovered that she no longer wanted to run. She wanted to defend herself and her backside. "That was never my purpose," she stated emphatically.

"And yet…" He gestured at the desk behind her, his meaning obvious.

"You weren't here, so I took the opportunity to—"

"Snoop?"

"To seek answers."

Unable to bear the suspense of waiting alone downstairs for news of Gisele's fate, she'd taken every opportunity to deliver coffee and food. If there'd been any excuse to stay, to offer comfort and support, she would have jumped all over it. Her sentiment had not been fake, and she resented the implication that she'd used the situation to her advantage.

It was only on this final occasion, when she found the room empty, that she'd taken any notice of the desk and the loose pile of papers. The temptation to look for a link to the Harrington name had been too great to resist. She had no idea what she'd thought she might find.

Certainly not a glossy publication titled *Now You're Pregnant*.

"I was waiting until the crisis with your horse had passed," she said tightly, "before seeking those answers."

"Go right ahead," he invited. "Ask away."

"Why are you here?" She lifted her chin and met his gaze. "Did you really have business in Melbourne or did Hugh Harrington send you?"

His pause before answering was telling. So was the glint of acknowledgement in his eyes. When he answered with another question—"I take it you know him?"—Isabelle's composure snapped.

Whirling around, she pushed papers left and right until she found the magazine, then turned back with it brandished in her hand. "You came here at his behest to, what? Find the woman who'd called him, whose call he didn't bother to return? And what is this, your research material?" She shoved the glossy cover at his too-close chest. A vain act—that hard wall of muscle didn't budge. "Were you going to compare pictures against the real thing?"

"I needed a reference point," he said in cool, casual contrast to her heated outburst. "I had no idea what three months pregnant would look like."

"Why should that matter to you? You're not the father."

"And Hugh Harrington is?"

Isabelle's brow pulled tight. "Are you suggesting that he isn't?"

"I am asking a straight question, Isabelle. Is Harrington the father of your baby?"

"*My* baby?" The syllables exploded from her mouth husked in shock. She shook her head and couldn't hold back a short, incredulous laugh. "You think that he slept with *me*? That *I'm* pregnant?"

His incisive glare cut through her astonishment. "Are you Isabelle Browne or not?"

"Yes. I am."

"But you're not pregnant."

"No, most definitely." Isabelle expelled a harried breath and held up a hand to stop any further questions. "Let me explain. My sister Francesca—Chessie—filled in for me back in January."

"Doing this job?"

"More or less. It was supposed to be a weekend appointment, cooking for your friend in a home at Portsea. He knew the owners through business or whatever." She made a dismissive gesture; the details didn't matter, only the outcome. "They loaned him the use of their holiday place. I came down with the flu, and Chessie stepped in. She'd worked for the agency before. She's capable, but she was no longer on the books."

"So she used your name."

Isabelle nodded. If she'd not been miserably ill at the time, she would never have agreed. "It was last minute, and Chessie was available. She convinced me that I shouldn't give up the job."

"Or the money," he added dryly, but condemnation narrowed his gaze and stiffened the set of Isabelle's shoulders.

"I've already told you that money is important in my situation."

"And I believed you were referring to the additional expense of a baby."

"I was! But that is an additional expense on top of my mortgage and every other bill that must be paid."

"It's your sister's baby," he said after a moment's pause. Their eyes met and held, and for the first time she saw that he was coming around to believing her. One small step in the right direction, but an immensely important one.

"My sister's," she echoed, "and your friend's."

His gaze fell away but not before she'd seen the edge of fierceness. A word that sounded like a curse fell from his tongue as he turned and strode toward the terrace. For several seconds he stared out into the darkness before he spoke. "Hugh Harrington isn't only my friend." Slowly he turned to face her, his expression so grim and forbidding that she felt a shiver of foreboding deep in her flesh. "He is my sister's fiancé."

The shiver turned to ice-cold shock in Isabelle's belly. She remembered what he'd told her a few minutes earlier: that he would feel the same commitment, the same despair, if any member of his family was suffering. She recalled the fierce edge to his expression and knew that he'd been thinking about his sister suffering.

She knew that fierceness. She understood.

"That's why you are here," she said softly. "For your sister."

"She doesn't know. While your sister has been growing his baby, Amanda has been planning their wedding."

Isabelle had to moisten her suddenly dry mouth before she could ask, "When?"

"The thirtieth of May."

Three weeks. She swallowed. "What are we going to do about this?"

"I think it's time we brought your sister into this discussion, don't you?"

The words were so cold, his face still so uncompromisingly hard, that Isabelle's indignation blazed anew. "Don't you think you should reserve your anger for the one who deserves it?"

"Believe me, Isabelle, I have enough to go around."

Francesca Browne was the woman Cristo had expected to meet when he arrived in Melbourne.

Blond with a cover-girl face and a body to match, she bore all the trademarks of Hugh's string of girlfriends of days gone by. She arrived at Pelican Point less than ten minutes after Isabelle's phone call, wearing a stylishly loose dress that disguised any sign of pregnancy. Murmuring an apology, she hugged her sister hard before turning a level gaze on him. "So you're Mr. Fix It," she said.

"I prefer Cristo," he replied. "I doubt this is a situation I can fix."

Her perfectly shaped brows rose slightly. "You don't think you can pay me off?"

"I have no intention of attempting to," he informed her. "Would you like to come through to the living room? I can assure you it is more comfortable than standing here in the foyer."

Cristo stepped back to let the sisters go first, and they did so arm in arm, talking sotto voce as they went. He followed. He didn't try to eavesdrop. It was enough to watch them, to see their attachment, to know that this version of what happened three months ago made unfortunate sense.

Francesca Browne may well have slept with Hugh Harrington. Isabelle had not. A selfish kernel admitted that he liked this version one hell of a lot better than the alternative.

"Do you often use your sister's name?" he asked after they'd settled.

"No," Francesca replied.

"I explained why she worked under my name," Isabelle added. She'd taken a seat on the sofa beside her sister, so they presented a united front of dignity and indignation. Cristo approved of this warrior woman prepared to do battle on her sister's behalf. He respected the tigerish set to her expression and the green fire in her eyes as she went on the attack once more. "She could hardly use her own name when she called Harrington. He wouldn't have had a clue who Chessie Browne was."

"He didn't have a clue who Isabelle Browne was."

"Are you saying he doesn't remember Chessie?"

"He denies ever meeting her."

"He met me," the younger sister joined in with bitter equanimity. She touched a hand to her belly. "I hold the evidence right here."

"*You* believe us," Isabelle interceded.

She posed the words as a statement rather than a question, and when Cristo's gaze meshed with hers he felt the power of that emphatic note. He wanted to reassure her, to wipe the last shadows of uncertainty from her expression, but he was not yet in a position to do so. His instincts about this woman—about the veracity of her story—were strong but he needed to be one hundred percent certain they were no longer adversaries but united in a common cause.

"I am not the one you need to convince," he told her with an apologetic hitch of one shoulder.

"Then why are you here, if not to answer that question? You said Harrington didn't send you. You said he didn't remember meeting Chessie."

Leaning forward in his chair, he strengthened the connection of their eye contact. "He came to me for advice on how to handle Francesca's claim of paternity. I was coming to Australia on business. He did not ask me. I chose to meet you."

"By employing me under false pretences?"

"I concede that did not work out as I had anticipated. However," he added, eyes still fixed on hers, "I would do it over again for the sake of my sister's future happiness."

"The end justifies the means?"

"When it comes to my family, yes. Always."

Cristo's focus was all on Isabelle, his expression as intense as his words. But in the short silence that followed, he heard Francesca clear her throat. Saw her raise her hand in an appeal for attention.

"Hello. Would someone like to fill me in on what is going on?" Despite the blithe tone, bewilderment clouded her eyes as they shifted from Cristo to Isabelle and back again. "What does my pregnancy have to do with your sister's happiness?"

Meeting Isabelle's gaze once more, he inclined his head,

silently giving his consent for her to go ahead. Her nostrils flared as she exhaled heavily. "I'm sorry, Chess, but there's no easy way of saying this. Hugh Harrington is engaged to Cristo's sister. Their wedding is in three weeks."

Francesca's mouth rounded in a silent O of shock. She blinked and dropped a barely audible profanity. Given the circumstances, Cristo could not blame her. "Does she know about me...about the baby and the call I made to Harry?"

Cristo registered her use of the nickname. Amanda used it, along with several of their closest friends, but very few others. No other single word could have provided such convincing—or condemning—evidence. "No," he said flatly. "She doesn't."

Francesca chewed her lip a second, digesting that knowledge. "I gather you are here on your sister's behalf, to find out the truth?"

Cristo nodded.

"And now you know, what do you intend doing with it?"

"Since he maintains no knowledge of you or any relationship, there is only one solution. You and Harrington in the same room, face-to-face."

"How is that possible?" Francesca said slowly.

He turned to Isabelle, who had listened to this last exchange in stiff-backed silence. Her eyes were huge in a face as pale as her sister's. "Are your passports up-to-date?" he asked. "You are going to need them."

Six

Isabelle started shaking her head before he finished speaking. "We can't just up and go to England. It's impossible."

"You don't have current passports?"

"We do," Chessie supplied helpfully. "We needed them for Bali last year."

"Then what is the problem?" Cristo asked. "Is money an issue?"

"It's always an issue and even more so now."

"It doesn't have to be." Despite Chessie's responses, he spoke directly to Isabelle. "I will fly you to London. You will stay in my home. All your expenses will be covered."

His hooded gaze fixed on hers with steadfast purpose, and Isabelle felt a trill of alarm. This was a man used to taking control, to getting his way. If she didn't stand her ground, then her impulsive sister would be swept along on the tide of his will.

She straightened her shoulders. "It's not only the costs involved. I have a job."

"It is my understanding that you are engaged by me for the remainder of this week."

"You still want me?" she blurted unthinkingly.

Something flared in his eyes, a slow note of danger. "Why should I not? I have a contract for your services, one week, paid in advance."

"But you can't want a housekeeper when you're returning to England. I imagine you have staff coming out of the rafters."

"Not quite," he said smoothly, but that banked fire still smouldered in his eyes. "I prefer my staff to be more discreet."

For a long moment Isabelle floundered in the treacherous undercurrents of the exchange, in wanting and services and discretion. She needed to keep paddling to stay on top of this conversation. "You don't need a housekeeper," she repeated with more force.

"Probably not, but I am attempting to make this easy for you."

Easy? She might have laughed if this subject weren't so deadly difficult.

"You implied that your job may prevent you accompanying your sister to London," he continued, "but your job is in my employment."

"For one week."

"Which I will extend, on the same terms. Let's say an extra two weeks—" he spread his hands in a gesture of appeasement, probably because Isabelle's eyes had goggled with a combination of shock and suspicion "—to make up for any inconvenience."

"I can't do that."

"Why not? Your next job for Miriam doesn't start for weeks

yet," Chessie pointed out. Isabelle gave her a withering look. A traitor at her side was not helpful.

"Your sister raises a valid point. Why not?"

"Because you admitted that you have plenty of staff. You can't possibly need me."

"But I do." Chessie exhaled with audible impatience. "Why are you being so stubborn? Why can't you just accept Cristo's offer? It sounds enormously generous. What have you got to lose?"

Chessie spoke the words. It was Chessie's blue-green eyes that reproached hers. But in her mind's eye she saw determined onyx, heard those same words in a dark baritone, felt a shiver of alarm and mistrust and, God help her, wanton excitement.

What did she have to lose? Oh, just her pride and any semblance of control over her unruly hormones.

"We have to think this over," she cautioned. Focusing on her sister, she shut out those watchful black eyes through sheer bloody-minded willpower and lowered her voice. "Don't be steamrolled into doing what's most convenient for anyone else. Have you thought about what's best for you and the baby?"

"You know I have, and this is exactly what I would have done myself if I could have afforded the airfare."

It was true. They'd been over this territory twice before, when Chessie first learned of her pregnancy and again little more than a week ago when, with her first trimester safely behind her, she'd decided to contact the father. Isabelle hadn't been able to talk her out of making that phone call, and now she felt a fatalistic sense of déjà vu.

When had Francesca Ava Browne ever done a proper risk evaluation before plunging into the unknown? From the first time she launched herself on chubby toddler's legs she had been unstoppable—not that this had ever stopped Isabelle from trying. "That's the point," she persisted. "You *can't* afford it. What if something goes wrong? You'll be stranded on the other side of the world with no money and no support."

"And if I don't go, I will be stuck here relying on you for support you can't afford to give." When Isabelle opened her mouth to object—she had always found money for Chessie; she always would!—her baby sister held up a hand. Suddenly she looked and sounded very grown-up. Isabelle felt the sand shifting beneath her feet. "I need to do this, for me and for the baby. I'm going, Belle. Whether you do or not is up to you."

They arrived in England on Wednesday evening and were whisked to the heart of London in a chauffeur-driven car. Settling into the luxurious leather-upholstered rear seat, Chessie elbowed Isabelle for at least the hundredth time since they'd left Melbourne, mouthing "Wow!"

That enthusiasm had become old somewhere over the centre of Australia, and Isabelle used her last remaining energy to grit her teeth. She'd snapped once already, at a refuelling stop in Dubai. Chessie asked Cristo if they were staying long enough for a look around, and Isabelle, tired and anxious and edgy, had snipped, "For Pete's sake, Chessie, this is not a holiday jaunt."

"I'm well aware of what this trip is about," her sister had responded calmly, "but that doesn't mean I can't enjoy the fringe benefits."

Of course Cristo overheard the exchange, and she'd felt his silent judgement slap her right through her travel-lagged irritability. She was supposed to be the serene, sensible sister. Somewhere around her twelfth birthday, Gran had first referred to her as Capability Browne and she'd hugged that reference close, unconsciously adopting the label as the person she wanted to be. Calm, composed, capable.

But these past days—ever since Cristiano Verón had stormed into her life—she'd become someone else entirely. Angry, argumentative, anxious. She'd blamed him and his unpredictability, she'd blamed the worry of Chessie's situation, but now it was time to put on her big-girl's blouse and take responsibility.

She was here to support Chessie, to ensure that her needs weren't overlooked in deference to Cristo's sister. She needed to be alert and on her game. She needed to forget her personal disappointment over how he'd deceived her, feigning interest in her life and her family and her dreams all in the guise of uncovering "her" pregnancy.

That didn't matter now. Protecting Chessie did.

As the big sedan glided to a halt outside a row of elegant town houses, she forced herself to relax the tension in her jaw and her shoulders. And when she glanced across, she saw the same tension etched in Chessie's face. She reached—and it was quite a reach across the width of the backseat—for her sister's hand and gave it a reassuring squeeze.

Chessie's fingers gripped hers for a second. They were ice-cold, but her smile was warm. It only trembled a little around the edges. "I'm so glad you came."

Isabelle smiled back. "So am I."

From the pavement outside, Cristo's home looked like all the others in the immaculately presented rows that lined each side of Wentworth Square. Isabelle blinked in surprise at the traditional facade. She'd expected something more unique, flashy, exotic.

Then she reminded herself that this was Cristiano Verón. Mr. Unpredictable himself.

Inside, she had to remind herself several times more.

Through her job, she was used to grand homes decorated to within an inch of their stylish lives. Most had graced the pages of at least one glossy design magazine. This place transcended anything she'd seen by, oh, about a thousand percent. And, she guessed, several million pounds.

As they trailed through room after room of Georgian splendour, even Chessie was reduced to gaping, wide-eyed silence by the exquisite detail of the cornice work and the marble fireplaces and the antique furniture. Not to mention the staircase that rose through the centre of the building, with galleried landings on each of the three upper storeys. All were lined with ornately crafted railings.

And then there was their guide on this tour of the house. Cristo had introduced him simply as Crash. No further explanation as to his position in the household or whether that was his first or last name. Isabelle had wondered if perhaps he was Krasch or Craczj or some other obscure foreign spelling, until he spoke in a voice that could have played all-England. He'd relayed a series of messages to Cristo, who soon after disappeared to his rooms on the first floor, and she'd pegged him as the butler. Although his unorthodox black jeans and T-shirt, shaggy haircut and unshaven jaw belied such a tame label.

Whatever his position, he showed immense pride in the house. "Cristo bought it three years ago," he told them as he showed them to their rooms…correction, their *suite* of rooms. "Previous owner had a rubbish eye for decorating. We only finished the refit late last year."

Isabelle paused in the centre of the sitting room that separated their bedrooms. "You did the whole place out? That must have been a challenge."

"The challenge was retaining the original design elements while making it liveable."

Chessie raised her eyebrows at that description. She almost touched the floor-to-ceiling drop of voile curtaining before withdrawing her hand. "Are we allowed to touch?" she asked.

"Everything," Crash replied dryly, "except the Renoir."

"You're kidding me." Chessie peered at the painting over the fireplace, then made a strangled sound. "You're not! Far out." She whirled around. "And those pictures in the drawing room… They're originals, aren't they?"

"You want to take a closer look?"

Chessie's eyes boggled, and Isabelle waved them off. Not that she wasn't interested in art, just not as passionately engrossed as her sister. And she was keen on talking to Cristo before he left for his country estate. He'd mentioned that to Crash earlier; he had to check that his beloved horse was recovering as well as his staff had promised. But despite this impatience, he'd noticed her worried frown and invited her to track him down after she had settled in.

Crash had pointed out his rooms on the first floor, and on her way down Isabelle chewed over the notion of ever settling in at this house. Artwork by the masters hung on every wall. The thick carpet runners that muffled her footsteps were works of art in themselves.

This world of million-dollar decorating makeovers and chauffeured limousines and private jets he copiloted…this was the world of Cristiano Verón and, she imagined, Hugh Harrington.

It was a world the Browne sisters worked in, not a world they lived in.

The only way she could pretend to settle in was as a working employee—not a token one—and only after she knew when Cristo planned to approach Harrington. She'd not had a chance to broach the question since that night in Melbourne. Caught up in the logistics of packing and leaving so swiftly, then in the travel with Chessie at her side, she'd not had a minute alone with Cristo. Now she would.

Hand fisted to knock, she hesitated just long enough to pray that she'd chosen the right door. Sitting room, not bedroom. The knock-knock of her heart resonated as loudly as her knuckles on the thick timber door.

It opened immediately, as if she'd caught him on his way out. Except he couldn't be—not unless he'd chosen to go out on a chilly London evening wearing nothing but a pair of jeans and the phone pressed to his ear. Beyond the impressive breadth of his bare-skinned shoulders, beneath the thickly muscled arm with which he held the door ajar, she could see a bed.

A big, broad bed smothered in a deep chocolate spread. It looked like velvet. It looked like him.

Her gaze rocketed from the bed to his face. There was something in his hooded gaze, a glimmer of heat and of predatory satisfaction, an invitation to come into his lair and do more than talk. Suddenly she was no longer tired; she was wide awake, alive with the tingle of anticipation and the whisper of danger.

Wrong door, she reminded herself with a snap to attention. *Wrong bed, wrong tingles and absolutely the wrong man.*

Cristo was expecting her, but not this soon—he'd barely had time for a quick shower, let alone to finish dressing—and not at his bedroom door. Not that he minded. Any interruption from this phone call was welcome. When the interruption was Isabelle Browne with her hair a loose tumble of honeyed curls and her eyes wide and warm and taken aback, it was even more welcome.

"I will call you back," he said into the phone, cutting off Vivi's rant about the wedding caterer. "I have company."

His company stood on the wrong side of the threshold, shaking her head and mouthing something about coming back later. Cristo held the door wider. "Are you coming in or not?"

"Not if I'm interrupting."

"You can always help." He lifted one unclothed shoulder to indicate his meaning.

For the briefest of moments, her gaze drifted with the notion, before she snapped to attention. "I meant the phone call."

"That was only my mother," he said dismissively. Then, when her eyes widened with disapproval, he elaborated. "She wanted to discuss a problem with the wedding arrangements."

"When there may not be a wedding," she murmured, picking up on his meaning.

"Indeed."

Their gazes met in a moment of solemn accord, a reminder of what still sat between them. Her being here in his house, in his bedroom, was not about them or the fizz of physical attraction. Yet. The seriousness of the situation with Harrington and her sister lurked, dark as a thundercloud, on the horizon. But when he'd opened the door and found her standing there, when he felt the heat of her gaze taking him in and the lightning-bolt response low in his belly, he knew there would be a time for them.

He could be patient. Opening his bedroom door to a willing Isabelle would be worth the wait.

Leaving the door wide open, he retreated to an armoire and deposited the phone. In the wall mirror he saw her swallow her reservations, lift her chin and step into the room...not very far into the room, however. Barely over the threshold she paused, her unsettled gaze skating from the bed to his shirtless back and on around the room. She looked uncomfortable and out of sorts.

Because this was his bedroom, because he was only half-dressed, because she too felt the crackle of awareness and wanted to run from it. A pity this was the wrong time. He would have enjoyed the chase.

Suppressing that desire, he turned to the bed, sat and reached for his shoes and socks. "Correct me if I'm wrong, but I am assuming that you didn't come down here to watch me dress."

"Have you spoken to Harrington?" she asked quickly, but he felt the warm glide of her gaze over his shoulders and back as he bent to pull on a shoe. He glanced up and caught her looking. He saw the involuntary flare of her nostrils, the softening of her bottom lip, the guilty flush of colour in her cheeks, and gave up the fight to suppress his elemental response.

She looked at him like that, his body responded. So be it.

"Unfortunately, I haven't," he said slowly in response to her question.

Her chin came up, her gaze sharpening on his. "Why ever not?"

"Because he isn't answering his phone."

"Does he know that you found Chessie? Did you leave a message?"

"With Amanda?" he asked dryly.

"What about at work," she persisted. "Surely he has a secretary or an assistant."

"That would be Amanda."

"Oh."

Cristo watched her chew at her bottom lip while the heat stirred in his belly and thighs and all points in between. "I may not hear from him for several days," he warned, predicting her next question. "He is out of town."

"Where?"

"Does it matter?"

For a second he thought she would question that, as well, but then she let go her indignation on a weighty sigh. Her shoulders slumped and that signal of defeat, small but definite, brought Cristo to his feet.

"This is not such a bad outcome," he said. "You and Francesca can use a day to recover from the flight. Catch up on your sleep, relax, and when he does arrive you will be ready to deal with the meeting and the outcome."

She did not look convinced. Worry creased between her brows as he closed down the space between them. He had no purpose in mind other than a need to be nearer, to ease that worry, to see her eyes spark once more. Through the open door he heard voices—Crash's gruff murmur, Francesca's response. He cocked his head, drawing Isabelle's attention to the sound. "Your sister will appreciate the time to get her bearings, surely."

"You're right about Chessie," she relented. Wary eyes followed him as he passed. She jumped a little as he closed the door, isolating them from the distraction of those voices.

"And what about you, Isabelle?" he asked, turning to meet her chary gaze. He could have smiled to ease the moment. He could have backed off and allowed her more space. Instead, he leaned forward and touched a thumb to the dark circle beneath one eye. "You didn't sleep on my plane. I hope you will feel comfortable enough here to make up for that lack."

"That depends."

"On?"

Her chin came up, her eyes met his with resolute purpose. "My role in your household."

"Guest doesn't work for you?"

"Not when you are paying me, no."

Cristo folded his arms over his chest and regarded her

silently for a moment. It was a pretence. He'd known she would not let this go, that she would insist on taking up some form of paid employment. "What do you have in mind?" he asked.

"That's not for me to say when I don't know your staff arrangements. I'm not even sure of Crash's position. Is he your butler?"

"Butler, cook, valet. He runs the house."

"Alone?"

"Pretty much."

She drew a strong breath, and her eyes darkened with a new determination. "Then I'm sure he could use help. Perhaps in the kitchen."

Cristo's lips quirked.

"Is that a problem?" she asked, noticing.

"Crash is, shall we say, a little territorial."

"About his kitchen?"

"About the whole house." When questions shadowed her expression, he continued. "Crash oversaw the renovations and the decorating. He lives here. I spend more time away than under this roof."

"At your country place?"

"Chisholm Park is home, but I don't spend as much time there as I would like. My life necessitates travel." He lifted a shoulder, a gesture of acceptance of what his life entailed. "This place is a convenience when I'm in the city, and a business asset. Clients are impressed."

"I imagine so," Isabelle said, looking around the room with a new perspective. As impressive as the formal rooms and the guest suites were, she couldn't place Cristo in them. He was too big, too uncompromisingly male and too comfortable with all that masculinity. This room, however, was different. "You had a hand here," she mused. "This is you."

"Well noticed," he said.

Just two words, offered with the same insouciance as all that came before, but the flame in his eyes sucked all the air from Isabelle's lungs. Beyond the door she heard muffled voices, but still she could not look away. She could not breathe. She could not do anything to break the overwhelming intensity of the moment.

"At some point you must tell me how you reached that conclusion," he said, his voice as dark and slumberous as his eyes, "and what you see as 'me.'"

Before she could think how to answer, a knock sounded at the door. A female voice that wasn't Francesca's was raised to a level that would have reached across to the depths of the dressing room. "Cristo, your goon says you are not to be disturbed, but I think he's having a lend. If you really do have a woman in there, you'd best say so quickly because otherwise I'm coming in."

"My sister," Cristo said smoothly, eyes still fixed on Isabelle's. "Shall I tell her to go away?"

Was he serious? Was that wicked message in his eyes for real? Isabelle's heart did a funny quickstep. Her mouth opened and shut, but no sound came out.

"Cristo?" Amanda rapped loudly at the door. "I'm serious. I really do need to talk to you."

Cristo's eyes met hers, the teasing heat now overlaid with regret. "We are going to need an explanation."

"For me being here?"

"For you being here in my bedroom, yes, but more importantly, for you and Francesca being here in my house."

Seven

Amanda burst through the door in a flurry of righteous indignation. She punched Cristo's arm, then she hugged him, all the while admonishing him for not opening the door, for not answering any of her messages over the past week and finally for disappearing to Australia without any explanation.

Cristo, Isabelle noticed, did not attempt to get a word in. He pretended to wince at the puny punch, and he hugged her back with what looked like genuine affection and a large dose of forbearance that Isabelle thought was largely for show. They made quite a picture—he a big cat, all golden-skinned power, his sister a kittenish beauty with a sleek brunette bob and porcelain-pale skin.

Without drawing breath, Amanda launched from general complaints into a specific and passionate tirade about unapproved changes to the menu for her wedding breakfast. At her indignant "Harry despises shellfish. I told the planner—she doesn't listen," Isabelle's stomach twisted. She hated high melodrama—that had been her mother's specialty; it still tied her in knots of anxiety—but after a minute of observing Amanda she knew Hugh's return and Chessie's revelations would not be received with calm, levelheaded stoicism.

Feeling like an intruder on a private family moment, she'd slunk back out of view, wanting nothing more than to blend into the furniture. This wasn't impossible; it was a skill she'd learned early in life that held her in good stead in her work.

But now she longed for true invisibility because Cristo was turning his still-fuming sister beneath his arm, his intent clear. Isabelle's eyes widened with a *no, please don't!* appeal. Which he, dammit, spoke right over.

"Take a breath before you hyperventilate," he told his sister. "And after you've done that, you might say hello to Isabelle."

"Oh, I'm so sorry," Amanda said. Her pansy-dark eyes took in Isabelle with undisguised curiosity. "I didn't even notice you there. You must think I'm completely self-absorbed."

"You are," Cristo murmured.

"I know," she agreed blithely. Her smile for Isabelle held genuine warmth and a complete lack of repentance. "This wedding has turned me into an utter bridezilla. I can't wait until it's all over and I'm myself again. Or myself under the new name of Mrs. Hugh Harrington," she added.

Isabelle's heart sunk. Her eyes sought Cristo's for help, for guidance, for anything to stop this conversation descending into complete hell. He obliged by releasing his sister and reaching for Isabelle's hand. He drew her close to his side and shocked her all the way to her toes by pressing a kiss to the top of her head.

"Isabelle is the reason I flew to the other side of the world," he continued, his voice dropping to a level that made all her female bits tingle, even while her sensible, logical self shrieked an objection.

Cristo squeezed her hand in warning, and she pressed her lips shut.

Amanda had not missed a thing. Her inquisitive eyes shifted from Isabelle to Cristo. "My, my, big brother, you are full of surprises."

What could she say? The biggest surprise is still to come? She's here in this house and pregnant with your lying, cheating fiancé's baby?

What if they bumped into each other, right now, on the stairs? With both Amanda and Chessie oblivious. Sick with the thought of that confrontation, she sent a beseeching look up at Cristo.

"Crash has got it," he said casually, but there was reassurance in his expression and in the strength of his hand holding hers. Crash must have been prewarned about keeping Chessie out of the way. Isabelle did not have a problem with that. Subtly she returned the press of Cristo's palm against hers, absorbing the heat and his energy and telling herself it was okay to enjoy the sensation. It was a necessary act; for Chessie and for Amanda she could play along.

A tiny frown creased Amanda's forehead. "What has your gorilla got?"

"Kitchen emergency," Cristo replied smoothly. "Isabelle was wanting to help with dinner. I've been convincing her that help isn't necessary."

Amanda turned accusing eyes on her brother. "If you had told me you were eating in, I would have cancelled my plans and joined you."

"Perhaps that is why I didn't tell you."

"Well, I know when I'm de trop," she sniffed. "I'll leave

you to whatever you were about to get up to, but please will you speak to the caterer? He pays no attention to me or to the planner, but you have weight."

Cristo assured her that he would deal with it. With that off her shoulders, Amanda kissed them both warmly on each cheek in a very Continental manner and assured Isabelle that she would call and arrange a date "to lunch at Ivy," before departing as abruptly as she'd arrived.

A second later her face reappeared at the door.

"I almost forgot. Vivi is in Rome for an exhibition for Patrizio." She rolled the *r* in the name and her eyes simultaneously. "She left strict instructions that I was to attend the Delahunty gala, but Harry won't be back in time and now you are, so I think I can quietly opt out." Her eyes slid to Isabelle and back. "I imagine you will be taking Isabelle, which will certainly make the night…interesting."

"Good night, Amanda," Cristo said firmly, closing the door on her cheeky grin.

Isabelle had no idea what that exchange was about. Her mind spun with names but also with a heady sense of relief because so much could have gone wrong and hadn't. In the post-Amanda quiet, she could feel the textured heat of Cristo's hand more intensely. Alone that connection felt stronger, more intimate. He stood too close, their arms aligned from shoulder to wrist, his thigh a whisper away from hers. She knew she should put an end to this charade—she would, once her mind stopped spinning.

"So that was your sister," she said, because something had to be said. "She is…" Her voice trailed off because she didn't know quite how to describe the pint-size virago.

"Loud? Exhausting? Overindulged?"

"Well, it takes someone to do the indulging," she said, and

he laughed, a lazy ripple of amusement that did crazy things to her pulse.

"I accept some culpability." He shifted slightly; Isabelle felt the brush of his hip against hers. Some parts of her body melted, others tightened, but she sensed a shift in the mood along with his stance, and her whole being tuned in to that weighty tension. Despite the laughter, she knew he was about to get serious.

"Amanda was born with a heart murmur," he said. "She was always this tiny little thing, fragile but game. She's had a string of operations, but she would not give up, even when her heart stopped beating. So, yes, we tend to indulge her. We have only ourselves to blame."

Her heart had stopped beating? Little wonder he was so protective. Isabelle had never faulted him for that, but now that she knew the full story…all the physical sensations were forgotten as she grappled with a new, deeper, more dangerous desire. She wanted more than her fingers curled in his. More even than to curl into his body, to wrap her arms around him, to reach for his mouth to taste that husky male laughter.

She wanted to know more.

She wanted to know *him*.

"And now?" she asked, the emotion gruff in her voice. "She looks healthy."

"Healthy as an ox. The last operation did the trick."

"I'm glad."

And she was sincerely glad. Amanda had such vivacity about her, and she hated the thought of that spark dimmed by Hugh's perfidy. She'd liked Amanda at first sight, loathed the perfidious Hugh without meeting him. "She sounds very attached to her fiancé."

"Unfortunately, yes. She believes this is true love."

Isabelle heard the cynical edge to those last words. "And you don't?"

"I believed they were well suited," he replied. Adroitly avoiding the issue of love, Isabelle noted. "Amanda has known Hugh a long time. She's great friends with his sister and knows all the family—and she's worked for Harringtons as his PA the past two years. Yet despite all she's seen firsthand, she set out to win him."

"All what, exactly?"

"He has a reputation for partying hard. I suspect that he's more than earned the tag of Heartbreaker Hugh."

In spite of the heat of his hand holding hers, Isabelle felt a coldness inside. Heartbreaker Hugh did not sound like a man who would stand by Chessie. "Yet you seem very involved in the wedding arrangements...."

"As Amanda's brother and guardian. Don't get me wrong, Isabelle. I didn't approve of their engagement at first. It has taken Hugh a year of devotion to Amanda to win me around. I thought he'd grown up," he said darkly. "I thought this marriage might actually stand a vague chance of success."

This marriage. Isabelle turned the telling phrase over in her mind, recalling what she'd learned of his family history in the Mornington restaurant. "As opposed to your mother's two?" she asked.

"Make that four."

Four? Isabelle swallowed. "Your mother has been married four times?"

"And currently considering a fifth. Patrizio, who entertains us all with his newfound career as an artist." His lips twisted into a cynical facsimile of a smile. "Vivi believes in true love, too, you see. She just hasn't quite found one that lasts longer than the honeymoon."

There didn't seem anything to say in answer to that. As much as she appreciated his frankness and this extra insight into his family, Isabelle was left feeling hollow and dispirited. She needed something to latch on to, to lash out at, and his manipulation of her presence in his bedroom seemed the perfect target. She tugged at her hand, and he, surprisingly, let her go without argument.

"How are we going to deal with what Amanda thinks she saw here?" she asked brusquely. "She thinks we are lovers."

"By the end of tonight, half of London will think the same thing."

Isabelle's head came up. She met his eyes, no longer dark with cynicism but steady and watchful. "What do you mean?"

"Amanda talks. A lot. I imagine she'll be on at least her sixth phone call by now."

"You don't sound very concerned."

"I'm not," he said evenly. "It would seem the perfect solution."

"To?"

"The question of why you and your sister flew into England on my private jet and now are ensconced in my house."

For a long moment, she stared back at him. Her heart was beating all over the shop. Was he serious? He looked serious. She puffed out a breath and shook her head. "No one will believe that you and I are lovers."

"Why not?"

"Because...look at me." Head high, she lifted her arms to indicate her ordinary looks, her plain clothes, her girl-next-door appearance, and Cristo did as instructed. He looked at her, slowly, thoroughly, intently. Hot from the inside out, she lowered her arms. "No one will believe us as a couple."

"Amanda didn't appear to have any difficulty."

"She doesn't know that I'm a housekeeper. You fly around

in a private jet. You live in Belgravia and play polo and do lunch at places I've never heard of. You do not date domestics!"

"You know this…how?"

He was being deliberately difficult. She had to make him see reason before he did something truly ludicrous, such as accepting Amanda's suggestion of taking her to this gala do. She sucked in a breath. "This function Amanda mentioned…"

"It's a charity dinner and auction," he explained, "for one of my stepfather's closest friends, who happens to be on the board of Chisholm Air. Alistair was a patron of the Dela-hunty Foundation. His company remains a major sponsor and supporter."

"Well, I couldn't go with you to something like that. I wouldn't know what to say or how to act. I'd be like Julia Roberts with the snails in *Pretty Woman*."

"I believe this year's theme is Russian. I'm almost certain snails will not be on the menu."

"That is not the point," she said through her teeth. She felt like grabbing him by the throat and shaking him. "I don't even have any clothes suitable for a formal function."

"A valid point," he mused after a moment's narrow-eyed consideration. Isabelle felt like breaking into the "Hallelujah Chorus." Finally he was taking this seriously. "I have to go to the office in the morning, but as soon as I can get away I will pick you up. Somewhere around one, I imagine."

The chorus in Isabelle's head stuttered to a confused halt. "Pick me up for…?"

"I'm taking you shopping," he said. "For whatever you need for this role."

"This role?" she echoed.

"As my lover, my girlfriend, my mistress, my woman. Which would you prefer?"

Isabelle went hot, then cold. It wasn't only the words he used, it was the tone. It was the dark flare of satisfaction in his eyes. It was the wicked notion tingling through her blood that perhaps he meant this to be real. "No." She shook her head adamantly. "I won't do it. I would rather scrub floors."

"Pity, because I am not in need of a charlady. You came here tonight to ascertain your role as my employee." Suddenly his expression was decisive, his demeanour all brook-no-argument business. "I do not need household help of any variety. I do not need a driver or a personal shopper or a valet." As if to reinforce that point, he crossed to his dressing room and emerged pulling on a shirt. "I need you here with your sister. I need you to keep Amanda's persistent curiosity satisfied and to run interference if her path should cross Francesca's. Do you understand?"

Isabelle's eyes rocketed from shirt buttons to his face. She nodded. This was better; this even sounded like a sensible idea. "Yes," she said with new enthusiasm. "I can do that."

"I have every confidence that you can."

"And what about the other role?"

"As my lover?"

"Your *pretend* lover." That had to be made clear right from the start.

And when he closed down the space between them, she held her ground and held his gaze. She didn't allow herself to be distracted by his hands tucking in the shirt or by the churn of heat in her blood as he stopped in front of her. "I have every confidence in you, Isabelle," he said, but there was a hint of wickedness in both voice and eyes as they drifted over her face. "I believe you will satisfy me in any role you take on, whether pretend or otherwise."

* * *

"He's paying you to be his mistress for a week? And buying you clothes?" Chessie grinned widely. "Hello, *Pretty Woman!*"

Isabelle did not grin back. She prowled the sitting room, unable to sit still. Unable to believe that she'd agreed to this ridiculous ruse or that she'd slept for twelve long hours after accepting the role. Cristiano Verón's pretend lover. In the clear light of a perfect spring morning, that idea made as much sense as her sister's movie reference.

"I'm not playing his mistress or dressing to impress his business associates. He's buying me an outfit so I don't look out of place at a charity dinner." She exhaled a soft gust of annoyance. "As if dressing me in expensive clothes will make a difference."

"Meaning what?"

"Meaning everyone will know I'm a fraud."

"Because you don't know which glass for red and which for white? Or which silverware to use for which course? Or how to unfold your serviette?" Chessie asked. "You can cook, plate and serve a formal seven-course dinner with your eyes closed, and you know it. What is the real problem? Is it Cristo?"

"It's Cristo, and it was meeting Amanda." Her gaze met her sister's and then slid away. She'd shared the gist of that meeting but not all the details. Chessie did not need the health issues influencing her decisions; that had to be between her and Harrington. "He expects me to play the part of his lover," she continued in a rush. "I know it's just acting, and an explanation for why we're here and to allay Amanda's curiosity, but he's paying me and now he's spending more money on fancy clothes."

"Necessary clothes," Chessie insisted. "Think of it as a uniform."

"A designer uniform that costs hundreds and hundreds of pounds?"

"Thousands, I imagine," Chessie said cheerfully. Then, when she saw the horror in Isabelle's eyes, "Come on, Belle, you know how these millionaires drop money. Look around you. How much would this room alone have cost to decorate? To Cristo an outfit that costs a thousand pounds would be like you dropping a five-cent coin. Why can't you just embrace it, have some fun? Like Cinderella, getting to go to the ball."

Isabelle gave her a look.

"You know what I think," her sister said thoughtfully. Wearing jeans and a sloppy joe, she still managed to look perfectly at home stretched out on an ornate cream and gold chaise longue that probably cost more than Isabelle's entire home full of furniture. "I think Cristo gets a thrill out of winding you up. I bet he's banking on more resistance. He's probably kicking back in his office right now with that wicked little smile he gets…you know the one…where just the corners of his mouth lift up?"

Isabelle swallowed. She knew that smile. It was a bone-melting mixture of rich treacle and pure testosterone. "And what do you suppose he's smiling about?" she asked her sister, intrigued despite herself.

"The prospect of another head-to-head with you. Imagine his surprise if you're waiting at the door, the ever-efficient employee, all ready to sweetly do your boss's bidding."

She could do this. Not because she subscribed to Chessie's suggestion of a game of one-upmanship—she was pretty sure that Cristo the grand master, with black belt, would have her on the figurative mat before the end of round one—but because Isabelle Browne was, at heart, an agreeable person.

After years of blocking her ears against the emotional melodramas played out between her parents, she preferred peaceable.

And no matter how aggravating she found this situation, Cristo was her boss. She had agreed to his terms; she was contracted as his employee. If a little part of her was wildly attracted to the notion of setting him off-kilter with unexpected compliance, who was to know?

She'd apprised Chessie in no uncertain terms that she wasn't playing games. That she took every one of Cristo's incendiary remarks with a grain of he-is-so-full-of-it salt. Ignoring Chessie's raised eyebrows and murmured "Methinks the lady doth protest too much," she set about locating her least-shabby jeans and underwear for the shopping expedition.

She'd narrowed the selection to a matched set of lace-trimmed lilac—a birthday gift from Chessie two years back and showing signs of age—and a basic white combination, plain but near new, when Chessie called her to the phone.

"Cristo," she said. "I can barely hear him, but I imagine he wants you."

Through the pitchy whine of jet engines, she could hear him clearly enough to recognise the all-about-business tone. He had to fly to Spain, urgent, unavoidable.

Isabelle didn't have time to summon any sense of relief before he told her he would be home for tonight's dinner. Amanda would be taking her shopping. She frowned through a ridiculous jolt of disappointment. "Isn't that a bit risky? I thought you'd be trying to keep us apart."

"Impossible. She called this morning wanting to meet us for lunch."

"Oh."

"Let her do all the talking," he advised, "and you'll be fine."

"But what about Chessie?"

"Crash will look after her."

Which is how she found herself crawling through thick London traffic in the backseat of the same chauffeur-driven car as yesterday—a Maybach, Amanda informed her, with doesn't-everyone-travel-like-this nonchalance. She'd tried to get out of the shopping trip, first when Amanda called to set a pick-up time and then when she arrived an apologetic fifty minutes late.

"Last-minute crisis," she'd explained. "Bloody job."

"You should have called me," Isabelle said, appalled that she'd dragged her away from work. "You don't have to do this."

"Oh, yes. I do." She shepherded a reluctant Isabelle out the door and toward the limo. "A couple of phone calls, problem sorted, crisis averted," Amanda continued. "Now I'm taking an extra-long lunch because I can. I have an in with the boss," she confided, wriggling her fingers so the antique-set diamond on her left hand caught the sun.

Isabelle couldn't *not* comment. "Your ring, it's stunning," she said, each word tasting thick and dry in her mouth.

"Isn't it? Harry found it at an estate sale in Bavaria."

"I suppose he travels a lot with his work."

"A lot and often. Usually I don't mind, but at the moment, with so much to do for the wedding…" Her voice trailed off, and for the briefest moment she looked exposed, almost forlorn. Then she inhaled through her nose and shot Isabelle a rueful smile. "I suspect he volunteered for this trip. 'Please, Justin, find me somewhere to go, anything to get me out of town.' This wedding has become a monster that's taken over my life."

That honesty, the deprecating humour—Isabelle was beginning to like Cristo's sister a little too much to continue the secretive charade. "Look," she said, barely able to meet her eyes. "You are much too busy for this."

"For helping Cristo out? Never. Do you know how often he's asked for my help?" Amanda raised her eyebrows, waiting for an answer.

"Um…not often?" Isabelle guessed.

"Exactly, and I want to redress the balance, just a little." Her gaze remained appealingly earnest, despite her carefree tone. "Besides, we're talking about shopping, which is one of my favourite pastimes, and spending Cristo's money. Which, according to him, is my other."

Isabelle looked dubious.

"Humour me," Amanda continued. "I've called ahead. It's all arranged. Nina is giving us private access to her whole collection."

"Nina?"

"We're here!" Amanda indicated an understated shopfront in a street of understated shopfronts.

Isabelle blinked. She had been expecting… To be honest, she didn't know. Perhaps Selfridges or Harvey Nichols or a sign that proclaimed Outrageously Expensive Couture.

"If I'd had more notice, I would have called in a stylist, but Nina is the next best thing. She has all the labels and exquisite taste. Come on," Amanda said, looping her arm through Isabelle's and gently urging her across the mile-wide seat toward the door. "Let's go spend an insane amount of my brother's money." Seeing the look on Isabelle's face, she smiled wickedly. "Don't worry, he has plenty. And when he gets an eyeful of you in full Nina-fied splendour, he won't mind a bit."

Eight

Cristo paused outside her door. The music playing inside was loud enough to recognise as Vivaldi even through the closed door. In all likelihood it would drown out the sound of his knock, but he allowed her a minute to answer regardless. According to Crash, whom he'd passed on the stairs, she was ready and waiting. According to Amanda's *mission-accomplished* text, she had the perfect dress, shoes, hairstyle.

Frankly, he'd expected more resistance. To the shopping expedition and to attending tonight's gala on his arm. Driving in from the airport, he'd thought about the upcoming clash of words and wills with much expectation and some impatience. The twenty-four hours since he'd last seen her seemed infinitely longer, and he'd stretched it another thirty minutes to shower, shave and dress. Dinner suit, black tie, standard for these events he was compelled to attend.

Tonight was different. For once he didn't feel compelled.

His body hummed with anticipation as he knocked once again. Then, done with waiting, he opened the door.

The sitting room was filled with the music's liquid notes and all the signs of a successful shopping expedition. Carrier bags, several pairs of abandoned shoes, a jewelled evening bag that caught the chandelier's sparkle and flung the light in a score of new directions.

But no Isabelle.

The door to her bedroom lay open, and through the concerto's diminuendo he caught the sparkling notes of laughter. A smile twitched at the corners of his mouth, and his body quickened with recognition. It was her voice that caused both reactions, although Francesca's was there in the background, no doubt spurring the laughter as she so often did.

Scooping up a discarded shoe from his path, he started across the room only to come to a stonewall halt when Isabelle hurried into view. Her head was turned as she flung a last comment back at her sister, and she didn't see him for several thick heartbeats. It was enough time for him to take in the picture—and, *Dios,* what a picture she made—and to pick his jaw up from the floor.

She turned, the laughter still in her eyes even as it died on her lips. She stopped. Blinked once. "You're here."

"So it would appear," he said.

The first impact had been all about her—the expanse of creamy skin, the ripple of her hair as she turned, the stimulating stroke of her laughter.

Now he took stock of the rest with a long, leisurely appraisal. Her dress, a column of scarlet. The fabric, soft and lustrous, cut and draped to make the most of her sensational figure. The rise of her breasts as she drew a breath, the shadow of cleavage that disappeared from view as she lifted a hand to the low-cut neckline.

At the other end the dress pooled over her feet to the carpet. Not quite ready and waiting. He held up the shoe in his hand. "Yours?"

"Yours," she replied, not echoing his question but answering it. The proud set of her chin let him know her meaning. She wasn't accepting his purchases. They would be worn; they would remain his property.

Their gazes met and held, a current of energy arcing between them. A new edge sharpened Cristo's anticipation. A knowledge that despite her stance and her words, she felt the same crackle of awareness. The same charged heat in her blood.

This was the Isabelle whose company he relished. The one who stood her ground, who met his gaze with steady strength to state her case.

Eyes locked on hers, he slowly closed the space between them. "If this is mine," he said, holding the delicate silvery straps in one hand and tapping the spiked heel against the palm of his other, "then do I get to put it on your foot, Cinderbella?"

At his play on her name, irritation flashed in her eyes. But before she could voice her objection, Francesca appeared in the doorway.

"Cheating," she said shortly, indicating the shoe with a wave of her hand. "Obviously that will be a perfect fit, given you bought it for her."

"Spoilsport."

"Not really," Francesca said. "Since I'm about to leave you to whatever sport you have in mind."

That earned an appreciative grin from Cristo and a cutting glare from her sister. "There's no need," she said briskly. "Once I put on the shoes, we'll be leaving, too."

"Then I will see you downstairs," Francesca replied. "I'm off to check out the coach and horses."

The door closed with a hollow thud, shutting them off. Alone. Their eyes met briefly as he handed her the shoe. "No coach," he told her. "Just the Maybach."

"Chessie likes to wind me up."

"Is Cinderella a hot button?" he asked.

"A warm one," she said, collecting the second shoe before sliding them both onto her feet. Three inches taller, she straightened and met his eyes. "Given my job, it's an old joke. Usually I pay it no mind."

"You think that tonight there is a reason to pay it mind?"

"The shopping, this dress, it's all a bit much."

"No, the dress is not too much," he countered softly. "In fact, it is precisely as I requested."

Her gaze sharpened on his, a frown tugging her newly shaped eyebrows together. "You gave Amanda specific instructions on how to dress me?"

Cristo hitched a shoulder. "General rather than specific."

"Such as?"

"I requested a dress that would enhance your beauty, not overwhelm it. This—" his voice dropped with his gaze, taking in the flutter of pulse at the base of her throat and the rosy flush in her exposed skin "—is almost perfect."

"Almost?" She stared at him, her expression a perfect blend of confusion and indignation. "The price you paid, there should not be anything lacking!"

"Just this one thing."

With a deft hand he fished a necklace from his inside pocket. Three rows of pearls fashioned into a contemporary choker, the piece was classic, simple perfection. Perfect for the dress, perfect for Isabelle.

"No." Her hand came up to her throat in a protective

gesture as she took a step back. "I told Amanda, the dress is enough. I don't need any jewellery."

"So she said, but I disagree."

"It's too much."

"Let me be the judge," he said, taking back the space she'd put between them and a little more. "Turn around," he said softly.

For a wilful second she stood her ground, shoulders squared, gaze fixed steadily on his. "Jewellery was not in the deal."

"Nor, as I recall, was hair or makeup."

Her eyes widened slightly. "If you object—"

"No, I approve."

"Good," she said darkly. "You paid enough for those, as well."

"Good," he retorted, smothering a smile. "I hope you gained some measure of enjoyment at my expense."

"You could have saved yourself a lot of money by sending me and Chessie."

"Would you have gone?" he asked, circling around her, taking in the dress from all angles. "And would you have chosen *this* dress?"

"No, there was this smoky grey one with—"

"I hate grey."

"I know."

Cristo laughed, and her frown darkened. "If you mean to annoy me, you will have to do better than that," he said softly. "I am in far too accommodating a mood."

"Your meeting in Spain, did that go well?"

That emergency seemed a lifetime ago. He'd solved it. He'd moved on. Now he wanted to concentrate on her. "Better than expected," he said, turning his focus to the tense set of her shoulders and the tumble of honey-gold hair that, although newly cut, still hit her shoulder blades. He gathered the glossy curls in one hand, baring her nape, releasing a subtle fragrance from hair and skin.

He hoped he'd wiped Spain and business from both their minds, but just in case he leaned forward to inhale the scent of warm honey and nectarine blossom and female skin. "Nice," he murmured.

"It's Jo Malone," she said faintly. "Amanda insisted."

"I must remember to thank her."

He pushed her hair forward over one shoulder and took his time sliding the pearls around her throat, absorbing the lightning spark of contact as his fingers brushed her skin. He may have imagined her quicksilver shiver of response. He did not imagine the heat rushing south in his blood.

The necklace clasp was a kindergarten task. Cristo could have managed it in the dark at any other time, but not on Isabelle's neck. His fingers preferred to linger on her skin, his gaze on the vulnerable curve beneath her ear. The temptation to lean forward, to press a kiss to that precise spot, sang with the violins in the air.

"We will never get there at this rate," she murmured, but the breathy catch in her voice was not impatience. And it spoke straight to his gathering arousal. "Let me get it."

"I wish," he murmured gruffly. Then, when she squirmed beneath his hands, "Hold still."

The catch clicked shut, but the temptation remained. He leaned close, pressed open lips to silky skin, and she leaped forward as if stung. Her hair whipped around her shoulders as she turned, but when her gaze fastened on his, something palpable churned between them. Awareness, knowledge, desire.

Her nostrils flared slightly, and whatever admonishment she'd been about to lay on him froze on her parted lips. One hand lifted, fingertips to the pearls. "Thank you," was all she said.

"My pleasure."

Cristo could have pursued the mood, could have pushed the energy swirling like the lush orchestral notes between them, but they were already late. The whole evening stretched ahead, a feast of Isabelle, a smorgasbord of opportunity.

"Ready?"

She nodded and gathered her bag. Then her gaze caught the time on the mantel clock, and the frown rushed back full tilt. "Will we be very late?" she fretted.

"Fashionably. Which could work for the better," he mused with a lazy smile.

"How is that?"

"We will be noticed, tongues will wag," he replied, taking her hand. "Arriving together, hand in hand, your hair slightly dishevelled. That should address any concerns about the credibility of our relationship, don't you think?"

Isabelle assumed he'd taken her hand as a demonstration of his point, but coming down the stairs she needed his hold for balance. She'd never worn heels so high. Amanda had dismissed her qualms. "It's a dinner," she'd said. "You'll be sitting." Nina agreed. Neither of them mentioned the perilous walking involved in getting to said dinner table, and she'd been having too much fun trying on clothes and soaking up every glimpse of Cristo offered through his sister's eyes. Amanda, as he'd said, liked to talk.

Inside the limo he took her hand again, which meant that despite the roomy interior—honestly, they could have held a charity fundraiser in the rear of this car—he was sitting far too close. Not quite touching, except when he leaned forward to point out one of the attractions beyond her side window. She leaned closer to the cool glass, peering out with feigned interest, although the passing sights barely registered.

Apparently Cristo Verón was the only attraction London had to offer her single-tracked senses.

Although understandable—handsome at the best of times, in black tie the man was truly a traffic stopper—it was an irritation that worried at her like a snappy terrier. Before and after the fact, she hated the extravagance of this afternoon's shopping, and yet at the time, she'd slipped into whatever the redoubtable Nina had passed her way. She'd walked out of the store with a staggering array of clothing, not only for tonight but to cover any likely outing over the next days.

Due to the efforts of Amanda and Nina and Perri the hair magician, she looked the part of a rich man's date, but that was only the external. What about the rest? What did Cristo expect of her at the charity gala? Would he continue to hold her hand, would they dance, would he whisper in her ear and kiss that sweet spot he'd hit upstairs?

Would that be their role, as new lovers unable to keep their hands from each other?

Heat rippled through her blood, the same sensation as when his fingertips had brushed her nape as he'd fastened the necklace. The same as every time he touched her.

Isabelle rubbed her arm in a vain attempt to dispel the tingle.

"Cold?" he asked.

"No." Far from it. "Just…nervous."

"There is no need."

"Even though we will be noticed and tongues will wag?"

His grip on her hand tightened, enough to draw her gaze around to meet his. Dark as the night, steady, serious. "I was teasing, Isabelle. There is no need for nerves. You will manage beautifully."

"You don't know me well enough to make that call. I might have appalling table manners. I might drink excessively and tell hideous jokes. I might trip over in these heels and land face-first in some duke's lap!"

"Lucky duke," he murmured, and Isabelle exhaled on a note that was part laughter and part disbelief. The awful thing? She could imagine him handling that situation with his usual sangfroid. As for her own sangfroid… Well, it hummed along with the rest of her over the compliment he was paying her with his confidence.

He'd trusted her to an afternoon with Amanda. He trusted her to play the part of his date. If she kept on remembering that—*this is a job, Isabelle, not Cinderella on her way to the ball*—then she might just get through the night.

"It would help if I knew more about this function," she said, forcing herself to concentrate on the job.

"What do you need to know? There will be an endless production of dinner courses. Some may even be edible. In keeping with the Russian theme, the entertainment may include ballet, although Cossacks on horseback are not out of the question. There will be an auction to benefit the Remember Rani Foundation, for cancer research. We will be seated at David's table."

Isabelle frowned. Names had flown at her from all directions these past few days, but that was one she did not recall. "Is David your stepfather's friend?"

"Yes. David Delahunty."

"Is there a Mrs. Delahunty?"

"The foundation is named for his late wife, Rani. He hasn't remarried." He paused, a brief beat of time, before adding, "His daughter will be there, and Rani's sister and her husband."

"What are their names?"

Isabelle prepared herself for taking mental notes, but Cristo lifted their linked hands and kissed her knuckles. "Relax, sweetheart, you are not expected to know any of these people. We have known each other for less than a week. Let's assume we haven't spent that time discussing London society."

His meaning shimmered a moment in the silence, replete with pillow-talk images. She felt the bloom of heat in her skin but she held his gaze. For the sake of tonight's role-play, she needed to know what they'd spent the past week doing. "If we're going to pass muster as a couple," she said steadily, "then we will need a believable story."

"I suggest we stick as closely as possible to the truth."

"So, we met last week when you came to Australia on business?"

"You were my housekeeper," he continued. "The fascination was instant."

"The fascination, yes," she agreed, falling into the fiction and into the dark heat of his heavy-lidded gaze. "But I was your employee. I would lose my job if I slept with you."

"Which is why I convinced you to accompany me back to England."

"To get me into bed? Would you do that?"

The pad of his thumb traced the delicate skin at her wrist and heat exploded low in her belly as he answered with one sure word. "Undoubtedly."

"And now we are lovers?"

"Is that a role you are willing to play?" he asked, his voice as dark and heavy as the heat in her blood.

For a long moment their gazes held, the atmosphere ripe with erotic speculation. Isabelle's heart thundered, too loud to hear her whispery caution. *It's a story, Isabelle. The role you are playing*. She moistened her lips. "Would anyone believe that we weren't?"

"Not for a second."

"This is a regular happening, then?" Her chin came up a notch to counter a silly pang of disappointment. Ridiculous, she knew, and yet she couldn't help herself. "You go away on a business trip and bring home a random woman?"

"Never random. I am very selective. Do you need details, statistics, my latest health check?"

"No," she countered quickly. "I just needed to know how I would be viewed. I have never been in this situation."

"Take your cues from me. Don't drink too much wine, leave the dukes alone, and you will do fine." His thumb traced the reverse path across her wrist. Then he nodded toward the window at her back as the car slowed and stopped. They had arrived. "Are you ready?"

There was comforting strength in his easy confidence, and Isabelle nodded. "As long as I don't forget myself and start bussing tables or—" a sudden thought widened her eyes "—I don't run into someone I've worked for!"

"Will they recognise you out of uniform?"

A good point. "You're right. They wouldn't."

Then the car door swung open to reveal a bevy of doormen in stunning livery and the pinkened glow of lamplight on flagstones and people…so many beautiful couples in dazzling evening dress and jewels—oh Lord, was that woman wearing a tiara?—and all as fashionably late as Isabelle and Cristo.

As she slid from seat to ground, Isabelle's stomach jived with nerves. She tried not to gawp but the beauty alighting from the next car looked awfully like the cover girl on the glossy magazine that graced her bedside table. "Is that Lily whatshername, the model?"

"Probably," Cristo drawled, all I-see-supermodels-every-day insouciance. His gaze barely shifted from hers as he took her hand and drew her close to his side.

To disguise her shiver of response, Isabelle turned into his body and inclined her head at the latest arrivals. "The man she's with, is that…" Her voice trailed off as her eyes widened in disbelief. "Oh my God, it is!"

"If that is Lily Whatshername, then I dare say it is." A smile kicked at his lips. "Would you like to meet them?"

"You know them? Really? No, you're winding me up!"

He laughed, a low, smoky sound that dappled her senses with shadowy heat. "I sold him a G5 last month. We're on speaking terms, although…" Taking her other hand, he pulled her closer still. Suddenly all her senses were attuned to him, this man, the slightly roughened texture of his fingers wrapped around hers, the brush of his jacket against her hip, the enveloping heat of his body. The double-shot potency of espresso eyes and voice. "I would rather you kept that sloe-eyed wonder focussed on me."

"I would," she said, "if I knew what that meant."

"It means we're playing besotted lovers, remember?"

"I haven't forgotten."

"Good." Although a smile still lurked around the corners of his mouth, the mood had turned oddly serious. Supermodels, pop stars, royalty in tiaras, the drift of orchestral music, all faded to dusk. And when he ran his hands up her arms to cup her shoulders, Isabelle couldn't do a thing to blunt her response. A tremor coursed through her, a powerful mix of hot and cold intensity that tightened her breasts and softened her belly.

For the barest of moments his gaze lifted from hers, long enough to break the hot spell of connection, enough to let in the muted chords of Russian music and German engines and posh English voices. When his eyes returned to hers, she saw the flare of intent and her heart tripped wildly as his mouth started its smooth descent. Stretching on tiptoes, she met his kiss with softened lips, breathing the citrus and bergamot on his skin, absorbing his dark male heat and spinning with the intensity of desire that swelled to fill her senses.

This is not a game, she thought. *This is absolutely real.*

But just as she ached to deepen the connection, his mouth was gone, hers left wanting more. In the time it took to regain her breath and gather her equilibrium, Isabelle felt the chill night air encroaching into her sensual cocoon. A second later she realised they were no longer alone. And as Cristo drew her around to perform the introductions to David Delahunty and his family, she realised that the chill dancing up her spine had nothing to do with the cool May night.

It had everything to do with the resentment radiating from the daughter's glacial blue eyes as they took in Isabelle's well-kissed lips.

Nine

"Did you enjoy yourself, Isabelle?"

As the limo pulled away from the kerb and commenced the return drive to Wentworth Square, Isabelle slipped out of her ill-conceived choice of shoes and pretended interest in massaging the ache from her feet. That gave her time to consider Cristo's tricky question and an excuse not to consider him. She knew he'd settled on the opposite side of the big car, that he'd loosened his bow tie, that he lounged at apparent ease as he waited on her response.

She *had* enjoyed the interesting menu and the superb champagne, the music and dancing and surreptitious celebrity-spotting. Although wide-eyed and quietly appalled at the extravagance, she'd enjoyed perusing the jewellery and art, the five-star travel and out-of-this-world experiences offered for auction. She would have enjoyed everything a whole lot more if she'd not been stewing over that kiss.

Why hadn't she realised that it was part of a carefully orchestrated show? A setup staged for Madeleine Delahunty's benefit.

On the heels of that stunner had come a second awful realisation. Despite all the self-talk about doing her job and playing a role, somewhere deep inside she had still harboured a kernel of Cinderella-going-to-the-ball hope. She'd believed in the crackling sexual energy when Cristo looked at her a certain way, when he held her hand, when he laughed low and smoky at something she said.

She'd believed in the possibility of a fairy tale, and she'd set herself up for the most crushing of letdowns.

Dumb, dumb, dumb.

And the dumbest thing of all? Her reaction. Standing there on the pavement with hot and cold chills of disappointment and mortification churning through her, she'd decided that the only suitable recourse was to play him at his own game. She'd cozied in even closer, she'd possibly even simpered and batted her eyelashes, and she'd thrown herself with uncharacteristic vengeance into the role of besotted can't-keep-my-hands-off-him lover.

Had she gone too far? Possibly. Probably. But, dammit, she wasn't going to apologise or back down now they were alone. He'd started it with that kiss. He'd invited her to follow his lead. If he didn't like how she'd followed—if *that* was the undercurrent she detected beneath the measured delivery of his question—then tough.

Setting her expression with her best attempt at cool, calm confidence, she turned to face him. "I enjoyed myself well enough, thank you."

"Perhaps a little too much."

"Did I overdo it?" she asked disingenuously. "This was my first appearance as a make-believe mistress. I wasn't sure of the boundaries, so I did as you asked and followed your lead.

I'm pretty sure that we established ourselves as a couple. That is what you wanted…?"

"I didn't know you were such an accomplished actress," he murmured darkly.

"Why, thank you. My mother would be pleased that all those drama lessons paid off."

His corner of the car rode in shadowed darkness, and she couldn't see his face clearly enough to judge his mood, but she sensed she'd surprised him. She wished that didn't please her quite so much. "So it was all an act?" His voice, too, was a tricky mix of shadow and dark. Hard to judge, hard to pick. "The way you never left my side, the little touches, your hand on my thigh."

"An act…and payback."

"For?"

"For putting me in that situation. For not telling me the whole story. For kissing me in front of your friends."

The car slowed at an intersection, and the fractured street-light caught his face, revealing his expression for the first time. The slant of his prominent cheekbones, the shadowed planes beneath, the darkening of beard along his jawline. The softened fullness of his mouth hovering close to a smile as he drawled, "Here I was thinking, *She's taken me at my word. She's trying harder to get under my skin.*"

He was enjoying this. Isabelle couldn't believe it. Her own jaw tightened with indignation. "I was trying to irritate you!"

He laughed, a rich rumble of sound that coiled around her in sexy loops and pulled tight. "Why does that not surprise me?"

"Does anything surprise you?" she snapped.

Although they had moved on and his expression was again hidden in shadow, Isabelle sensed a shift in mood. She knew the smile was gone. Her heart beat a little harder, a lot quicker.

"You do, Isabelle," he said, soft, serious. One arm stretched across the backseat, his knuckles grazed the bare skin at her shoulder and suddenly the vast space shrunk, all the air sucked up in that one slice of a second. "Constantly."

She frowned hard, fighting his insidious charm and the expectant leap of her hormones. With a handful of words and one featherlight touch, he'd managed to turn her outrage inside out. She would not have that. She would not let him get away with such a cheap and obvious distraction. "Is that because I've shown such remarkable restraint, going along with every one of your manipulative plans when—"

"Manipulative?" he cut in, still sounding far too unrattled for Isabelle's liking. "How so?"

Turning in her seat, she fastened him with an incredulous glare. "*Everything* in the past week fits under that umbrella. The way you employed me with the sole aim of working the truth about Hugh from me, without any hint of what you were about. The way you used my concern for Chessie and my need of paid employment to coerce me into coming to England and then into playing this role of your lover. I should have known you had an ulterior motive."

"And if I had told you that my ulterior motive was getting to know you, would you have agreed to continue as my employee? Would you be here with me now?"

Getting to know her? Isabelle's heartbeat stuttered. *No.* She'd enjoyed the very fine champagne but not enough to succumb to his smooth talk. Her frown deepened to a borderline scowl. "I was talking about how you used me and our 'relationship'—" she drew the word out, each syllable served with a heavy dash of sarcasm and a side of fully justified pique "—to deliver a we're-through message to your last girlfriend."

"Are you referring to Madeleine?" He sounded surprised, unsure. As if he didn't know. As if he needed to think it over. As if!

"Unless there were other exes that I missed the pleasure of meeting tonight, then, yes, Madeleine."

"Is that what she told you? That she is my ex-girlfriend?"

"Not in so many words, but that is the message she delivered." With every barbed word, with every murderous look. "I felt the daggers in my back. Would you care to check for wounds?"

His breath checked, as if that answer had amused him again. "Later," he promised. Then, when Isabelle's glare darkened, "Do not believe everything Madeleine tells you."

"Are you telling me she's not an ex?"

"Neither girlfriend nor lover."

He'd leaned forward to capture her gaze, and despite the deception of the shadows she could not ignore the sincerity in his voice or eyes. *Damn him.* "Then her possessiveness is…?"

"A misunderstanding."

Isabelle puffed out a breath full of scepticism. "She misunderstood your interest in her? You're really 'just good friends'?"

"Exactly. I've known her from the weekend I arrived in England. David and Rani and Madeleine were the first to welcome me. Our parents were the closest of friends. We spent a lot of time together growing up. Our parents jested about us as a couple." He paused, raked a hand through his hair, and despite the matter-of-fact delivery Isabelle realised that he was uncomfortable with the subject. "My mother has, unfortunately, not given up on the joke."

"She wants to arrange your marriage?"

"Exactly," he said darkly. "In spite of her track record, Vivi believes everyone should be married."

Obviously *he* didn't. Isabelle remembered their conversation about Amanda's engagement and his cynical comments on true love. She also remembered Madeleine's cutting verbal skills—the woman's blood might run cold with venom, but her mind was as sharp as her tongue. "Surely Madeleine couldn't believe that possible, not without some encouragement from you."

"After her mother died…" He shook his head, expelled a harsh breath. "David took it hard. Madeleine needed a friend."

And Cristo was that friend, the old family connection. He'd already spoken and demonstrated his desire to do whatever was needed for his extended family. "She got the wrong idea," Isabelle said slowly, "about your interest."

"Madeleine has always been headstrong and overindulged."

Isabelle thought of a few more pertinent adjectives, but she didn't voice them. Already she had pieced together a picture she understood. Cristo at his kindest would be devastatingly hard to resist. How could she fault Madeleine for wanting him? "She is used to having whatever she wants, and now she wants you."

"Something like that."

In the lee of this exchange, Isabelle felt deflated and incredibly vulnerable. She hadn't needed this extra insight into Cristo's compassionate side—she was struggling enough with the powerful physical attraction—and now she felt unexpected sympathy for Madeleine and a degree of shame for her actions. This event was named in Rani Delahunty's honour. The charity raised funds for the cancer that had claimed her life. It would have been a difficult night for Madeleine without having Cristo's supposed new girlfriend flaunted in her face.

"So you took me along tonight," she stated tightly, "to show Madeleine what she couldn't have. Don't you think it would have been kinder to tell her straight out that you're just not that into her?"

"I have done so, many times, in many ways, but not tonight. I took you," he said with the same quiet intensity, "because I wanted to."

"Not to keep Madeleine at bay?"

"I've been keeping her at bay, as you put it, for half of my life. I do not need you for that, Isabelle."

"But you kissed me because of her," she persisted, because she had to maintain the fight. She could not start thinking about what he did need from her.

"I kissed you because I'd been wanting to ever since we met."

"Even though you thought I was pregnant with Hugh Harrington's baby?"

"I never wanted to believe that. *This* is what I wanted to believe." Again he brushed the bare skin at her shoulder, this time as a deliberate demonstration of the man-woman awareness, the lightning streak of sunfire that burned in her nerve endings. "This chemistry, Isabelle, and the honesty I believed in your eyes."

"Honesty?" She wanted to laugh, to scoff, but her bravado was going up in flames. "How can you believe that anything between us is genuine?"

This time he turned his hand, cupping her shoulder, clouding her resolve with the textured heat of his skin and his voice. "Would you be more inclined to believe if I demonstrated?"

"No," she said quickly. Too quickly. She drew in a calming breath. "There is nothing to prove."

"I disagree. You are sceptical of my intent." He took her hand, twined their fingers, used that leverage to pull her closer. "What if I kissed you again, with no audience and no ulterior motive?"

"Except to prove your point. Madeleine might be—"

"Forget Madeleine."

"—used to having whatever she wants," she continued

strongly over his interjection, "but you are no better. I think you two have a lot in common. You should reconsider."

"You are right on one score. I have grown used to having what I want, and I am honest enough to admit that I want you." He stroked his thumb over the corner of her mouth. "How about you, Isabelle?"

She knew a challenge when it looked her in the eye, and this challenge held her gaze with unflinching boldness. Then he slid his hand from her shoulder to the bare skin of her back. A caress, an encouragement, a gentle pressure that brought her forward to meet his lowering mouth. "One little kiss," he whispered against her lips, "as proof this chemistry is real."

One. Little. Kiss.

Oh, no, this was so much more. It started where the last kiss had ended, a sweet, sensual seduction of her lips and her senses, but as soon as she surrendered—as soon as the hands that had come up to ward him off yielded to the temptation to touch—it plunged into so much more. It was a bold and thorough exploration of lips and tongues and skin, a yielding and a taking and a hunger that ripped through Isabelle the instant her mouth opened beneath his. She felt the tremor deep in her body, heard his throaty sound of satisfaction, tasted the satisfaction in a big dizzying gulp of acknowledgement.

This *was* real, this chemistry, this mutual wanting.

Then his hands took possession, pulling her onto his lap, drawing her tight against the hard heat of his body. It was shockingly raw and primal, his hands on her thighs, thumbs tracing the edge of her invisible knickers as he licked into her mouth. She shifted in his lap, finding a better angle for the kiss and a closer contact with the hard proof of his desire.

Lost in the potency of the moment, she forgot time, place, propriety, the thousand cautions she'd issued herself over the past days. She was greedy for more, for her hands on more than his shirt, more than his throat and his face. She wanted to feel his heat without barriers. She was too close, not close enough. She itched with the craziness of need, and when he swore softly the foreign word, his exasperation, the exhalation of breath hot against her skin, only inflamed her more. She turned in his lap, hands on his shirt buttons, her laugh a husky reflection of her impatience until she realised that he'd gone still and why he'd sworn.

His hands were no longer on her thighs but restraining her hands. The car was stationary, not as part of the slow crawl home through London traffic but because they had arrived at Wentworth Square. And someone was knocking at the car window.

Calmly Cristo shifted her to the seat beside him and straightened her dress, but when he opened the window he took her hand in a reassuring grip. She sucked in a deep breath, the world stopped spinning and the dark figure outside materialised into Crash's craggy features.

"This had better be good," Cristo said darkly.

"Hugh called," the butler replied shortly. "From Farnborough."

Pressed close against his side, Isabelle felt his muscles tense as his irritation with the interruption turned to instant alertness. "I thought he wasn't due back until the weekend."

"Apparently he called Amanda last night, and she mentioned Isabelle."

"Of course she did."

"He's on his way here now. I thought you should know."

Isabelle hadn't thought that anything could wipe that kiss so quickly from her mind. This news had managed the impossible. Uncaring about her kissed-clean lips and mussed hair, she leaned forward into view. "Does Chessie know?"

"She was in the room when the call came in. She's waiting in the library."

Waiting for Hugh's arrival was torture. A diplomatic Crash suggested that she might like to "freshen up," but she shook her head. Nobody cared if her ridiculously expensive dress was slightly crumpled, her feet bare, her hair and makeup ravaged. Chessie hadn't even noticed, a sure indication that despite her outward signs of preparedness and her assurances that she was more than ready for this meeting, her sister was jangling with nerves.

Isabelle forced her to sit and practice her breathing. "It's never too early," she said, taking her sister's hand and demonstrating with a couple of exaggerated Lamaze-inspired breaths. Chessie laughed and almost relaxed until they heard someone outside the door and her grip turned almost punishing with sudden tension.

But it was only Crash bringing them tea, and a few minutes later Cristo returned from the male version of freshening up, which meant he no longer looked as though he'd been run over by a wildly turned-on woman. He'd changed into jeans and a light sweater. His eyes found Isabelle's right away, steady, questioning, and she nodded a silent answer. *We're good.* And she realised with a warm settling of her own nerves that this wasn't a platitude, that with the calming strength of his presence they would get through this.

He took a chair opposite and distracted them both by asking Chessie about her visit to the National Gallery and then updating them on his horse Gisele's improving health. He was so easy to listen to, so easy to watch as he explained the rudiments of polo to Chessie with words and hands and a stray ball he found on the desk. Chessie relaxed enough to ask questions, to laugh at his answers, although every so often her gaze flicked to the window overlooking the street.

When the doorbell rang, she lifted an inch off the sofa. "He's here."

Her words were superfluous—who else would be calling after midnight?—and barely audible despite the sudden silence. Cristo stood, his tension marked in the rigid set of his jaw and the flexing of his hands into fists. She wondered if that was merely an easing of tension or a sign of intent, but she could not feel any alarm on Hugh Harrington's part. He deserved whatever was coming.

In the hallway outside they heard voices, Crash's and another, but when Isabelle reached for Chessie's hand, her sister shook her head. "I'm good," she said. "I can do this."

When the door opened and Crash stepped back to usher in the new arrival, Isabelle's eyes remained on Chessie's face. She saw her sister's slight recoil, the small shake of her head as she looked from Hugh to Crash to Cristo. He was the first to speak, his voice as hard and dark as the ebony timber that dominated the room.

"Hugh," he said. "I'm glad you saw fit to return home and face the music."

"No." Chessie was still shaking her head as she looked from one man to the other. "What's going on? This is not Harry."

Ten

Cristo watched the bewilderment on every face following Francesca's declaration and Hugh's equally adamant avowal that he was, as recently as one hour ago when his passport was last checked, Hugh Harrington. When Francesca argued that point, Hugh reached into an inside pocket and produced the document, which Chessie refused to look at.

"Are you Isabelle Browne?" Hugh asked, and Cristo had to step in and referee the confused melee of answers. Finally he managed to explain, to everyone's satisfaction, the story of the sister swap in Melbourne.

"I am the pregnant one," Francesca reiterated in case anyone was still in doubt. "But you are not my Harry."

"No, I'm not," Hugh said thoughtfully, and then he laughed softly with what sounded like wonderment. "I'll be damned."

"What?" Cristo asked at the same time as Isabelle.

"I am *a* Harry," Hugh replied, and Cristo went still.

"Justin?" he asked sharply.

Hugh nodded. "He flew to Melbourne for the auction."

"He stayed at this client's house?"

"Just for one night."

"Apparently that was enough," Cristo murmured.

"Who are you talking about?" Isabelle stepped forward, her forehead creased in confusion. She placed her hand on Cristo's arm and instantly had his attention. "Are there other Harrys?"

"Justin is Hugh's elder brother. I didn't know they shared the nickname. It didn't cross my mind that it could be Justin."

"I'll say." Hugh still looked bemused. "Would never have picked it."

"Why not?" Francesca asked into the beat of pause that followed this announcement. "Please don't tell me he is married or engaged or a serial—"

"No," Hugh cut in. "Justin isn't married, at least not anymore."

Under a barrage of questions, the story finally came together. Hugh had been Harringtons' man in situ in Australia back in January, doing the groundwork for a major estate sale. Justin arrived to oversee the auction before flying back to New York. According to Hugh, that encapsulated his brother's life since the death of his wife last summer—constant travel, little sleep, working like an automaton. Which is why it had never crossed his mind that Justin could be the "Harry" Francesca sought.

Yes, they'd both been dubbed Harry at school, as had their father and grandfather and all Harrington men since time immemorial, but the nickname hadn't stuck to Justin. Cristo understood why. Unlike his younger brother, Justin Harrington had never been one of the party-hard players around town. He'd always been serious—not a Harry but a Lord Justin Harrington, viscount and future earl, head of a traditional and ultra-conservative family business.

And, according to Hugh, he'd become a complete social hermit since Leesa's tragic boating accident. "To the best of my knowledge, he has not even casually dated," he confided to Cristo. "Must say I'm somewhat flummoxed by this evidence to the contrary. Do you think Chessie is on the up-and-up?"

"Do you think I would have brought her here from Australia and put her up in my home if I didn't?"

"From what Amanda says, I thought that might have more to do with the sister."

Cristo didn't give him the benefit of an answer. It didn't matter what any of them thought; the truth would be determined by Justin. Crash had turned up an auction brochure bearing his picture, and Francesca identified him with a conclusive nod before tapping a finger against the advertised sale date. "Is he in New York for this?"

"Not only for the auction," Hugh replied. "A key executive resigned early this year. Left the Manhattan office in a bit of a jumble."

"Is he expected home soon?"

"For the wedding. But with the Carmichael sale only days before, there's some doubt he'll even make the rehearsal. Your best bet would be to call him, although I wonder..." Harry ruminated for several seconds, his expression turning from thoughtful to diffident. "I wonder if you would mind terribly much if we kept this under our hats, as it were, until after the wedding. Justin is my best man, and I would rather he were at my side than dashing you off to Vegas."

"That is not going to happen," Francesca said with feeling.

"Then I beg you not to break this news to my family before the wedding."

"Will they run me out of town?" she asked. "Or force me to the altar with a shotgun?"

Hugh reassured her that neither would be the case, although they might expect a wedding before the baby. "Rather old-fashioned in that regard," he said, "but you've nothing to fear. Justin will insist on doing the responsible thing. That's why I'm concerned about telling him now, you see. It's not only the wedding—this Carmichael sale is crucial to Harringtons' reputation in America. Your news would prove somewhat of a distraction, I'm afraid."

"Another two weeks won't make any difference to me," Francesca replied, "except we may have overstayed our welcome here."

"Not at all," Cristo assured her evenly. "You should not feel pressured to rush yourself from under my roof or to accept Hugh's request for a delay. I can fly you to New York."

"Thank you, but I don't want to turn this into a chase around the world. I can wait until after the wedding." She rested a hand on her belly. "I have months of patience left."

Isabelle attempted to argue, but Francesca's mind was made up. Pleading tiredness, she excused herself and went upstairs, her stormy-faced sister at her side. A satisfied Harry left soon after, but Cristo was neither satisfied nor ready to retire. He had a feeling Isabelle would return—she would want to pursue this new development, to know where she and Francesca stood—and he did not have long to wait for her knock at the door.

"Can I pour you a cognac?" he asked, ushering her across the room to the massive ebony desk where Crash had left a ray bearing bottle and glasses. She looked pale, agitated, in need of both a drink and reassurance.

"Does it help?"

"It certainly doesn't hurt." When he passed her the glass, their fingers brushed and a frisson of heated memory flickered across her face. Cristo's body stirred in response, but he said nothing; this was not the time. Leaning back against the desk, he watched her take a tentative sip. Accepted her murmured thanks.

"Not only for the drink," she added, swirling the golden liquid for a second before taking a visible grip of her fretfulness. "You were very fair, offering Chessie the opportunity to go to New York."

"Did you manage to change her mind?"

She laughed ruefully and shook her head. "I'm afraid I have never had much success on that score."

"Tonight must have been quite a shock for her. Perhaps she needs the extra time to adjust to this turn of events. To allow this new picture of her baby's father to take shape."

"Can I ask…" She turned her glass a slow, measured circle within her hands and inhaled deeply. "Is he everything Hugh suggested?"

"Justin is a decent man, highly thought of, honourable. Francesca and her baby are in good hands."

She took her time digesting that, but gradually the storm in her eyes settled as if she'd accepted his judgement. A small thing, Cristo told himself, to produce such inordinate pleasure. "You must be happy with how this has turned out," she said. "Given the alternative."

Oddly, he hadn't given any consideration to what had been averted. Not until now. The ramifications for Amanda and Hugh were huge, and that realisation ramped his pleasure to a new level and brought a smile to his lips. "This drink should be a celebration." He leaned closer, touched his glass to hers. "To satisfactory solutions."

"And happy endings," she added, "for everyone."

Cristo toasted that, but she must have noticed the unspoken cynicism in his salute because her gaze drifted away and the smile tugging at the corners of her mouth faltered. She sipped at her drink, swallowed, swirled, before her gaze lifted again to his. "What now?" she asked. "How are we to keep this secret until after the wedding? Amanda is so…"

"Nosy?"

"She is curious because she cares about you and she thinks we are a couple. She invited me to lunch next week. She pressed me to commit to a day, and she asked if I was coming to her wedding. I can't keep lying to her, and if she meets Chessie and notices she is pregnant… I can't keep up this pretence for two weeks, Cristo. I think it would be best if we went to stay somewhere else."

"I agree," he said mildly, and she blinked in surprise. He could think of nothing better than taking her somewhere else, a place with no Amanda, no Francesca, no Harrys of any variety. "I was wanting to spend this weekend at Chisholm Park. You will come with me," he decided. Not the perfect solution, but one Cristo could warm to…especially if he could ensure they were left alone.

"But won't that defeat the purpose?"

"The purpose being?"

"To avoid Amanda's attempts to embrace me into your family. I was thinking Chessie and I should go somewhere remote—a hotel or a B and B."

"Somewhere I'm not?" he challenged. "Is that more to the point, Isabelle?"

"No," she retorted quickly. "I was only questioning whether Amanda and your mother and the bridal party would be descending on your family home for the wedding."

"Thankfully, no. Our village church wouldn't accommodate the masses, so the wedding is in Sussex, near the Harrington estate. I can assure you that the wedding party will be heading south from London, in the opposite direction to us."

She'd been playing with her drink again, turning the glass within her hands, but they stilled on the last word. Her gaze lifted to his. "Does *us* include Chessie?"

"She is welcome," he replied. "Although earlier she mentioned how much she is enjoying London and the galleries."

"Her idea of heaven."

"Then perhaps she would prefer to stay here."

She took less than a second to catch on, for her shoulders to straighten. "You would prefer her to stay here. Be honest—that is what you are really saying, isn't it?"

"I would prefer you to myself, Isabelle, with no interruptions."

His voice slowed and deepened, his message clearly reflected in her eyes. Suddenly they were back in the car, his hands on her thighs, hers fumbling with his buttons, their breathing hot and impatient. But when he signalled his intent to act, putting down his glass with a decisive thunk and shifting his body weight to his feet, she backed away. Just a few steps before she changed course, circling around to put the huge desk between them.

From that position of safety, she levelled him a steady gaze. "What are you proposing?"

"A weekend in the country, no pretence or coercion, just you and me and a dozen polo ponies. As to what else…" Without losing eye contact, he reached down and snagged the polo ball from the desk. He rolled it slowly across the impressive breadth of timber and into her hands. "That ball is yours to play, Isabelle. I'm in your hands."

"I don't need you as a babysitter, and you know it. You're using me as an excuse," Chessie accused after hearing of last night's invitation. Isabelle had badgered her sister into accompanying her on a morning walk—not Chessie's favourite activity—to talk about her reaction to "Harry's" surprise identity. But within a block Chessie had hijacked the conversation and turned the walk into a stroll. Feigning fatigue, she sunk to a bench in the centre of the square and narrowed her perceptive eyes on Isabelle's still-standing figure. "You're afraid of what might happen. A whole weekend alone with the delicious Cristo. You are such a chicken."

"You're a fine one to talk about cowardice," Isabelle countered hotly. She couldn't sit; she itched with the need to keep walking, to clear her woolly head after a sleepless night. To feel like her normal, sensible self again. "You could have gone to New York. You've already flown halfway around the world to find this man."

"And what I found out last night is enough for now. Give me a week to digest all that…."

"A week? Your decisions usually take less than a second."

"Usually I'm not considering anything more important than blue dress or skinny jeans." Chessie's eyes held hers, her expression serious for at least a second before she gave a rueful shrug. "Course, in a few days I'll probably wish I had taken up Cristo's generous offer, but for now I'm happy with my choice. You, on the other hand, are not."

Trust her little sister to see right through her restless irritability. Last night Cristo hadn't accepted what he called her knee-jerk answer. Initially that had revolved around her employment contract—how could she go away for a weekend when her job was to keep Chessie and Amanda apart?

He'd responded by giving her the weekend off and suggesting she sleep on it—ha!—and he would ask again when he returned from wherever he'd flown today. He'd told her where, but the name was unfamiliar and possibly unspellable. Yet another sign, she'd reasoned during the hours she'd lain awake and then paced her spacious bedroom, of the disparity in their lifestyles. Yet another reason to resist this mad attraction.

"I'm not happy because of all this." She gestured widely around her, at the rows of stately town houses, the chauffeur opening the door of a Rolls Royce at number twelve, the woman emerging decked head to foot in high couture. She waved her hand at her own chain-store jeans. "Belgravia is not me, Chess."

"Then perhaps you need a break in the country."

"You think Chisholm Park will be anything less?"

"How do you know? Aren't you curious, just a little bit?"

"No," Isabelle snapped. But when Chessie caught her hand and tugged, she subsided to the seat at her side. She sighed heavily. "Not a bit curious. A lot."

Ever since he'd told her that Chisholm Park was his home, and she'd sensed his impatience to be there. That hunger to know more had been fed last night, when he'd diverted Chessie with news of Gisele and polo and she'd eaten up every scrap of information. She remembered the man in Melbourne, so pumped and fizzing with earthy vitality after a morning riding with Judd Armitage.

This was the man she hungered to know, the real man, the one who'd looked into her eyes last night and spoken with stripped-bare sincerity.

No pretence or coercion, just you and me and a dozen polo ponies.

"I am afraid," she admitted now, "of how much I want to go. You know me, Chess. I don't do weekend romps."

"I know, but what if it's more than that?" Chessie argued. "He's invited you to his home."

Isabelle scoffed dismissively. She had to, to counteract the mad skitter of her heart. "It's only a weekend."

"If that's all it is, then why not go and satisfy your curiosity? What have you got to lose?"

Eleven

Cristo didn't return from places unpronounceable to seek her answer; he sent a car. According to the message delivered midafternoon in a clipped, haven't-a-second-to-waste tone by his executive assistant, he'd been delayed unavoidably. A car would collect her at 8:00 p.m. sharp.

"Like a package to be delivered," Isabelle grumbled after the call's abrupt disconnection. "I wonder if his housekeeper will have to sign for me?"

"Probably won't need to," Chessie replied. "Isn't his country pile quite close to the airport he uses? He might well be there when you're tossed out on the doorstep. Just waiting to unwrap you."

He wasn't.

After spending the interminable stop-start drive on tenterhooks, trying her best not to imagine those clever hands undressing her, Isabelle was left deflated. Not because she was

looking forward to that doorstep unwrapping. She was too
annoyed by his presumptuous sending of a car. She should
have sent it packing; she shouldn't have been swayed by
Chessie's prodding or by the whispery hopes of *what if....*

*What if he really did feel the same attraction, the same ex-
plosion of sunfire in every touch? What if this was more than
chemistry, more than a passing intrigue?*

Unfortunately, a part of her had succumbed to that notion.
Just a small part, mind, because she was altogether too prag-
matic to imagine that plain, ordinary, been-nowhere, done-
nothing Isabelle Browne could be anything but a momentary
novelty to a man like Cristo Verón. Another part of her—a hot,
dangerous, newly awakened part—ached to be that passing
novelty. She'd always thought ahead, made the sensible
choices, gone with the unselfish options. If she was ever going
to throw caution to the wind and do something just to please
herself and hang the consequences, this was her chance.

It was a heady, exciting notion. She could almost hear her
sister cheering her on…and that was enough to create huge
trepidation. Chessie had a habit of throwing caution to the
wind, and now she was dealing with the consequences.

Despite her emotions careening in every direction, somewhere along the A1 Isabelle managed to doze off. She missed
the anticipated rush of seeing Chisholm Park for the first
time, which only added to the disappointment of being met
by the housekeeper. Meredith, a tall, stylish redhead who
didn't wear a uniform, told her that Cristo would not be home
for hours yet. There followed a quick tour of the house,
peppered by directions of "this room is" and "over there you'll
find" that Isabelle was too unfocussed to take aboard.

After Isabelle declined the offer of supper, tea or anything
from the kitchen, Meredith prepared to leave. "Cristo said you

should make yourself at home. Do you remember where everything is? The kitchen and the library and his sitting room with the big-screen tele?"

Isabelle said yes, she remembered, since she had no intention of exploring the endless corridors or of sitting up to welcome him home. Unsure whether she would stay, she didn't unpack. She took her time preparing for bed; she imagined she would still be tossing and turning long after eleven. But after a cursory round of tosses and turns, she surrendered to the thick embrace of her down duvet and slept dreamlessly until after six. For the first time in weeks she felt deeply rested and ready to face the day. Outside birds chattered with early morning industry, but the house slept on. She hurried down two flights of stairs and out the front door without drawing breath. She craved her morning walk, her thinking time, before she faced any conversation or decisions.

It was a splendid morning for walking. In the splintered sunlight of the tree-lined driveway, the air was shivery cool despite her sweater and jeans and she set off at a brisk pace, her mind only on the task of exercise. But soon it grew impossible to ignore the birdcalls, and the drumming vibration of an unseen woodpecker slowed her pace as she skimmed the treetops in a vain attempt to locate the creature. As her view widened, she was captured by a cluster of horses, sleek and glossy beneath the clear sky, and as she continued to turn in a slow circle the house came into view and her eyes boggled.

If she'd thought the Belgravia town house was something, then this was something else.

Three storeys of red-brick stateliness stood like a rosy castle amid endless acres of verdant parkland.

"Chisholm Park indeed," she murmured as she scanned the sweeps of grass broken by uncontrived plantings of leafy herbage and trees. Oaks and beeches and ashes—and, over to the west, beyond a dense wooded thicket, she caught the gleam of sunlight on water.

Intrigued, she turned off the driveway and cut across an open field, her stride lengthening as she followed the downhill slope until she found a better vantage point for what turned out to be a small lake. It was picture perfect, a movie set, beyond anything she'd imagined.

Seeking a closer view, she continued on, following a pathway until the ground levelled out. She paused when she heard the distant sound of galloping hooves. Curious, she changed direction through a wooded grove and exited onto a closely mown field where a trio of horses and riders raced in hot pursuit of a polo ball. She recognised it from the one Cristo had rolled across the desk. She recognised Cristo in the same heartbeat, despite the face-shadowing helmet. In white breeches and long tan boots, he manoeuvred his shiny black steed to overtake the others with languid ease.

Isabelle was riveted.

Yes, she'd seen him at polo practice before—she'd commented on his prowess at the Mornington restaurant—but that day she had watched from a distance. She'd not been close enough to feel the ground reverberate beneath thundering hooves, to smell the earthy mix of horse and turf, to hear the urgent calls that signalled the next play. Today she'd wandered right onto the edge of the action, and she watched transfixed as the threesome powered by. Cristo led the charge at breakneck speed, and when he leaned precariously low over the horse's side, her breath caught in alarm.

But with effortless skill he swung the stick in a smooth arc and smacked the ball beneath his horse's neck and out of the others' reach.

They wheeled to follow, and Isabelle's heart resumed beating with renewed exhilaration. Grinning widely, she lifted her hands to applaud and then realised that the ball was rocketing across the grass toward her. She didn't want to interrupt their practice; she would have scooted back into the shelter of the trees, but then Cristo spotted her.

His head came up, a new alertness in his posture, and Isabelle knew his gaze had locked on her. She felt the ripple of awareness down her spine, the jump of her pulse, the curl of honeyed heat in her stomach, and she couldn't move. With an infinitesimal lift of his hands, he slowed his horse, and she heard him call the others to stop play.

The ball's pace slowed on the thicker outer grass, and Isabelle's heart thumped hard as she threw caution to the wind and took a decisive step to meet it. Intent on her rash purpose—would she roll it back or hand it to him?—she didn't notice the approaching horse until it cut through her path. The mallet's powerful swing was so near she felt the shift of air in its wake.

As she jumped out of harm's way, the rider lifted her head, and she recognised the venomous smirk of crimson lips. Madeleine. She recoiled reflexively, the punch of shock driving all the breath and heat and exhilaration from her body. Vaguely she registered the cold bark of anger in Cristo's voice as he called Madeleine to task, and then he was cantering toward her and vaulting from the saddle and striding to her side.

She was pretty sure he would have wrapped her in his arms if she'd not taken an evasive step and held up both hands to ward him off. She didn't want cosseting, and she didn't need his soothing sounds of concern. "I'm fine," she assured him, her voice brittle with sudden anger. "Obviously she needs the practice. Her shot was way off."

He cursed, or at least that's what she gathered. The word was foreign—she was going on tone and the way he ripped off his helmet and glove and tossed them the way of his mallet. Helmet hair, she noted snippily, but then he raked a hair through the flattened crown and turned his fierce gaze on her and for a moment her synapses tied themselves in knots. Which, when she started to think again, only made her madder.

"I'm going to resume my walk now. Is it safe to continue this way—" she indicated the path along the side of the field "—or should I go back the way I came?"

"I'll walk with you," he said.

"Protection? Is that necessary?"

She started to move away, but he stopped her with a hand on her shoulder, turning her back toward him. She felt like slapping the hand away, but beyond his broad shoulders she could see the two horses, two riders, waiting and watching. She was not about to give Madeleine and friend the benefit of front-row seats to any display of disillusioned fury.

"You had a right to be angry, even before Madeleine's stunt," he said. "I meant what I said about this weekend. I didn't invite her here."

"You don't owe me any explanation," she said tightly.

"Yes, I do." Cupping both shoulders, he held her steady. Forced her to meet his gaze. "Madeleine is playing in a charity tournament tomorrow. This morning she discovered that one of her ponies is lame. She needs a replacement."

"And she thought of you."

"She thought of me, the team sponsor, who she knows is not playing tomorrow and will therefore have spare ponies."

Oh. She swallowed. "Why aren't you playing?" she couldn't resist asking.

"I have other plans."

Those other plans pulsed between them for a long moment, and Isabelle felt a change in his grip, saw a new tension in the set of his jaw. He was waiting for her to object, to tell him that her plans had suddenly changed, and three seconds ago he would have been right on the money. But now… "You were going to play?" she asked, needing to know for sure. "Until these other plans came along?"

"Yes."

"You didn't have to do that on my account. I might have enjoyed a day at the polo."

"With Madeleine playing?" he asked dryly. "Not a good idea."

"She wasn't meaning to run me down." The ache of conflict eased from her chest and suddenly she felt magnanimous, even toward Madeleine. "She knew there was room to spare."

Again his grip tightened and so did the corners of his mouth. "Whatever she meant, it was a foolhardy stunt. I shouldn't have let her onto the field this morning. She was already in a snit."

"Because you're not playing tomorrow?" she guessed.

"Because of my replacement," he corrected.

"Is there someone else she dislikes as much as me, or is it because the stand-in is not as good a player?"

He laughed, the sound unexpected and acutely sexy. "My replacement is the great Alejandro Verón. He is a ten-goal player."

"This is better than you?"

"That's as good as it gets," he said. "My brother is a professional. I don't play nearly enough to approach his standard."

He spoke as a matter of fact, not arrogant, just supremely confident that with sufficient games he too would be one of the best. Isabelle wondered if there was anything he didn't do supremely well. A shiver danced through her, and when his gaze narrowed intently and the tenor of his grip changed, she knew he'd sensed it, seen it… For whatever reason, he knew. Perhaps it glowed like an aura of lust around her.

It was too much, too soon, and she flicked her gaze toward his horse. Still standing, obediently still, where he'd been abandoned, except… "Is your horse supposed to be eating your glove?" she asked slowly.

Amusement glimmered in his eyes as they flicked over the horse and then returned to her face. "Perhaps he is hungry. Have *you* eaten, Isabelle?"

Her stomach had bottomed out. Hunger, yes, although not only for food. "Not yet."

"Let's return to the stables, and then I will treat you to the best breakfast in the home counties."

The village pub was only a couple of kilometres across country. They could have walked, and another day they would, but by the time they'd finished up at the stables and he'd showered and changed, Cristo was starving. He grabbed Isabelle's hand and tugged her toward the garage. When she caught sight of the array of vehicles, he had to tug even harder.

"Are these all yours?" she asked. It was the same question and the same awed expression as when she'd walked into the stables and clocked all the heads poking out into the central alley.

"Not this time." He towed her toward his Aston and popped the doors. "This one's mine. The rest were Alistair's. They're Amanda's now. She hasn't the heart to sell them."

When he gunned the car down the drive, he spied Isabelle stroking the leather seat and that brought out a satisfied grin. "It does that, doesn't it?"

Their eyes met and shared the moment, the purr of the powerful engine, the warmth of a perfect May morning, the silent promise of the weekend ahead. He reached for her hand, felt the rocket of response from that simple touch. "I'm glad you came," he said.

"And if I hadn't?"

"I would have driven to London. I would have changed your mind."

Breakfast was in the restaurant attached to a quaint village pub that was full of old English charm and customers. Unsurprising, really, given the breakfast was as good as Cristo had promised. They ate and they talked, picking up the conversation started on the short drive.

Isabelle discovered more about Chisholm Park, including how Alistair had bought the place as a failed means of keeping Vivi happy. He'd renovated extensively, adding stables for horse-mad Cristo and a poolhouse for Amanda and the lake for his wife. "And for himself?" Isabelle asked.

"He chose this location convenient to the headquarters of Chisholm Air. When marriage failed him, the business he loved did not."

She learned more about the business, casual information interspersed with telling observations that suggested Cristo had inherited his stepfather's love of Chisholm Air along with his chairmanship and stock holdings. Isabelle's mood was a peculiar mix of comfort from the easy conversation and gathering despair because every anecdote reinforced the disparity in their positions and their beliefs.

His cynicism toward love and marriage and his attitude to business do not matter, she reminded herself. *This is make-believe. Just enjoy the moment.*

A neighbour stopped by their table and asked about the prospects of the Chisholm Hawks in tomorrow's tournament.

Briefly they analysed the competition, expert opinion maintaining that if Cristo's brother was in form, the Hawks would win with several goals to spare. "See you tomorrow, then," Will said, "and you, Isabelle."

"I hope so." She returned his hearty smile, then watched him leave.

"I trust you were only being polite."

"Yes…and no." Isabelle worried at her bottom lip. "Look, I know you're not playing and that was on my behalf, but from what Will said, this Sovereign's Plate tournament is a big deal, and your brother's appearance even more so."

"I can see A.J. anytime," he said with an offhand shrug, but there was nothing casual in the banked heat of his gaze when it lifted from her mouth to her eyes. "Unless there is a reason you want to go to tomorrow's game?"

"Other than meeting your brother?"

"You don't want to meet him."

"Why ever not?" Isabelle asked, her curiosity piqued. "Are you alike?"

"I'm told there is a resemblance, but only in appearance. I am the good brother," he said, an edge of humour sparking his dark eyes.

"And Alejandro is bad?"

"The worst."

"Is this why I don't want to meet him?"

"This is why I do not want you to meet him," he said, and the possessiveness of that statement caused a delicious tightening in her stomach. A heaviness in her breasts. And the certainty that this brother—the good one—could make her feel very, very bad. "Nor do I intend sharing you with every inquisitive neighbour who stops by."

"Isn't that what you wanted me for at the gala?"

"Unless you want me to remind you exactly what I want—" again those eyes glittered, again her body tightened —with half of Herting Green leaning sideways in their chairs to eavesdrop, I suggest we get out of here."

"Will you tell me, then?"

"Better than that, Isabelle. I will show you."

Twelve

He showed her with a steamy kiss the instant they wer
cocooned in the privacy of his car. It was hot and open
mouthed, a kiss packed with carnal intent and controlled ag
gression, the kiss they'd started in the backseat of the lim
turned up another ten notches.

It was exactly what Isabelle needed to wipe her mind fre
of the nagging what-the-hell-are-you-doing-here? doubts tha
had resurfaced while he settled the bill.

Closing her eyes to the late-morning brightness, she sur
rendered instantly, completely, absorbing the scent of leathe
and man, the enticing pressure of his thumbs at the corner
of her mouth, the strong taste of coffee on his tongue. She'
given up the brew, fearing her reliance, and now she knew th
taste would be forever etched in this long, hot tangle o
mouths and the shudder of longing deep in her core.

When he finally broke away, the passion of their embrac

throbbed in the overheated air and in the dark smoulder of his eyes. "Home?" he asked.

"Yes."

Two words, their first since he'd ushered her from the restaurant, and perfectly enough. He strapped their seat belts and started the engine, and the Aston's bark of response echoed through her blood. Pulling out of the car park, they had to wait for an elderly lady to pass. Cristo's fingers drummed an impatient beat on the steering wheel. Isabelle wondered if her need was as nakedly apparent.

Across the street, a family exited the village store, two children intent on ice creams, their mother on talking a toddler down from a tantrum. A normal day, with people going about their Saturday morning activities, while she was being whisked back to a country estate in a midnight-blue Aston Martin by a polo-playing millionaire.

That should have freaked her out, but she felt unusually confident. She also knew that her emotions could quickly cartwheel out of control, especially if she allowed herself to think. "Do you have music?" she asked.

He flicked...something...and the seductive rhythms of Ravel filled the silence.

She smiled at the choice, and when he lifted an enquiring brow, she told him how she'd imagined his entrance music as Ravel the day he arrived in Melbourne. "Not 'La Valse,'" she added, recognising the obsessive darkness in this piece. "Something smoother."

"I saw you dancing that day," he said. Her eyes widened in surprise. "Past one of the windows. You were not what I expected."

"What were you expecting?"

"Superficial beauty...the kind that used to attract Hugh."

"I didn't strike you as Hugh's type?"

"No." Briefly his glance left the road, caught on hers. "You struck me as mine."

Then he reached for her hand, brought it to his thigh, and the hard muscle shifting with every gear change honed her desire to a sharp edge. She wanted both hands on him without the denim barrier—without any barrier—and she wanted his hands on her and his undiverted gaze when she asked him to tell her again.

You struck me as mine.

She'd been achingly aware of him, of his eyes following her as she'd shown him around the house, but she'd never allowed herself to believe it was personal. That he might be drawn to her despite her ugly grey uniform. But when he turned off the engine in the garage and unbuckled his belt and then hers, perhaps he saw the hint of wonder in her eyes because he paused and his expression narrowed.

"You are not having second thoughts," he said. No question, a statement of fact.

"No." Isabelle swallowed, unaccountably nervous despite the certainty of her response. "Although now might be a very good time to remind me of what you want."

"In words?"

"That would depend on the words."

"Indeed," he said slowly, drawing the word out and studying her with enough erotic speculation to burn the clothes from her body. Words did not matter when he looked at her that way, or when he turned an ordinary word into a thing of honeyed beauty with his clever tongue.

All the way from garage to bedroom he put that tongue to wicked purpose, telling her in rich, raw detail exactly what he wanted to do with her, to her, in her. Halfway up the stairs he paused to study her feverish face. "Hot?" he asked.

She managed a strangled *hmm* of assent, so he peeled away her sweater and camisole in one smooth motion. The glancing heat of his hands against her skin almost brought her to her knees. The flare of his nostrils as he studied the swollen rise of her breasts did cause her thighs to tremble. She might have melted right there, a pool of undone woman on the ornate staircase, if he'd not scooped her up in his arms.

It was so unexpected that she released a breath of surprised laughter. "You didn't mention your need to carry me."

"Humour me."

"Happy to."

He'd reached the landing and paused, his expression all male satisfaction as he looked into her face. "On all counts?"

The detail of his very specific requests burned hot in her skin, but her female parts danced with unembarrassed excitement. She smiled, a softly wanton curve of her lips that caused Cristo's nostrils to flare and his eyes to glitter with piercing heat. "Are we starting with the staircase?" she asked.

"We are starting in my bed."

"And finishing where?"

"Paradise."

She laughed, an earthy ripple of sound that stroked every massively aroused cell in Cristo's body. He felt like he'd been hard for hours, days, weeks. He felt like he could remain so, riding this crest of desire until he could no longer stand, until there were no ways left to have her. One weekend was too finite, too short, and the thought tore at his patience.

He shouldered open the door to his suite, kicked it shut behind them, and the solid thud shut down the clamour for instant gratification. He did not want quick, not this first time. He wanted it exactly as he'd spelled out on the stairs.

Slow. Deep. Thorough.

He turned to lower her against the door, holding her upright between the hard throb of his body and the thick slab of timber. He kissed her with the laughter fresh on her lips, lost himself in the sweet passion of her mouth and then in the torturous ache of her hands on his skin. They'd burrowed beneath his shirt to skim his back, his shoulders, the curve of his biceps, but it was not enough.

"Pull it off," he breathed between kisses, and when she'd dispensed with his shirt the spill of her breasts from low-cut lace burned against his chest. He held her higher, enough that he could lick at the swell of flesh and tug the engorged nipple between his teeth. She cried out, a tortured pant of wanting, and he obliged, dedicating himself to each breast in turn until she writhed beneath him.

He needed skin against skin.

Dios, he ached to be inside her.

She hooked arms and legs around him as he carried her to the bed, as he pulled back and discarded the covers and took her down onto the cool sheets. He reared back, enough to strip her of bra and jeans and underpants, enough to dispense of his, and then they came together in a crackle of lust. The perfection of her softly rounded body, the mix of vanilla sweetness and earthy spices, the throaty gasp of his name on her lips when his fingers delved between her legs—everything about her drove him crazy with greed. He could not kiss her in enough places, caress her long enough, when all he wanted was everything at once.

When she took him in her hands, her touch was a contradictory mix of boldness and explorative innocence that snapped his restraint. He pressed a long, hot kiss to her mouth, to each breast, to the feminine curve of her belly, and then he rolled away to don protection. She arched up to meet his return, and he linked their hands and stretched them high above their heads as he lowered himself between her thighs and sunk into her welcoming heat.

"Look at me," he said thickly, compelling Isabelle's gaze back to his as he slid deeper and started to move in a slow, rolling pace that sealed their connection and rocked against every sweet spot. He maintained that deep eye contact when he took her mouth, when he kissed her with the same sensual rhythm, and when she arched her back with the first shuddering grasp of her climax, he could no longer control his response.

The tension gathered in every muscle, coiled around the base of his spine, and her fingers clung tightly to his as his synapses snapped with the powerful surge of his release.

Isabelle hated the aftermath of sex. She didn't know how to act, what to say, whether to speak at all. To her inexperienced mind, there seemed dangers at every turn, when the mind turned mushy with lust suddenly clicked back to clarity and thought, *Uh-oh. Was I too wanton, too passive, too needy? Should I ask after the nail marks in his hand, offer to apply Band-Aids if I broke the skin? Is it better to take my cue from him, or to be proactive and ask what happens next?*

And that was without the practical aspects of retrieving clothes strewn from here to midday.

God, she'd let him strip her on the stairs.

The thought of Meredith finding her things on the staircase caused her to jackknife upright. Cristo hadn't said anything since returning from the bathroom; she'd wondered if he might be asleep, but she felt the weight of his hand on her back, the gliding touch of his fingertips against her shoulder blade. "What is it?" he asked. His voice sounded heavy with a yawn, and that very human sign gave her the courage to turn and meet his gaze.

"I just remembered my clothes are on the stairs," she admitted.

The mild enquiry in his eyes turned warmly teasing. "And your tidy housekeeper's mind is offended?"

"I was thinking more of your housekeeper, actually. I don't want her picking up after me or thinking…"

"That you're spending the day in bed with me? I'm sure Meredith wouldn't give that a second thought."

Because she's used to it? Isabelle wanted to ask, but didn't. Afraid the miserable jab of jealousy might show in her face, she looked away. "I would rather she didn't find them," she said stiffly, "that's all."

The weight of his hand shifted, its pressure encouraging her to relax back into the pillows. She resisted, waiting for his response. "Unless you leave them there until Monday," he said, "none of my staff will find them."

"Don't they work on the weekends?"

"Not this one. I told you, Isabelle," he continued when her gaze shifted back to his, "I planned for these days to be just us."

He hadn't wanted any staff on duty. Because of all the places he wanted to strip her? To have her? Heat bloomed beneath her skin at the memory of his incendiary words, of each and every steamy promise. "Were you that confident?"

"No," he replied, but his expression, his posture, his satisfied smile were all supremely confident. "I was more…hopeful."

"Did your hopefulness extend to us ending up here in your bed after you took me to breakfast?"

"This has pretty much ruined my plans for today."

Teasing, Isabelle knew, so she took no umbrage. "What had you planned?"

"A long drive."

"To show me the sites of Hertfordshire?"

"To have you to myself, to let the Aston work its magic.

For sightseeing, nothing beats a helicopter," he added, "especially when you take along a picnic and put down wherever takes your fancy."

"That was quite a day you had planned," Isabelle said, impressed despite herself.

"I thought I would have my work cut out," he admitted, and although his tone maintained the lightness of the preceding banter, there was something in his gaze that coiled tight in Isabelle's stomach. Then he grinned, a ridiculously sexy and satisfied smile that belied any question of doubt. "For you, Isabelle, I had planned a serious day of wooing."

Wooing. It was such a delightfully old-fashioned word and such a romantic notion that Isabelle couldn't help being charmed. She would not allow the tender loop of warmth to take hold, however, because it was only a word...a word wrapped up in that cockiest of grins. His plan had been to woo her into his bed, not to romance her, and for that he'd needed no fancy props. He'd only needed the beguiling directness of his tongue.

"You don't have to impress me with grand gestures," she said, "or with your expensive toys."

"Not even the helicopter?"

"Not even."

"I see." The tilt of his smile shifted from cocky to unholy as his hand drifted from her shoulders to the small of her back. "In that case, I shall have to impress you in other ways."

"Will this involve us leaving this bed?"

His fingertips traced the curve of her buttocks. A languid, tantalising signal of intent. "Not for a very long time."

"Stay," Chessie implored on Monday morning. "There is no reason not to."

Only guilt, Isabelle thought, because when Cristo suggested that she stay on at Chisholm Park until the wedding, her acceptance had come easily and without any consideration for her sister's plight. Perhaps because he'd asked while looking deep into her eyes and filling her just as deeply with the heavy heat of his desire.

"Why don't you come out here?" Isabelle said into the phone. "There is no reason not to."

"There is, actually," Chessie replied after a beat of pause. "Colin has tickets to the Chelsea Flower Show."

"Colin?"

"Crash. His real name is Colin Ashcroft, but I am so over nicknames. Did you know he was at school with Cristo? And he paints. Seriously good stuff."

Isabelle frowned, uncomfortable with Chessie's familiarity with the intriguing butler. "You're not getting too friendly, are you?"

"Romantically? Good grief, no. Colin is looking after me, which I'm sure is the job he's been assigned with you and Cristo out of town. Plus, he knows people." Chessie managed to imbue those last few words with enough profundity that Isabelle knew she meant Justin Harrington. "I would rather be picking his brain than mouldering away in the country."

After being assured there was little mouldering in Herting Green, Chessie consented to come out early the following week, after she'd pored over all the exhibits and Kew Gardens and several other must-sees for an apprentice landscape designer.

Isabelle tried not to be too selfishly pleased to have Cristo and Chisholm Park to herself for a whole week. She loved the place and the effortlessness with which she fitted in. Even when he was working, sometimes at the Luton offices, sometimes in lengthy phone conferences from home, she didn't rattle around or feel lost. She pitched in and helped Meredith and the stable staff. Chloe was even teaching her to ride on the quietest of ponies. Those regular doses of reality helped balance out the fairy-tale aspects of being Cristo Verón's lover.

She vowed to maintain that make-believe, to keep things light, to remember that he'd not promised anything beyond the wedding, but her vows were tested from day one. That was the polo tournament, when he capitulated to her wishes and took her to see the final games. It should have been easy to keep her perspective, seeing him greeting friends in the posh and privileged crowd, but he moved just as easily amongst the grooms and spent most of the afternoon at Isabelle's side.

She wasn't sure if she liked the frantic pace and violent clashes; she found it easier to watch Cristo, to revel in his exhilaration and the pride he took in Chloe's game. Driving to the grounds she'd learned that his young groom was replacing Madeleine on the team. "I will not allow her to get away with yesterday's stunt," he said shortly. "She put you and the pony in needless danger."

Chloe, it turned out, was well up to the task.

"She's good," Isabelle decided, watching her slight figure ride another player off the ball with fearless gusto. Cristo nodded, an answer to her question and a signal of approval when his brother pounced on the loose ball and fired an effortless goal to put the Hawks into the lead. Whatever else he said was lost in the roar of applause and in Isabelle's response when he swung her up in a close embrace and kissed her soundly. Not a peck but a full-blooded this-is-my-woman kiss for all to see.

"Is that how you celebrate every goal?" she asked.

Cristo's grin grew warm as he slid her down his body until her feet touched ground. "You should see how I celebrate a win."

Isabelle did get to see that night, when he swept her home

and made good with another of his promises. Champagne sipped from her skin, he told her, tasted sweeter than any victory. And Isabelle kept her perspective by noting that the champagne was an obscenely expensive vintage. The stuff of fairy tales, it bore no relation to her real life.

Another day he took her sightseeing in a helicopter bearing the Chisholm Air logo. *His* logo, to all intents and purposes, because he casually admitted that he owned a majority share in the company. She'd figured as much, but this confirmation of his wealth put him in a different stratosphere. One where she could not exist without an oxygen mask or a housekeeper's uniform.

Then he brought her down to reality by taking her to dinner at the village pub, this time on foot so he could introduce her to Gisele, the mare who'd almost died while he was in Melbourne and who was now recuperating nicely. Watching him stroke her neck, listening to the deep affection in his voice as he told her about the pony's courage and bravery, turned Isabelle's heart upside down and inside out.

Another evening he brought home an extravagant picnic basket and drove her in the Aston to a secluded spot by the lake. "I had tickets to Glyndebourne tonight," he admitted later, stretching out beside her on the picnic rug. His hand dipped lazily beneath her skirt. "I hope you don't mind, but they frown on making out on the lawns there."

"Stuffy of them," she replied. "I'm glad we didn't go."

"Because you fancy making out on the grass or because you don't like the opera?"

"I've never been."

His hand drifted higher. "So you're an opera virgin?"

"I guess I am," she managed, although his questing fingertips made her feel very unvirginal.

"How do you know you don't like something you've never tried?"

Isabelle's eyes drifted shut. She didn't want to talk, especially about opera. She wanted those clever fingers to really apply themselves to something she did like. But they'd stilled, and when she peered beneath her lowered lids she found him waiting patiently for her answer. "I don't care much for operatic melodrama," she said. "Had enough of it in my childhood."

"Your parents?" he guessed, giving up the seductive intent and turning her until her face rested on his sun-warmed chest. "Tell me about them."

"It's a long story."

"As is many an opera."

She huffed out a laugh. "Then I guess I will start with the opera, which is where my parents met. Working," she added. "My mother was a moderately successful soprano, my father a set director."

"Your love of music is no accident, then?"

"There was always music," Isabelle said with a shrug. "At home, and the lessons they signed us up for. Piano, drama, voice, art. Luckily neither Chessie nor I had the talent or the desire to pursue them."

"Luckily?"

Usually she hated talking about her upbringing, but in the sun-tinged evening with his hand idly stroking her hair she felt relaxed and encouraged. He wanted to know—he wanted to know *her*. "I would not want the life of my parents," she replied with heartfelt fervour. "They travelled constantly, often not together because they were working on different productions. They didn't even have a home."

"Did you travel with your mother?" he asked. The play of

his hand in her hair was no longer lazy; its weight rested a moment, strong and comforting.

"When I was a baby, yes, but then I needed to start school and my mother was pregnant with Chessie. We moved in with my grandparents in Melbourne—Poppy was alive then, too— and that was a disaster." A rueful smile ghosted across her lips. "So many fights, about everything. My father left and my mother started taking jobs, as well. In the end we just spent more and more time with our grandparents."

"What happened to your parents?"

"They visited between seasons, they sent cards and presents for our birthdays, but then my father died. I don't know what happened, but after the funeral there was a big row—Mother brought this horrid new man with her—and we didn't see her again. It was okay," she hastened to add. "In fact, after all the clashes, there was finally some peace in the house, and Gran...she was wonderful."

"I know."

Intrigued, Isabelle rolled onto her side and pushed up onto her elbow. "How do you know?"

"She taught you everything you know, and look how you turned out."

Isabelle smiled into his eyes, unable to hide the pleasure she took from that compliment. It was the perfect ending to the conversation, the perfect endorsement of the grandmother she'd adored, and when he reached for her, his hand strong and warm on her neck, and drew her down into his kiss, she felt an overwhelming swell of emotion inside.

She loved him, not only for this perfect evening or the connection they'd forged this past week, but because of everything she knew of him. His responsibility to his family, his protectiveness of Amanda, his regard for his staff and his animals, his loyalty to the Delahuntys and his stepfather's memory. Even his exasperated dealings with Vivi reflected his deep affection. Every day there was something else, some new facet, and yet she had barely scraped the surface of Cristo Verón.

There was still so much to learn, and for an instant she felt a mild rush of panic because she had so little time and soon this idyll would be over. But then his hands slid up her thighs to cradle her buttocks, and the kiss took fire and burned through her anxiety, leaving only the purest of truths.

She loved him, and for now that was enough.

Thirteen

"Are you expecting visitors?"

Chloe waved her polo stick in the direction of the driveway, and Isabelle turned in her saddle—gingerly, since she still didn't trust herself not to spook her horse with a clumsy movement—and caught a familiar silhouette gliding in and out of view between the trees. Tonight Cristo was flying to Russia, an unavoidable meeting, and for a moment she'd hoped he might have cut short today's business. But no, this was the town car not his Aston Martin.

"My sister," she told Chloe. How like Chessie to arrive a day early and without warning…although she rather fancied shocking Chessie with her brand-new skill. In jodhpurs and long boots borrowed from Chloe, she even looked the part. "Can we ride down and greet her?"

"Don't see why not." Turning her pony around, Chloe whistled her dog Otto to heel and led their sedate procession across the parkland toward the house. Isabelle's intrepid skill was yet to progress beyond a walk. "Keep a firm hand on your reins," Chloe called over her shoulder. "Dini has quite a fondness for the shrubbery."

Isabelle kept a firm hand on her reins and a firm eye on her pony in case appetite overwhelmed his calm nature. She paid no heed to the car or its occupant until Chloe said, "Your sister doesn't exactly travel light, does she?"

The driver added another piece to the mountain of matched luggage at the foot of the stairs, and Isabelle shook her head. "I don't think that's Chessie's." In fact she knew it wasn't, even before a stylishly attired stranger stepped from behind the car and into view.

From this distance she bore no physical resemblance to Cristo, and yet Isabelle instinctively knew that this was his mother.

"It's Vivi," Chloe confirmed. "I wonder what she's doing here?"

"Another wedding emergency, I imagine."

"Could be that." Chloe's eyes twinkled above a cheeky grin. "Or she's come to scope you."

"No," Isabelle said weakly. Then more strongly, "She has no reason to do that."

"You're the first girlfriend Cristo has ever brought here. I imagine that is reason enough."

As that message sunk in, Isabelle's heart skittered again. *The first girlfriend he'd brought here.* If Vivi knew—Vivi, who wanted him married to Madeleine—then that might explain her arrival. It certainly explained the sick pitch of Isabelle's stomach.

"Do you want to ride up and say hello?" Chloe asked.

"Good grief, no!"

And before she could laugh off that horrified response, the distinctive sound of a helicopter's approach had Otto barking and spinning in mad circles and Isabelle grabbing a better grip on Dini's reins. Chloe narrowed her gaze at the sky overhead before declaring, "The cavalry has arrived. You're saved!"

The cavalry was only one—but the right one, Isabelle reminded herself as she hurried from the stables to the helipad. With nerves threatening to chew holes right through her, she needed his reassurance as badly as her next breath. A quick word explaining that Vivi had called him home to discuss a wedding-planning issue. A smile, a kiss, an arm flung around her shoulder and an invitation to "Come meet my mother."

Any of the above would have worked, but then Isabelle saw him appear from beneath the whirling beat of the craft's rotors and straighten. She'd seen him in a suit and tie before—this past week she'd watched him dress from naked skin into full business attire on many a morning—but there was something in his bearing right now that pulled her up short. Shadowy wisps of foreboding fluttered through her, halting her headlong rush to intercept him.

Perhaps it was the dark aviator shades. Perhaps the flat set of his mouth, the tightness of his jaw. And perhaps it was the manner in which he'd arrived, sweeping in by helicopter in answer to his mother's summons. Whatever the cause, suddenly the stretch of lawn between them opened into a chasm of doubts. She'd spent a week in his company, she'd witnessed one sliver of his life and she'd allowed herself to believe she might fit. Standing there in her borrowed clothes, she felt like a fraud and a fool. The places she fit best were alongside Meredith in the kitchen and Chloe at the stables.

She would have turned tail and scarpered back to the stables if Meredith hadn't appeared from the back of the house, gesturing for her to come. Damn. In the mudroom she pulled off her boots and took stock of herself in Chloe's too-tight breeches and a no-longer-clean polo shirt. She wanted to run upstairs and change, but before she made the stairs the phone started to ring and she paused a moment too long. Meredith hurried through from the kitchen bearing a tea tray, and when she spotted Isabelle her relief was instant. "Will you take this through to the morning room for me, Isabelle? I'm expecting a call from Colin. This is likely him now."

What could she do?

Approaching the room, her feet grew heavy. The door stood ajar, and she could hear the two voices clearly. Vivi was bemoaning her morning's travel at melodramatic length. "My son owns half the private jets in this country," she sniffed, "and I am forced to fly commercial."

"No one forced you."

"You did, holing up down here with this Isabelle who I am hearing about from all quarters. Of course I needed to see what the fuss was all about."

"You are reading too much into this," Cristo said, his voice dismissively cool.

Apparently his mother could not be dismissed so easily because she went on, undeterred. "Madeleine tells me she works as a house cleaner. Is this true?"

"Yes," Isabelle said. "Quite true."

Years of practice came to the fore as she glided into the room and across the Aubusson rug to the tea table. The silence was perfect—not one rattle of cups, not a tinkle of spoons. She put down the tray with smooth efficiency and prepared to pour.

"Tea, Mrs...?" She left the query hanging, since she did not know Vivi's present name.

"Marais," the woman supplied, her smile warmer than Isabelle had expected. Up close she bore quite a likeness to her daughter, and like Amanda her eyes shone with undisguised interest as she took Isabelle in. "But you, Isabelle, shall call me Vivi as all my children do."

There was a beat of pause, an awkward moment. Isabelle did not know quite what to say. She'd been prepared for Vivi's coolness, hostility even, but this apparent amiability had thrown her.

"Speaking of children," Cristo interjected smoothly, but his eyes sparked with irritation as he moved to Isabelle's side and encouraged her to sit. "Where *is* your toyboy?"

"Patrizio has a showing," Vivi replied, seemingly unperturbed by her son's barb. "He will be following in a few days. I came early because I could not wait to meet your Isabelle."

Cristo said something low, foreign.

"Don't be rude," Vivi snapped.

"I learned my manners from you, Mother."

"Rubbish, we both know you have far better manners than I. Now—" she turned her attention to Isabelle "—I believe you are coming to the wedding? My son has not told me, but Amanda says this is so. We will need to rearrange the tables slightly, but this is not a problem."

"Amanda was kind to invite me, but I haven't decided if—"

"Why ever would you not?" Vivi interrupted. Then she looked from Isabelle to Cristo, her expression disingenuous. "Oh dear, have I put my shoe in it? When Amanda told me that Isabelle was your date for the Delahunty event and that you'd brought her to stay at your home, naturally I assumed this was more than an *amourette*...."

"What this is," Cristo said evenly, "is none of your business."

Vivi even managed to make her scoffing reply sound elegantly European.

"Aren't you needed in Sussex?" Cristo continued. "Surely the wedding preparations cannot run without your interference."

"Everything is ready," Vivi said, "according to that wedding planner who has not earned her overpriced fee. If she does create any more dilemmas, we shall manage them just as well from here. In the meantime, I am going to enjoy a few restful days with you and Isabelle. Now, the tea. Are you pouring, Isabelle?"

On the outside Cristo maintained an unaffected facade— over the years, he'd learned it was the only way to shake Vivi when she sunk her teeth into something. If she couldn't create a drama, she grew bored and moved on. Unfortunately she had latched on to his relationship with Isabelle today, of all days, and he did not have the luxury of wearing her down, nor could he delay his trip to Moscow.

He hated the necessity of leaving Isabelle, halving the time he had left with her before Saturday's wedding. If it were possible, he would take her with him, but the negotiations were delicate, the accommodations uncertain, and now there was Vivi. Ever since he received the message from his driver— too late to change the course of his mother's actions—he'd been quietly fuming. Mostly because he'd been so obsessed with getting Isabelle into his bed, he'd missed the obvious.

Of course Amanda and Madeleine and Lord knows who else would have told her about Isabelle. Why hadn't he anticipated her reaction? He did not bring casual girlfriends to Chisholm Park. He didn't take them to the polo or walk hand in hand with them through the village and French kiss them against the courtyard wall of the Maiden's Arms.

Now Vivi had met Isabelle and declared her approval. Taking the stairs two at a time, Cristo shuddered. He did not trust Vivi at the best of times; an acquiescent Vivi roused all his suspicions. He'd brought Isabelle to Chisholm Park to escape his family and their machinations. Now he would have to make other plans.

Isabelle had excused herself a little while back, saying she needed to change out of her riding clothes, and he found her just out of the shower and pulling on clean underwear. Brief. Lace. Dusky blue. The sight distracted him for a good long moment, until she shrugged into a clean blue shirt and started buttoning. If not for Vivi's arrival and the changed plans he needed to put into effect, he would have stalked across the room and started unbuttoning.

"I will have the car run you into London," he said. "You can spend the next few days at Wentworth Square."

She paused in her buttoning. Her expression was trickily composed, and he had no idea what she was thinking or feeling. "Because of Vivi?"

"What do you think?"

"I think you don't trust me to deal with your mother."

"I did not bring you here to deal with my family," Cristo said, "especially my mother, who will have you measured up for a wedding dress before I return."

Something shifted in her gaze, something he couldn't catch before she shook her head and laughed softly. "I'm pretty sure I can prevent your mother booking the church. You have nothing to worry about there. I am used to difficult clients and…"

"You are not the housekeeper," he said curtly.

"If you prefer me gone—" her gaze fixed on his, steady and searching for a long moment "—I can have my bag packed in five minutes."

Backed into a corner of his own making, Cristo had to let her stay. He was not happy. The edge remained until he'd unbuttoned her shirt and backed her against the dresser and used his fingers and mouth to bring her to a quick, shattering climax. And when he finally stripped away the lace and buried himself in her silken heat, he leaned forward and spoke with hot intensity against her ear. "This is why you are here and why you are staying. This—" he backed off slowly, enough that he could look into her eyes "—is why I will be doing everything in my power to finish this business swiftly. So you will be here in my bed when I return."

He had thought sex would settle his malcontent; that and putting the basis of their relationship into clear words. But Cristo's dissatisfaction escalated from the moment he left Chisholm Park. The caveman approach was not him, and it niggled that Isabelle had accepted his dictate without any response.

It niggled more when every attempt to call, to explain, to apologise failed.

In the morning she was out riding with Chloe; later she'd taken Vivi to lunch; and when his late-night call went unanswered, he could not settle without knowing she was all right. That neither his boorish tactics nor Vivi's demanding temperament had sent her running for the hills. He tried Crash, who knew nothing, except that Chessie was to remain with him for a few more days.

Stewing over his lack of foresight—not only regarding Vivi's guerrilla tactics; why hadn't he given Isabelle a mobile phone?—he paced and waited until Meredith returned his curt message. "There's no need to worry," she assured him. "Isabelle and Vivi are getting along famously. They've gone into London to meet with Amanda. Something to do with dress fittings."

That explanation did nothing to soothe Cristo's aggravation. He could just imagine Vivi railroading Isabelle into doing her bidding…and Isabelle allowing it. Jaw set tight, he punched the keys to Amanda's number. She answered sleepily, but when she recognised his voice and his cutting tone she immediately launched into a lengthy explanation.

"I suppose you're put out about the bridesmaid thing, but honestly I had no choice. I needed someone who would fit into the dress without major alterations. I was going to ask Madeleine, but I couldn't risk pairing her with Alejandro in the wedding party. You know what those two are like together," she said with an audible shudder. "But Isabelle is perfect."

Cristo swore softly. "As a replacement bridesmaid?"

"Harry's sister took a tumble from a horse. She's broken her collarbone and banged up her shoulder. Gia said she'll be fine by Saturday, that she'll do it with her arm in a sling, but her mother won't hear of it, and Vivi agrees. She suggested Isabelle as a replacement, and for once she has got it right!"

"Did Isabelle have any say in this?"

"She took some convincing," Amanda admitted. "She was talking about not coming to the wedding at all, and I rather gather that's because of you. Are you afraid she'll get ideas?"

"No," he said sharply, remembering with a flash of irritation how she'd coolly told him he had nothing to worry about on that score. "Isabelle is far too sensible for that."

"She is sensible, isn't she, and very capable. I suspect she is the queen of organization. I wish she'd been around to help me plan the wedding. She is going to speak to the caterers tomorrow, just to make sure everything's sorted. Oh, and she's arranged for Vivi to have a facial at Aylesbury while she's doing that, so she is also smart, your Isabelle. You should not let her get away!"

Cristo had spent the past week getting to know *his* Isabelle; he did not need his family's approval. Nor did he need her virtues spelled out, especially not in such a heavy-handed, she's-the-perfect-woman-for-you fashion. "I give you enough latitude in other areas," he told Amanda sternly, "but my love life is off-limits."

"Well, yes, but it concerns me that she says she is returning to Australia. Even though Bill and Gabrielle Thompson offered her a job."

Cristo went cold. He knew nothing of this job offer from a high-profile professional couple, nothing about any future decisions. During the past week, they'd skirted around that topic; he'd assumed she would wait until Francesca's plans were decided before looking ahead.

Yet she'd discussed this with his sister?

His antsiness snarled into more, and his tense silence was enough encouragement for Amanda to keep on talking. "I only know because we ran into them outside the Ritz tonight. Apparently Isabelle worked for them when they were in Australia last year, and they said to call them whenever she wanted a change of location. When they saw her here, they immediately made a firm offer, but she said she was going back to Australia."

"That's her home," Cristo said shortly, but as he ended the call he felt hollow. Cold. Impotent being so far away and unable to speak to Isabelle. Suddenly the Antovic contract didn't matter as much as being where he needed to be. Home. With Isabelle. Sheltering her from his ravenous family and convincing her to remain after the wedding.

Fourteen

Isabelle didn't remember agreeing to the bridesmaid gig, yet here she stood in a fairy-tale concoction of shimmering pink with lace and pearl embellishments. Apparently she and Georgina Harrington were a similar size and shape, and the gown was sent with accessories to Chisholm Park. By chauffeured limousine. The only transportation more fitting would have been a horse-drawn glass coach.

"I can give you a tad more room here," Vivi decided, tugging somewhere in the back where Isabelle couldn't see. Nor did she care; she was more interested in the concept of Vivi doing the work. So far she'd been very adept at making work and offering suggestions—Isabelle as bridesmaid, for example—but not so big on the doing.

"Do you sew?" she asked.

Vivi's perfectly made-up face appeared from beyond the gown's voluminous skirt. "Beautifully," she said with the trademark family confidence. "I did my apprenticeship on Savile Row. That is where I met my first two husbands."

Isabelle tried not to look too astonished, but failed dismally. "Not both at the same time, I hope."

Vivi laughed, then sat back on her heels. "If Alistair had been in the same room as Juan Verón I would not have noticed him, and that would have been an immense shame." Her eyes met Isabelle's in the mirror. "All the good in Cristo, that is from Alistair. He was a good, good man. Too good for me."

Afraid that everything she felt might show in her eyes, Isabelle let her gaze drop away in feigned contemplation of the gown's adjusted fit. Over the past days she'd grown adept at parrying Vivi's questions and avoiding the deeply personal, but now she was trapped in weighty folds of pearl-encrusted taffeta and by the new gravity in the woman's dark eyes. There was no escape.

"I am not all bad," Vivi continued, "but I have made some impulsive decisions that were not always in my family's best interests. My heart is in a rush and I am a selfish woman. When I left Juan, he did not want me to take a thing."

Isabelle knew she wasn't talking about fripperies. She knew but she had to ask.

"Not even your children?"

"I tried to take my sons, but Alejandro ran away. I had to make a choice, you see, to leave with one son or to take Cristo back to his father and leave with none. Cristo did not understand why he had to leave his home and his brother—he hated this ugly, grey country. But I hoped that this one time, my selfish heart made the right choice."

"Why are you telling me this?"

"I suspect that Cristo will not, and I want you to understand." From her seat on the floor, Vivi reached up and touched Isabelle's hand. "He is everything that you see and he is so much more, Isabelle, with so much love to give. Yet I fear that I have spoiled his view of love and marriage. He is a man and so he is stubborn. He is my son and so he is a cynic. If you love him, Isabelle, you need to know this. That is all."

After completing the alteration, Vivi and her copious luggage left for Sussex. Chisholm Park seemed cavernous and empty and as she awaited Chessie's arrival, Isabelle found herself with too much time for reflection. Too much time to chew over the implications of what she'd learned from Vivi…and to fill in the gaps.

Vivi hadn't mentioned the marriages after her first two, and how those upheavals in her household had affected Cristo. Every time Vivi followed her selfish heart to a new man, her child also had to follow. To a new home, a new country, into the care of strangers. How could he not equate falling in love with disruption and change and loss, all inextricably linked? Could a belief entrenched from such an early age be over-turned, especially by a man with no need to change? He had so much that he loved already—his business, his home, his horses, his family—how could he possibly want for more?

And beneath the flickering doubt in Isabelle's heart, a new hurt burgeoned. He hadn't shared much of his life at all. Despite all the time they'd spent together, all the long walks and pillow conversations, she had only grazed the surface of his past.

Walking and thinking brought Isabelle to her bedroom, the one she'd taken the first night she arrived at Chisholm Park and where she'd eventually unpacked and stored her things. She'd only slept here the one night, but maintaining the pretence of her own room had been her safety net. She'd used it after Vivi's arrival, when she'd been spooked by the reminder of this family's wealth and position. When she'd needed a hole to scamper to. This is where Cristo had found her afterward, when he'd wanted to send her away and she'd resisted. When she'd chosen to block out the message he'd delivered so clearly in words and in action.

In two days her commitment to Cristo and his family would end. It was time to start thinking about her future. Time to call Miriam to confirm her next position, time to pack her bags. The fairy tale was over.

Cristo returned to find his home as he liked it—blessedly free of uninvited guests. On her way out the door, Meredith confirmed that his mother had departed after lunch. Isabelle was upstairs packing. "Happy to be home?" she asked.

"You have no idea."

With the remnants of shattered tension shooting through his blood, Cristo longed to bound up the stairs, but the power of that desire lent him restraint. Wanting this strongly did not sit comfortably, but he'd not examined the reasons. He would convince Isabelle to stay; that was all that mattered.

Packing meant the room she'd insisted on keeping, and that's where Cristo found her...or at least the signs of her presence. The plain black suitcase she'd brought from Australia sat open on the bed, several neat piles of clothes beside it. Something about that innocent sight sat wrong, and by the time he'd prowled around the bed and inspected the partially packed bag he knew why.

He picked up white cotton underwear he'd never seen before, fingering the soft fabric as he inspected the rest of the contents. Everything was plain, clean, serviceable. No lace bras or silk camisoles or sheer panties. He saw nothing of what he'd bought her from Nina, nothing that looked suitable for the wedding weekend.

Sensing her imminent arrival, his head came up as though tugged on strings of anticipation. She stopped on the threshold to the bathroom. Her deepwater eyes widened with surprise and a fleeting glimpse of pleasure. He hated how she shut that down. How she limited her smile to a tentative welcome.

"I wasn't expecting you until tomorrow," she said.

"Is that why you're packing?"

Her gaze slid away to the suitcase, and she shrugged slightly as she came into the room. "I was feeling a bit lost, actually, and I decided to get a start on. I wasn't sure what time we'd be leaving tomorrow."

"Unusual choices for a wedding," he said, running his hand across a stack of T-shirts.

"This is my own stuff."

"I can see that."

"For when I leave here."

A simple exchange, it should not have been incendiary. But her cool, calm manner as she picked up the panties he'd discarded and placed them back in the case acted like gasoline on the fire of Cristo's mood. "Tell me about that," he said, folding his arms across his chest and narrowing his gaze on her carefully composed face. "When are you leaving?"

"That depends on Chessie, but after the wedding. I spoke to Miriam today, and she has a job for me next weekend."

"What about the job with Bill and Gabrielle Thompson?"

Shock flared in her eyes. She blinked it away. "How did you know about…" She puffed out a breath. "Amanda. It doesn't matter. I'm not taking it."

"Why not?" he persisted, shifting his body to block her

attempt to turn away. "What if your sister stays in England to have her baby? Have you considered that possibility?"

"It's one possibility, but I can't make plans based on maybes. Nor can I risk my current job."

"As a housekeeper."

Isabelle's head came up. "What is that supposed to mean?" she asked sharply.

"I mean it's a job you can get anywhere, with any service or any number of private clients, as demonstrated by the Thompsons' offer."

Irritated and ridiculously hurt by his put-down of her job, Isabelle struggled to maintain her composure. This could decline into clash of tempers too easily—she'd sensed him spoiling for a fight the instant she came out of the bathroom—and the recognition of her feelings and the continuing flutter of hope that he might yet return them had her on an emotional edge. She could not do verbal sparring right now. Not without the risk of revealing too much.

"I have a home in Melbourne," she said with admirable calm.

"You could have a home here."

Despite every good intention, her stomach clenched with longing. "Are you saying that you want me to stay?"

"Yes," he said staunchly. "I am."

"And do what?" *This was long term, not a weekend, not an extra week of a fairy-tale affair. This was real life, and she had to be sure; she had to nail down the details of that reality.* "If I took a job with the Thompsons, for example, I would be expected to live in and to travel with them. And when you or Vivi or Amanda came to one of their dinner parties, I would be greeting you at the door and serving your meal. Is that how—"

"No." His head came up a fraction, his nostrils flared and

his eyes flashed with primitive fire. "You won't be living in with these people, and I want you by my side at the table."

"What are you asking?" she managed, her voice husky and barely audible above the singing of joy in her ears.

"That you stay here with me."

Isabelle moistened her dry lips. "I have no money, no income…"

"You don't need any. I will give you whatever you need."

He took her by the shoulders, brought her close enough to feel the lure of his body heat, and the temptation to yield was ever so strong and wrong, so wrong. Sucking in a breath Isabelle steeled her shoulders and her willpower. "You are asking me to stay as your mistress, all expenses paid." She saw the truth of that in his eyes, felt the dismay like a punch in her stomach. "What will I do all day while you're working and travelling? Do I go to the spa, make myself beautiful, wait for you to bring me home jewellery and more fancy clothes?"

"You enjoy the stables. You can help Chloe and continue your polo lessons."

"That's a holiday, Cristo, not a life."

For a long moment she held his gaze without wavering, absorbing the reflexive tightening of his grip and the hardening of his black-eyed glare. Then she turned abruptly within his hold, breaking his grip and allowing herself a brief respite as she fumbled blindly with her clothes. What a fool she was to have expected more.

"What are you angling for, Isabelle? A proposal?"

His voice was low, flat, but every hair on the back of her neck stood up. She should have denied it, shouldn't have taken so long to respond, and when it came her laughter sounded brittle and unconvincing. "Of course not. I've known you less than a month."

"Some women believe that is enough time. They mistake lust for love."

Isabelle's shoulders tightened. The injustice of that comparison snapped in her eyes and her voice as she turned back to face him. "Some women might, but I am not Vivi. I do know the difference, Cristo, and I do not expect a proposal from you."

"Not even a proposal that we continue our current arrangement? If you prefer, I can get you a place of your own."

"Thank you, but no. This was always temporary—a weekend, a week, until the wedding. I want to keep my job and a shred of pride," she said. "I cannot do that as a kept woman. Now, please, let me finish packing."

Everything inside Cristo screamed *no.* He wanted to bend her to his will, make her see reason, wipe the frosty control from her face, but what else could he offer? How could he make her stay? If she had faced him with defiance or counterdemands he would know how to argue, how to respond, but he did not know how to deal with such a simple, composed request.

Let me finish packing.

He turned away, took several steps before his gaze fastened on the contents beyond the open closet doors. The red gown he'd worn to the gala. A heather-grey jacket she'd worn the night they walked to the pub. The bright sundress he'd slipped hands and mouth beneath, the day they'd picnicked by the lake.

When he heard the quiet snap of her suitcase closing, Cristo saw red. "You have forgotten these." In six quick strides he'd snatched up all the hangers. He tossed them on the bed. Returned to open drawers, gathering underwear and shoes and bags, everything he had bought for her.

"Stop," she said, the single word wrenched from her throat with the first uncensored emotion he'd heard all afternoon.

Horrified, she watched him dump another bundle on the bed
"Stop it, I said!"

"All yours, Isabelle. Consider them perks of the job."

"They were my uniform, that's all. I don't need them
anymore."

"Nor do I."

Now he was done, Cristo stood back from the evidence o
his panicked petulance and wanted to kick himself. Isabell
turned away again, but not before he'd seen the shimmer o
moisture in her eyes. *Dios,* he was a dolt. He'd acted like a
child deprived of his favourite toy, but he would not see he
cry. She started to pick up the mess of his doing, and his jav
set with a new resolve.

"Leave them," he said, and when she kept on tidying he
forced her away from the clothes and the bed. Feeling he
tense up beneath his hands, seeing the trapped look on her fac
as she slapped at his hands, was too much to bear. He pulle
her tightly held body close against his and wrapped her in hi
arms. "Forgive me," he murmured against her ear. "You ar
right. I did not want to hear you say no. I wanted to find a wa
to make it yes, and I could see you walking away. I lost it."

That was all he could think to say, but against his shirt h
felt her hot tears, and those he had to stop. He smoothed a
hand over her back, bent to kiss her face, felt the gradua
melting of her tension beneath his hands, and despite th
complexities of emotion that rampaged through his body, h
could not stop. His hands dipped lower, pulled her closer t
his quickening heat, and the comfort of his caress change
tenor. There was no other way to show her how well they fi
no other way to communicate the depth of his feelings.

When he undressed her, she did not resist. When he too
her down onto the floor amid the mess of discarded clothes

she went willingly. When he made love to her every part with slow, thorough intensity, she responded with the same cries of fulfillment—but there was a sadness in her eyes and an inevitability tapping at the edge of his consciousness.

What if this is the last time? What if you never again taste the sweetness of her mouth and her skin? What if you never again experience this wild, soaring connection?

No matter how many times he turned to her that night, no matter how many times and ways he showed her how well they fit, he still felt oddly unfulfilled.

"Stay," he breathed against her sweat-dampened skin late in the night, and Isabelle nestled against his body and listened to his promises. He would get her a cottage in the country. He would find her a job, her own business if she would prefer. And each promise of what he could buy her or what he could make happen with his wealth and position only deepened her conviction to leave.

There was only one gift that would change her mind, one that didn't cost a penny, the one she feared he would always hold back.

His love.

Fifteen

The wedding was everything Isabelle had expected and feared. A beautiful, wonderful, miserable, emotionally exhausting roller coaster before she even arrived at the church. She did her bridesmaid's turn down the aisle without drawing unnecessary attention to herself, particularly from the man standing at the groom's side. As predicted, Justin Harrington had missed the rehearsal, and this was her first glimpse of Chessie's one-night stand. Tall, his bearing stiff and aloof, taking no interest in the procession of bridesmaids. *Phew.*

One by one they took their places and then, over the first trumpet blares of the processional, she heard the creak of pews and rustle of rich fabrics as the guests turned to watch the bride's entrance. Isabelle glanced sideways past the line of extravagant pink frocks and caught Hugh drawing a deep breath, and beyond him the ice-cold expression of his brother. She'd heard nothing but good about the responsible, dutiful lder Harrington since he'd been revealed as the father of Chessie's baby, but now—a shiver tingled the length of her spine—he looked so cold. Quickly she shifted her focus back to Hugh, found his attention riveted and his face wreathed in pride and love and simmering excitement as his bride approached. The bottom dropped out of her stomach.

This is what she ached for—not the ring or the pretty dresses, not massed roses and glorious music, but the meaning behind today's ceremony and the look on Hugh's face that said it all.

Sudden tears choked her throat, but that was all right. It was a wedding. She could disguise them behind a smile of feigned happiness. Her peripheral vision filled with tear-blurred white, and blinking rapidly she turned enough to see Cristo handing his sister over to her new life. And as he stepped away, his gaze lifted and caught on Isabelle's—a brief capture, a heartbeat, an intense stab of longing, that only compounded her I-want-this-for-myself wretchedness.

She was such a fool, thinking she could get through this day without revealing the extent of her feelings. She should have run when she had a chance; now she was trapped by the occasion and her duty. If only there'd been somewhere in this ridiculous dress to stow her iPod, she could have blocked out the solemnity of the vows and the depth of meaning behind them.

But music would not have blocked out the huge smile that spread across Hugh's face when the minister pronounced them man and wife. Nothing could have blocked out his whoop of delight as he grabbed Amanda by the waist and swung her up and around in an open display of triumphant joy. Spontaneous applause broke out through the church, the mood so buoyantly infectious that even Isabelle laughed.

Then she was swept up in a joyous procession from the

church, formal photos, and an endless greeting line at the ex
ceedingly grand Aylesbury Hall. She'd thought the reception
might be easier, but she'd not counted on the unusual interes
in her…and the story of how she'd met Cristo. Someone—
Vivi, she presumed—had embellished the story with enough
dramatic flair that every second woman she met sighed, "How
romantic." Several asked if there would be another wedding
soon, and Isabelle wanted to shout the truth: he has everything
he wants—why on earth would he marry me?

At her side, taking this all in, was Alejandro Verón
Absurdly handsome and an outrageous flirt, he should have
proved the perfect partner. But his touch created none of the
zing of his brother's, and his interest in her affair with Cristo—
apparently he'd not been taken in by Vivi's version—made her
uncomfortable. His questions seemed to seek a reason for
Cristo's interest, and in the end she told him straight. "No, we
don't have a lot of common interests other than sex."

"You are a realist," he said with calming approval as he
ushered her to the floor to join the bridal waltz. "I can see tha
you are not taken in by all this wedding bull."

Obviously she was a better actor than she'd thought; thos
childhood lessons had really paid off.

"This is good," Alejandro decided, taking her into his arms
"You will deal well with my brother."

Usually Cristo dealt well with the strictures of duty, espe
cially when they pertained to his family. Today they'd kep
him from Isabelle at a time when he needed her close, remind
ing her how well they fit together and attempting to regain the
connection they'd forged last week. But they hadn't spoke
more than ten words, and he seethed beneath the weight of
his responsibilities as host. Even now, with the traditiona

aspects of the reception finished, he could not relax and enjoy the party he had paid for. Everyone wanted to congratulate him on the splendid event. All he wanted was to cut in on his brother, to hold Isabelle in his arms.

"She and Alejandro seem to have hit it off," Vivi commented. She'd not missed the reason for his distraction; his gaze had been following the other couple around the floor. "She has won us all, your Isabelle."

"She is going back to Australia."

His graceful mother missed a step, but recovered quickly. "Have you asked her to stay?"

"Yes," he said tersely. "I have offered her a home, a job, her own business. I have done everything but beg."

"Then perhaps it is time to go down on your knees."

She was not suggesting he beg, but the notion of matrimony as a relationship cure was laughable when it came from Vivi. Cristo could not laugh, not even with the cynicism reserved for her. For the length of this exchange he'd lost sight of Isabelle in the swirl of dancing couples, but now he found her again.

Dancing with Justin Harrington.

Luck had been on their side. Harrington's last-minute arrival for the wedding meant no time for introductions or to learn that the last-minute bridesmaid was Isabelle Browne. Now Christo manoeuvred close enough to see Isabelle's face. She needed rescuing, fast.

Vivi had no complaint when he cut in on the other couple. Slipping from one man to the other, she took Justin's hand and steered him away with smoothly practiced skill.

"Thank you," Isabelle said shakily. "That was very well done."

"Vivi has her moments."

She tried a smile, but it trembled at the edges and Cristo fastened his hold. "He knows?"

"Someone was talking, he heard my name. I had to tell him about Chessie."

Dios. "You told him she's pregnant?"

"Only that she's here, at Chisholm Park. The rest is not mine to tell."

Relieved, he tucked her closer beneath his chin and dipped to press his lips briefly against her cheek. A small kiss, but the contact he craved. The rest of this dance was his to enjoy.

All day Isabelle's emotions had been building, a giant weight pressed against a wall of tightly masked composure and all it took was the butterfly touch of Cristo's lips to bring that wall tumbling down. The shudder started deep inside and moved through her in a rush of heartfelt longing.

"Are you all right?" he asked, his breath warm against her ear.

Isabelle shook her head slightly. She could have blamed Justin, the shock of that ambush, but she was tired of make-believe. Sick of hiding the truth of her feelings. And when he drew back—enough to lift her face, to look into her eyes—she could not lie. "You were partially right," she said quietly. She lifted her hand from his shoulder, brushed her fingertips along his jaw. "Some women do fall in love in less than a month."

His head came up reflexively, and her gaze fell away with her hand. She did not want to see the shock in his eyes.

"It's all right," she continued quickly. "You don't have to say anything. I just wanted you to know."

Now it was done, she couldn't slip back into the bittersweet dance. She needed space to breathe and compose herself.

perhaps to lash herself for that burst of honesty, and when a couple dancing energetically by bumped into Cristo, she took advantage of their profuse apologies to tug her hand free of his and slip away.

The knowledge that he would follow and demand further explanation—possibly even use her vulnerability to change her mind—leant her feet desperate speed. She didn't know where she was going—she just needed solitude, and she headed out into the maze of gardens, kicked off the constrictive heels that hadn't fitted her properly and kept on running.

She didn't stop until walls of hedges halted her progress, and she sank onto a nearby garden bench. Winded, her breath rasped painfully in her lungs, and when she leaned forward to ease the pressure, the wetness of tears spilled from her face to mark the bodice of her frock. It was a shock to learn she was crying. It was a bigger shock to discover she was not alone.

"Trouble in paradise?"

She recognised the sneering edge to the voice without looking up. More than two hundred guests, and it had to be Madeleine. She didn't answer; there was nothing to say, but that didn't stop her tormentor. Isabelle heard the swish of her dress coming closer, and she tensed reflexively.

"If you're trying to escape, too, there's a gate down here."

That sounded surprisingly helpful, and when the dress swished on by, Isabelle caught the edge of agitation in the movement and looked up. Shoes in one hand, purse clutched in the other, Madeleine was stalking toward the far end of the garden room. Escaping, too?

When she stumbled unsteadily, car keys and shoes tumbled from her hand to the ground. Isabelle sat up straighter. "You're not driving…?"

"I don't intend walking all the way home."

Alarmed, Isabelle bit down on her irritation. "Since you can't walk straight, that would not be a good idea."

Hunkered down and still struggling to gather up her shoes, the other woman cut her a look. "Do you have a better one?"

A smile ghosted across Isabelle's lips as she remembered where Madeleine's home was located. *Oh, the irony of chance.* "Actually, I do." She rose on steady feet and held out her hand. "If you give me your car keys, I will drive you."

She'd gone. Cristo didn't know how or where to, but Isabelle had disappeared. At the wedding he found only her shoes, a pair of ridiculously high-heeled sandals discarded on the terrace steps. In the room they'd shared the night before the wedding, where he'd intended to woo her again tonight, he found the bridesmaid's dress and an insultingly brief note.

"Thank you for everything. Love, Isabelle."

It was enough to get his hackles up, to send him chasing back to Chisholm Park, but somehow she'd managed to outrun him. The suitcase packed with her own things was gone; the clothes from Nina's hung neatly in the closet. There was no second note—perhaps she thought everything had been said, but she was very much mistaken.

Wherever she had gone he would find her and he would have the right of reply. He didn't know if he could change her mind, if what he had to offer was enough to make up for his wrongheadedness when he'd returned from Russia—even if he was what she wanted.

But the thought of his life without Isabelle stretched before him, infinitely longer and more dismally grey than his first

English winter, and he knew that he would offer everything that he feared and more. To keep Isabelle in his life, he would offer whatever it took.

Isabelle could hardly believe her unexpected good fortune. Madeleine had proven a most worthy accomplice, not only in providing an escape from the wedding, but she'd then offered Isabelle the loan of her family's seaside cottage. "Why are you helping me?" Isabelle asked, suspicious.

"You're leaving Cristo," the other woman said. "Why wouldn't I help?"

She hadn't wanted to take up that offer, but in the end it was her only option. Justin Harrington had beaten her back to Chisholm Park, he'd spirited Chessie away to London and although her sister sounded confident of working out a solution, Isabelle remembered the man's haughty demeanour and she worried.

She couldn't leave England yet, not without knowing that Chessie's plans were solid and in *everyone's* best interests, not only that cool-eyed aristocrat's.

And as if to clinch the deal, she learned that the De-lahuntys' cottage was in a quiet Cornish village, a stone's throw from the beach. Isabelle never felt more at home than walking on the beach and around the cliff tops. Every day she walked and she chewed over her options. If her sister stayed in England, she liked the idea of being close. Part of her growing family. She could get a housekeeping position, perhaps cook or butler, but she hated the thought of running across Cristo. Or even Vivi or Amanda or Madeleine.

When she grew tired of the incessant eddying of her thoughts, she plugged in her earphones and filled her head with music. That was today's choice. That's why she didn't hear the helicopter zooming in from the east or hovering above the cliff top in preparation for landing. That's why she had no warning at all until she reached the end of the beach turned and there he was at the foot of the stairs leading up to the cottage. Even from this distance she knew it was him, by the set of his shoulders, the exact way he held his head, the loose roll of his limbs as he started toward her. And mostly by the crazy leap of her heart.

She stood stock-still in the sand as he cut down the space between them. She didn't consider running. She didn't even think to pull the buds from her ears and turn off the music. She heard nothing but the mad, out-of-control thunder in her heart

He stopped in front of her, tall and unbearably attractive with the wind whipping the ends of his hair and plastering his shirt to his chest. Sunglasses hid his eyes and his expression gave away nothing. Not even the hint of a smile as he reached out one hand and removed the earphones.

"Thank you." A silly thing to say, but that's what came out She cleared her throat. "How did you find me?"

"By the trail of shoes."

Isabelle frowned, not understanding, but then he reached behind him and pulled one of her flip-flops from his hip pocket. "Yours?"

Of course it was. She'd left them on the stairs. "I mean here, in Cornwall."

"That was considerably more difficult," he said with great solemnity.

"I'm sorry."

"Are you?" One corner of his mouth quirked. Almost a smile, but one edged in tension. "I rather thought that was the point."

Yes, of course it was, but he'd thrown her with his out-of-he-blue appearance. The *sorry* had just slipped out, an automatic response to being put on the spot. "I suppose Chessie old you I'd come here."

"Eventually. And only after extracting a promise."

"Oh?" As far as intelligent responses went, that ranked up here with *sorry,* but Isabelle was busily backpedalling, trying o recall what she'd told Chessie in their phone conversations. Trying to work out what kind of promise she might extract from him. And since he hadn't jumped in to tell her, she had to ask, "What have you promised?"

"That I won't break your heart."

Her heart had not settled down from its first thunderous leap, but now it took off at a frantic gallop of fear and hope and expectation. "How can you make such a promise?"

"Because I had to," he said with a hitch of one shoulder. "You ran away, Isabelle."

And he had to chase—he still could not accept no as an answer. She shook her head slowly. "You are not used to women running away, I'm sure."

"Not after they have told me they love me, no. That *is* what you were saying at the wedding?"

"You didn't have to make idle promises," she said in a rush, ignoring the directness of his question. "Chessie should have old you that I am sticking around a while, at least until she decides where she's having the baby. Then I will decide what I'm doing."

"She told me." He tipped the sunglasses to the top of his head, revealing eyes that burned with grim determination and something else she dared not attempt to identify. "I'm not here to make idle promises, Isabelle. I'm here to ask why you didn't give me the right of reply before you ran."

"I didn't want you to say something you didn't mean."

"I hope I am not a man who says things I do not mean, although this past week I have talked all the way around what I need to say to you, Isabelle. I have thought about my life without you and my life since I've met you." He lifted a hand to her face, mimicking the way she had touched him on the dance floor at the wedding. "Perhaps this colour you bring into my life is love."

"Perhaps?" she managed, a bare whisper of breath. A big beat of hope in her chest. "You are willing to risk breaking my heart for perhaps?"

"I will look after your heart, Isabelle, if you will look out for mine."

And when she looked into his eyes, she saw the vulnerability, and her own heart melted. "I do not fall in and out of love," she told him. "For me, this is it, once and forever, the only time I have ever felt this craziness. So please do not lead me on. Please do not offer anything unless you are certain that I am the one—not just because you want me now and not only for the weeks you spend at Chisholm Park where I do fit in, but for all the parts of your life where I do not fit."

"You fit me just fine, Isabelle Browne."

"In the country doing ordinary things, yes. At the stables, yes. In bed, yes."

His eyes glittered narrowly. "A point I would rather you didn't share with my brother in future."

Isabelle opened her mouth and shut it again.

"My family likes to talk and to interfere. They love to create drama. They're not good at leaving well enough alone, but in this instance they are right. You are the one for me, Isabelle. I cannot offer you the peaceful life that you prefer, but I can give you the home that you crave and I can offer you my heart."

To her amazement and soaring delight he went down on one knee in the sand. "You don't have to do this," she said. "Not unless you're sure."

"I am sure," he said, and the look in his eyes was everything Isabelle had ever wanted. "You are the colour in my life, Isabelle, the one I want to wake up beside every morning, to make love to every night. Will you be my wife, for better and for worse?"

"Yes," she breathed, sinking to her knees in front of him. His hands cupped her face, hers touched his lips and all she could feel was the better. "For ever after, yes, please."

* * * * *

A Christmas bride for the cowboy

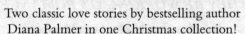

Two classic love stories by bestselling author
Diana Palmer in one Christmas collection!

Featuring

Sutton's Way
and
Coltrain's Proposal

Available 3rd December 2010

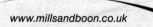

2 FREE BOOKS
AND A SURPRISE GIFT

We would like to take this opportunity to thank you for reading this Mills & Boon® book by offering you the chance to take TWO more specially selected books from the Desire™ 2-in-1 series absolutely FREE! We're also making this offer to introduce you to the benefits of the Mills & Boon® Book Club™—

- **FREE home delivery**
- **FREE gifts and competitions**
- **FREE monthly Newsletter**
- **Exclusive Mills & Boon Book Club offers**
- **Books available before they're in the shops**

Accepting these FREE books and gift places you under no obligation to buy, you may cancel at any time, even after receiving your free books. Simply complete your details below and return the entire page to the address below. You don't even need a stamp!

YES Please send me 2 free Desire stories in a 2-in-1 volume and a surprise gift. I understand that unless you hear from me, I will receive 2 superb new 2-in-1 books every month for just £5.30 each, postage and packing free. I am under no obligation to purchase any books and may cancel my subscription at any time. The free books and gift will be mine to keep in any case.

Ms/Mrs/Miss/Mr _____ Initials _____

Surname _____

Address _____

_____ Postcode _____

E-mail_____

Send this whole page to: Mills & Boon Book Club, Free Book Offer, FREEPOST NAT 10298, Richmond, TW9 1BR